SWORDS OF SECUNDA

ADRIAN COLLINS

DEDICATION

For Rosemary.

"I can't leave yet. I'm a mother. I don't have that choice."

Rest in peace.

ACKNOWLEDGEMENTS

Simon, AB and Bob – the storyline and editing would have been a lost cause without you. Cheers lads. To mum, for another wonderful cover. To Fi, for supporting me through my passions and my obsessions in another step towards realising my dream.

PROLOGUE

Brother Archenon Sokar's closest friend was going to die, tonight. The man was his liege, his lord, a man he had followed into the very teeth of the hellish war that had all but destroyed his people. His liege was an almighty hero who had rebuilt a nation from a shattered and displaced populace and a scant few hundred knights and soldiers. He loved this man like the blood brothers he'd left lifeless upon the dirt many so years ago as they'd battled the horrors of the Black Lands that had nearly swept them from the realm.

Archenon ran a hand down his face, feeling the ravages of time on the bristled wrinkles. His eyes, beginning to cloud over with cataracts, looked at his leather-skinned hand and then wiped the moist tears onto his thick white cloak. His legs struggled under him as he leant heavily upon his tall walking staff. Archenon's hunched back ached almost incessantly in the cold of the winter. His shoulders had long since lost the power that had earned him such regard amongst fighting men. His arms had even lost the strength to hold his king's standard. At seventy-three summers old, the knight had outlived all of his friends and comrades, bar one.

Archenon looked through tear-fogged eyes at his eldest son, standing by his side, hand out in a warm offer of help. He

1

bit back more tears and gently pushed the hand away, muffling a sob as best he could. Fifty-seven years of friendship and loyalty was about to come to an end. It'd been a long time coming. His king had not left his bed in two years. He'd not even been lucid in the last month or two. Archenon had watched him sleep away most of the last fortnight, barely waking long enough to take on water and food.

The chief apothecary had come and woken Archenon long before dawn. "It is time," the man had said gravely. "Best be quick, Lord Archenon. He will depart soon."

Archenon thought he had steeled his soul for this, prepared his mind to lose his greatest friend. Now that the moment was upon him, he knew he had fooled himself. Nothing could have prepared him for this. His throat and eyes burned, his body ached already for the loss to come, and his chest trembled as his heart longed for them both to be young once more.

To be young once more. Archenon closed his eyes a moment, reaching out and holding his son's arm for balance. *To wear the armour we were given when we earned our knighthoods. To stand side by side in the shield wall, daring the horror of battle to test our courage. To stand triumphant as the foe were beaten off and sent back beyond the new frontier. To love, to live, to stand by your side as you led our people back to the first step on this great journey to return us to our true greatness. To set plans in motion to one day re-take Mother Secunda.*

"Father?"

Archenon burst painfully from his memory. He didn't have much time. He had to see his brother. He needed the chance to say goodbye. He needed to be there when he left. The gods had abandoned them all decades ago. Archenon was all the king had from those lost days of glory when knights had marched in their tens of thousands and Mother Secunda was safe from savages. He had to be there. *Hold strong, my friend. I'm coming.*

He nodded to his son. Talian, fifty years old and still a bull of a man, reached out a meaty fist and rapped lightly upon the door. Archenon took a deep, shuddering breath. *Hold strong.*

The great oak doors creaked open to reveal a large, dimly lit bedchamber. At the centre of the room, surrounded by kneeling warriors, a massive four-poster bed sat like an island in a sea of armour. Almost one hundred knights and lords filled the room, every one of them garbed in full plate. The thick high inner collars of the Secundan knights' stereotypical pauldrons flanked each short-cropped head of hair.

As Archenon walked, tear-filled eyes looked up to meet him. He reached out and placed a hand on the steel-shod shoulder of the warrior who had replaced him to hold the king's banner, then gripped another brother's forearm as he recognised a grandson of one of the men he had fought with in their last stand against the barbarian horde. Men stood to greet him, solemn and respectful.

He and the king were the last of an age of heroes these warriors worshipped, the last of the knights who had fought the barbarians to a standstill. They were the last of the few hundred survivors of the entire war where Mother Secunda had been lost. They were men who had helped plan and build the White Frontier. They'd lobbied the nations around them to stand together and create the Lands of the Light. Archenon had been the first lord to lead a Secundan garrison on the White Frontier.

All seemed like a lifetime ago, and as he arrived at his king's bedside, all was lost to horrible memory as the withered body of King Armenius Faramon came into view. Already he could see the dark purples and blacks of dying flesh creeping up Armenius' chest and throat and temples. The king's lips were tight and pale, his flesh pallid and his eyes closed. Deep, shuddering breaths wracked his ailing frame; too few, too far apart, and made with too much effort.

Archenon reached out and took his king's hand, feeling a clammy coldness he had known well from holding too many of his brother knights in their bloody last moments. The king's eyes opened, their brilliant blue still sharp, just the way Archenon had always remembered them. A thin smile creased Armenius' face.

"My brother, you are here," wheezed the dying king.

3

"My king," said Archenon, fresh tears welling.

Armenius smiled again. "My brother, do not cry. I go to see our ancestors, wherever the absent gods have allowed them to gather."

Archenon could not find words. They evaded him, though he wasn't sure he wanted to find them.

"Silent for once, brother?" said the king, huffing out a painful laugh. "If only I could have experienced this during our youth at some point. It is somewhat pleasant."

"Wouldn't have got this old if I'd kept my mouth shut, you old fool. Pulled you out of way too many scrapes," said Archenon, the last few words coming out in a blubbering laugh.

Armenius began to laugh and then folded a little as a vicious cough racked his body. Speckles of blood flecked his lips and the white sheet up around his armpits.

The dying king wheezed, his eyes closing for a while as he tried to get his breath. Once more, those piercing blue eyes opened and rested on Archenon.

"My brother, my friend, my confidant," said Armenius. "Enjoy your last years, forgive me my faults, watch over my sons and tell me of how great our nation has become when you join me in the shield wall in the sky."

"The shield wall in the sky?" asked Archenon.

On any other day he might have laughed at such a whimsical notion.

"The gods have abandoned us, but their realm remains. I shall gather our gloriously fallen there, and watch over our nation."

The king's eyes closed as he rested a moment. Archenon wiped his eyes with his sleeve and blew out his cheeks as he watched his friend's chest struggle through shallow breaths. *The Shield Wall in the Sky*. It was a nice notion.

As he watched Armenius' face, an aide handed him a piece of parchment. Archenon looked up questioningly.

"Words from our king, spoken only days past while in a fever dream. His son bade I write them down for you."

Archenon looked down at the paper, his old eyes struggling to focus on the small hand. Painstakingly slowly, the words coalesced for him.

> *"One sundered soul,*
> *Outside the circle,*
> *The beast within awoken.*
>
> *One sundered soul,*
> *Infused with one sundered spirit,*
> *The instincts of a thousand years,*
> *Coursing through his veins.*
>
> *One sundered soul,*
> *The dark son,*
> *The strongest and bravest of them all.*
>
> *One sundered soul,*
> *Doomed to stand,*
> *When all around him fall."*

Archenon read it again while his friend slept. The words of a fever dream were worthless, but they were some of the last words of his dearest friend nonetheless. He would not, could not, discard them.

The king's head rolled to the side, his eyes lolling over to look at the warriors surround his bed. His jaw worked and his tongue clacked as he tried to moisten his mouth.

"My brothers. Remember always that this land relies upon you. My sons will rely on you. But we are nothing without the land and its people. As a whole: peasant, blacksmith, miner, soldier, knight and lord; we are Secunda."

The king took a shuddering breath.

"Your people, your armour, and the man beside you. Say it."

"Your people, your armour, and the man beside you," intoned the congregation.

The king's eyes rested upon his sons, his daughters, and their sons and daughters who stood at the end of the bed.

"Rule well, my children. Secunda needs you."

Finally those blues rested once more on Archenon.

"Until we meet once more... in the shield wall in the sky."

Archenon felt the slackening of Armenius' light grip. He listened as a few last spasmodic breaths cleared from his lungs as a heart as mighty as any that had ever lived finally gave out. He bowed his head and kissed his king's hand one last time. Immediately, Archenon Sokar felt alone.

The last man of an age well on its way to legend, he had the only two old eyes left that had seen the greatest battles of the century. One last whitebeard left to his last few lonesome years before the loss of Mother Secunda went from memory to history, and in time, legend.

He felt his skin tingle. Warmth, like the heat of the sun on the lost battlements of Mother Secunda, flowed over and through him. There were cries of alarm, and someone drew a blade behind him. He held out a hand and looked up, intent on seeing Armenius' face, but his eyes were blinded by the golden brightness.

Archenon reached out, though not in fear. Something within told him it would be all right. Something told him there would be no more pain.

His bony fingers grasped something — something small and hard attached to the tiny links of a silver chain. It burned his hand pleasantly. It slipped over the king's head easily and hung lightly from his fist, no heavier than a silver talisman or pendant. He lifted it to the ceiling and stood as the light shone all the brighter and illuminated the room.

Archenon had seen sorcery of the darkest kind in his time. He'd spent his life fighting it. He'd watched brothers he'd thought slain rise, their eyes milky and their mouths distended, to slay friend with such power it made strong men look like children. He'd watched the heavens, dark and roiling, lower down to the battlefield to pluck the loyal and the good from the field of battle and wrench them to their horrible deaths, only their rain of blood splashing back to the battlefield to show they were ever there at all.

The gods had abandoned the Secundans decades ago. No churches were built in the new Secunda, no places of worship and no priests to tell them which invisible deity to kneel to. For the first time in close to forty years, Archenon felt something he'd almost forgotten: faith.

As the light shone brighter, the hurt he felt began to recede. His back straightened a little and his shoulders squared, though not without pain. Summoning himself to speak, he took a step towards the shocked men before him.

"Until I see you in the Shield Wall in the Sky, my Lord."

Men looked at him, confused but hopeful, feeling something wonderful was happening.

"He is still here, my brothers!" he cried, feeling his momentum gathering as his heart soared and breathed life into his voice that reminded him of days long past. "He watches from above, waiting for us upon the green fields the gods left bare when they abandoned us, calling our fallen brothers to him. Calling them to His shield wall! Calling them for as long as Secunda stands and Secundans draw breath! Watching over us, for ever!"

Men were standing now, in awe as the light shone from Archenon's fist like the light of the sun.

"He is our Eternal Lord and under his gaze we shall not fail!"

CHAPTER ONE

"And Lo! Armenius, our Eternal Lord stood tall amongst his brothers," thundered the voice of Warrior Priest Trethore Sokar over the hundreds strong congregation, his heart alight with the fiery vigour.

Trethore launched himself into his well practiced, but nonetheless energetic, follow-up. "He was a mighty oak reigning over a forest of devout followers, his face the strength of the mountains and his words the last of a man and the first of a god."

Trethore halted in his delivery of the sermon, allowing the moment to build. Many of the fighting men and camp followers around him had heard his sermons before. In fact, many of the faces before him had been listening to his voice since childhood. This was the moment he enjoyed most, when he would lift their hearts from the horrors of this war and see light in the eyes of those who had seen too much death, when he would once more renew their courage and vigour and pull them up from the quagmire of ice and mud they were camped in outside of the charnel house the once glorious city of Gall had become.

He sought a face he knew by name, his blue eyes searching out from beneath greying eyebrows to finally rest upon his man. He found the youthful knight, perhaps twenty summers old if he remembered correctly, and already a hero with his own legend being written. *The knight who slew the warlord. The hero of Gall.*

Uthiel Caellar.

Almost translucent blue eyes locked back on his. Dark sandy hair shifted in the cool breeze as the darkness of night closed in around them. Trethore poured all of his will and his belief into his next words and watched as the shoulders and head of the kneeling knight lifted, as if a great weight had fallen from him. The men and women around that young man lifted with him.

"My ancestor, mighty Archenon Sokar, four centuries past, was there. He was there when Armenius told us of the Shield Wall in the Sky. He was there when the hole left in our lives by the desertion of false gods was filled with a new one. He was there at the glorious ascension of the Eternal Lord!"

The congregation was lifted now. Trethore's heart soared with theirs.

"'Brothers!' our Eternal Lord did cry. 'Brothers! Rule our lands and our people with strength, courage and honour. Defy the foe, defy the darkness, defy all who would sully Secunda's sons and daughters!'"

Trethore's voice lowered, almost to a whisper. The silence around him was so great and his voice so well trained that it carried over the few hundred he presided over easily.

"Then there was quiet. A thousand times a thousand men and women knelt, listening to his words as holy light began to shine from his armoured body. A ring of steel-garbed men around Armenius and the free folk around them all listened. A voice spoke, it was my ancestor, tall and proud and full of righteous might."

Trethore paused again, smiling, his eyes breaking from Uthiel's smoothly and catching many more sets as he expanded his audience.

"'My lord?' said Archenon, 'my lord, we need you here. We need you to lead us.'"

Trethore reached out one of his arms, his face saddening as if he were saying those words himself, four hundred years ago.

"The Eternal Lord strode forward and placed a hand upon my ancestor's armoured shoulder. His hand blessed the very pauldron I wear upon my own shoulder, now, and he spoke.

"'My brother, fear not, for I go to our fallen brothers. They stand alone above us, on the sky-plains left vacant by our false-gods. They stand beset by a mighty dark foe, fell and terrible. I have to draw them together, to unite them under my banner once more.

"I go to form the Shield Wall in the Sky. I shall see you there."

All was quiet around Trethore. He could see the light of the Eternal Lord in every man and woman's eyes.

"He said that, and then he locked eyes with my ancestor's once more.

"'Watch over my sons, as you have watched over me,' said the Eternal Lord.

"Archenon promised he would. He swore upon this very sword and this very armour that his descendants forever more would watch over the descendants of the Eternal Lord, and the people they ruled over."

Trethore allowed the room to go silent again, his eyes locking on Uthiel once more. He'd helped to turn this boy into a knight.

A memory flashed past his eyes: the months-old memory of a discussion with the knight before him, a fleeting discussion where Uthiel had almost let something slip. Something secret. Something dark. Something that had not made sense until months later, while Trethore had been leading the warrior priests in the cleansing of the tainted city of Gall.

His fist clenched involuntarily as he pictured the body he'd found, a slain barbarian wearing the blood-covered, desecrated and holy plate and mail of the Grey Wolves. Trethore could taste the rage all over again, that same sour-spit taste he'd had as he had torn the pauldrons from the corpse's shoulders, the helm from his head, gorget from around his neck and the cuirass from his torso. His wrath had risen and risen that this beast should sully the holy steel that had been dug from Secunda's bosom and fashioned into armour for her defenders.

Finally his raw fingers had pulled off the cloth and chainmail undergarment to reveal the pale flesh beneath. There it was — a betrayal of the most heinous kind — an anathema to the purity of the Grey Wolves knight Order. He'd located the pink scar of the wolf's head branding all young Grey Wolves had burnt into their flesh upon initiation.

It was the very same mark that Uthiel had burnt into his flesh; the very same brotherhood this great hero belonged to. Trethore's eyes hardened ever so slightly as he struggled to keep his outward calm.

Already this war had claimed one of their knight Orders in the year and more it had raged. The Knights Aggressor, led by the king's own brother, had fallen to the unknowable darkness. Hundreds of knights, the elite and supposedly most devout of the warriors of Secunda, had turned on their home land and the Lands of the Light and led these foul barbarians to ritual slaughters that claimed the lives of hundreds of thousands.

Could the Grey Wolves have also turned? Could fully two of the seven great knight Orders have allowed their souls to darken and their thoughts turn a berserker red? Could traitors to the Eternal Lord be kneeling before me right —

Trethore's jaw clamped hard, nostrils flaring as he took a deep breath and sought the calming influence of the Eternal Lord. He spread his arms in a well-practiced gesture, his palms facing skywards.

"Let us pray for those brothers we have lost, for the lives of those who could not defend themselves. And let us damn those who would assail our home. Tonight, let us pray for the soul of Tanin Caellar, and the men of the mighty Fifth who fell around him in Gall.

"Brother Uthiel, with your permission, I shall recite the family prayer gifted to your father by the Lord Pomen."

All eyes turned to Uthiel. The youth bowed his head into shadow, his grief-stricken features quickly hidden. His face rose a moment later, his expression hard and his eyes red.

11

"I would be honoured," came his strained voice, "as would be my father."

There was a murmur of assent from the men. Trethore watched as the hands of the men around Uthiel rose to land on the blond youth's armoured shoulders and upper back in moral support. The first was Tarren, the last surviving knight of the initiates Trethore had sent to fight for the Wolves. Also there was First Captain Solanthur Verutus, champion and mightiest of the knights arrayed against the great foe. Trethore had once believed he could trust such men. But these men all wore the grey tabard of the Wolves. All bore the brand. All could be cancers he would need to excise from the body of Secunda.

Trethore took another deep breath, and began.

"As long as I fight in his name,
And draw the blood of those that would sully Mother
Secunda, for Him,
The Eternal Lord shall be my blade.

As long as I fight in His name,
And protect those that cannot protect themselves,
The Eternal Lord shall be my shield.

As long as I fight in His name,
I shall fear not the blade's kiss,
For the Eternal Lord watches over my body.

As long as I fight in His name,
I fear not the pain of glorious death,
For to die in His name,
Is to be welcomed into His arms."

Trethore opened his eyes as he finished, gazing out over the hundreds of bowed heads before him. Many were still praying, silent lips in communion with the Eternal lord, and he felt a wave of relief wash over him as he saw the men in grey doing so also. He quelled that quickly and angrily.

He was a warrior priest. His was not the lot of the fat bellied abbots Gall used to employ, nor the opulent sun priests of the far north. No, his was the honour of wearing the steel that had sheathed knights who stood and fought side by side with the Eternal Lord. His was the holy duty of keeping the very soul of Secunda cleansed of taint. He looked down to his sword. If the Wolves were treacherous, it would be a bloody duty indeed.

Trethore stood and watched them all for a while, arms crossed upon his chest. Some began to make their way from the clearing and to the tent city around them earlier than others. Trethore noted with reluctant approval that Uthiel and some of the Grey Wolves stayed longer than most, well into the night until the stars shone clear and bright above and the sun had spent some time below the horizon.

Uthiel stood and walked over to him, bowing with respect.

"I thank you for your prayer, father. It has lifted my soul and applied a balm to my grief," said the young knight.

Trethore nodded, reaching out and placing a hand upon Uthiel's shoulder.

"Your father stands with Him in the shield wall, Uthiel. He was a good man, a good Secundan. You should be proud."

Uthiel lopsidedly turned a grimace into a grin. "I am. He was a great man. I only hope I can live up to his expectations."

Trethore stood solemn. "A hope that we all have for you."

Uthiel sighed. "Rest well, father. I shall retire."

Trethore watched the young knight go.

Do you stand loyal or cancerous, young knight?

CHAPTER TWO

Wind whistled through the burnt-out city like stagnant breath through broken, rotted teeth. Hot, damp cloth flapped wetly in the fetid breeze as the gusts moved a hanging sign here, or gave a burnt door or shutters enough of a shove to creak loudly there. Uthiel Caellar, knight of the Grey Wolves, stood with his brothers around him, encased in his full plate from helm to greave. Within his helm he could hear his own breath above all else, ragged and tiring, smelling like his last meal had been rotted rat flesh.

A shutter banged closed and he felt his brothers compress the line around him. They presented a steel wall: greaves upon their shins, mail skirts, kite shields, large pauldrons with a high inner collar sitting atop their mighty shoulders, and bucket helms. The knights boasted a brotherhood built on courage, sacrifice and blood. They moved forwards in perfect synchronicity, eyes peering from helm slits just over the flat rims of their shields. Uthiel felt confident as his men advanced step by carefully measured step over the poorly laid cobblestones.

"Movement, brother captain," said one of his knights, the man's voice lent a tinny reverberation by his armour.

It took a moment for Uthiel to realise the man was addressing him. *I am a Captain of the Grey Wolves. These are my men, my company. They will follow me anywhere, into the garden of Death herself should I feel it our duty to lead them there.*

"Brother captain?" asked the man once more.

Uthiel realised he had not responded. He looked back, twisting his torso to see past the collar of his pauldrons. The knights around him were similarly armoured: cases of battle-dulled plate, joints filled with the steel cloth of finely made chainmail. Torn and blood-specked grey tabards hung lank over their cuirasses. Hundreds of glorious knights in the armour of their forefathers were marching with him. Uthiel felt his spirit lift.

Uthiel's gaze was drawn quickly back to the front. Shapes were looming ever closer. Silhouettes of axes and furs and gauntly muscled heathen swayed in the shadows like fur trees in a storm. Uthiel smiled in anticipation.

"Brother captain, your orders?" came the voice, more insistent this time.

Uthiel licked his lips. "Forward, my brothers, ever forward," he said, hefting his shield up to his eye-line and advancing, his bright blade parallel to the ground and ready to stab out as his brothers kept tight formation beside him.

Uthiel and his company broke in to a jog, war whoops and challenges being yelled out as their formation slowly began to drift apart. Men ran harder as their cries of excitement turned into bellows of rage or screams of fury. Brothers, faceless brothers, first as individuals, and then in an ever-increasing torrent of steel, dropped their shields and sprinted heedlessly forward. They roared and screamed incoherently at the enemy that charged headlong down the street at them.

Chest heaving and burning with effort, Uthiel was more than a little surprised to find a second blade in the hand where his shield had been but a moment before. No memory of discarding his shield came to a mind slowly drowning in a red haze, as his legs propelled him across the cobblestones at an ever-increasing rate.

The man beside him tore off his helm and flung it into the air. Uthiel ducked as the steel flashed past his head. Annoyance flashed through his haze, and he called out to the brother. The man's face turned to him, it was arrogance personified: matted black hair, wolfish eyes, and filed teeth punched the joy of battle from Uthiel's chest. Uthiel snarled as he realised who this was.

Murderer. Traitor. Brother.

Uthiel threw himself at Kael. Swords clashed once, twice, three times in exchanges so quick they barely registered to the eye. Then, there was nothing.

Uthiel stood alone at one corner of a crossroads. His breath rasped through his dry lips as he searched for the man he had slain back in Gall, seeking the beast he had chased halfway across a butchered kingdom. He couldn't see the treacherous Grey Wolf who had sacrificed half the population of Gall in a mad attempt to bring a blood-drenched god to walk the land and lead the barbarians he had brought across the White Frontier in the sacking of the Lands of the Light. Uthiel whirled around, trying to look everywhere at once for the monster he'd stopped from destroying the Lands of the Light.

At the other corner of the crossroads he spotted a shadow. The man was tall and broad, with the stereotypically large pauldrons of the Secundan knight Orders upon his shoulders. The figure walked towards him. Uthiel recognised his bastardised Secundan armour immediately and bared his teeth and prepared for the charge. The appearance of two alike figures, either side of Kael, stalled him a moment.

Uthiel's jaw dropped as he recognised brothers from the training yards of his youth, both of whom he'd seen die. They had been boys he'd grown with and men he had been taken to the knightly Orders with. One had left to join the Knights Aggressor while the second had saved his life by killing the first and denying the dark god his vessel.

Nikhael emerged from the shadows. That soulless stare was locked unwaveringly upon Uthiel. Shoulders flexed from under a thick coating of blood at different stages of drying and coagulation. Some flaked into the wind, some still dripped from his body and from the forearm-length blade held in a white-knuckled grip.

Branor emerged next. He was meek and frightened, not the beloved brother Uthiel grew up with, who had been so cocksure and confident. This young man was lost. His empty gaze washed over Uthiel without seeing. He stumbled as if blind, but strode on next to the two men beside him a moment later.

The jaws of the three men before him distended, lowering beyond the capability of man, black viscera drooling from blue lips and patting to the ground like lamp oil.

"Brother," came a voice, sickeningly from the three men's lungs.

Uthiel hesitated.

Branor's eyes cleared and he hid his face, ducking behind Kael as if in shame.

"Bran," said Uthiel, reaching out his hand, pleading for his brother to come back. "Please Bran, you're all I've got left. You have to hold on."

It was too late. Branor disappeared from sight. Kael and Nikhael advanced further, their shoulders sprouting demonic blades and their cheeks hollowing out as their jaws dropped, the black shadows within their gullets terrible. Their skin grew paler and more translucent by the moment. Muscles bulged a dead crimson beneath wet parchment skin. They became seven foot tall. Eight.

They melded into Branor, begging him with pleading eyes for salvation. Fat drops of black rain the viscosity of tar began to fall from the sky around him. Uthiel held out his hand, wanting to reach out and touch his life-long friend lost in the horrors of Gall.

Branor's jaw gaped wide to envelop him, his entire body morphing and splitting, stretching and breaking into one immense lamprey mouth, the gullet darker than a starless night sky.

Help me, brother. Uthiel please, come and save me from him! Help me!

Branor screamed. Another voice, like a thousand twisted souls baying for blood took over the scream as it died and ended. Uthiel fell to his knees as each word, every syllable, hit him like a forge hammer to the skull.

You are mine.

My champion.

A lord of the darkness awaiting his crown.

A harbinger of death and a butcher of the innocent.

A traitor to your people but a general of my cause.

You shall bring me to the lands of flesh once more.

You are mine.

"No!" Uthiel yelled, his voice quivering in the face of such malicious evil.

You have no choice. I will have you.

The image of a young woman's mouth screaming, her gap-toothed aperture covered in blood, flashed across his mind.

Then a piece of white cloth soaked in crimson was bound around his eyes. The metallic smell of blood filled his senses as his vision went dark.

Finally a baby wailed in terror, and Uthiel felt the air punched from his lungs like his soul had been ripped from him.

Every piece of Uthiel screamed.

Uthiel sat up, his naked body drenched in sweat, his chest heaving and his mouth closing around the sound of his yell. He looked down beside him to where Emilia would normally have been, but she was gone, off to work in the army hospital before he had woken. In the early morning dark of his canvas tent, there was naught but himself. His covers were strewn upon the floor, his ragged breathing misting instantly in the cold air. Uthiel's pale skin was covered in cold bumps, his scars already turning purple. Grabbing the coarse blanket, he wrapped himself in the material and tried to bring his body back to some semblance of warmth.

With a growl of annoyance as he spied the wan light of daybreak sliding through the tent flap, he pressed his feet down on the ice-hardened dirt floor and walked from the tent. Outside, the world was white with fresh snow, tents sitting two feet shorter than they had at dusk the night before under the clean white piles.

Uthiel took a deep breath. He loved and hated what he was about to do. There were few better ways to wake up, other than perhaps with Emilia teasing him awake, but also few better ways to leech whatever warmth the night had left a man from his bones. Uthiel saw another man come bleary eyed from a tent across from him. The man had the decency to wear a loincloth, but Uthiel could not care less as his manhood quickly retreated upwards.

Reaching down, he grabbed two handfuls of fluffy ice and, with a gasp and quick movements, he rubbed himself marginally clean of the dirt that had accumulated on his pale skin. As the ice rubbed over his face, his bent nose and scars ached, as they did each morning he went through this routine. They were painfully constant reminders of treachery, bloodshed, and the loss of his friends and brothers etched in his flesh and bone.

The man across from him gave him a wave. "Morning, brother Uthiel," the man called, before turning and hurrying out of the cold and back into his tent.

Uthiel half-waved to no one in particular, as his brother knight had already disappeared as the tent flap had closed. He took a final moment to suck in a giant lungful of the cold air of winter, his chest burning icily before he exhaled, and then turned and hurried back into his tent.

It took only a few short moments to don his clothes, clip on his belt and force on his boots before he made his way out once more, trudging through the snow at knee-height. He tramped through a forest of tents and men of war waking to this gloriously peaceful morning.

Uthiel's gaze swept out and took in the Secundan host. They were camped in their thousands before the ruined walls of Gall. Hordes of men moved in the mid-morning sun, stomping through the snow to their morning duties. The air was full of the clamour of voices, steel, horses, the hammer and anvil, and a hundred other noises that had started to feel to Uthiel Caellar like home. Somewhere a pipe started up a reedy tune.

The young knight stood motionless within the clamour, the stiff breeze tousling his hair and sweetly stinging his pale blue eyes. As his eyes squinted at a particularly icy gust, he felt the two thick scars that crinkled his youthful features begin to lessen in their aching as his body warmed. He ran a finger over them, tracing their lineage of brutality. One ran from the end of his eyebrow down past his jaw to his neck, and the second cut across the bridge of his nose and horizontally across his pale cheek.

His grey tabard, sign and symbol of his position as a brother knight of the Order of the Grey Wolves, flapped harshly despite its cinching at the waist with a black leather belt. His thick shirt and leggings beneath the hallowed grey were lined with fleece and kept some of the cold out of his lean warrior's body. Some of the lords and nobles often wore thick furs and fleeces, bears, wolves, and others, but Uthiel was no lord, and such things were beyond him.

As he had each day since the battle for Gall for some, and since before then for others, Uthiel instinctively waited for the young men he'd grown up with and fought with to appear from their tents. *Ghosts, to the man.* He listened for their banter, their goading, arguing, complaining, bragging. *Fighting by His side in the Shield Wall in the Sky.* He could almost hear them making fun of his usually dishevelled morning appearance. *I lost them. My brothers: Keldon, Eliem, Umbar, Bran.... My father...*

As it had each day since the battle for Gall for some, and since before then for others, Uthiel's heart broke just a little bit more as he remembered their deaths. The balm from the previous night had not healed his grief, as it had not every night for months.

A strong hand clasped his shoulder from behind. Uthiel had to stop his own hand, already gripping the leather bound handle of his forearm-length knife, from drawing the blade in anger. It was a habit three months of fighting guerrilla warfare behind the barbarian lines had instilled in his reflexes. Blue eyes, dark hair and a stern young face that had shared much of Uthiel's experience looked at him. *Not all of them lost. He fought with me, shared the battles, the hardships. Not Gall, though. Not where the world changed.*

"Brother," said Uthiel, before Tarren could speak. "How fares the leg?"

Tarren winced a little and shifted his weight off the leg that had taken an arrow in the ambush at Rouen and still pained him in the cold. The knight was of an age with Uthiel, still not yet even twenty summers, not by a couple of years at least by Uthiel's memory of the summers he'd lived through, and stood perhaps half a foot shorter, but stockier. He wore the same garb as Uthiel, a hard earned grey tabard upon his chest.

"Hurts," said the young knight. "Probably be limping like some cripple for the rest of this life, till He takes us, anyway. This rate, probably won't be so long before He does."

"A ray of sunshine, as ever, brother," said Uthiel.

Tarren grimaced and spat into the snow. "Just telling it like it is. If the first captain keeps insisting we lead the bloody van of every march we'll not live to see Mother Secunda freed from the barbarians, especially if I have to follow you around everywhere."

Uthiel felt his jaw clench at the thinly veiled insult, then relaxed and enjoyed the friendly jape for what it was. The days when Tarren challenged his leadership were gone. *I hope.*

"The final envoys should get here today," said Uthiel, letting Tarren's comment go by. "Men from Imonetia, Tarren! Hundreds, maybe thousands of leagues away where the fortresses of the White Frontier sit in sand and not snow…"

"Just another jumped-up lord probably," growled Tarren. "Someone born with a silver spoon in his mouth and the ability to send thousands of good men to their deaths."

"Would you say the same of our lords? Pretty soon they'll be sending thousands of us to our deaths," retorted Uthiel.

"You mean Thomak? Pomen? Well, Pomen's all right. Served with your 'da so must be a good man. Thomak? He's an Armenius gifted hero, we're lucky he's in charge and not some bastard like Ryun. Heard some horrible things about that lord."

"Like what?" asked Uthiel.

"Like what he did to some of those barbarians wearing our armour. Burned alive. Flayed. Tortured. More than even they deserve."

Uthiel frowned, his voice almost a whisper of a whisper. "They deserved every lick of flame and blade."

Tarren looked at him sharply. "No man deserves that. Worse than a traitor's death."

Uthiel's stare hardened, instinctively wanting to challenge his subordinate, to tell Tarren the truth of what happened. Every piece of him screamed to break the oath of secrecy he'd sworn to the man who had commanded the united might of the Lands of the Light.

Uthiel's shoulders slumped. *Duty.*

"You weren't there, brother. You would not understand what we saw of them," said Uthiel resignedly, futilely hoping that would be an end to the conversation.

"What? I miss one fight and all of a sudden everything we've been through is for naught? I no longer understand what it's like to stand in a shield wall or skirmish line, with bloodied blade in my hand and foes held back by the strength of my shield arm?" stormed Tarren, his face reddening.

"Brother, no," started Uthiel, but stopped, *How can I possibly explain this? How can I tell him Kael the great betrayer was a Grey Wolf brother turned traitor? How do I say 'a Grey Wolf ten years thought dead, a first captain as mighty as our own, marshalled a million barbarians to destroy the Lands of the Light and sacrificed a hundred thousand innocent Gall women to bring a god of blood to the earth to rule the realm? I can't tell anyone, though, because Thomak will hang, draw and quarter me if I do.' Just how in the bloody name of Armenius do I tell him that!?*

"That's not what I meant," he said weakly, shrugging his shoulders. "You don't understand. What we saw... Those men in our armour... they..."

Aw, shit.

The stockier knight did not speak for a while, allowing the silence to grow.

"What happened, brother?" asked Tarren, his voice far away. "What happened to Keldon and Branor? How did they die? If you spin me some story of glory I'll hit you. I know that you have told me before of their deaths to be a lie."

Keldon was crushed by the invisible fist of a shaman, his flesh and blood exploding from his armour. Bran... Bran turned on me... tried to tear me apart... I almost saved him... Could have saved him. I didn't... couldn't. Armenius forgive me.

There was an awkward silence between the two as the conversation died. Uthiel tried to think of something to say as Kael's filed teeth smiled at him in his mind's eye. Tarren grunted and left without a word, his limp as evident as his discontent.

With another sigh, Uthiel's gaze lifted above the row of dirty white canvas tents and looked upon the charred grey stone walls that had once protected the people of Gall. Their seventy-foot high strength had seen the people she'd protected through thousands of years of peace and war. *Wasn't enough to stop the Black Wolves. Wasn't enough to save hundreds of thousands of innocents and the king's men who tried to protect them. Wasn't enough to stop Kael.*

Uthiel shivered at the thought. The image of the forest of seven-foot high trestles crowding the cobblestone streets with lifeless women strapped naked to the top of them, their throats slashed, would be burned in to his very soul for as long as he lived. Taking a deep breath, Uthiel wondered if the image would ever leave him, even when Armenius called him to do battle in the Shield Wall in the Sky.

Uthiel turned away from the city, away from the pale smoke rising to the clouds above, away from the horrible memories of slaughter, away from Kael and the treasonous Black Wolves, away from the deaths of his friends, and finally away from the fall of his father. Immediately his chest tightened and his throat constricted. His eyes began to sting and he felt a tear roll down his face.

So much death. So much horror. How he and the survivors had stood in front of the tidal wave of blood and violence, the overwhelming urge for depravity, that had spilled forth from

23

the pillar of light that flashed down from the sky to claim many of their lives and some of their souls, Uthiel would never know. Why he still breathed to continue to worship and honour Armenius, when so many of Secunda's knights and soldiers had fallen, was something he genuinely feared he could not come to terms with.

He was about to make for the cook fires that were beginning to spew black smoke from wet wood into the sky above, when he heard the clobbering of hoof beats. Forty feet away, Tarren stopped and turned back, locking eyes with Uthiel through the crowd. A rare smile crossed that craggy face as he jog-limped his way back to Uthiel, their conversation seemingly already forgotten.

"Bit excited to see another jumped-up lord, are we?" ventured Uthiel, eyebrow raised.

Tarren kept going past him, towards the sound. "Not every bloody day you get to see the sand-dwellers. Probably not much else to do."

"We could go get in queue for food," said Uthiel, feeling his stomach growl.

Tarren paused for a moment, looking to be truly torn between the two options, then grunted and kept walking towards the thunder of whatever mounted company was coming in to camp. They quickly joined the hundreds of men that lined the main road in anticipation of the spectacle to come. Knights, soldiers, armourers, cooks, whores, hunters, healers, the lightly wounded and a massive array of other camp followers, all stood together. Body heat and breath misted into the air above in wispy clouds as they looked to the outer earthen ramparts of the immense camp.

Uthiel spied his father's friends, who fought with the Fifth, standing amongst the crowd. He waved to Antony and Argo. The two men waved back, smiling. Uthiel could still see the pain of the loss of Tanin upon their faces.

Uthiel shouldered his way a little forward, trying not to bump anyone too hard, past some of his taller brothers despite their growls, so he could see properly. Tarren was less careful, hammering his thick shoulder into anyone in his way. Were it not for the horses coming from the gate, there probably would have been a fight.

The first thing Uthiel noticed, even before the weird dress styles and armour and swords of the men riding them, were the horses. They looked like ponies, maybe geldings. His brow furrowed. Their saddle must have sat at least five hands lower than a Secundan mount. He wanted to laugh a little, but the men upon them stowed that. Their bodies were wrapped in travel-stained silk and cloth, immaculate and sleeveless chainmail coats covering them from neck to ankle, hand-width bands of steel flowing over their shoulders like segmented pauldrons.

Gold and steel skull caps with more flowing chainmail, that covered from the back rim of the cap down over the neck and hung down the mens' backs, flapped with each thundering trot of their horses. From their belts, curved swords bounced and on their backs round bronze and steel bucklers and roundshields hung on black leather straps.

It only felt like a short moment before they were gone in a spray of splattering mud, heading towards the centre of camp where the envoys from Pandur, Lemug, and the other knight Orders had thundered days, in some cases, and weeks in others, ago.

"Well, that's it then," said Uthiel. "With all of them here, we can expect to be on the march again soon."

Tarren spat on the ground. "Not likely. I think they'll be more than happy to just sit in their warm tents while we freeze our arses off out here through winter. Lords, all 'talk' and no 'do'."

"With Lord Steward Thomak in command?"

"Mark my words, hero," snapped Tarren, back to his surly self. "Winter'll be long gone before we pull up these tents."

As Tarren turned and left, still grumbling, Uthiel kept his stare on the quickly disappearing horses.

"If only that were true," he said, before a grim smile spread across his face.

CHAPTER THREE

"M'lord?"

"M'lord, can you wake?" came the voice again: friendly, respectful, familiar.

Lord Pomen slowly opened his eyes to a room full of fog. *Not fog. Cataracts.* Immediately the itch at the back of his throat and in his lungs roared to life and that hacking, phlegm-coated cough started. A cup was offered to him by a wrinkled hand, attached to a bent arm, attached to a thin chest in a grey coat, attached to a face: friendly, respectful, familiar. *Grullen. Faithful Grullen.*

Pomen accepted the cup, his coughing fit abating but his breath coming out in wheezes, as he recovered from what had become his morning ritual since the second week of camp. He drank deeply. Warm watered wine with honey soothed his throat somewhat for a moment, but a few breaths later he exploded into another coughing fit.

"My lord, are you alright? Should I fetch a healer?" asked Grullen, as Pomen once more gained control of himself, thick mucus rattling in his chest.

He shook his head, afraid that if he spoke he would fall into yet another fit. All over, he ached. Body, mind and soul, he ached. Pomen had long accepted this would be his last campaign, his final battle against the great enemy before his body failed him and his mind lost its edge.

Before the winter he had felt strong and tall and proud, as he had for his many years of servitude to the Grey Wolves and Secunda. But this winter, this camp, and this war had finally sapped his life's last reserves of strength. Grullen backed away to an almost standard and well-practised distance as Pomen swung his skinny white legs out from under the cover and placed his bare feet upon the cold, hard-packed dirt ground. The chill shot up through his legs from the soles of his wrinkled feet and immediately his knees started throbbing. Marching at the head of thousands of men from Secunda to Gall was something his body just wasn't built to withstand any more.

Pomen looked to his armour: his beautifully artificed and polished armour. He could see his own blurry reflection in the polished steel of his cuirass. The early morning sun's rays glinted from those stereotypical Secundan knight Order pauldrons. They were huge, with their ear-height inner collar, upon his armour rack. His heart lifted at the sight of his second skin, but then sank immediately as he tried to stand. The weight of his own body was getting hard enough to carry, let alone the weight of his glorious armour.

Armenius, give me strength.

Pomen looked up to his servant. "Breakfast, Grullen. Bring me some hot tea. No more wine. Wine is not for breakfast for a man my age. Dulls the wits."

Grullen bowed his head. "M'lord." He left through the tent flap.

Pomen yawned and stretched his old bones. He rubbed his face with his grizzled hands, stifling a second yawn, before rubbing the sides of his chest to combat the winter cold. He needed to get his mind in order. He needed to be sharp. If his body wasn't up to the task of running the Grey Wolves, then his mind damn well needed to be. Standing, he headed over to his chest of clothes, his knees complaining with every step and his throat burning with every breath.

A short while later he was garbed for his day's duty in thick leggings and shirt under his dark grey tabard. His dark leather boots held his feet snugly and he used them to pace towards the opening that led to the expanse of the Secundan camp.

He grabbed a thick bear fur cloak and wrapped it around his shoulders, shoulders that had not been so skinny since he was a boy, maybe thirteen or fourteen. He rested a hand on his cuirass, looking mournfully at the armour he was beginning to believe he might never wear upon his wasting form again. The cloak quickly added some warmth to his bones, and he shuddered a little at the simple pleasure of the building heat of his body.

Grullen took that moment to duck through the tent flap, his eyes settling on Pomen's pale, bony hand upon the polished plate.

"No offence m'lord, but you're too ill to be weighed down by all that steel," said Grullen apologetically. "M'lord needs his strength. The Imonetians have arrived, I've been asked to bring you to the lord steward."

Pomen took a deep breath. *This is it.* It was time to attend the final war council before the winter campaign an almost dead king had ordered before his wounding, and a war-hungry Secundan steward had committed the five kingdoms of the Land of the Light to. *Four kingdoms,* he reminded himself, *Gall's strength is no more. Her soldiers, her sons and her daughters were slaughtered by the servants of the dark god. Kael, you black-hearted bastard, how could you do this?*

Grullen seemed to take his quiet reflection as an invitation to keep speaking. "M'lord, shall I grab another cloak? Perhaps a second pair of leggings will help keep the cold at bay. This winter'll be a horrible one, spent away from hearths and the protection of stone walls."

"My father taught me that to lead men you must be strong," he told Grullen. "To wrap oneself up like some woman or commoner would be unbefitting. These men follow me. I would not have them look at me like I am some unshorn sheep, warm and comfortable while they struggle in the cold in a worse-for-wear tent, if they have tents at all."

"They might see you as a six-foot tall ice statue if you don't stay warm, m'lord," retorted Grullen.

Pomen frowned, grimaced and went on, doing his best to ignore Grullen's comment. "I'll be needing a belt, yes, the thick black one would be good. Now pass me my sword and scabbard."

With a final look at his frame, Pomen clasped his bearskin cloak under his chin, brushed himself with his hands and then walked out of the tent and into the harsh and bitter cold wind of the Gall winter. Clenching his jaw, he turned back to Grullen.

"Alright Grullen, I'll take the second pair of leggings."

A short while later, his breath rasping from his body in itchy and irritating bursts of mist, his knees aching like Death herself was giving them a cold tickle, Pomen walked from his tent. He nodded his reluctant thanks to Grullen, and turned away from his servant as the four Grey Wolf knights of his personal bodyguard formed up in a square around him. He welcomed their company.

"Hadar, how fares the wound?" he asked of one of his men.

Hadar met his eyes for a moment. "It fares well, lord general, my limp is only irritated by this damn cold."

"Winter and age, eh?" said Pomen.

Hadar hesitated a moment — Pomen easily had twenty-five years on the man — before nodding once more with his eyes averted to the camp around them. "Yes lord, winter and age."

Pomen sighed inside, his face hiding his jealousy as he looked at the thick plates of blessed armour upon his bodyguards. Licking his ice-dry lips, he pulled his attention away from his men. He remembered how he had looked at knight lords his age in his youth — with scorn at their inability. Even in his middle years when hours in a battle line was not beyond him, he'd thought himself invulnerable to time. By Armenius, even in the last few years, foolishly, as the oldest knight probably in Secunda, he still thought of those old men and revelled in his ability to hold his armour and sword and fight.

The weight of his years had come crashing down on him — finally. His winter illness had stripped his strength and stamina. He needed to accept that and move on. He needed to keep his honour for when Armenius finally called him to the Shield Wall in the Sky. At this moment, that didn't feel too far away. *Months, perhaps. A year, maybe.* Men in his vocation rarely lived to his age, but many of the townsfolk he'd seen in his life, wrinkled and old and bent backed with cataract-coated eyes and drooling mouths, never lived long once the cough begun. Soon blood would spit from his mouth, his mind would cloud and wander, and his body would fail. Piece by miserable piece, it would fail. If he was young again, most probably he would have survived and only lost a few pounds.

"My Lord Pomen?" came a questioning voice.

Pomen realized he'd stopped walking. Inside, the spark, that spark that made a man what he was, flared brightly with anger. *By Armenius, no!* Pomen took a deep, searing breath. *I'll not fade into the night! I'll not be left to die in some room like a leper, forgotten by my brothers! I am the Lord General Pomen and I wield the might of the Order of the Grey Wolves, the mighty Secundan Fifth and the unstoppable Seventh! I am a servant of Armenius, and I shall not falter!*

Pomen growled, his body firing and for a beautiful moment feeling like his old self again, before he almost doubled over as a vicious coughing fit wracked his body. One of his bodyguards reached out to help him but Pomen held out his hand.

"No, Hadar, I am fine," gasped Pomen, his gravelly voice reasserting some of his authority. "Take me to the lord steward."

Pomen and his men moved on, their boots trudging through the brown tracks in the snow that hundreds of men had already trod that morning. All around him cook fires had been lit and men huddled around the flames to get warm. Thousands of tents rippled loudly in the harsh wind as it swept over the plain from the mountains to the west. Secunda sat many leagues to the west, bereft of a massive portion of her men as they moved east to retake the White Frontier. Mother

Secunda sat in the opposite direction, her ancient walls and towers and castle lost to the Lands of the Light for some four centuries and more.

As he walked, Pomen took in more of the sights and smells of a war camp. There were longs tracks of mud through the snow upon the ground. Men stretched stiff backs from sleeping upon the cold ground in their tents. Food cooked over open flames and inside burnished cooking pots. Woodsmoke floated lazily up until it was snatched away by the wind. Sentries changed shifts as some men took up positions and others clambered exhaustedly for a few hours of sleep. Horses whinnied, people laughed and shouted, and the steady rhythm of a blacksmith's hammer rang out. A whore, bags under her eyes and a pocket full of clinking coppers, walked past, heading to where the baggage trains were set up.

Pomen smiled and looked to the sky, the sounds and smell of a war camp full with the brave men and women of his homeland lifted his spirits and helped him forget his melancholy. Armenius, the Eternal Lord, god of the Secundan people, had put him here for a reason, and that was to lead men into battle. He had been given years beyond those of most of his brothers. His days of standing in the front line of a shield wall were over two, perhaps more decades gone, and oft in those years he had thought himself useless, but here, now, he had found his purpose once more. His lot was no longer to slay individuals in combat with weapons of steel, it was to destroy armies in war with regiments of flesh and courage.

Eventually, as the sun began to rise further into the sky, he and his bodyguard arrived at the king's tent. Before he even entered, he could hear the voices of Thomak and his war council arguing over one thing or other. Pomen took a deep, calming breath, held in a cough as his throat flared again, pulled his shoulders back, dismissed his bodyguards, and entered the tent.

There were at least fifty men crammed in there, some knights, some soldiers, many serving other purposes, standing around a massive painted canvas map upon a large oak table.

Hard packed dirt was underfoot and wood smoke clung to the ceiling of the thickly canvassed tent.

A few of the knights wore their full plate armour, and the tabards of the other five remaining Orders Pomen understood had been deployed many miles to the north and south of his forces. Pomen regarded them a moment. *Such pride, such strength. Thomak will be pressed to keep such men in line. The King, with some of last words before closing his eyes, may have given him stewardship, but by Armenius, he'll have to work to keep it. They will follow him for now, but as soon as things don't go their way, he'll be pressed.*

Among the dignitaries of the Orders were men in the mail and strip plate with underlying silk of the Imonetians in the north, puffy sleeves and silk wrappings and leggings clasping tight around their ankles and wrists. Curved cavalry scimitars hung from their belts. Pomen spied one man with a thick but groomed beard in the plate armour of the Lemugian's elite First Cavalry from the deep south, his weapons and arms of similar origin to the Secundan knight class, though markedly different.

He admired the man's armour a moment, wondering how many glorious charges that steel plate had seen from atop the finest warhorses in the realm, while being worn by the finest cavalrymen in the known world. He smiled at the thought of the Lemugians and the Grey Wolves fighting together. *The finest heavy foot beside the finest cavalry marching to glory —* *magnificent.* The thought warmed his fighter's heart.

Beside the knight a handsome woman in her forties stood tall and regal. A thick bearskin edged in gold thread hung over the shoulders of her heavy winter dress. Upon her head, atop her greying blonde hair that had been harshly pulled back into a ponytail, sat a thin crown of gold with a single inlaid green emerald aligned with her nose. Pomen stared for longer than was appropriate for a man of his age. Queen Valissa of Lemug was a woman of attractive power.

Valissa stood calm and composed amongst the ruckus, her gaze coolly judging every man around her. Pomen dipped his head before those dark green eyes could land on him, lest he not be able to look away.

Disconcertingly, the Pandurs had no representative at the table.

"Ah! My Lord Pomen!" called out the lord steward over the hubbub of voices. "Please, attend us immediately, we've had news from the other fronts. Some of it good, some of it bad, I'm afraid."

Pomen nodded his welcomes to those he knew and then immediately turned his attention to the map. He scrutinised the canvas quickly, and took in the numbered pieces of carved wood representing the army groups and their last known position. Straight away he saw that they were only a few days' march from the White Frontier town of Archenon Creek, holding the centre of the line. To the immediate north the forces of three knight Orders along with the First and Second Armenian armies had made it almost to the White Frontier and presented a bulge in the line, twenty miles forward of both Pomen's forces and the Lemugians and Pandurs in the deep south.

Most concerning was in the far north, where elements of Sixth, Eighth, Ninth, and two more knight Orders had only managed to push out a couple of days' march from the Secundan border. The news got worse the further north Pomen looked. Imonetia had fallen. Her shattered forces had pulled back and west across the sand and rock and managed to evade the barbarian advance as winter fell, but her cities and towns were gone, as were a great deal of her people and soldiers. *That news must be a month old. For all we know, they are gone and the barbarians march for a poorly defended Secunda.*

The reserve armies lay in camp to the west awaiting deployment orders. They were small and spread sparsely, consisting mainly of the combined remnants of badly mauled army units. They lent ever more weight to the knife's edge the ownership of the realm lay upon, and the grandiosity of the plans the king had put into action before falling.

A few more men had entered the king's tent as Pomen surveyed the maps. Thomak addressed each by name before turning back to the general assembly. Scribes were in constant deep conversation with the men around the table, taking notes on fighting strength and supplies and then passing the detailed scrolls to the centre to be piled in front of Thomak.

"Silence!" called a voice over the din. "Silence for the words of the lord steward of Secunda, marshal of the military might of the Lands of the Light!"

The Lord Steward Thomak, marshal of the military might of the Lands of the Light, waited a moment as the voices died down and the eyes of the leaders and envoys of the largest army assembled, across the largest front in written history, settled upon him, Pomen's included.

"My friends, let us reappraise the situation briefly for the latecomers, while the scribes finish their work," began Thomak. " At the centre of the line, here, under command of the Lord General Pomen of the Grey Wolves, we have the Secundan Fifth once again at near full strength, having rolled two reserve forces into it. Six thousand men. The Seventh is below strength at approximately four thousand with no further reinforcements available before we march on Archenon Creek. Do I have this correct, Lord Pomen?"

Pomen nodded his assent at the figures, though added one correction. "We also still have around a hundred men from both the Fifth and Seventh who are healing in the field hospital. We can expect them to re-join the ranks before we march."

Thomak accepted this in his stride, a hundred men in the greater scheme of the war effort was probably not much to consider. "Noted. The Grey Wolves are far below strength with only a hundred and sixty five brothers ready to march. Many of the heroes of our first company are gone, but I have seen them all training hard and the integration of the thirty new initiates into the ranks looks to have gone well. You would do well to reform the Order around men like First Captain Solanthur, Captain Laurenn, and the hero Uthiel Caellar. What progress has been made on this since they were appointed to you?"

"Little, Field Marshal Thomak," admitted Pomen. The Order had only been his for less than a week, so slow had Thomak been to relinquish command. "Today I shall be setting up a general staff to help me manage my forces efficiently.

There is much structure to be put in place before I change the current setup of the Wolves."

Pomen noticed a small clench in Thomak's jaw but nothing further was said on the Grey Wolves.

"As stated yesterday," continued Thomak, "half of the king's guard shall remain here with the king to return him to Secunda when he is fit to be moved, while the other half shall remain available to you as an additional cavalry wing. You'll have approximately a hundred men plus destriers. They are to return from their out riding duties this afternoon, upon which moment you shall be appointed their services. They are the best cavalry available to the Secundan army, Lord Pomen. Use them well."

Pomen nodded his understanding as he covered a cough with his hand. *I know how to lead and command men. I've been doing it since you were a sparkle in your father's eye.* "Of their unparalleled prowess on the field there is no doubt, lord steward. Who is currently in charge of the king's guard? I shall seek him out upon his return."

"Captain Duram leads them. He is an absolute mountain of a man, easily the biggest of them and should not be hard to spot," said Thomak.

"We only have enough supply to march for a week, lord steward," continued Pomen.

"Take whatever food you can from the area around us and ration harshly, Lord Pomen. Supplies from Secunda are still two weeks away and you'll need to make do until then. I cannot afford special favour to you just because I once commanded the Wolves," said Thomak, turning away from the lord and beginning to address a man in a red tabard with stitched white rose on the breast.

Bastard. We are your brothers.

"Lord General Colle Gill of the Order of the White Rose," said Thomak. "To confirm, your Order stands three hundred and twenty strong in the south, along with a further four hundred men of the Order of the Black Falcon and the Sons of Armenius."

"Correct, lord steward," responded the booming deep voice of Colle Gill. "The First and Second Secundan armies both stand at six thousand strong, with an additional one and a half thousand fighting men in reserve."

Thomak nodded. "A stronger front that we have here. You will order your men to hold for three days and then march on the White Frontier. This should allow enough time for us to straighten the line. How are supplies?"

"We've received supplies from both Secunda and Lemug. We've enough to last the month."

"Good man," said Thomak, reaching out his hand and receiving a hearty warrior's handshake from the lord general of the White Rose, who visibly lifted.

"Queen Valissa, The deep south?" said Thomak, addressing the Lemugian emissary, Gill already forgotten.

Gracefully, Valissa took a step forward. The bearded man took a step with her, looking threatening and ready for violence, garbed in the Lemug knight's dark plate. He wore no tabard but a sword wrapped in brambles was inscribed and painted with black on his chest.

"Lemug had raised forty thousands of men on top of our fifteen thousands standing army before the winter," she said in a strong and confident voice. "Pandur were only able to manage some twenty thousands. We have lost the White Frontier fortresses of Tyrri and the Pandur Plain, though we held on to the fortress at the Baht Pass from the onset of the war. The first two major battles cost us twenty five thousands of men and the Pandurs half their number, but we held them and pushed them back through the first months of winter to stand within six days march of the two lost fortresses.

"As I left it two month's hard riding past, the two Lemug armies stood well supplied at twelve thousands, heading to both lost fortresses and the remaining six thousand to the held fortress at the Baht Pass. Lemug is clear of the barbarians behind our lines and we are ready to push back to the Frontier. King Trygun of Pandur has taken his ten thousand remaining men and pushed down the line of the mountains to ensure we are not flanked. He asked that I bring news of their progress."

The way that Valissa almost spat out King Trygun's name left no doubt of her opinion on the king, and the people who bordered the lands of her own.

"What of reserves?" asked Thomak.

Valissa bowed her head a little. "Every fighting man with any sort of training either lies dead under a burial mound, or stands ready to march forward. We pulled men from our mines and farms and smithies — good strong labourers — but they are not soldiers. They will take time to be fit for war. Whether their hearts have more than a moment's courage in them we'll not know until the enemy hits our lines."

"How many?"

"A further fifteen thousand," said the Lemugian queen. "Though this leaves our labourers with so few that we expect production and gathering of supplies to be unable to keep up with demand of the standing army."

"You shall have assistance if we can provide it," promised Thomak.

Pomen laughed bitterly inside. *A well-intentioned empty promise at best, a lie at worst.*

Thomak turned to another Secundan knight. "Lord Helion, appraise me of the north."

A knight of average height in full plate and a dark green tabard decorated with a red, leafless tree took a step forward and leaned down over the map, placing leather gloved fists on the table, as if to support himself. His double chinned face was the mask of tiredness held up by raw courage and commitment.

"Armenius damn it, but those bastard barbarians came at us in force two months ago," he said gruffly. "We had pushed them back some forty miles towards the White Frontier, but then they hit us from the side. Ten thousand soldiers, a thousand knights, hundreds of smiths, cooks, labourers, whores, and a great deal of our supplies — gone. Shit covered bastards snuck in and slew our outriders and then hit us a hammer blow from absolutely nowhere.

"We've been fighting skirmishes as we've retreated, losing more and more as we go. Our count stands at just a few thousand. Apart from a few older or infirm of my brothers left

37

back at our fortress, it pains me to say, the Order of the Blood Tree, my Order, has been all but wiped out."

A tear rolled down his cheek and splashed to the map, leaving a dark circle on the canvas. His chins wobbled a little as he forced a sob down. Pomen choked a little. Helion was generally a pompous arse. He was fat, though slimming through the harshness of war and winter, arrogant and mean-spirited, but Pomen would not wish his lot upon any man. To see your brothers, a thousand of them, dead to the man around you was an experience he had narrowly avoided ten years ago during Kael's great betrayal. Not since Armenius had lost near ten thousand men in one red afternoon and night, and then fought clear, had a brother Order known so much pain. Immediately after, Helion's face hardened. There was resolve there once more. Pomen's respect for a man he had never liked took a step up.

Helion's eyes snapped up to focus on the emissary from Imonetia. "How did you let so many of them through? How could you lose your entire bloody city! You cost me my brothers! My family!"

The face of the Imonetian emissary went red and he immediately shouted a response. "You lost ten thousand men? I spit on your ten thousand men!"

Helion stood upright, his fists clenching and his wobbling face going pale with rage. "I'll have your tongue for that!" he screamed, reaching for his forearm length knife.

"Fifty four thousand men gone! Fifty four thousand of Imonetia's sons, brothers and fathers! Most of our army! That's not even counting the people we lost as they ran to seek refuge in Secunda!" yelled the Imonetian, spittle flying on to the map.

"Is your army full of boys and old men, Prince Aphiti? How could you have a force so large, and lose? Are you stupid, or are you all just so retarded from all of your princely inbreeding that you cannot wield an army any better than trying to wield a spoonful of shit into your own mouths?" shouted back Helion.

Stupid. Back down a step you go, Lord Helion, thought Pomen.

"I'll gut you like a Dunesnake!" screamed Aphiti, his blade rasping from its sheath. All around the table, knights drew their swords and faced the raging prince.

"Enough!" roared Thomak. "Lord Helion, hold your tongue. Prince Aphiti, remember whose table you stand at. Much Secundan blood will be spilt to help regain your kingdom, do not forget that. The rest of you, if anyone *ever* draws their blade unnecessarily again in my presence I'll have you hanged. Is that clear?"

Helion and Prince Aphiti continued to glare at each other malevolently. The room seethed with anger and nervous energy as blades slid back into boiled leather sheaths.

Thomak let out a growl of anger and frustration. "Lord Pomen, attend me here, the rest of you get out. Lord General Gill and Queen Valissa, you have your orders. Replace your horses as needs be and leave immediately. The rest of you, we will reconvene at midday."

Valissa stood still. Thomak's eyes narrowed.

"You may leave, honoured queen," said the lord steward levelly.

Valissa shook her head. "No, I shall stay. My king expects me to be a diplomat to this camp and to the leader of this war effort."

Thomak's face hardened. "That will not be necessary. I shall send riders to keep the south appraised."

The Lemugian queen smiled, though there was no humour in her eyes.

"I have brought many men and messengers with me. I shall do as my king commands me. What I shall *not* do, is bend to the will of a steward."

Thomak's face darkened.

Valissa smiled once more. This time there was genuine humour in the act.

"I grow weary. The air in here has become far too stuffed with ego for my liking. Send for me when you are ready to appraise me of the army's movements."

Inside, Pomen enjoyed the confrontation immensely. Rarely was Thomak brought down by any but the king. The aging lord general watched the sway of Valissa's hips as her bearded knight shepherded her out.

Too young for you, old man.

Give me ten years of youth and I'll show you too old. Pomen suppressed a chuckle.

As the moment passed, and Pomen waited for the men and servants to leave, he sighed to himself. With the Lemugians and the Pandurs having been at each other's throats for ten centuries and not looking to resolve their differences any time soon, with fresh anger growing between the Imonetians and the Secundan Orders, the Order of the Knights Aggressor turning traitor some four months prior and the barbarians running rife through the lands, would anyone survive the winter?

Pomen took a breath, felt the itch take over, and coughed explosively, spit and phlegm flying through his ice-cold fingers. As he wiped his hand on a cloth left upon the table, Thomak locked eyes with him.

"Lord Pomen, how do you fare?" asked the commander of the Lands of the Light.

"Strong and in good health, lord steward," said Pomen. *Lie.*

Thomak smiled. There was the slightest hint of a smirk being covered by that smile. *Like I am a sheep, thinking this Wolf is my friend.* A small cough, that quickly turned into a series of bone jarring, spittle expelling, back bending coughs quickly showed his lie for what it was.

As he calmed and stood straighter, Pomen saw the smirk on Thomak's face was more forthright. Thomak trailed the tips of his fingers over the line of the white frontier, stopping on Imonetia.

"Tomorrow, my old friend," said Thomak, "the Grey Wolves, the king's guards, and the Fifth will begin the long march to escort Prince Aphiti north into the desert to take back Imonetia and straighten the front."

Pomen nodded solemnly, his mind already working through the thousands of logistical decisions to make and orders to give to get some six thousand men to break camp, muster, and get moving. He'd need outriding scouts, a wagon train, last minute scavengers and hunters to be sent out immediately, he had to decide which wounded could be taken and which to reassign to the Seventh remaining for the march on Archenon creek, what...

"Lord Pomen," said Thomak, pulling Pomen's mind back to the present.

Another knight entered the tent. He was old, like Pomen, perhaps less than a decade his junior, perhaps a little more. Soft torchlight glinted off polished steel pauldrons. It was a brother he'd fought with for close on half a century. *Lord Ryun?*

"Lord Pomen," said Thomak again, pulling Pomen's eyes back. "Looking at you, today, coughing and spluttering and hobbling like an invalid mere days from Death's embrace, I have realised that putting you in command of the Grey Wolves was a mistake. Your image, I can tolerate. Your tardiness in restructuring the Wolves, I cannot. You shall no longer be leading them. The honour shall fall to Lord Ryun."

CHAPTER FOUR

Uthiel awoke on his back the next morning, the same canvas tent above him holding back the same fresh powdered cold, but this time with the warmth of Emilia's light breathing whispering across his chest. Yawning, he looked down at her breathtaking beauty, snuggled against him under their coarse blanket. He could feel her lean leg rested over his manhood, still slightly tender from their love making the night before, her small foot curled against his opposite thigh. A delicate hand, residue dried blood and grime still stuck under her fingernails from her work the previous day with the apothecaries, rested in front of her face amongst the smooth splays of her dark hair upon the other side of his steadily rising and falling chest.

In this moment, this fleeting moment, he knew would not last to the beckoning sunrise, Uthiel was unequivocally happy. The advance to Archenon Creek, his losses of the past years, his tears, his rages, his agonies, the blood, the screams: none of it worried him in this profound moment. He was in the eye of his hurricane. He reached up with his hand to stroke her hair. The movement of the shoulder and arm she slept upon roused her.

Mesmerising green eyes, flecked lightly with brown around the irises, looked up at him drowsily from amongst fair skin lightly coated with freckles. The corners of her mouth creased as her lips broke into a welcome smile. She inhaled deeply through the nose, seeming to enjoy the smell of his chest as she moaned and stretched her limbs, rejuvenated.

"Good morning, my lover," she whispered. "Did you dream?"

Uthiel smiled, the memory of a rare peaceful sleep coming back to him to make this morning moment all the more pleasant.

"I did."

"Was it a good dream? Did *he* come for you again?"

Uthiel closed his eyes, reliving the dream as he'd explained it to her.

It had started out as nightmarish as most of them did of late. He stood in a dark city, under a dark sky. Brothers unknown to him slowly succumbed to raging madness. Nikhael, Bran and Kael had approached him once more, melding and splitting. Then the darkness had come for him. It had massive yellow teeth and a gullet blacker than the purest of pitch, with breath like a five-day-old battlefield in summer.

The mouth, twice as tall as he was, had leapt at him. Uthiel had drawn breath to scream, but golden light had coalesced into a shield before him, warding off the evil. The light shone bright and soon he had felt his feet and hands in the lush grass of a great field.

His vision had returned, shapes going from dark fog to sharp figures in Secundan plate before his very eyes. Kind faces looked down at him. An arm stretched out and gripped his own in a warrior's shake, pulling him to his feet. He had looked into a strong face, a man he did not know but had stereotypical Secundan features. Uthiel had peered beyond the man, looking at the line of warriors arrayed in an immense battle line hundreds of thousands strong.

War trumpets had blared and banners had flapped in the cool wind. Somewhere distant, cavalry had thundered, out of sight.

A golden figure had walked towards him and Uthiel had drank in the vision of the man. He'd stood tall and heroic, and immediately Uthiel had known who the man was. His chest swelling with pride and awe, Uthiel had watched as Armenius Faramon, Eternal Lord of the Secundan people, reached out his hand in a warrior's shake.

Uthiel had taken the god's hand, squinting his eyes in the brightness of Armenius' spirit.

"Welcome, brother."

"Have I fallen?" Uthiel had asked, struggling to remember a battle.

"No, my son," said Armenius. "But glories and great danger rest upon your shoulders in equal measures. A great darkness comes to this land, and you alone have the strength and the spirit to unite the realm against it. As I foretold, as my mortal form lay dying, *one doomed to stand, when all around him fall.*"

Uthiel frowned. "Doomed?"

His god's lips had thinned a moment before continuing. "A great challenge shall face you. You shall become a champion of the light, or you shall fall. Either way I shall be there with you."

Armenius had reached out and placed a hand where the wolf head talisman normally would have hung around Uthiel's neck. Uthiel had felt a burning warmth.

"The future is not certain, though what is certain is that if you do not become what I need you to be, Secunda shall fall."

Uthiel's face set. "I shall be your champion, my Eternal Lord."

"I expected no less, my son."

Uthiel looked out beyond the battle line. Dark clouds hung low on the horizon, the silent streaks of far off rain falling in stillness below them to a shadowed land.

"A storm comes?" asked Uthiel.

"Like none before," responded Armenius.

Uthiel had watched for a moment, and then started as he felt the pull of his flesh calling him to wake.

"Is my father here?" he'd burst out suddenly.

Armenius nodded, but changed the subject quickly as Uthiel felt the call to return to his flesh grow stronger.

"Remember my son, your rage makes you deadly when it is cold, when it is pure and controlled with faith."

The voice seemed to be coming from a far distance now.

"He will also use it against you," warned Armenius, his gaze moving back out to the clouded horizon.

Uthiel smiled, a warm fog having enveloped his mind before Armenius had spoken.

"My father stands at His side..." was the last piece of the dream he had remembered.

"A wonderful dream then?" cooed Emilia coyly, her fingertips running over his skin. "My champion of the light."

He smiled and rolled onto his side to wrap his other arm around her small frame, coarse hands sliding over soft skin and coming to rest on her waist. His eyes quickly flicked to the other cot in the tent but Tarren was not there, nor did it seem he had been there all night. Right now, it bothered him not at all. They lay in comfortable silence, just smiling and listening to each other breathe.

Uthiel felt her tense up for the smallest moment, feeling more than seeing or hearing her sudden change in mood.

"What is it?" he asked.

"Do you love me?" asked Emilia, absent-mindedly toying with the wolf's head talisman around his neck.

Uthiel laughed. "Of course, what sort of a question is that?"

"Why?"

Uthiel thought for a long, drawn out moment before answering. "I have watched the sun rise from the steps of the Armenian cathedral in Secunda, marvelling as the sky went from black to purple to red to orange, yellow and then finally blue. I marvelled at the way the sun crept across the towns and forests and farms, like a slow wave of glorious molten gold, like the very touch of Armenius himself. Naught is as beautiful as what I see when I wake up with you. Nothing but the Eternal Lord himself stirs my heart so much."

She cocked her head a little while Uthiel sucked in a breath, surprised at his own eloquence.

"If we survive this war, would you want children with me?"

Uthiel frowned, taken aback by the forwardness of the question. "I am a knight, I... I will always be away fighting... I'm not sure I would be..."

Emilia pulled back from him, sitting up to look him in the eye. "So, no, then? You would sleep with me, sow your seed within me, and leave?"

Uthiel sat up also, further taken aback by her sudden anger. "Emilia, you... you surprised me with the question is all. There will come a day, if I survive this war, when I will want sons. By Armenius, if this war would end right now and I could sire a strong boy in our image with you upon this very cot, I would take you right now!"

Emilia smiled, her mood immediately changing before Uthiel's befuddled eyes as she rolled onto him, his hand resting in the curve of the small of her back. "I am glad to hear it, my lover."

Her eyes looked down at his chest, her hand following her gaze as her fingers traced aimlessly across his skin. Her cheeks flushed.

"Emilia?" Uthiel asked, his heart quickening.

"Uthiel," she said hesitantly. "I do not know for sure, but my blood is now a week late..."

Her voice wavered, her beautiful eyes earnestly searching for his reaction. Uthiel's mouth hung open, his mind slowing the world around him as his hammering heart tried to push him into overdrive to provide a response. For the briefest of moments the greatest terror threatened to overcome him, to send him running. It threatened to send him charging away to war and away from Emilia, anywhere but in this cot in this moment under Emilia's searching gaze.

His head railed fearfully, but his heart overcame it with sudden power. A golden warmth that started in his chest, spreading like wildfire across his limbs, exploded in to a happy laugh and a broad grin as he grabbed her and lovingly crushed her body into his. He grabbed her shoulders and with easy strength lifted her up off his chest so he could look her in the eyes.

"Truly?"

She nodded, her face begging for more reassurance one moment, and then demanding it the next.

He wrapped her up in his arms once again and laughed. "By Armenius, let it be a boy!"

She sat up, obviously feigned disapproval on her face. "And if it's a girl?"

Uthiel shrugged and laughed some more. "Then I'll cut her hair short and laugh as she beats all the young lads at their own games!"

"Brother!" came a voice from outside the tent. "What is all that bloody racket in there? The sun is rising, I need my armour, and you need to get up! Some lord or other is probably looking for you!"

"Tarren!" half barked, half laughed Uthiel. "I am to be a father, you ugly bastard, give me a bloody moment!"

There was a long pause, then Tarren spoke, but not to Uthiel. "My Eternal Lord, is there anything else you want to bloody well gift to his bloody hero-lordiness? Perhaps a pretty horse of his own? Estate near the Cathedral? Discover his last name is actually bloody Mirator or bloody Faramon even? Ah, shit on me," finished the man gruffly.

Uthiel and Emilia laughed as Tarren's grumblings continued, but faded, as he walked away.

Uthiel was sure he was gone until Tarren yelled back at the tent from a distance. "Best celebrate quickly, brother. Word in the Order and amongst the Fifth is that we march."

Uthiel's heart leapt a moment, *we march*. "Where to?" he called out.

His heart dropped immediately as he said it, *I am to be a father. What if I don't come back to hold my son?*

"Who knows? Somewhere where a whole bunch of bastards are trying to cut us to pieces is my best bloody guess," called out Tarren.

There was already a tear in Emilia's eye as Uthiel sat up, his face set. He looked down to her. "I swear to Armenius, I will return to hold our child. The Eternal Lord willing, we shall reclaim Mother Secunda soon and I shall be by your side as you birth, to give our child a name."

47

"And if you are still at war?" asked Emilia.

"Then name him Tanin," said Uthiel with a smile as he donned his woollen drawers and shirt and reached for his mail skirt.

Emilia smiled at him and Uthiel smiled back bravely, doing his best not to allow the thought of impending battles to break through his heady joy. Quickly, he laced on his skirt and part mail hauberk before slipping on his boots and greaves, while he could still comfortably bend over, before reaching for his cuirass. Emilia stood, and as she got dressed Uthiel's eyes searched her flat belly for any signs of the swell of life. None was yet visible, but the sight of her lean body brought a smile to his face anyway.

She helped him buckle his cuirass to his body, as she had been doing for a month now, and then his goussets to his biceps before attaching his pauldrons over his well-muscled shoulders to almost complete the suit of armour. Uthiel buckled on his waist sword belt and then his shoulder sword belt, the grip and crosspiece rising up over his left pauldron.

Finally Emilia passed him his most prized possessions, two polished vambrances that he slipped his forearms into. Upon the thick outer edge of the two armour pieces, the words *Shield of Secunda* had been inscribed carefully by hand. Uthiel took in their magnificence greedily, as he did each time he placed them upon himself. They were pieces of armour gifted to him by the Lord Pomen himself, worn by heroes long past. That he wore it now was an honour grander than any other.

Finally, Uthiel picked up his shield, which had lain dormant in his tent since it had been returned to him after the battle of Gall, its dark red face broken only by a brass *Armenius* bolted onto the front. Threading his left forearm through its loops, he placed his free hand upon Emilia's stomach and then leaned down and pressed his lips to hers. Without further word, he turned to leave.

"And if it is a girl?" asked Emilia, straightening her thick woollen dress.

Uthiel paused a moment. "Then name her after your mother."

He strode out past the impatiently waiting Tarren and into the light and sounds of the muster for war. Tarren stank of ale and sweat and was heavily favouring his good leg. He gave Uthiel a look that could have boiled a live chicken without water and then moved to walk into their shared tent, only to stop and ungainly step back to allow Emilia out. Grumbling under his breath, Tarren finally made it in.

Emilia stood before Uthiel, their toes and bellies touching, her neck craning up and her eyes searching his.

"Come back to me, my love."

Uthiel smiled, stooping down to kiss her quivering lips.

Words didn't seem to be needed. Emilia smiled back and walked away, hand on her flat belly. Uthiel admired the sway of her hips as she disappeared into the crowd towards the cluster of apothecary tents.

A father. Me, a father.

Uthiel grinned a widely. Tarren bumped into him from behind.

"Oh for..." started Tarren. "How long am I going to have to put up with that stupid bloody grin?"

Uthiel just laughed, impervious to Tarren's foul mood, as the shorter man's hung-over hands fumbled to tie up a sword belt. He took a deep breath and placed a hand on Tarren's pauldron.

"Come, brother, I'm so hungry I'm looking for low flying ducks," said Uthiel.

Tarren stopped fussing over his gear and looked up. "I could eat."

Uthiel watched as the three bodies swung from a tree, tongues lolling, unseeing eyes goggling at the crowd around them. Piss tricked in quick droplets from their bare toes onto the mud below. Their trousers were browned and fouled. The knee of the one on the far right spasmodically kicked now and then as life after death continued to die. The winter wind picked at their Secundan Fifth tabards, flapping and snapping against freshly dead flesh.

Lord Ryun stood watching the men sway in the breeze out in front of the crowd, his dark blue eyes alive with righteous fire. His short-cropped receding hair framed his hard face, wrinkled and craggy with age. His cold frown was brightly reflected in the beauty of his well-crafted plate.

"And thus, the punishment for thievery! Those of you who would slay, rape, steal, or cheat your fellow countrymen in Secunda's most needy hour shall suffer the same fate!" Ryun's voice rasped out, loud like the wind.

Uthiel scratched his eyebrow, averting his eyes.

"Not got the stomach for it, eh hero?" said Tarren.

Uthiel never got to respond.

"Best get a stomach for it, brother, time shall come soon you'll be leading and disciplining these men yourself," said Lord Ryun, only some ten feet away.

"My lord?" asked Uthiel.

The Lord Ryun walked over to Uthiel, every step drawing the attention of more of the soldiers and knights who had gathered to watch the three thieves hang. Hard eyes locked on Uthiel; studying, judging, measuring.

Uthiel stood tall, doing his best not to wilt under the lord's gaze. He'd met the king of Secunda twice — twice been under the gaze of a direct descendant of their Eternal Lord. *I can handle this.*

Ryun stopped before him. Respectfully, Uthiel lowered his gaze to the snow-specked mud at his feet. Lord Ryun's expensive-looking boots were remarkably clean of grime or mud or blood. Uthiel looked to his own. They were still tinged red to the ankle from walking the cobblestone streets of Gall. The silence lengthened.

"Brother Uthiel Caellar," said Ryun. "The boy who slew the warlord. Hero. Brother. Now? Captain."

Uthiel stood dumbfounded. "What?"

"My lord general," said Ryun.

Uthiel didn't understand, and his slack face must have shown this.

"I am a lord general, brother, you shall address me correctly," said Ryun, though he were chiding a youth.

"Yes, lord... lord general, sir," stammered Uthiel. "Lord Pomen?"

"Pomen?" breathed Ryun. "Old, sick, weak. He's past his glories and useless to an army on the march. Lord Steward Thomak has retired our brother to a position on his war council."

Uthiel's face must still have looked as clueless as a cow to the butcher's blade.

"I am the lord general of the Grey Wolves, brother, and you are my newest captain," stated the Lord Ryun.

"Not my first choice," continued Ryun before Uthiel could interject. "Nor my second or third. By Armenius, there are at least twenty men who deserve it more but you have the favour of the lord steward for your ridiculous antics in front of the king. 'Hero of Secunda' he calls you."

"Thank you, lord general," responded Uthiel.

"Don't thank me," said Ryun. "Prove yourself a worthy captain. Do well by your men. Prove my impression of you wrong or you'll be replaced."

Uthiel blinked.

"Midday, be at my tent with the other captains. We've a march to get moving, and you have brothers to introduce yourself to," said Ryun.

As the lord general of the Grey Wolves walked away, Uthiel looked to Tarren.

"Bloody hell, more gifts from Armenius. He must love you, *captain*," grumbled Tarren as he motioned for Uthiel to walk before him. "I had to bloody ask, didn't I."

Uthiel opened his mouth to respond, but nothing came out. Tarren huffed and turned away, walking swiftly to disappear into the crowd. Watching his brother walk away, Uthiel was lost in his own gaze, looking at nothing in particular as his mind tried to settle on what had just happened.

"Uthiel, lad," came a voice: an old, familiar voice from his childhood and his youth. He'd last heard that voice almost two years ago, the night before entering the Bastion of the Chosen.

He turned and saw father Trethore. As always, the old priest's face was warm and accommodating, his specked black hair now perhaps a little bit more white around the edges than grey, but his stance and power no less diminished. As always, Uthiel's eyes were drawn to the ornate suit of armour the old priest wore.

Four centuries old and it was still polished enough to shave in its reflective surface. It had not a scratch or dent, just pound upon pound of strong Secundan steel shaped into the second skin of the elite warriors of Armenius. Twenty-seven names were inscribed down the left breast of the cuirass. The glorious list ended in Trethore's own, and began with his ancestor; a man who had stood next to the Eternal Lord in a shield wall when He'd still graced the Lands of the Light with his tread.

Uthiel bowed his head reverently, his eyes closing after flowing down the priest's long white, travel stained cloak. "Father."

Trethore reached out a hand and pressed onto Uthiel's shoulder.

"Some great news this morning, I hear," the old priest said.

Uthiel's face lit up, like the sun across the plain on a cloudless morning. He felt a huge grin, that couldn't be smothered, cross his face. Father Trethore reciprocated encouragingly.

"You heard?" said Uthiel. "I only found out this very morning, amazing isn't it?"

Trethore grinned broadly and placed a hand on Uthiel's pauldron. "Much glory in His eyes awaits you. I always knew you would lead men into war."

"Lead men..." stammered Uthiel. "Oh, yes, a great honour, father."

Trethore frowned. "Something else on your mind?"

Uthiel couldn't help but let that grin cross his face once more, news this good was far too difficult to keep to himself. *I am to be a father!*

"Something else has happened," said Trethore, more fact than question.

Uthiel stood straighter in front of the priest, feeling his chest swell fit to burst with happiness.

"I am to be a father," beamed Uthiel.

Trethore pushed forwards and grabbed Uthiel into a hug. "My heart bursts with pride, young man. To see you become the man you are today, and then to bring life into this world that you defend. Surely the Eternal Lord smiles upon you."

Trethore held him a moment longer, like a proud father would a son, before he released the young knight and backed away. *A little bit like Tanin would have held me.*

"Tell me, who is this young lady, the mother of your child?" asked Trethore.

Uthiel smiled again, more goofy and youthful this time, feeling a fool. "A Gallite, Emilia."

Trethore stuck out his bottom lip and nodded his head. "Good luck to you, Uthiel. May the child be healthy and strong. I must away, I have duties to attend."

As Trethore turned and walked away Uthiel hesitated a moment, suddenly feeling extremely vulnerable as he thought of his new family. He half-reached out to the warrior priest. "Father."

Trethore stopped, pausing a moment with his back to Uthiel before turning. "Yes?"

"Word has it we are to march today or tomorrow…" said the youth. "If we do, my Order will be in the van. I will be in the van. I need someone to look after her, to look after my unborn, while I fight."

Trethore's face held blank a moment before it turned solemn. "I can take her on as a servant, Uthiel. Her safety I cannot guarantee, for we are at war, but I shall keep her close and protect her as best I can."

Uthiel felt his spirits lift a little. Trethore was not just a priest in pretty armour, he was also a formidable warrior. Uthiel took a deep breath, relieving some of the momentary stress.

"I must away," said Trethore once more, turning and walking away.

Uthiel watched him a moment, then looked around to get his bearings so he could find his way to the Lord Ryun's command tent. *Why had Trethore hesitated?*

Uthiel dropped the thought after less than a heartbeat. Trethore was one of the people he trusted most in the world. *If you cannot trust a warrior priest of Armenius to watch over your innocent family, who can you trust when all of your brothers, bar one, are dead?*

If you knew of the Black Wolves, was there anyone you could trust?

A brother-priest in full ceremonial armour appeared from the shadow of a tent to walk beside father Trethore. He was young and had a face that spoke of a vicious ability to visit violence upon anything that lived and could bleed. He had a fighter's body, broad shoulders under those polished pauldrons tapering down to a slim waist above powerful legs.

Trethore acknowledged him with little more than a glance.

"That him?" asked the young man, his voice quiet, almost a whisper.

"That's him."

"He one of them?"

Trethore paused a moment, rubbing a callused hand over his light stubble, squinting against the sun's reflection from a snow drift. "If he's not, he knows something. He tries to hide it from me, but I have known him since he was waist height. I trained him in lore and combat, prepared him for the initiation into the Wolves, made him the man he is today as much as his own blood father did. I just need to find a way past his defences."

"I can make his defences crumble," said the youth. "A chair, a skinning knife, a few lengths of rope, and one night and I promise I'll have him singing all the secrets of the Grey Wolves to you. Probably even secrets he didn't know he knew."

Trethore sucked in a breath through his teeth. "I don't believe there will be a need for that. The lad has a family now. Has asked me to look after her while he fights in the van."

The young warrior priest smiled.

Trethore stopped, grabbing the youth by the pauldron. "No harm is to come to her, Tyran, she is under my protection. For all my suspicion, I could be wrong."

Tyran raised an eyebrow.

"About Uthiel, Tyran, not about the Wolves. I have seen their treachery first hand. I will do what I must to excise the cancer from their ranks, or I will amputate the Order from Secunda."

Lord Pomen stood watching the muster of what should have been his men. His bitter heart railed at his position — slunk under a tree, his back bent and struggling to stay vertical under the weight of his thick fur coat, and his shame. His bodyguards stood a respectful distance away, only watching his silently jealous rage from the corners of their eyes as they did their best to divert their gaze from what they hoped never to suffer.

A hacking cough shook Pomen's rapidly deteriorating frame, his chest wetly rattling with each desperately drawn inward breath, his throat and tongue burning with each body-shuddering hack. As he felt warmness spit onto his lips and drip onto his chin he raised a white kerchief to his mouth and dabbed away the saliva he'd expelled.

Damn.

He felt his spirit die a little more as he looked down into the cloth to see red mixed with the yellow and green and black.

Not long now.

His bodyguards knew his illness well enough now to know that Pomen would not want them helping him as he clawed each piece of strength and bodily control he could to still his coughing and remain upright at the same time. His wrinkled, pale hand with skin that seemed to the old man to be thinning by the day, reached out and shifted some of his weight to the tree he stood beneath.

"My lord steward," said one of his bodyguards.

Pomen turned to see Lord Steward Thomak pass by his guards with barely a nod. As usual, the man looked regal, rich, proud, and strong.

"Lord Pomen," said Thomak, an overdone look of concern crossing his face. "How do you fare?"

"Just fine, lord steward," responded Pomen. "A slight ailment, no..."

"I've not seen a knight look so pathetic in my years," mused Thomak, interrupting the old lord like he had not even opened his mouth to speak. "You understand I had no choice when it came to replacing you. You'd simply not have been able to keep up with the column."

"I..." started Pomen in response.

Thomak raised his eyebrows to stall the old man. "Do you deny your condition? By Armenius, man, you would be fit for a night in bed with Death herself!"

Pomen's shoulders sagged. He knew Thomak was right. He was in no state to lead men in to battle. No state to do much other than cough himself to a debilitating, slow and horrible death.

"The restructure..." started Pomen.

"Taken care of," said Thomak. "Ryun to lord general, as you already know. First Captain Solanthur and Captain Laurenn will remain as leaders of our one hundred and sixty odd brothers. You'll be most interested to know that young Caellar will be given a command as one of the newly promoted captains. He'll lead twenty brother knights. A pity you shall not witness the heights to which I shall expand his legend. He is but steps from greatness, and it shall be I who will lead him there. Not you."

Thomak eyed Pomen's reaction, his face not quite holding back his enjoyment of the situation. The old lord may have been sick, but he knew when he was being goaded and kept his face stoic. *How did Thomak and I come to this? What is it that I have done to earn his ire? Or what is it I haven't done... or will not do?*

Pomen exhaled deeply, stifling a cough with his ice-cold hand, but finding some semblance of calmness.

"Brother Caellar is not ready," he said gruffly. "You overextend him beyond brothers far more experienced and ready."

"He'll be leading one of three regiments heading north to march on Imonetia," continued Thomak, once again ignoring the old lord's words. "The first captain will also go."

"And the third regiment will be led by?" asked Pomen, not entirely sure Thomak would deign to respond to him.

"Lord General Ryun's eldest son shall lead the third regiment. He has also been newly promoted to captain. With the Fifth and sixty of our brothers at their backs we should have no problem completing our mission in Imonetia," said Thomak.

"Our mission?" asked Pomen. "On behalf of the Lands of the Light, you mean? To restore the Imonetian Royals to their city?"

Thomak smirked. "Correct, Lord Ryun, to restore order to Imonetia."

Pomen held his steward's eye for a moment and then broke away.

"And what of me, lord steward?" asked Pomen, adding some meekness to his tone as his stepped into the game Thomak was playing.

Thomak snorted. "A man of your standing cannot be left idle. You have a responsibility to your Order and a duty to partake in this war until your last breath is expelled from your body. You'll remain with me and the Seventh and the remaining Wolves as we march on Archenon Creek. You shall be assimilated into my war council."

Pomen didn't quite manage to catch his facial expression before it appeared on his face.

"Don't confuse this generosity of position with an actual need of your council, Lord Pomen," snarled Thomak. "You will be there to order the Pandurs and Lemugians to action when I need it. You'll pass on messages as your status lends weight to any missive: no more, no less."

Thomak turned and walked away without further word. Pomen stood a while, his mind working through Thomak's words. There was something in those eyes that disturbed him, something in there that the lord steward was not being honest about. Pomen, despite his illness and his physical weakness, still possessed a mind as sharp as a freshly honed blade. He latched on to that moment like a bloodhound.

Thomak was hiding or planning something. Deep within his soul, where Armenius spoke with Pomen through action and thought and impulse, there a semblance of purpose blossomed once more in the ailing lord. Pomen may not have much time before the Eternal Lord called him to take his place with his brothers in the Shield Wall in the Sky, but in whatever time was left to him he would find out what Thomak was planning, and should it be against the greater good of the Lands of the Light and Secunda, he would find a way to stop that bastard.

He returned his gaze to his brother knights forming up near the Fifth. *What's happening to my Wolves? What in the name of Armenius is going on?*

CHAPTER FIVE

Uthiel sat within the quiet confides of his tent, pauldron removed from his armour in his hand, looking for a quiet hour before his midday meeting with the lord general. Outside, the din of thousands of men moving throughout the camp was as nothing to the tumult within the young captain. In his solitude, his mind wandered. *Bran, where are you when I need you, brother?*

A tear threatened to spill from his eye as he thought of his brother. Obliterated, Branor was lost forever, never to raise tankards or sons. Branor still haunted his nightmares, partly as friend in dire need, and partly as a black-eyed beast slavering for death. To be unable to bury his friend and say prayers to what remained of him had hurt. At least with his father, he had been able to say goodbye, in his fashion, to something he could look at. He'd had no such luck with his lifelong friend. Not a single piece of Branor, or Nikhael, had remained. *What happened to you, Nikhael? What stole the life from you, brother? What replaced your soul with only the lust for slaughter?*

He pushed the thought from his mind. He needed to find peace. He found some of that peace as he sat rubbing a polish-covered cloth over his cuirass. He paid special attention to every small detail he could lay eye upon, losing himself in the simple motion of cleaning the forged metal that had protected him against sword, arrow, axe, and... *and whatever Carn, Nikhael and Bran became.*

As he worked his cloth over the metal, he began to whisper prayers to Armenius, his voice barely a dull murmur, his words for himself and the Eternal Lord alone. Eventually, he came to his two swords and forearm-length knife. Unsheathing all three, he laid them next to their scabbards upon the cot. Both of the longer blades had the names of their previous owners etched up near the crosspiece. When he looked at each name the memory of his brothers came back to him. *Ghurkar*: a mentor, harsh and unbending. *Lokhi*: one of the young men he had gone through initiation with, and as finer knight as Uthiel was ever to meet. Lokhi had been there when he'd slain the warlord. Each blade already shone brilliantly with an unblemished edge that could cut through flesh like it was paper.

Spitting on his whetstone, Uthiel picked up the sword he had taken from his old mentor, Ghurkar Storm, and began to smoothly and rhythmically hone its edge, the slow rasping of stone on steel a soothing melody to his ears. Still, his lips kept up their continuous murmur.

> *"As long as I fight in His name,*
> *And draw the blood of those that would sully Mother Secunda, for Him,*
> *The Eternal Lord shall be my blade."*

The words his father had adopted from the Lord Pomen as their family prayer before the march on Gall seemed to help him clear his mind, pouring water onto the fires that burnt within him. Placing the blade upon the cot next to his thigh, he lost himself in thought, his hand raising to fiddle with his talisman and his eyes seeing only memories. His lips continued to murmur.

In his mind's eye he watched again as Branor fought with the rage within himself and then begged for the mercy of the release of death. He watched as his lifelong friend barrelled into Nikhael, who had but a moment before been on the cusp of ending Uthiel's life. He remembered the look on Branor's face as he glanced up from the dark of the ruined keep, knowing full well that although his life was measured in heartbeats, he had slain Nikhael and saved his brother.

Until we both stand at His side, brother.

The memory of Branor's last words to him surprisingly brought a smile to his face. As young boys they had both laughed at death, boasting that it would take the mightiest of foes to bring them to their glorious ends. Uthiel sighed. Branor had taken down the mightiest foe he had yet met. Nikhael had been even mightier than the barbarian warlord Uthiel had killed. If only Branor had known just how much of an abomination he had slain, he would have died laughing. *If only I could have told him just what we faced.*

And there he had it. The crux of Uthiel's unhappiness dawned upon him. He'd lied to his best friend and all of his brothers, and now they were dead, gone to fight alongside Him in the great Shield Wall in the Sky. They had all joined the knights knowing that both glory and death came hand in hand for fighting men, though their acceptance of the latter reality was blinded by their youth-perceived invulnerability.

Uthiel mourned them, no less than he'd mourned the death of his own blood brothers in his youth. The souring of their memory came not from their horrific demises, but from lying to men he called brothers. It was a knife to his guts to know he was keeping the knowledge of the treacherous past of their own Order from them.

Without thinking he dropped to his knees, his hands upon his thighs and his eyes skyward, seeing straight through the canvas roof to the clear winter sky above, and quietly begged their forgiveness. He had been there for long enough for the sun to almost reach its pinnacle when he heard Tarren walking to the tent, bawdily joking with another.

Uthiel sat back upon his small bunk, once more working polish back into the beautiful planes and recesses of his plate as the faces of the past faded into dark memory. Tarren eventually finished his conversation and walked in, limping less now than earlier in the morning.

"Brother," he started. "Captain," he corrected himself. "The Grey Wolves have been chosen as a part of the van for the march on Imonetia. Finally, we can stop growing fat here in this bastard camp and go make war on our enemies."

Uthiel raised an eyebrow. "Are you so keen to be thrown back into the fighting?"

Tarren barked a rough laugh and arched his back, knuckling his hips. "By Armenius, this camp's stench overwhelms me. The competition in practice bores me, the whores are so bow-legged they can barely walk, and I'm sick to death of all your bloody moaning as you languish here. Poor little hero of the Grey Wolves, deprived of all his glory. Let's get you some more bloody men, find us some bloody barbarians, and go have some bloody adventures!"

Uthiel smiled, despite himself. "That'll be 'Captain Poor Little Hero of the Grey Wolves', thank you, brother."

Tarren huffed. "Come, brother-captain, best you get out amongst the men."

Uthiel nodded. "I have a meet with the lord general first. I need to be allocated my regiment and we must prepare to march."

"Suit yourself. I'll go hone my tremendous skills while you go play at captain," said Tarren, and turned to leave.

Uthiel looked up. "Tarren."

The young knight turned back. Uthiel held his gaze a moment.

"As of today I lead men, brother, you amongst them," said Uthiel.

Tarren frowned, his face becoming serious.

"We've not always seen eye to eye," said Uthiel, raising a hand as he saw a protest rise on Tarren's face. "We've come close to blows, once or twice. At best, we've survived each other. At worst, you've outright questioned my ability to lead men into battle effectively."

"Captain, respectfully..." Tarren trailed off.

"Your jokes, calling me 'hero', does not go beyond this tent," said Uthiel, a clear warning in his voice. "You are my friend, a brother, but also now under my command. In front of my men and my superiors, you will show me the due respect."

Tarren's mouth worked for a moment silently before clamping shut. His lips thinned and his eyes closed resignedly for a moment. "As you would have it, brother-captain."

Uthiel sighed as Tarren turned to leave. He'd become very good at pushing people away from him after the loss of Branor. "Tarren, wait, I could use the practice."

Uthiel spun away from Tarren, ducking his head as he heard the dulled blade slice fatly through the air above his hair. Uthiel moved well for a man wrapped in plate and mail armour, his footsteps swift and sure upon the muddy training ground as he pivoted on his toes, turned, and levelled one of his practice blades at his opponent, the other dangling cockily behind him for a moment before he pulled it up stiffly to his rear hip. Opposite him, Tarren stood in his fresh plate, also helmetless, a longer sword in one hand and a wide buckler strapped to the other.

Tarren looked surly and angry, more so than usual, after they had last met in their shared tent. The young knight moved sideways, his blade ever pointed at Uthiel's heart and his eyes locked down its length. Tarren feigned with his blade as he darted in, but Uthiel read the move, stepping aside and whipping a sword out to playfully clang against Tarren's longer blade. Tarren leapt in, seeking an opportunity to win the bout, hacking and slashing skilfully, using his buckler as much for attack and defence as his sword, as Uthiel whipped back lightning fast ripostes.

Without warning, the flashing blades stilled, their vibrations still ringing in the air as each man drew back two swift steps to be out of the others' reach. They circled each other once more, eyeing warily. Uthiel darted in without warning, not so much as a dropping of the shoulder or twitching of the eye to give away his intent, his lunge bouncing from Tarren's midriff. Tarren flinched backwards and then struck down with his blade, smashing the shorter sword from Uthiel's grip. Before Tarren could follow in with his buckler, he found the rounded edge of Uthiel's other sword resting on top of his gorget, against the flesh of his throat.

Uthiel smiled. Tarren was a good opponent, but he knew his brother's style of fighting too well, knowing what to look for every time. "You still do not trust in your armour to protect you, my brother," he said.

Tarren shook his head in annoyance. "After my wounding I struggle to trust in it."

"You need to, my brother. A sword lunge will always bounce off your cuirass or pauldrons. The strength Secunda gave it from her iron bosom, and the spirits of the brother who wore it before you, ensure that," said Uthiel.

"It didn't bounce off so well when Carn slew our brothers," mumbled Tarren gruffly, and immediately the mood turned darker at the memory of their leader turned against them: of the awesome power that pushed Carn's blade through the steel plate of their brothers like it was no more than blood soaked, wafer-thin parchment.

Uthiel was silent a while, memories of the fierce melee echoing through his mind. He grimaced at the thought of the disgustingly skinny shaman the first captain had killed to end Carn's second, horrible life. The sound of footsteps squelching through the mud broke his reverie.

A brother taller than he by almost half a foot, in full armour and grey tabard, approached them. The man had broad shoulders and a leanly muscled neck that spoke of a body rippling with strength. His gaunt face held no scars, odd for a brother in his late twenties, and was darkly handsome for it. He had black eyes and pale skin, and his head was shaved almost clean, the receding widows peak visible. *Nikhael. Those eyes are just like Nikhael's.*

The man's armour was impeccable. There were no dents, no scuffs and his tabard hung perfectly down to the base of his mail skirt, the slit in the material even lining up exactly with the slit in the intricate rings. Only the smallest spatter of mud could be seen upon the well-kept black boots and the base of his greaves.

This tall visage was not what interested Uthiel the most, however, not by a long way. It was the man's light swagger: well hidden, but there all the same. His surefooted manner of moving and his quiet confidence was matched by a fierce aggression held within the deep dungeons of his icy eyes, waiting for its master to unleash it. The man held out his hand, and first Uthiel, and then Tarren grasped their brother's forearm.

"I am brother Pavel," said the knight, his voice quiet and deep.

"Finest sword of the second company," whispered Tarren in awe, his eyes flicking down to the long blade scabbarded across Pavel's back.

"Uthiel Caellar, first company," said Uthiel, ignoring Tarren.

"And you would be brother Tarren," said Pavel, his stony gaze locking on Uthiel's companion.

Tarren nodded, standing straighter.

Pavel's eyes remained locked on Tarren. "Brother Uthiel is right, you must trust in your armour. Ignore the lunge, step in and hammer your buckler into his skull next time. Perhaps that will help rid our young brother of his cockiness."

Tarren snorted. "Would take a few knocks on the head to belt that out of his lordiness."

Uthiel shot him a look.

Pavel did not deign to laugh, or smile, or provide any expression that may have been mistaken as taking part in the levity.

Uthiel turned back to the tall Grey Wolf. "Brother Pavel, you honour us. We've heard fine stories of your skill with that blade. Can we be of service?"

Pavel's eyes turned on Uthiel, measuring up the young knight in a heartbeat.

"Rid yourself of those training blades. Get your real steel and I shall show you a duel," said the knight.

Uthiel laughed, hiding his nervousness. "We are marching tomorrow, brother Pavel. Accidental injury to either of us at this time would be foolish with our numbers already so low."

Pavel responded, his voice deadpan. "I assure you, little brother, I am at no risk."

Uthiel smarted. "You would insult me, brother?"

With his right hand Pavel reached up above his pauldron and reverently gripped the black leather bound handle just below the small crosspiece and drew the blade out gracefully and slowly. Uthiel's eyes watched the polished steel, engraved down the centre with words of worship, as it slid out inch by inch, with only the lightest whisper to herald its arrival. The blade was single edged, a rare master's blade, and curved upwards slightly towards its sharp tip.

"It is not an insult, merely fact, brother," stated Pavel, resting the flat edge of the beautiful sword against his pauldron.

Uthiel licked his lips, noting all of a sudden the small crowd of brothers who had drawn up around them, watching intently. He had known, in his fighter's heart, that he was just as outmatched now against this brother, as he had been when Captain Phyrus had soundly beaten him in practice fresh from initiation, all those months ago, before the war. *Phyrus. Yet another ghost from the past year.*

"Is the great hero afraid?" said a voice condescendingly.

Uthiel turned to try to find Tarren, a sharp rebuke already making its way over his lips, but Tarren was looking at another of his brothers. The man reminded Uthiel of a young mountain bear, standing perhaps five and a half feet tall and heavily muscled, made even more enormous by his armour. His face was almost hidden by a thick beard and heavy eyebrows. Shaggy dark hair hung limp with sweat upon his creased brow and pale blue eyes stared at Uthiel with complete and utter contempt.

From his right hand, a well-kept sword hung limply in his thick fingers, while a dented kite shield was strapped to his left. On the opposite hip from his empty sword sheath hung not only his forearm-length knife, but also a three-foot long, notched, dark-steel sword breaker.

Uthiel knew of the man, he'd seen him in combat with the first company. Theon was one of the first captain's hardest men, a man as cruel as he was brutally effective in combat.

"Brother Theon," breathed Uthiel.

Theon smiled without camaraderie, dropped his shield and drew his sword breaker from its belt loop. "Brother Pavel, let me handle this upstart. He's one of my company and in the first, we beat our upstarts ourselves."

Pavel's eyes narrowed, the toe of his foremost foot shifting its point slightly to open his hips and shoulders to both Uthiel and Theon. He did not speak as Theon strode forwards threateningly.

"Do not make me beat you once more, brother Pavel," sneered Theon. "I have already defeated you once for the honour of the first. Remember your place."

Pavel's eyes twitched in the tiniest show of his bristling irritation. Still, his mouth remained shut. All the while Uthiel stood agape at the two knights, knowing full well he was the match of neither.

Theon stopped his chunky form to create a triangle with a knight, a brother, at each tip. Uthiel raised his training blades and prepared to defend himself. With a growl, Theon drew back his blade. Uthiel put up both of his in preparation to ward the blow. It never landed.

"If that blow lands I'll have to hang you, brother," came the deep voice of First Captain Solanthur Verutus, the Light Bringer.

Theon stopped in shock, and Uthiel immediately dropped his guard while Pavel had sheathed his blade faster than quicksilver, his head already bowed to the first captain and the man who strode in his wake.

"Uthiel Caellar. You are late. The command tent. Now," ordered the Lord Ryun, already walking away towards his tent.

Uthiel looked to Solanthur, who watched him for a moment, before locking eyes with Theon. "Theon, Pavel, as of now, you are reformed into Uthiel's company. He is your captain. You shall be as his Shields, as the warrior kings of old once had."

Without hesitation Pavel turned, head still bowing as he took a knee, and looked under his fine brow to Uthiel. "My apologies, my captain. My sword is, of course, yours. Second company has always had a Shield to guard its captain. A set of eyes and a strong arm to watch over you while you lead our brothers. I offer you my shield as your own. My life as your Shield."

Theon hawked and spat loudly upon the ground, glaring at Solanthur, and then at Uthiel. With a shake of his head and an incredulous snort, he turned and walked away through the fifty-odd strong throng of brother knights that surrounded them. Uthiel stood rooted to the spot, not quite sure he'd heard right. *Two of the finest swords in the Order under my command? Both of those men should be a captain a hundred times over before me.*

Someone called to him, trying to get his attention. Uthiel was almost too dumbstruck to notice.

"That means you, brother-captain," said Solanthur, taking a deep breath. "Your time under my leadership has been short. I hope you have learned enough to lead the men as they deserve to be led. Honour them, and they shall honour you. Now, come."

Uthiel nodded dumbly and looked over to Tarren, who shook his head and walked away, muttering under his breath. Hearing further mutterings around him, he looked other men he knew in the eye, wondering which ones would be his. He wondered if he was strong enough to lead such men; wondered if they would be like Pavel, or more like Theon.

Clenching his jaw, he walked towards the crowd of knights, all of their eyes locked on their newest captain. He watched as brothers whispered of his virtues and flaws. He could barely hear the young men, fresh from initiation, debate his heroic legend with the veterans who questioned his experience. Uthiel took a deep breath. *Armenius, let me lead these men to glory with honour and dignity.*

Mud squelched beneath his boots as he made his way past the men of his Order and towards the command tent of the Lord General Ryun. As he approached, he spotted a group of knights some sixteen or seventeen strong. Most were younger than he, five or six were older knights, one of them a grey beard and quite long in the tooth.

Lord Ryun stood in conversation with them, and Solanthur moved by his side. As Uthiel broke through the throng of his brothers, camp followers and men of the Fifth and Seventh, those knights, as one, looked over to him. In unison, irrespective of the denial or anger or acceptance or excitement in their eyes, they lowered their heads reverently and spoke in one voice.

"Captain."

Uthiel was taken aback a moment before shaking himself to response. "Brothers."

Lord Ryun stepped forward. "Captain Uthiel Caellar, these brothers are your charges, twenty of the finest men in Secunda: your company."

Despite himself, Uthiel smiled. *My company.*

A soldier in a tabard of the Fifth approached the Lord Ryun.

"Captain Darian, twenty-second company of the Fifth, at your service, my lord general."

The captain was old, perhaps past forty or fifty summers, and his face was hard and embittered.

"Not my service, captain," said Lord General Ryun, pointing to Uthiel. "His."

Uthiel stepped towards the captain, hand outstretched in a warrior's handshake offering. "Uthiel Caellar, captain of this company of Grey Wolves."

The old captain hesitated a moment, his eyes flicking back to Ryun, before taking Uthiel's hand. "Honoured, sir. Your orders?"

Before Uthiel could speak, Ryun interrupted. "Your men assembled to the north of camp by day break tomorrow, captain. Be prepared for a march into hostile territory, under command of young Caellar here."

Uthiel gritted his teeth as Darian saluted and walked off, back to wherever his men were currently picketed.

"You too, brothers," said the lord general to Uthiel's company.

Those men turned away and left also, each to prepare for the coming march. They would drink their last ales, polish their armour one last time, have final bouts of practice-duelling, and pack their tents and meagre belongings. Some would rush off to see their sweethearts or whores and plant their seed in or on bellies.

Ryun looked to Uthiel as the last of the men left, his stare hardening. "Let me be absolutely clear with you, Caellar. You're very lucky with your friends and family. Were it not for Thomak and your father and the Lord Pomen, you'd be a rank and file brother knight for some time until you earned your captaincy or someone put you in the dirt."

Uthiel's face reddened, his eyes flicking over to Solanthur's for a moment and seeing no support, before defiantly locking back on to the lord general's.

"You have a simple company, a small one, mostly initiates apart from a few experienced brothers I have been forced to remove from better companies, to babysit you and yours," said Ryun coldly, bringing the full force of his venom to bear. "The first captain, a captain of the king's guards, and my own son will be there to lead with me. You do as you're told, lead your men where you're told to lead them when you're told to do so, and you'll be fine."

Uthiel looked once more to the first captain. The man's gaze did not waver as the lord general continued his harsh lecture. The Lord General Ryun was still looking at him like a rat-infested corpse pit.

"I am stuck with you as a captain, in that I have no choice, Caellar," continued Ryun, his voice softening a modicum. "But the men I've been forced to put under you deserve better. Do not fail me, or them."

Uthiel struggled for a response as Ryun walked away with Solanthur. His mind finally kicking in to action, he raised a hand futilely.

"Lord general!" he called out. "Do you still require me in the command tent?"

The Lord General Ryun looked back and snorted. "It's unlikely your input will be required. Just be north of the camp at daybreak with your men."

Uthiel nodded to himself and turned away, feeling like he had been physically struck.

The Lord Pomen's chest heaved desperately for air as he watched the exchange between Ryun and Uthiel from afar. He'd seen it from the outset and tried to hurry on over. Some thirty or forty feet later he'd had to stop and lean on one of his bodyguards to catch his breath as his body threatened to give out.

Uthiel looked set to walk away, but Pomen called out, his wrinkled hand reaching for the youth. The young knight turned and spotted him, and then walked swiftly on over to the ailing knight lord.

"Lord Pomen, are you alright?" asked the young knight, almost translucent blue eyes honest and earnest.

Lord Pomen smiled, falsely. "Armenius smiles upon me this day, brother Uthiel, and you?"

Uthiel's face was troubled. "I've had better days, truth be told."

"Do not let him get to you, Uthiel. You are your father's son. You are strong, a leader of men, a true son of Armenius. You were born to be a captain of the Grey Wolves, to stand pauldron to pauldron with men like the Light Bringer," insisted Pomen. "Born for the glory of the battlefield."

"Just not ready for a meeting of lords and captains," mumbled Uthiel.

Pomen stopped. "What?"

"The meeting of the Order's lords and captains before we march come the morning. Surely you are on your way there?"

Pomen's heart sank, at the same time as his mind raged. *A meeting of the Order's leaders without me? I am a foremost lord!*

"My lord? A problem?" asked the young knight.

"No, young captain, I am late for the meeting, is all," lied Pomen. "Best get to your men. Remember, each man under your command is a direct reflection of yourself. Be a strong, honourable, and fair leader, and your men will be strong, honourable, and fair. Be aught else, and failure as a leader, and the loss of the confidence and lives of your men, will haunt your remaining days."

Uthiel nodded. "My thanks, lord."

"Your father would be proud of you, brother. I must hurry to the council," said Pomen as he walked away, his guards around him.

It was a short walk, made long by his illness, but eventually Pomen made it to the council tent. He could hear voices through the thick canvas. Pomen strained to hear the heated debate and agreement of fast planning sessions. Voices murmured and then shouted. A harsh laugh interrupted someone. A droning tone picked up once more.

Pomen broke through the tent flap into the council meeting. All eyes turned on him. All voices stopped.

The first thing that Pomen noticed was that not all of the captains were there. Uthiel, of course, was missing. The Light Bringer wasn't there. He was less surprised to see the Lord General Ryun, his son, a few lieutenants, and two captains of the Secundan Fifth present beside Thomak. Colle Gill and the representatives of the Order of the Black Falcon and the Sons of Armenius turned to look at him also.

Immediately a map was folded from the table at the centre of the tent and moved away by a scribe. Missives were hidden, certain men up and left without a word or look, and quickly the entire room's attention was centred on him. Pomen stifled a cough as his throat tickled and spasmed.

"Lord Pomen," said Thomak. "You were not summoned here."

"My lord steward," responded Pomen. "This is a meeting of lords, is it not? Of the men that lead our Order and the Fifth?"

"Of which you are neither," snapped Thomak.

Pomen licked his lips as the men around the lord steward snickered and laughed at him. *Time to dispense with this game.*

"What are you doing, lord steward?" asked Pomen.

"Why, Lord Pomen, I am planning to restore Imonetia and the Lands of the Light to their former glory."

The men around Pomen smiled or glowered.

"You mean to restore the royals to rightful place at the head of their nation," stated Pomen.

Thomak stopped, all mocking looks gone from his face. "With or without the royals, Imonetia will be restored."

Pomen felt a chill run down his spine. It had nothing to do with the winter or his illness.

CHAPTER SIX

Come sunrise, Uthiel stood before his new company and supporting soldiers from the Fifth in parade ground order. His men were to the right of Solanthur's men in the centre, while Captain Ryun's stood on the left. Solanthur looked magnificent in front of first company. Uthiel admired him from in front of his own men. The knight was everything Uthiel prayed to the Eternal Lord he would become. He was every inch the hero Uthiel and his friends had grown up idolising. Solanthur was one of the finest leaders, blades, and knights ever to don Secundan plate. His men stood tall and proud behind him, battle hardened veterans to a man, ever the reflection of their leader. The first captain noticed Uthiel and nodded his greeting solemnly.

Uthiel returned the gesture, his heart quickening at the perceived approval of the first captain, before turning back to look at his own men. While they each stood tall and proud, they did so as individuals, too haughty to acknowledge each other or too green to understand the true brotherhood forged in the battle line. In comparison to first company, his men looked disharmonious in the extreme. Uthiel muttered a prayer to Armenius as he watched his men.

Tarren looked to him. After a moment the stout brother's head inclined almost imperceptibly. Uthiel appreciated the gesture, knowing the irascible youth to be the only knight in his company who would give the word 'brother' any truly heartfelt meaning. Theon's glare rested on anything he could lay it on, as if his unhappiness could burn the world around him. Pavel was impassive, his face sombre and serious, but ultimately uncaring. The tall swordsman offered Uthiel a nod, but the motion was empty and bereft of the brotherhood Uthiel craved from his men. *I'll earn my brotherhood,* Uthiel promised himself, his heart steeling.

Behind them, the remaining five and a half thousand men of the Fifth stood to attention with their wagon train in the background. The black banner flapped in the wind above, the silver 'S' with a stylised black '5' sewn into its bottom curve snapping in the stiff winter morning's breeze. Either side of the black banner, long, thin off-white pieces of material twisted and swirled in the wind, the names of the fallen stitched in tiny hand in seemingly endless columns. Name after name of the young men obliterated at Archenon Creek flowed like spirits riding the breeze. They were the names of the fathers and sons and brothers of the men who had once again raised the Fifth to march for vengeance.

Uthiel's father's name was on that list, sewn into that banner in tiny hand.

The slopping of hooves through mud and snow heralded the one-hundred knights of the king's personal guard sitting upon their mounts to the flank, the red dawn clouds above reflecting from their polished armour. A massive captain sat upon a huge destrier to the fore of the column, a banner bearer behind him carrying a sewn image of the king above.

Before the Secundan host the two princes of Imonetia, the last remaining royals of their land, stood with a meagre group of bodyguards. They spoke amiably with the Lord General Ryun and his own personal guard. Uthiel watched their movements: proper and well mannered, straight backed yet relaxed in the saddle as they spoke with the lord of the Grey Wolves as if they were about to embark on no more than an early morning stroll.

While both princes were obviously of the same pedigree — sun-tanned dark skin, dark hair, a sharp chin with a dark and short goatee, and dark brown eyes — the likeness ended there. The elder was obesely fat, his chest labouring to keep his body powered. Sweat gleaned upon his forehead, despite the chill. There, his softness ended, however. Eyes as sharp as razors, constantly moving around and judging everyone and everything around him, laid on Uthiel a moment before moving on. Fierce intelligence burned in those orbs that seemed to be suffocating beneath fat lids. Uthiel felt the hackles upon his neck raise as he watched the man. Here was a warrior of politics and the mind, a fierce bear wobbling with fat and what seemed like amiable meekness, but had the power to do as much damage as Uthiel could with a sword.

The younger's face was a map of barely suppressed excitement and anger held in check by royal-trained will. Uthiel watched the young prince, perhaps a couple of summers older than he and Tarren, as he shifted in his saddle, obviously eager to get the column moving towards the reclamation of his brother's throne. The man disappeared from view as his bodyguards interspersed themselves between the host and the gathering of princes and Uthiel's lord general. Without thinking Uthiel took a half step forward, his fingers brushing against the leather-wrapped handle of Ghurkar's sword at his waist.

Seeing one of Ryun's bodyguards speaking with one of the prince's bodyguards with no hint of aggression or anger eased Uthiel's concern quickly. *We await the pleasure of our lords to unleash our righteous anger on the black foe.* Uthiel smiled to himself. *Well, to walk a month north first, through the winter snows and then sands and then... then we can unleash our righteous anger.*

As the sun began to slowly make its way up the horizon, the clouds above shifting through the hues of flame, trumpets blared and the knight companies began to form up to create the van of the host. Uthiel felt a quick pang of annoyance that the less experienced Captain Ryun's company were given the honour of following first company as the Lord General Ryun's son and his men, and attached company of the Fifth, were ordered forward.

Uthiel waited impatiently for the men to pass. As they moved by at an easy pace, he felt a presence by his side.

"Captain," said Captain Darian. "The men are ready to march. With your permission?"

Uthiel nodded his approval.

Darian turned and began to walk away. Uthiel knew enough of fighting men to know displeasure. In the set of the old man's shoulders, the craggy look thinly veiled upon his face, and the dragging feet, it was as plain as day to him. This was a man not happy with his current lot in life.

"Captain Darian," called out Uthiel.

Darian stopped, hesitating a moment before turning around. "My lord?"

Uthiel walked over to him, a few short steps at most. "I am no lord. Low born, like you, only my life led me to the Orders, whereas yours led you to the Fifth, like my father."

Darian's face tweaked a moment. "I did not know him, though I knew of him and marched under him on Gall."

"You were there when my father fell?" asked Uthiel.

"No, my company was still at the mouth of the bridge when the front lines were hit."

Uthiel sighed and fell silent for a moment.

"May I speak frankly, Captain?" asked Uthiel.

"You are a knight captain. You outrank me. You may speak as you please," responded Darian, a little dash of venom at the mention of rank.

Uthiel allowed the tone to pass by, picking his battles. "As you wish. You are older, far more experienced than I. You have fought upon battlefields along the length and breadth of the frontier, survived the ravishes of war to retirement, and now been pulled out of your quiet life in Secunda probably due to the death of a son, brother, or friend. Am I on the right track?"

Darian nodded, his eyes wary and a little defiant.

Uthiel took that as a sign to continue. "On the other hand, I, only may seem seventeen or eighteen summers old to you, am an up-jumped knight with but a little more than a year of field experience and new to command who has ridden the coat-tails of either his famous father or one action in which he slew some great big barbarian, and is now your commander. Am I still on the right track?"

Darian's head didn't move. But his eyes remained wary.

Uthiel let the moment hang, holding the old captain's stare. It was time to take a chance.

"Counsel me."

Darian's surprise was obvious. "What?"

"I *am* young," said Uthiel. "I *am* inexperienced. Those are my faults and I own them, I control them, and I can conquer them like I have conquered the foes of Armenius."

Darian's face switched from surprise to dubiousness.

"You have led men for years, those years both bloody and peaceful. My father was a general: your general. He made sure you men were fed and well led. He cared for you like a father cares for his sons," continued Uthiel. "He led you to victory after victory and died defending our king. A lesser man would have left hundreds more of you strewn upon field after field, in town after town, your blood soaking into the dirt."

"A fine speech," interrupted Darian. "But what do you want of me?"

His line of thought interrupted, Uthiel spoke his want once more. "I want you to counsel me."

"Counsel?" snapped Darian, pausing a moment to gather his thoughts and take a calming breath. He rubbed his face with his hands before continuing. "I can help you, a little. I know of soldiering, not of being a knight. But I do know that there is more to leading men than having the courage to shoulder your shield and lean into the charge of the foe."

Uthiel nodded. "And?"

Darian smiled, though there was little warmth to it. "I said 'a little,' captain. I cannot lead these men or your knights for you."

One of the lord general's messengers appeared next to Uthiel, his face red with exertion from running.

"Captain Caellar," said the man. "The lord general demands you get your men moving immediately."

"What?"

Uthiel looked back at the two companies of his brothers marching off north and quickly realised his discussion with the captain of the Fifth had made him forget to get his men moving. He swore loudly.

"Brothers!" he called. "We move! Follow me!"

Darian turned to walk away, and stopped for a moment. "Uthiel, you should think."

Uthiel looked back at him, confusion written on his features. "Of what?"

"What more there is to leading men, or course!" called out Darian. "I can but only direct you to the enemy bastion, captain, you are the one who needs to get in there and conquer it."

Uthiel smiled to himself as he lost sight of Darian behind his marching brothers. Tarren moved up next to him as he took his position at the head of his men.

"Making friends already, captain?" he said gruffly.

Uthiel snorted. "Why, jealous?"

"About as jealous of the piece of dirt beneath the fresh cow-pat," retorted Tarren.

Uthiel laughed, his spirits lifting. He looked back to the camp, spying the tips of tents, earthen walls, and penned horses but not seeing her, the woman who held his child. He sighed. *Time to go to war.*

The sun had passed the pinnacle of its arc above and was well on its way down. Uthiel and his men, and the host around them, were still walking ever north. Uthiel's feet had surpassed pain and gone numb. He could barely feel them at all. His calves suffered as if they had become as taut as iron or stone, every pull or push agonising. His armour weighed him down, his strong physique now struggling, and his breath deep and laboured. *Should have stowed it upon the baggage train.*

Immediately Uthiel quelled the thought, picturing his men without their plate, at the end of the day's march, when the barbarians of his imagination swept upon them. *There is more to leading men...*

Uthiel was thinking of the wiry captain, a man now perhaps a friend, perhaps not, when he once again felt a presence beside him. He turned and immediately dipped his head.

"Prince," he said. "How may I serve?"

The leaner of the Imonetian princes was right beside him, his segmented pauldrons nearly brushing Uthiel's own, a glowering bodyguard watching the young knight with intent. The young prince studied him, but did not speak. The prince's eyes were alight, though his face remained calm, holding its excited edge.

"I am Phiti," said the prince, his accent odd but easy to understand. "Younger brother to the king."

"Captain Uthiel Caellar, of the fifth company Grey Wolves. I am honoured," returned Uthiel.

Phiti smiled and nodded, and paused for a while. Before Uthiel could build the courage to speak once more, but well after the silence got awkward, the prince spoke again.

"I look forward to our nations warring together," said the prince.

"As do I, Prince Phiti," responded Uthiel. "I look forward to seeing how the Imonetians make war."

"Taking back my homeland shall be gloriously remembered through history as a moment when Imonetia and Secunda stood shoulder to shoulder and slew the great foe side by side, as equals," declared Phiti, zealousness lighting his eyes with a hungry fervour for battle.

Uthiel didn't respond immediately, his gaze darting from the immense columns of the Secundan army and knight companies and then back to the meagre offering of men the Imonetian royals had brought with them. He noted their flimsy looking armour and curved swords, short horses and satin wrapped limbs with gold chain that looked more ceremonial than functional.

The prince picked up on his line of thought quickly and astutely.

"You think us weak?" he asked, his face hardening a little, almost imperceptibly.

When Uthiel didn't immediately respond, the prince took a deep breath and continued. "I spoke in haste. You are young, like me, though you are not as well travelled as I am. Our perceptions are lacking in experience."

Uthiel nodded. "I should learn control of my face as I have over my swords."

"You misunderstand me," said Phiti. "I mean that to me, you knights look slow, cumbersome, your shield walls like trying to steer a herd of stubborn bullock around a field, easy fodder for the speed of the Imonetian cavalry. Your nation has already fallen once, and yet the histories say you fight the same today as you did when you lost your homelands to the darkness. What do you think of that?"

This time it was Uthiel's eyes that flared with anger, but even as his mouth opened to retort, he clamped it shut and stared forward.

The prince watched him, openly staring at the young knight captain. "In my lands, it is considered rude to ignore your betters."

Uthiel's eyes blazed and he turned. "Prince Phiti, in Secunda, it is considered rude to speak ill of those who have mustered their strength, in your time of weakness, to help you."

Immediately, Uthiel knew he should not have spoken. Inside he cursed, but externally he held the prince's glare. *I am a captain of the Grey Wolves! A hero of Secunda! You're not my prince, nor my royal, nor my liege.*

In his peripheral vision Uthiel noted the prince's bodyguard's hard stare narrow at him, large hands at the end of arms thick with muscle lowering towards a pair of curved blades crossed in sheaths upon his lower back. Uthiel's hand instinctively dropped towards Ghurkar's blade at his hip.

Prince Phiti smiled and laughed, and his bodyguard relaxed. "My friend, may I call you a friend? My friend, you have missed my quip. Cool your rage a moment and think, I was only offering a perspective much alike your own, just through my eyes instead of yours."

Uthiel's jaw was still clenching and unclenching rhythmically as he pushed down his wounded pride and thought for a moment about the conversation. It only took him a moment to see that he had done no less to the prince with his face than the prince had done with his words. Immediately his anger broke like a storm whose wrath was spent.

"I apologise, Prince Phiti," he said immediately.

The prince only laughed again, tapping the side of his head with his finger.

"I think I shall enjoy our friendship," he said, his accent thick. "You are honest. We shall talk more. Perhaps I shall honour you with a training duel. Perhaps you will show me that you are not all slow and cumbersome like the bullock, while I shall show you my countrymen are not flimsy warriors that a light dune breeze would blow from the battlefield."

Uthiel nodded, happy at this turn of their conversation. "It would be my honour to draw blunted blades with you, prince."

The prince smiled and turned, paused a moment, and turned back. "A prince must choose his friends wisely. In Imonetia, a royal's friends are quite often those that would gain from a prince's untimely demise. This is why I must always have guards, men who are not my friends, close by with blade ready to defend me."

The prince's eyes had narrowed as he spoke, the intensity replacing any sign of levity or camaraderie. "For a prince's bodyguard, in Imonetia, is a prince's slave, his life tied to that of his master."

Uthiel's gaze shifted to the bodyguard. The man was like a coiled up viper, waiting for an excuse to launch himself at something with those curved blades.

The prince turned to look at his slave. "Khin I call him, though such men are often not named. His youth was spent in the fighting pits, his teenage years in the gladiator arenas, and his adulthood by my side plotting, counter-plotting, and killing those who would do me harm."

The prince let that sink in, allowing Uthiel to fully appreciate the meaning behind the words. Uthiel nodded his understanding, measuring up the bodyguard as his warrior spirit rose to the challenge in the slave's eyes.

Uthiel relaxed, however. "I take your meaning, Prince Phiti."

The prince smiled again, a severe mischievous edge on his lips and in his eyes. "My meaning? Why, my friend, I was merely telling you of Imonetian politics and my bodyguard's role. As there are no longer any who may lay claim to Imonetia other than my brother and I, there are no longer hidden dangers for me to worry about!"

The prince left Uthiel in a state of confusion.

Tarren approached from behind. "The friend of a prince now, brother captain?"

Uthiel's gaze watched the prince and his bodyguard as they returned to the Imonetian contingent of the host.

"A friend?" he said. "Truly, I would not know, brother."

Emilia stood watching the Secundan host head north with the Imonetians at the front as the sun rose, turning the sky the colours of flame. Without her noticing, as it had been wont to do lately, her hand moved to her flat stomach, searching for the first signs of the bulge of life. As usual it found nothing, as it had ten or fifteen times already that morning.

She searched for him: her lover, her knight, the father of their child. Emilia strained, wishing she could see his scarred face, the light shine in his eyes whenever he saw her. She loved to watch that light let the duty and violence and honour and horror of his life flow from his form as his arms wrapped around her, his hands resting either side of her waist.

Where are you, my Uthiel?

Strain as she might, he could not pick out one group of knights from the others over the distance. In their armour and grey tabards they mostly looked the same.

Why are you leaving me? Leaving your child?

The thought came unbidden to the forefront of her mind, its bitterness like a bucket of ice tipped over her body. The morning she'd told Uthiel of her lack of moon's blood had been the most frightening and happily rewarding of her young life.

That moment, when he'd frozen as she'd told him, had seemed to last forever as half of her demanded he smile and stay, while the other half expected him to turn and run and never return. That moment had lasted the blink of an eye and a lifetime.

That moment that had ended with his smile, his laugh, his love, and his commitment: everything she had wanted and more.

And now he was gone.

One mere night later and he had once more gone to war. He was gone to fight in the far off battles that had destroyed her people, the wars Uthiel had fought in, all but one of his friends had died in, and that had almost claimed his life many times over.

The thoughts brought back the memories of Gall.

She'd been stripped of her clothes and dignity, brutally marched from her town on the border of Gall and Secunda by barbarians and Secundan knight traitors, and trussed up to a seven foot tall trestle with her neck and head hanging over the end, awaiting a blood-drenched death.

Emilia had eventually gotten free as the traitor had come through the forest of sacrifices, drenched in blood so thick he looked like he was covered in vermillion mud, thousands of lives having already slipped by the blade dangling drunkenly in his grip. She remembered hitting the ground and running, her feet pounding over the cobblestone streets of Gall as she sprinted from the monster chasing her.

In her mind's eye he grew like a demon, horns and rippling musculature covering his body as his eyes burned red, an undulating heat haze emanating up and over his eyebrows. He bayed like a maddened beast as he charged for her, teeth gnashing viciously.

Emilia's memory flashed white and returned to her as she drove the meat cleaver into the bastard's head, splitting it like a melon. His, and a thousand others', blood splashed on to her. Then came the relief of surviving, mixed with the horror of murdering someone that had almost overwhelmed her.

Then she'd found him. She'd been cold, shaking, beaten, malnourished, and numb. He'd been betrayed and had just watched his best friend vaporised in a pillar of flame bred by a fell god. He was scarred, and broken, and unconscious.

She'd sat on the cold ground and pushed her lean thighs under his head, too numb to feel the weight of the jagged edges of his damaged armour digging into her legs as her hands cradled his head. Instinctively, back in the here and now, she found her hands over her belly once more as her eyes rose to the sky, looking for the gods who had abandoned the hundreds of thousands of her country men and women in their time of need.

I can't lose him. He's all that I've got. Everything. Gods, if you've any honour left in you after what you've done, let him come back to hold his son. Armenius, you are Uthiel's god, not mine, though I pray to you to bring him home safe. Just bring him back to me and let him watch over his child as a man should. Let his duty be to his family and no longer to the butchering of others.

"Emilia?" The voice was kind, soft, friendly.

Emilia turned, wiping a tear from her face. Her heart lifted for a moment as she saw dark hair and blue eyes between a set of tall steel inner collars. That lasted less than a moment as she saw the hair was heavily rimmed in grey, turning to white. That face was age and weather beaten, though fatherly and soft. The armour was polished to the point where she could easily see her own reflection amongst the intricate inscriptions of scripture.

His sharp blue eyes held kindness and depth of knowledge, and an ability to pierce the soul to its very depths to bare the deepest thoughts mistakenly believed hidden. It was this last thing that pulled Emilia back as she realised what this man was.

"Yes?" she responded uncertainly, remembering the warning Uthiel had given her.

"My name is Father Trethore," said the man. "I have known Uthiel since he was a boy, tutored him in thoughts and combat, watched him ascend to knighthood and leadership and most importantly..."

His face creased into a warm smile.

"...fatherhood."

"How can I help you, father?" she asked.

"Uthiel has asked me to watch over you," soothed the priest. "I cannot guarantee your safety, but you'll be well behind the lines as a part of my servants."

Emilia's eyebrows rose and her arms crossed.

"Though not as one of my servants, of course," said Trethore hurriedly. "However, the war effort, and I, will need some of your energy."

Emilia looked at his armour. "I shall keep your armour clean, father, and attend you as you require to earn my keep and your protection."

Trethore reached out a hand and placed it upon her slight shoulder. "You need not earn it, being Uthiel's has earned it already. But I am short-staffed and could use your help, to be honest."

Emilia smiled, none of her initial fear gone.

"When do I start?" she asked.

"Take the remainder of the day to move your tent and belongings to stand next to mine. I'll send a man to help you move and find my tent come noon," said Trethore, his voice and manner growing ever more friendly and warm. "I'll see you then."

Emilia nodded. "My unborn and I thank you for your protection."

"Until noon, child," said Trethore before turning and walking away.

As Emilia watched him go, her mind once more wandered back to when she'd had her Uthiel in her arms.

He will protect you, Uthiel had said. *He is the only one I know I can trust with you and our child.*

But you harbour a secret he will stop at nothing to find out.

Do you understand me Emilia? She had nodded. *He suspects nothing of you for now, but will stop at absolutely nothing to find out what we know about the Black Wolves. And when he finds out, he will kill everyone and anyone who had* anything to do with it to protect the purity of his nation and his religion.

Why would you leave me with such a beast? She had asked.

His head had dropped, his shoulders slumping in defeat.

I have no one else.

CHAPTER SEVEN

Uthiel drank in the scene around him. The host's camp was sprawled over the sparsely grassed field and the campfires were beginning to brighten the evening gloom in their hundreds. The knights of the Order of the Grey Wolves were in the centre, their travel stained white tents pitched already, and the horses of their lords heavily guarded along with the steeds of the king's guard towards the southern end of the camp.

The tall black banner of the Secundan Fifth snapped lustily in the crisp wind, the long, thin white strips of cloth with the names of their dead stitched into it whipping around wildly. Men in chainmail, tired from a long week of marching, either took early night watch positions on the camp side of hastily dug trenches and stakes driven into the hard winter ground, or they milled towards the fires in the hope of finding warm beef and onion broth and dry bread.

Those not on watch often shook free of their tabards, many reverently touching the stylised '5' stitched on the chest as they folded the garment and placed it on top of their heaped chainmail hauberks. The men moved quickly to huddle around the fires as they waited for the camp cooks to finish their work. The camp was full of the sounds of life: laughter, jovial banter, the calls of the patrolling sentries, and the cries and moans as the camp whores plied their trade. Even the caustically blunt wit of the unfortunates digging the latrine pits while desperate men dropped their pants nearby to relieve themselves, floated and coalesced in the centre of the camp where the knights stood with the Imonetians.

Uthiel stared openly as Prince Phiti's bodyguards produced a garish tent of rich cloth and satin stitched with silver and gold string, and began to pitch it inside the protective cordon of the Wolves' tent circle next to Lord General Ryun's plain white canvas tent. The prince stood stock still, appraising the work of his men silently while Khin fiercely eyed any knight who watched the prince too long. Eventually, those dark, almond eyes rested on Uthiel. The bodyguard slave took a step towards Uthiel.

Uthiel still wore his plate, as he imagined befitted his rank having seen Solanthur still in his, and his blades were still securely strapped to his body in their baked leather sheaths. The prince wasn't paying attention but Khin had moved a few more steps and half drawn his blade. Uthiel moved to grab his but a body moved before him and interjected its tall armoured form gracefully between Uthiel and the bodyguard. The tall knight reached up and slowly pulled a long, single edged sword from a shoulder scabbard.

Prince Phiti finally took notice and turned to watch, a small smile flicking over his lips. Around them, knights and Imonetian warriors alike had begun to take notice. Swords were drawn, shields hefted, the air hung heavy with violent anticipation.

"Brother Pavel," said Uthiel, drawing one of his blades. "I am more than capable of defending myself."

Brother Pavel turned his head slightly back to Uthiel, not taking his eyes from the menacingly advancing bodyguard. "As your sworn Shield and company champion, the right to defend my captain is mine."

The tall knight's knees sunk a little and the blade drew back behind him, one hand near the pommel and the other against the small crosspiece. Khin strode closer, his face intent on Pavel. Only when a second body interceded between Uthiel and the bodyguard did Khin stop. Sword breaker and Secundan steel in opposing hands, brother Theon stood beside Pavel.

"Khin," came the prince's voice. "That is enough."

"Theon..." started Uthiel.

The big knight turned back to look at him fiercely. "Don't flatter yourself, captain. A knight Shield is earned, not awarded. But I'll be damned if there is a company that I'm in where I am not champion."

Pavel's eyes narrowed and his stance subtly shifted towards this new threat. Uthiel saw the move and read the next moment before it could happen.

"At ease, brothers," he warned. "I'm sure prince Phiti's guard was just being overly wary."

The two knights ignored him and began to square off. Pavel's face showed the slightest hint of anger while Theon's face was open with the relish of facing off against his brother.

"Brothers!" roared Uthiel. "I may not have earned your respect yet, but I am your captain and you will be at ease!"

Theon and Pavel stopped. Both turned to look at him. Pavel immediately dropped his head and sheathed his sword with a flourish. "As you will, captain."

Pavel backed off into the crowd but Theon glared at Uthiel further.

"Captain Caellar," came an elegant voice.

Prince Phiti had pulled a dulled practice blade from one of his kneeling bodyguards.

"Will you duel with me? I have yet to test the mettle of the Secundan knight."

Theon looked about to jump in, but Uthiel silenced him with a look that brooked no argument. "It would be an honour, Prince Phiti."

Uthiel drew his second blade and turned to walk to where the practice kit cart sat. One of his younger charges leaned against it, watching proceedings wide-eyed. Uthiel reversed the blades and handed them to the young knight, reaching past him to then pull two short practice blades from the cart.

He rolled his shoulders and took some practice swings to loosen his arms and back, twisting at the hips to free the tired muscles of his lower back before dropping in to a crouch and bouncing a few times to get his legs moving. Phiti watched him calmly as he reached out his arm and a beaten roundshield was slipped on to his forearm. The prince rolled his head and stalked towards him, shield out in front and blade back to strike.

Uthiel stood ready to take the prince, side on with blade pommels held at either hip and the rounded tips aimed at Phiti's face. The prince hesitated a moment and Uthiel bunched and leapt forward, his blades cutting through the air to slam in to the shield before he spun away. The prince smiled and moved forward, shield up once more. Uthiel feinted to one side, parried the prince's first strike with his right blade, slammed his second blade down on the curved scimitar near the crosspiece and lunged, hammering his weight through his shoulder in to the prince's shield and sending him back a few shaky steps.

The prince held his own, however, good footwork keeping him from falling and a solid grip on his blade preventing Uthiel from smashing it from his hand. Uthiel smiled, his confidence growing, and moved in once more. Three more heavy blows landed on the shield, one further parried, and with a yell his departing strike just missed the top of the prince's helm. From the sidelines Uthiel's company cheered him on while the bodyguards of the prince yelled for their liege.

Uthiel moved in once more, and met a very different opponent. All of a sudden he felt slow and clumsy in his armour as the prince moved like quicksilver, dodging and ducking his strikes as opposed to trying to block them. Uthiel desperately defended himself, refusing to allow a blade to reach his armour or body. His feet slipped and slid in the mud as he fought for firm purchase. Defensive offense was barely even an option as he felt the angles of his blades he normally used to deflect strikes lessening, and the crunch of the prince's blade bear more heavily on his arms and shoulders.

Sweat poured down through his lank hair and in to his eyes as he ducked, blocked, parried, and disbelievingly found himself searching for the incoming blade once more despite wielding two himself. Before Uthiel realised what was happening, the rain of blows stopped. His chest sucking in great lungfuls of air, and his swords held low, he looked up to see the prince dance away from him a few feet.

"Heavy, in all that armour, is it not?" the youthful royal teased.

Uthiel didn't respond, not wanting to waste his air on returning taunts. He brought his swords up.

The prince shrugged his shoulders at the lack of response, and leapt forth once again. His blade twirled through complex moves and his shield was everywhere, blocking whatever ripostes Uthiel could manage with ease. Almost before Uthiel realised, the shield became a weapon as the prince spun lightly, the beaten steel edge swinging around like a disc intent on beheading the young captain. Already knowing it would hurt, Uthiel didn't bother to block the rounded edge, but trusted in his armoured shoulder's tall inner collar and leant into the blow. At the same time, he hammered the crosspiece of his blade into the prince's stomach.

While the shield slammed into him and sent him stumbling sideways, Uthiel's own punch did little damage, like hitting a sack of grain as the prince lithely twisted with the blow. Before he could stand upright once more, the right hand blade was slammed from his grip and the prince was upon him once more. Uthiel kept stumbling backwards, his remaining blade weaving a desperate defence before him until he finally found himself on his back in the dirt, to the roar of the Imonetian crowd.

The prince soaked it up, raising his blade and shield to the sky, while Uthiel sat up and tried to get to his feet. The prince viciously kicked out and landed him back on the dirt and snow, before stepping forwards to put a boot on Uthiel's cuirass to pin him down.

Before the expensive riding boot could land, Uthiel rolled hard to his left, his vambrance striking out with all his strength to knock the other grounded boot sideways and bring the prince crashing down.

There was a sharp intake of breath as the crowd took in Uthiel's final move. He once more lay on his back. His remaining blade was held up horizontally. The prince's throat rested upon the dulled edge, his non-shield arm thrown out too late to stop his descent on to the blade. The two were face-to-face, mere inches separating their flaring noses.

Uthiel watched the prince, inwardly disbelieving the man could try such a foolish and vainglorious move to finish the bout when a blade to the throat from arm's length would have sufficed. The young royal's features quickly went from surprise, to anger, and then back to their practiced smile. A few of the Grey Wolves threw up a ragged cheer.

"I believe the bout is mine, Prince Phiti," growled Uthiel, the effort of holding a large portion of the prince's bodyweight on the blade telling.

The prince's smile grew a little wrier as he pushed himself up, wiping mud and snow from his clothes and holding out his arm for one of his guards to rush forward and take the roundshield. The guard shot Uthiel a fierce glare as he took the beaten steel from his liege's arm. The prince took a few steps back. Uthiel got himself to his feet. There was a pregnant pause, as all waited on how the prince would react.

Uthiel felt Theon and Pavel by his side, though he could not see them until they moved into the fore of his peripheral vision. Khin stormed forward to stand before his prince once more, his face a map of rage begging to be unleashed. Uthiel felt one of his blades pushed in to his hand and without turning to look gave a nod of thanks to the young knight who had probably put it there.

"Captain Caellar!" roared a hoarse voice.

Uthiel's head dropped a little as Lord General Ryun burst through the crowd.

"Caellar, you damned young upstart, what in the name of Armenius to you imagine you are doing?"

Uthiel offered no response, but turned to face his lord general.

Ryun stormed up to stand before him, his hard stare flicking between the muddied prince and his captain.

"Well? Can you explain this stain on the honour of the Wolves? To strike a prince! Have you taken leave of your senses?"

The prince walked forwards, pushing past his bodyguard.

"Lord general, if I may. I asked the young captain to show me the worth of a Secundan knight," said the prince.

Ryun stood still, his cheeks quivering and his face incredulous.

"I was bested fairly, your Order's honour is in tact. There is no ill will," finished the prince, with a sly look at Uthiel. "In fact, I would consider it an honour if the young captain would bout with me further on the way to retake my homeland."

Ryun stood there. His mouth opened and closed once or twice before his eyes narrowed once more at Uthiel. "As you wish, Prince Phiti. I'll leave you in the care of the captain, for now, but will expect you for supper tonight."

Phiti bowed. "It would be my pleasure."

As Ryun walked away, Phiti stood next to Uthiel and watched the lord general stalk off next to the young captain.

"You taught me a valuable lesson today, Captain Caellar," said the prince.

Uthiel smiled. "Stow the showmanship and make the practical kill?" he offered.

"Gods no," mused Phiti. "Next time I'll make sure my opponent is properly disarmed *before* I get theatrical with my victory."

The prince offered Uthiel his forearm and hand in a warrior's handshake. Uthiel took it firmly, noting the thick golden bracelet around the wrist and the slim gold royal seals around Phiti's index finger.

"A Grey Wolf is never disarmed, Prince Phiti," promised Uthiel.

"We shall see, my friend. We shall see."

During the day, the winter seemed to dissipate somewhat as the Secundan and Imonetian host reached the end of the third week of their march north. Under Uthiel's feet the thickly clotted dirt and mud was gradually changing into a finer grade of soil, but was not yet the coarse sand the desert lords called home. Chill winds still whipped through the men and fluttered their hair and cloaks with icy fingers. Above, an unblemished sky allowed the sun to radiate heat that was just beyond pleasant, but not unbearable.

Uthiel marched at the head of his company, his shield hung on a leather strap over the shoulder opposite to where Lokhi's sword poked over his pauldron. He was the tip of the vanguard, the northernmost soldier of the Lands of the Light. By his side his twenty knights stood fanned out, ten to twenty paces between each of them as they strode over low grass clumps and between sparse trees with segmented trunks and blade-like leaves. Pavel was, as ever, beside him to his right while Tarren walked on his left. Theon was a few men down the picket line, speaking in a low voice to the younger knights of the company who seemed more intent on his words than on the job at hand. Uthiel gave a low whistle to get their attention and then placed two fingers over his eyes before pointing outwards.

They took his meaning, though Theon kept speaking, which in itself wasn't an issue so long as the youths kept watch. Any foe waiting for them would see the Secundans long before they heard Theon's low voice, so little was the tree cover. Uthiel's own eyes moved back to the fore. He was a cautious man, well used to being in the van of an advancing army after his time with first company during the advance from Secunda to Gall. He smiled a little, remembering times when brothers like Keldon, Lokhi, Eliem and Umbar were striding by his side.

He laughed a little to himself as he remembered Eliem and Umbar, one so skinny he looked as if he were wearing his father's armour and the other the exact opposite. He thought of the way Keldon used to tease them incessantly. *How did you two possibly become knights?* Keldon would say. *By Armenius, one of you could feed an entire tribe of barbarians while the other is little more use than a toothpick!*

He thought of Lokhi, and the massive ears the quiet young knight had sported. He had been Branor's chosen target of playful ridicule. Uthiel had loved his brothers. He still loved their memories, painful as they could be at times. He pulled in a deep, cool breath, savouring life in the moment. *Bran, you would have loved this,* he thought as he turned around.

Behind him, the one hundred men of his company of the Fifth, the twenty-second company, were spread out further in a double line fifty men wide. Their spears were leant on shoulders and wobbled above them, the heads dulled with charcoal. Tabards flapped in the wind over their neck-to-knee chainmail hauberks, and shields hung on leather straps. Captain Darian marched at their centre, his weathered face pinched and squinting as he looked north beyond the knights.

The old captain caught his gaze and gave Uthiel a wave, quickening his step to catch up. Uthiel didn't stop, turning his attention back the way he was walking and waited for the man to arrive by his side. He had grown to like the captain, though Darian was over twice his age.

Many men in Darian's situation would have chafed at a young man, even a knight, not yet twenty summers old, taking command. Not Darian, the captain had taken it in his stride, using the time they spent on the march to try to coach Uthiel. Darian arrived by his side, grunting a greeting to Pavel and then offered his hand to Uthiel.

"Captain Darian, how fare the men?" asked Uthiel, taking the hand in a warrior's shake.

"Their legs are growing weary, though they will be fine. They are soldiers of the Fifth and shall not rest until their banner stands on the graves of their sons and brothers and fathers lost at Archenon Creek," responded Darian, his face hardening as memories of lost family flittered by.

Uthiel felt for the man. He too felt the loss keenly, for although his father had not died at Archenon Creek, he had fallen leading the Fifth into Gall.

"They do me proud. Not much longer before we must find a campsite. Any word from the outriders?"

"Last I saw, the cavalry were off west, making sure none of those bastards were trying to cut around us. No word has been passed to me. Probably wouldn't lower themselves to talk to a lowly foot soldier," huffed Darian.

Uthiel smiled. "No, probably not."

They walked a while in companionable silence before Darian broke the quiet.

"I fear we may be pushing too far ahead of the host," he said, without alarm.

Uthiel looked back over his shoulder. He could see a few specks of men, and the banner of the Fifth, but they were more than a mile off.

"True, I had noticed. However, we sit in a shallow valley, we cannot allow the host to arrive without knowing what lies around," said Uthiel, looking at the hills around them. "To be caught here would be a mistake."

"If we send men up on those hills the enemy may see them outlined against the sky. They'll know we are here before we see them."

"The foe are canny enough to already have men in all the high places watching us. There is not much we can do about that."

"I'll get my men on to it," said Darian.

"Groups of five, one man to leave his mail with the company and act as a runner, you at a centre point well behind the lines with two fresh runners. I'll send some of my younger brothers back to inform the lord general that we have reached a high vantage point—"

"Where shall we set our strong point for camp? In the valley or on the high point?"

Uthiel rubbed his chin, not the least bit annoyed at being interrupted, his gaze wavering between the low ground before him and the high ground above.

"Get your men up there, get me a lay of the land on the other side. I'll recommend to the lord general that we push on down the other side and settle upon the rise. We'll be stationary for the night, best we have a position where we can rain arrows down upon them from above, as opposed to the other way around."

"It'll reveal the size of our force completely to the foe, put us all on display," warned Darian. "Some leaders would frown at such a strategy."

Uthiel's sharp eyes picked out a dark figure upon one of the rises. It stood slowly and ran at a crouch down the other

97

side. Uthiel stretched out an arm and pointed at the quickly disappearing figure.

"Like I said, they already know we're here. From up there, they already know how many we are. Surprise is no longer a luxury we have, we must therefore rely on our assaults landing like great hammers and our defence being impenetrable."

Darian smiled, ever so slightly, a look of approval flashing across his eyes momentarily. "As you say, captain."

Darian stopped walking and turned back, waving his men forward. They came up at a jog and neatly assembled into ranks. The captain of the twenty-second company of the Fifth barked out his orders and immediately the men broke up and ran off, a few staying behind to bear the weight of the runners' mail and spears, awkwardly awaiting the baggage train.

The sun had sunk deep towards the horizon and the shadows from the surrounding hills put large pieces of the valley into darkness before Lord General Ryun and the Secundan host arrived. The prince was by his side as Uthiel made his report of the day's movements and the inactivity of the foe.

Ryun looked up at the rises around them, his eyes settling on where Uthiel had suggested camp and his brow furrowing as he contemplated Uthiel's site.

"I see no flaw in the site. Word from the scouts?"

"We've almost reached the desert. There are broad plains beyond the hills sweeping from the east around to the north-west, with small rises and dells, but nothing major. A river bisects the land. It is broad, though I know not its name. A few small towns, five or so miles off in our current direction, are based around the river. To the south-west, there is a broad forest twenty, maybe twenty-five miles off. More than a day's march or ride at least."

"Any sign of the foe?"

"A scout saw us arrive and ran off, though I doubt he was the first one to see us."

The lord general stuck out his bottom lip a little and nodded to himself. "True."

"The yellow sands stain the horizon just below the sky, we are not so far from Imonetia's borders."

Ryun smiled wryly. "In the desert, little brother, it is never that simple. A man's water skin holds a day's worth of water, maybe two in desperate times. We must follow the line of the river, lest our men run out and perish of thirst. If it is the river I believe it to be, we've a week of marching through the sand to look forward to before we see the walls of Imonetia."

Uthiel blew out his cheeks, soaking up that piece of knowledge.

Ryun regarded him a moment. "Take me to the camp site. We've only a few hours of daylight left and we've defences to dig and stakes and tents to pitch."

Uthiel beamed inside. Taking advantage of a chance to prove himself was a satisfying feeling. "I'll lead, lord general, though first we need more men on those rises. The men of the twenty-second need to be strengthened."

Ryun turned and called out, "Solanthur! Captain Ryun! Get your companies out on those rises and start pushing down on the other side. We camp up there tonight."

Solanthur moved past with his men and gave Uthiel a pat on the pauldron. Captain Ryun gave him a glare. Uthiel glared right back as he walked ahead of Lord General Ryun with his men in tow. The *clip-clopping* of hooves turned him around once more and he jumped back a little as Phiti's horse nearly took a bite from his hair.

"What's that?" asked the prince.

Uthiel raised his eyebrows. "Pardon, prince?"

"In your hand, whatever you are toying with from around your neck," said the prince, pointing at his right hand.

Uthiel looked down and realised he had the wolf head talisman between thumb and forefinger and was twisting it on the thin chain absent-mindedly.

"A gift, from my father."

"May I see?"

Uthiel lifted it over his head and handed it to the prince. Immediately he felt naked without it and yearned for its return.

The prince tuned it over in his hand before passing it back.

"Your father was also a Grey Wolf?" enquired Phiti.

Uthiel shook his head. "No, a general of the Fifth. He died in Gall."

Phiti made a gesture with his hand. "The gods of the sand, their dunes and storms taking and returning what they will, surely know this great warrior's name."

Uthiel thought of Tanin for a moment: the booming laugh, the games of his youth, the pride in the man's eyes as his son was selected for knight training from amongst thousands of other boys, dinner at the Blue Goose in Secunda on the last night before he left for the Grey Wolves — there were so many memories.

"It is a hard thing," said Phiti, holding out the talisman for Uthiel to take, "to lose one's father before his time. A hard thing indeed, I feel your loss, my friend."

Uthiel looked up and saw the pain in the prince's face. "May your own father stand firm by His side in the Shield Wall in the Sky."

Phiti laughed.

"Our roundshields and silks would look funny in your metal walls, my friend," said the prince, his face then taking on a more sombre set. "But I am honoured that you would say so. I look forward to when we draw blades as allies and spill the blood of those who ransacked my home, when these endless days of marching are over and duelling with practice swords is at an end. I'll stomp the life from the barbarian and take my brother's seat back. Then Imonetia will be a land of the light once more."

Uthiel turned to the prince. "I truly cannot wait."

CHAPTER EIGHT

"An almighty cry of fear erupted from Xantis' foul horde, as the imminent death of their leader dawned on them. With one fell stroke, Armenius broke the backbone of what remained of the enemy. One gleaming, glorious arc of sun-reflecting steel as he carved his way into the annals of history as the saviour of Secunda."

Father Trethore paused to give well-practiced weight to the moment. Emilia watched him reverently, enjoying his oratory in his deep and resonating voice.

Trethore stood tall amidst the hundreds of knights and soldiers of Secunda, with a peppering of cooks and surgeons and other camp followers. Secundan men and women, even the whores, knelt in the icy mud of the camp with their heads bowed, their minds at ease while Trethore rebuilt their spirits after the day's efforts with sermons and tales of their Eternal Lord, Armenius Faramon.

"He is our father, our protector, and our shining guidance against the dark night that lingers menacingly beyond the White Frontier. The dark night that strives ever towards the destruction of all we value and deem holy. It is the dark night that will stop at nothing to murder everything that you hold dear in this world – everything that your soon-to-be brothers spill their blood every day to protect and everything that you will soon spill your blood to protect.

The warrior priest himself looked magnificent, standing tall in the centre of the congregation, his zealous faith the epicentre of the host. His armour shone brilliantly, and Emilia took some quiet pride in knowing its appearance was due to her hard work with polish and cloth and a small stiff brush.

"I want you to close your eyes," finished Trethore, his breath misting before him in the cold air. "Close your eyes and pray to Armenius Faramon, our Eternal Lord, to guide your sword and strengthen your armour. But most importantly of all, pray to him to steel your courage and allow you to protect those who cannot protect themselves from the Dark beyond the Light that is our Eternal Lord and his chosen representative here; the King."

"My soul, my blood, my life for you my Eternal Lord. Praise be to you Armenius, for my life and my family's I thank you," intoned the congregation, hundreds of voices melding together in a soothing wave of devotion.

Emilia smiled. Though the gods the Gallites worshipped may have deserted her, and what pitiful remnants of a people were left of her lands under the stewardship of the Secundans, it warmed her soul to see people in the harshest of conditions still worshipping her lover's god. She may not have believed in Armenius, but that belief in the good of gods could still exist after the horrors she had seen was a nice feeling. *Shit, could there even be gods left if a war of this scale could be allowed to happen?*

Emilia giggled to herself as she repeated the word under her breath. "Shit."

The Secundans began to stand as the sermon finished, slowly dispersing into the rows of tents surrounding the small clearing. Trethore was shaking hands and offering words of courage and condolence in equal measures to men and women who had lost family and not seen home in over a year. They'd sat in this camp for months, snow hammering down from above at night, the sodden ground turning to ankle and then knee-deep sludge as they tramped it by day, and the ever present smell of the latrines encroaching further throughout the camp each waking moment.

The cold got into the bones, through even the thickest of garments. Mildew had sunk into every absorbent material in the camp, and the mud was in *everything*. Her once pristine white work dress now sported a gradient of colour of almost black brown covering her feet up to a light mixture of sweat stain yellow and off-white at the armpits and shoulders. As with most of the camp followers, apart from the whores and the lords, she lived in abject poverty. Emilia did not have the heart to press for a new dress.

Much of the host's store of clothes had been requisitioned by the surgeons and nurses to use as bandages for those still healing from the battle for Gall, or those injured in the training fields. *And the battle to come*, thought Emilia. *Always the battle to come.*

The thought brought her mind back to Uthiel, the young and strong father of the child growing in her belly, many leagues north marching once more into the jaws of danger and battle. He was leaving her and their baby here with the one man who could protect her best of all. Trethore was the one man who commanded the respect of the Secundan host from the lowliest latrine digger to the lord steward himself: a man who could call upon any other Secundan to die for him and her.

"Emilia," came the warm voice of warrior-priest.

Emilia tried to hide an involuntary flinch. Trethore was also the man who would torture her until she told the truth of what she knew about the treachery of the Grey Wolves. To let slip the horrible memories of what she had seen in the very heart of Gall would doom her child and her man to death in one fell swoop.

"Are you alright, lady?" asked the warrior priest.

Though she was not of noble birth, the old man kept calling her that. She had corrected him a few times, on each occasion he had smiled warmly. *You are with a young knight of Secunda. You hold one of us in your belly. If you do not deserve the title, then none do.* Often were the times when Emilia looked at the aged warrior priest and wondered if what Uthiel told her about him was true. Could this man be capable of such horrible cruelty as to murder a young mother with a son of Secunda in her belly for merely seeing the betrayal of the knights her Uthiel should have been calling 'brother'?

"I am fine, thank you sir," she lied.

"Did you enjoy my sermon?"

"It was warming to witness the worship of my Uthiel's people, and you deliver your words well."

"The Eternal Lord watches all of us, Emilia. He watches and He judges and He lends His strength to those of us who would fight the darkness for Him," said Trethore. "I see His strength in you, in the story of your survival."

"You do?" she asked, a little sceptical.

"I do. You have fought the evil of the black lands. You saw the horror of the great sacrifice of the foe to their dark god. You tore your limbs bloody to escape. You grasped cleaver and your courage, and naught else, and slew the great foe—"

"I only fought to live," interrupted Emilia. "An animal has that kind of courage. The foul barbarian was a fool, I should not have had a chance."

"Nonsense, your bravery should be an example to all."

"I am most certainly not brave, I—"

"You attacked a *trained knight* in naught but what you were born in, with a meat cleaver," his voice was like a delicate sword thrust.

Emilia saw it for what it was immediately. *He suspects... does he know? Uthiel!*

"A trained knight?" she laughed nervously to cover her fear. "Surely not. A trained knight would have killed me a hundred times over! Besides, Uthiel says the barbarians do not have knights and lords like we do, only foul warlords in furs and bronze."

Trethore's face smiled, as if he were enjoying her supposed naiveté. His eyes didn't smile, however: they were ice-cold, hard, calculating and they were scything through her defences and looking into the depths of her soul. With all of her courage she held his stare, allowing her eyebrows to slowly move up in the middle to improve her look of bewildered innocence.

Then, with no warning, Trethore's eyes were once again those of the priest. Soft, yielding, warm and welcoming, they matched his face perfectly.

"Too true. A slip of the tongue. Apologies. My armour shall be requiring a cleansing tonight, Emilia," he said. "And you make sure to get yourself a hot meal when you gather food for my supper. Your child needs it just as much as you do."

She wasn't ready for him to reach down and place a hand upon his belly but this time she didn't flinch. In a low rumble he blessed her child, eyes closed. When he finished and looked back up to her, she smiled, *beamed*, to have been honoured so.

"Armenius watch over your child, lady," was all he said before walking away.

Emilia watched those massive pauldrons, dirty white tabard and grey-white hair quickly disappear into the crowd. She sagged with relief.

Uthiel should be here watching over my child, she thought.
He should be here, protecting us.
Protecting us from you.

Uthiel squinted in the pre-dawn light. The Lord General Ryun knelt in amongst the tufts of grass on the dry, hard packed, dirt, looking from their vantage point atop the rise and down into the broad plains before them. His three captains stood behind him, staring down at the faded map the lord general held.

They were still a week's march from the city of Imonetia, capital of the surrounding lands, but they would cross into the borderlands of the desert lords this very morning. Uthiel had sensed the excitement within the young prince Phiti. He could almost taste the youth's lust for the battle to cleanse the lands of the barbarian foe that had slain all but two of his family and many tens of thousands of the people his brother would rule.

"Uthiel's company scouting for the day," said Ryun. "First company in reserve, my son with me in the van. The king's guard split in two on either flank."

Uthiel acknowledged with the other men. "Lord general."

"I must attend the prince," said Ryun, his tone suggesting annoyance. "He has some fool notion that he and his men should be scouting with our companies. Says he would like to experience our methods of war."

"Best he'll experience is Caellar's drollness," sneered Ryun's son. "At worst, he'll be slain out in the fields before we can get there."

He turned and locked eyes with Uthiel. "Or perhaps I have those the wrong way around."

Uthiel bristled on the inside, but kept himself in check. He'd worked hard to avoid the ire of the lord general. Bringing displeasure upon himself by insulting Ryun's beloved son would not do the men under his command any good, though it may make him feel better. He turned to the lord general.

"My lord general, with your leave, I'll take my company and get moving out to a half mile distance until you're ready to move. There will be seven groups of three of us, spread fifty paces, which should give us enough coverage based upon the sparseness of cover upon these plains."

Lord General Ryun sniffed and nodded. "Make it so."

"Armenius be with you," said Uthiel as he left the men.

Only First Captain Solanthur Verutus responded in kind, the lord general engrossed in his map and the man's son with a scowl of distaste locked on to his face. The first captain rose and walked after Uthiel, catching him quickly with his long stride.

"Brother."

Uthiel turned his head, though did not slow down. "First captain? You honour me."

"Ensure you keep your correct scouting distance, you moved too far from the column yesterday and you'll not have your army company at your back today if you run into trouble," said Solanthur.

"That is a fair statement," responded Uthiel, doing his best to take the criticism as constructive. "I shall keep that in mind."

"I also think thirty paces spacing should be enough, the riders of the king's guard should be more than enough to cover the flanks of the line, and if you are ambushed, three brothers would not be enough to fend off many."

At this, Uthiel took affront. "I have done more with less."

Solanthur nodded. "Calm, brother, I meant no insult. Remember, however, that you have young knights fresh from initiation. Not all share your experience."

Uthiel bowed his head. "True, first captain. As ever, your experience is invaluable to me."

Solanthur offered his hand in a warrior's handshake. "May you finally find our foe, that we may smite him side by side in the shield wall."

"Armenius be with you," said Uthiel.

The first captain smiled. "So long as I do my duty, he shall be."

Many hours later, Uthiel and two of his brothers, young knights and not yet blooded on the battlefield, walked through a small field of knee-high, dry grass. The tips of the long blades were quite sharp, and on more than one occasion Uthiel cursed as they slipped between his greave and chainmail skirt and spiked him through his cloth pants.

A lazy breeze blew through the grass, rustling it in long waves of both sight and sound. It reminded him of a time when he had stood by Carn's side, walking towards yet another ransacked Gallite town. He smiled at the memory of the veteran and then sighed, yet another brother gone. He looked around to the two men who stood with him now.

Brother Axom held his crossbow parallel with the ground, keen eyes watching their surrounds, his helmet held to his belt by a leather loop through the eye slit. Axom had a young face, to Uthiel like that of a boy, though he could not be more than a summer or two younger than himself. Stereotypical dark hair framed his handsome features.

To Uthiel's left walked brother Linyn, short and stocky, heavily built with a permanent frown upon his face that deeply lined his forehead, long before age should have introduced itself to his features. A red painted shield was tight upon one forearm and a blade leant upon his pauldron.

Both knights wore polished plate covered in a grey tabard. Both young men were untried in combat but had showed promise in the mud-slick training grounds of the Secundan host in Gall. But practice and actual combat were as different as male and female. All the training available to all the fighting men and women in the world wasn't worth a phlegm filled blob of bloody spit once a foe swung a blade, or a cudgel, or even a fist, at you.

Uthiel took a calming breath. Only combat would tell. Axom and Linyn's courage would hold and their training would take over, or it wouldn't and they would run and probably die. There was little room for cowardice at the front end of the army, even less out beyond the van. Little room for anything but days and weeks of quiet reflection and fearful anticipation mixed in with swift bouts of blood-drenched glory, or terror.

His second calming breath brought him to a more restful state of mind as he began to pick out more and more details of the small town in front of them. Still a mile or two off, with no building above a single storey tall, it was the first town of Imonetia the Secundans had seen since crossing the border.

Uthiel's head whipped around as he heard hooves beating towards them from behind.

"Cavalry?" said Linyn, giving voice to Uthiel's question as he looked to his captain.

"Should be scouting the flanks," said Uthiel, more to himself than to his young brother.

Sun glinting from gold is what he spotted first amongst the massed marching host behind them. Then the tall forms of mounted men — but not as tall as he was prepared for, nor as bulky.

Phiti.

Uthiel swore under his breath. Out on the scouting line is *not* where the prince and his bodyguards should have been. The young captain watched as the thirty or forty elite horsemen approached. He began to walk over to intercept.

The prince drew a blade and lifted it above his head, roaring an incoherent scream of rage as he raced past Uthiel, nearly smashing him to the ground. Uthiel backpedalled quickly as the prince's men followed by in a broader column, a few lengths behind the furiously accelerating Phiti.

As Uthiel watched them race past, he spotted the first of the barbarians overturning carts to create blockades between buildings.

"Armenius' balls! With me brothers!" yelled Uthiel, running forward.

He spotted Linyn pulling his shield from his forearm to remove its awkwardness from his loping stride.

"You bloody well hold on to that shield, brother Linyn!" he roared at the young knight as he pushed his legs at a steady pace.

Linyn nearly tripped as he desperately tried to keep a hold of his shield.

"Keep your feet, Linyn!" called out Uthiel. "Axom! Hold back, steady pace! You'll be useless if you sprint the whole way there."

His chest heaving with the exertion of yelling at his subordinates, Uthiel kept his steady pace, seeing the brothers led by Theon and Pavel either side of him closing the gaps in the line. Tarren and his two brothers were amongst the last to fall into line from the far flank. As his company closed around him and matched his pace, Uthiel heard the cavalry impact on the line of the barbarians ahead of them.

The crash was loud but far off: steel on steel, steel on flesh, screams of pain and vicious joy. Uthiel swore again and picked up his pace as he watched the prince's men get bogged down in the defences the barbarians had erected. Men, swathed in leathers and furs and wielding half-moon axes, charged into the prince's bodyguard and starting hauling men from their saddles to hack them into chunks upon the ground.

The prince fought like a cornered wolf, his blade licking out and blood exploded from every barbarian-slaying strike. The roundshield was everywhere at once. His horse whirled and kicked out, caving in another man's skull.

Phiti's bodyguards were fierce veterans, but they were falling, one by one. Already a third of them were butchered upon the ground.

As Uthiel and his brothers came within a fifty paces of the battle, Uthiel drew his blade. In front of him, he watched a bodyguard throw himself between an axe and his prince, and pay for his loyalty with his life.

At twenty paces Uthiel called to his brothers, "Slow to march! Lock shields!"

As one, his company closed ranks, eleven in the front centred on Uthiel and ten behind ready to stab over their brother's shoulders. The barbarians noticed them, as their shields locked together with the crash of steel, and some swung to face them. The men from the Black Lands died swiftly, their bodies stamped into the dirt, and their fellows ran from the wall of death that faced them, straight back into the vicious melee.

There the prince was dismounted, a curved blade in each hand and a thick coating of blood sprayed over his expensive clothing and armour. Uthiel pushed his men forward harder, their blades finding flesh and enemy axes finding their shields more and more often. As he dragged his blade from the throat of a gurgling barbarian, Uthiel deflected an axe onto the shield next to him with his vambrance and plunged Ghurkar Storm's gleaming sword through the man's throat.

As the man fell, Uthiel felt the crush of his brothers around him relax. Heavy breathing and the moans of the dying replaced the clash of battle. Like a fierce storm blowing itself out, the fight was over. Only the backs of the barbarians still able-bodied enough to run could be seen as they made their way in all directions, blind with panic.

"Wounds?" Uthiel shouted, looking at the field before them, watching the prince's bodyguards follow him immediately into the heart of the town and disappear behind the mud brick and warped wood walls.

"Someone help me find a bandage," came a voice, young and gruff and annoyed. "Blood keeps going in my bloody eyes. Can't bloody see properly."

"That you, brother Tarren?" called Uthiel.

"He's been cut on the forehead, captain!" called out another voice, which quickly lowered. "By Armenius, I think I can see your skull in the cut, brother."

"Wrap him up, brother Inen, staunch the wound. That skull would stop almost any blade I'd wager."

There was some laughter amongst his men. Uthiel smiled.

The smile disappeared as a shrill scream pierced the air. There were shouts, more screams: horribly piercing, gurgling wails that spoke of pierced lungs drowning in blood. They were the high-pitched screams of women and children. Uthiel launched himself forward, his men following a heartbeat later.

"You lay with them?"

Uthiel heard the roar, so filled with hatred he could scarce believe it came from a man. Voices begged for mercy in response.

"You harbour their offspring like your own?"

Uthiel pushed himself harder, reassured by Tarren and Pavel's presence either side of him as he cut through a row of buildings and into the town centre.

Uthiel stopped dead, his limbs slackening and his mouth opening. The tip of his blade lowered and brushed against his greaves. "Sweet Armenius, save me..."

"Whores! Stinking, goat-bred whores!"

Another shrill scream was cut off abruptly.

Pavel stopped next to him, horror crossing even his features before turning to anger. His shorter blade was sheathed and the long swordmaster's blade slid out with a whisper.

Tarren's mouth gawped open. For once he had no words, for there were no words that a fighting man could use to describe the scene. There could never be words, only horrible memories to sit on a pedestal above all the horrible experiences Uthiel and his men had lived through in the last year.

"Phiti!" thundered Uthiel, spittle flying from his lips as he strode forwards, his eyes wide with incandescent, disbelieving fury. "Phiti!"

The Imonetian prince looked up at him, his face a mask of rage. In his right hand, a curved blade shone red with blood. In his left hand, down by his knee, he gripped a young woman fast by a handful of long dark hair. She was well in to her pregnancy. Three other women of varying ages and looks, their stomachs distended with life, lay slain upon the ground.

As Uthiel strode over, Phiti threw the woman to the ground and rounded on the incensed knight captain.

"Do you see, Uthiel? Look to their bellies! In their cowardice they lay with the enemy while their husbands and sons and brothers fought and died for them."

Uthiel didn't speak, but stormed forwards, sheathing his blade.

"They would breed barbarian bastard children! In Imonetia! Tainted blood forever rooted in our lands! Filthy, shit-covered *barbarian bas*—"

Uthiel's fist hammered into the prince's jaw. There was an audible crack and half a tooth flew from Phiti's mouth in a spray of blood. Like a lightning strike Khin lashed out with his curved blades. The first missed Uthiel's face by a hair's breadth and the second slammed into his pauldron and vambrance with astonishing force. Uthiel stumbled and crashed to the ground.

Khin leapt at him, and was smashed from his feet by Pavel, his two-handed blade slamming into the slave's segmented pauldron and sending him flying back. A second guard came at Pavel. In a move almost supernatural in its speed and fluidity, Pavel spun and carved through the man's side, spilling a rope of intestine out through the gaping wound.

Uthiel got to his feet, swords in hand. His brothers were fighting their way to him, but they would not make it in time. Twelve of Phiti's bodyguards ran at them, blades and roundshields at the ready. Uthiel prepared himself, slipping into his well-practiced stance.

In his peripheral vision he saw Theon use his sword-breaker to crush a man's forearm before knocking him senseless with a strike to his helm. Tarren duelled with two of them, using his shield to ward off one while calling to his brothers to get to Uthiel.

"Armenius be with you, my captain," said Pavel.

As one, Uthiel and his Shield launched themselves forward.

"Stop!"

The voice commanded power. The power a royal was used to owning in a land that obeyed him without question.

Phiti strode through the throng of men. "Weapons down! My guard, weapons down! No more blood."

"Do you know what you have done?" roared the prince as he rounded on Uthiel.

Uthiel let him get close, and then dropped one of his swords and flashed another punch at him. The prince swayed back, caught Uthiel's wrist and then placed a knife against his throat with snake-like speed.

Before the prince could speak or move again, Pavel's blade snicked royal skin right beneath the prince's jawline. Immediately ten blades were aimed at the Shield in turn. The cries went up once again. Phiti pulled his blade back and put on a reconciliatory smile.

"Captain Caellar—" he began.

"What did you think you were doing?" asked Uthiel coldly, placing a hand on Pavel's blade and lightly pushing it away from Phiti's throat. The air sat heavy and thick with violent tension.

"They—"

"They survived your inability to protect them when you had an army fifty thousand strong. They survived the barbarians who slew their families around them. They survived the horror of rape and the disgust of mothering children to these beasts, *but they could not survive you, whoreson bastard!*" finished Uthiel with all the venom he could muster.

Phiti looked at him questioningly. "Uthiel, you must understand, they are tainted—"

"They are your people!" shouted Uthiel, once more feeling his temper flare like the deep rumblings of a once-dormant volcano. "They relied on you, they trusted you, their families died for you!"

Petulantly, Phiti turned away. "They are Imonetians. They are mine and my brother's to do with as we please."

Uthiel tried to calm himself. "Phiti, how could you do this? How could you treat people so?"

The prince stood staring at him. All around them was just the panting breathing of the living and the moans of the wounded. Somewhere, those lucky enough to survive Phiti and all that came before him were screaming as they ran.

Hard, royal features let slip for a moment. Phiti looked at the bodies around. Women and children stared back in horror, their bodies still warm enough to give a false notion of life to their faces. The prince half reached out his hand and took a step towards one, stopped himself, and looked back at Uthiel. Phiti sniffled wetly and deeply, rubbed his eyes and turned away.

Uthiel just watched him. He had no more words as the prince walked away, and his bodyguards interspersed themselves between him and Phiti watchfully. Uthiel spat upon the ground, his mouth tasting of ash and bile.

Phiti lived in a world Uthiel would never understand. His far-off stare rested on one of the dead women. Her face, in its youthful beauty and innocence, made him think of Emilia. He felt sick.

CHAPTER NINE

The Lord Pomen accepted a cup of mulled wine from Grullen and took a deep draught. The last coughing fit had taxed him dearly. A blood and phlegm stained kerchief sat upon his bony legs, which were bare and stripped of the powerful muscle that had carried him well into old age. Not for the first time, Pomen noticed his hands shaking slightly.

Grullen noticed this also.

"My lord, time we got you dressed, don't you think? It is very cold this fine morning."

Pomen handed his manservant the half empty mug, the wine sloshing around as the ailing lord tried to hold his outstretched arm steady. He snorted, it wasn't a year ago that same arm would have been holding up a blade as he led the men of the Fifth into battle after battle on the long march to, and into, Gall. It was a sad acceptance.

Grullen came to him with a pair of black breeches and helped the lord put them on while seated. Pomen grunted as he lifted his backside from the tough mattress to allow his manservant to pull them up to his skinny waist and tie them tight above his protruding hips.

The ailing lord stood and raised his arms to allow his nightgown to be removed. As it came over his head he looked down at his body: all ribs and liver spots and scars gone blue-purple with age and cold. He looked to the ceiling of his tent. *How much longer, my Eternal Lord? How much longer will you give me?*

As Grullen finished dressing him by gingerly placing a heavy bear-skin cloak over his shoulders, Pomen's mind began to tick over. It had been a few weeks since Uthiel and the Light Bringer had left with the Lord General Ryun and his son, and all of their combined might, to take the youngest royal of Imonetia back to the land he called home. Prince, *no, King* Aphiti, the eldest of the two brothers, had remained in camp with the Secundan host, playing his role as the diplomat of his nation while his brother surged off in search of glory and vengeance.

The king was a haughty being, his dark eyes missing nothing. The man rarely strayed from the company and confidence of his bodyguards, rarely speaking in tones that could be overheard by Secundan ears. He'd barely spoken more than a few civil words to Pomen, despite the old man's attempts to speak with him over the last fortnight. He was therefore incredibly surprised to find King Aphiti standing before his tent as he exited into the biting cold of the mid morning air.

"Lord Pomen, warmest greetings on this coldest of days," said the king, his body swathed in rich and thick furs linked with golden chains.

"King Aphiti, it is an honour," stammered Pomen, fighting the shiver of his jaw as his body accustomed itself slowly to the cold.

"I would like to speak with you, as one man to another, as brothers of the Lands of the Light. Will you treat with me?"

"Happily, King Aphiti. Though my tent is not fit for your presence..."

"It is a fine morning, the sun is out. Walk with me."

"Grullen, my guards please. Bring kindling with you. A fire may be pleasant on the outskirts of camp."

Aphiti nodded at the notion and then turned and started walking. Pomen had to push himself to catch up. It took them some time, due to Pomen's lack of strength, but soon they found themselves upon a sturdy log on the edge of the camp, as far away from the latrine pits as possible. Together they watched the flames of a fire their bodyguards had brought to life for them. The two spoke, almost from when the sun was at its pinnacle until only a quarter of its cycle remained before it would plunge into the darkness of the horizon.

The king had just finished regaling him with stories of his younger brother's heroics in their retreat and eventual rout from their homeland: of glorious charges, and bitterly fought rearguard actions. Pomen had been speaking of Uthiel, of the nephew he had been gifted by a hero general of the mighty Fifth; by a man who had been his only friend outside of his Order since he had been inducted at the age of sixteen summers.

"Lord Pomen, my friend, I hope I may call you that now?"

"It would be my honour, King Aphiti."

"My friend, I am concerned."

Pomen lifted a hand to assuage his fears, but the King signalled silence politely.

"I am concerned that I have not seen a strategy from your lord steward in regards to how he plans to take my homeland back. All I know is that he has taken my dearest and only brother north. There has been no word, no messenger. I am left without eyes for the most important campaign of my life."

Pomen said nothing for a moment, marshalling his thoughts. While the king professed the easy camaraderie of friendship, Pomen was sharp enough to know that his words were being examined on every level and committed to memory, his body language scrutinised against his tone and the sincerity in his eyes. The royals and lords of Imonetia were infamously vicious and conniving towards each other, and their skills at this game were second to none in the Lands of the Light.

Pomen took a long, rattling breath and then stifled a cough. "I assure you, King Aphiti, the lord steward's strategy meeting will have worked out a plan of attack that will return you and your brother to your rightful places on the throne of your homelands. We have our most capable men with him."

Aphiti had stared at him, not giving away anything with his stern gaze.

"My own nephew is with them."

Aphiti's face turned into a smile that Pomen immediately picked up as false.

"He is not your blood nephew, my friend. Not your true kin."

Pomen bit back his anger.

"He is worth more to me than any who have come before him. He is all that is good of the Wolves and the men who worship the Eternal Lord. Though I have known him only a short time, I loved his father as the truest of brothers, and I love Uthiel as the son I could never have."

Aphiti stared at him for a while, the king's face softening in a more honest manner this time.

"I had nine sons, from the age of eight to the age of twenty-seven," said Aphiti, staring into the flames before them. "Good, strong sons for the most, almost all of them wed and with sons and daughters of their own."

Pomen smiled genuinely. "You must be proud."

Aphiti shook his head slightly, his jaw trembling. He looked up to his guards and with a nod they pushed themselves another ten paces from the king and the lord. Aphiti took a deep breath.

"I watched most of them die in battles. I watched from behind lines of men as they were crushed in open field slaughters. I watched from behind the walls of our great capital as they butchered us upon the battlements and a stormed keep. I watched my eldest and most glorious son as he led most of my bodyguards, and the few remaining soldiers left to him, in a final charge up the escape tunnel to buy me time to flee. I watched his two sons and three daughters starve or pass away in their sleep from grief as we marched south and west to the safety of your lands. And now I watch my braver younger brother go north..."

Pomen risked putting his hand on Aphiti's shoulder as the king choked back a tear.

"Not all of us were born to wield the blade. Not all of us were made that way."

"No," said Aphiti, much of the hardness returning to his eyes. "Some of us were born with minds sharp enough to traverse the perils of court like a battlefield of will, to understand the flows of diplomacy like the dance of blades, to know when a friend that you've trusted is secretly honing his knife in anticipation of burying it in your back."

Pomen frowned. "King Aphiti, I am but an old lord. My body is frail and failing. I know I am not long for this world, I see the pieces of my lungs that are coughed out in my fits and I know I shall be going to join Him in the Shield Wall in the Sky in weeks, maybe months if I am lucky."

Aphiti looked to be about to interrupt so Pomen stopped him.

"King Aphiti, hear me out." He took a breath as he felt the familiar tickle begin to work its way down his throat and into his chest. "I may be weak, but if you insinuate against my honour again, I shall walk away lest I be driven to draw blade against you. I may not be one from your court, but I am not some mindless barbarian incapable of understanding your point."

The king sat back, looking hurt. "My dear Lord Pomen, my friend, this is no insinuation. Had you of allowed me to finish my musings you would have found me quite forthwith. Allow me to demonstrate."

Aphiti's jaw set as he locked his dark eyes with Pomen's.

"Lord Pomen, if I find out you or your countrymen are harbouring secrets from my brother or myself, I shall kill you all. That is not an empty promise. Before I was king, my father sired five other sons. I was the second youngest, the weakest, the fattest, the ugliest, but before the barbarians brought war I wore the crown of Imonetia. I wore this because my older, stronger brothers died of festering cuts that turned gangrenous. They passed in the night as their hearts gave out from too much good living. They drowned in their own vomit from drinking too much. They fell from horses while out riding alone. They all had one thing in common.

"Do you know what that was, Lord Pomen?"

Pomen pushed himself painfully to his feet. "I've lost the taste for your company, King Aphiti. I shall take my leave. Grullen? My staff please. We are leaving."

As Pomen walked off Aphiti called out to him one last time.

"They all underestimated me, Lord Pomen. They all thought strength at arms and heroic leadership rendered them invulnerable to a fat, scheming wretch like me. And now they all are as dust, lost amongst the grains of sand like they never existed at all."

The Lord Pomen closed his eyes as he walked, one hand on his staff and the other on Grullen's forearm to guide him. Aphiti made him sick, the bastard was all that Pomen despised in men. He was the brains without any of the brawn. He was the thinker with none of the courage required to put his body on the line when his plans went in to action. He was a coward: a dangerous coward who'd caught on to something and was nuzzling it like a scavenging dog to see if there was life in his theory.

Pomen had a feeling the man was right.

Damn you Thomak, what in Armenius' name are you doing?

Emilia lay in a small tent, looking at how the wind played and tousled with the canvas above her. The warrior priest Trethore had been kind to her and found her a thick fur to keep her and the life growing inside her warm. She placed one of her small hands upon the swelling of her belly. She was sure she could feel the little life in there, drawing strength from her.

She closed her eyes, enjoying the knowledge that Trethore was not expecting her until he took an early lunch before noon. His armour was polished, his clothes clean, and his linen turned the night before. Emilia was free to lie in this morning and let her mind rest and recuperate from the fatigue of camp life mixed with pregnancy.

As always, when her mind was allowed to wander, she thought of Uthiel. As always, in these recent weeks, she was quick to anger at his departure; at his choice of duty over family. She allowed the heat to dissipate. Uthiel was protecting her and their child in the best way he knew how.

As long as the barbarians ran loose beyond the White Frontier, there would never be the assurance of safety. As long those filthy bastards could get past that line where the light of courage and honour met the darkness of hatred and foul worship, she and her child would never be safe.

She cringed a little as flashes of memory assailed the thickly built bastions of her mind. She'd built those bastions within herself to guard her from the horrors she had witnessed from where she was captured with her family, where she had watched them slay her father. From there her mind raced to the very heart of Gall where she had been one of the very few survivors of one hundred thousand women the Black Wolves had sacrificed to make the cobblestone streets run red.

Forests of seven foot tall trestles filling the streets, dark wet hair hanging lank from lifeless heads and vermillion tears on pale white skin dripping the last vestiges of life onto the ground.

Emilia shook her head, desperately trying to find the face of her lover to calm her horror.

A beast in a horrible parody of Secundan knight armour smashing through the trestle legs, wood and pale limbs flailing in the torrential downpour as he crashes towards her, heart hammering at her chest as she tries to free herself of the last ropes.

Picking up the cleaver and smashing it into the face of a traitor: blue eyes, jet black hair.

Watching Uthiel betrayed, and saved, and betrayed once more.

Uthiel...

Uthiel.

And then, like the sun shining through the dissipating clouds above Gall after the mass slaughter, there she had his face. Scars, pain, youth and all, she had him. As quickly as she had him, Uthiel's face twisted in pain and was gone to the clouds of fear and anguish that billowed towards her.

Her father dead on the ground.

121

Her stomach twisted. With a cry, Emilia opened her eyes and sat up. Breathing heavily, the sound of a rushing river in her ears and her hand resting protectively on her swirling belly, she stood and began to dress. She needed to stay occupied, needed to have something to keep her busy to keep her free of the memories.

Of late, they had seemed worse. She struggled to fight them off with the happier recollections of her short life. She even tried to imagine what their child would look like. It would be the perfect mixture of both of them, having all of their virtues and none of their flaws. Their child would be perfect in time, but for now her mind's eye was unable to even picture whether the eyes would be his almost translucent blues or her own.

Emilia walked from the tent. One of the camp whores waved to her.

"Good morning, Emilia! You look lovely today!" the whore called out.

Emilia smiled. "As do you, Relanna."

Relanna laughed. "Nonsense, child! I've been up all night entertaining the men of this wonderful war host. I'm tired, I'm sore, and I'm in need of a good scrub."

"Good day to you Relanna, enjoy your rest."

Relanna waved and ducked into a shabby canvas tent.

Emilia continued walking. Around her the day was in full swing. Men lounged around, spitting on whetstones and honing their blades, dicing, squabbling, eating, preparing arms and armour, complaining, laughing, and so many more actions and noises and smells that Emilia had come to expect. Men and women who knew her waved and said kind words.

Buron the baker, a fat man in his mid fifties who always leered at her when he thought she wasn't looking, gave her a quarter loaf of fresh baked bread.

"For you and the babe. Best you kept fed as well as you can now lass, we'll be on the move again soon and food will dry up quickly."

Emilia thanked him, and did her best to ignore the fact he had spoken to her breasts while handing her the bread. There were so many tasks to complete in a day when you were surrounded by many thousands of soldiers and camp followers, but Emilia found she had not the stomach or skill for them this morning.

She didn't feel like introducing herself to the women who knitted winter clothes, nor did she like being leered at for longer than necessary by the baker. She didn't want her arms up to the elbows in guts, either with the butcher or with the apothecarion. She didn't want to be at the river cleaning clothes or fetching food for the cooks. She didn't really want to be around anyone that wasn't Uthiel, she realised. She glanced north for a moment. *No point wishing for the impossible. Patience is what I need.*

She did, however, want to do something that reminded her a little of him. Emilia set her sights for Trethore's tent. With any luck the warrior priest would be out of his armour and leading a sermon somewhere, and she could sit in the peace and quiet of his tent with cleaning brush and polishing cloth and work on the steel pieces. It wasn't hard work, and she didn't mind it. She would be occupied and alone.

It did not take her long to circle back and come upon the white canvas of father Trethore's tent. On the way, she spotted Relanna allowing a tall man into her tent. She laughed a little to herself as Relanna spotted her and winked cheekily before closing the flap and tying it to a peg embedded in the ground.

Emilia shook her head lightly, a smile still playing upon her lips. She reached out to open the tent flap to go into Trethore's quarters but stopped.

"The cancer runs deep," came a voice. "This much we can tell. They reek of corruption."

Emilia stopped, her hand lingering only a finger's breadth away from the tent flap, and then turned to go.

"The Wolves, they are in control of Secunda and Gall. Soon Imonetia also. If there is corruption, we must cut it from the body of their Order swiftly."

That voice was Trethore's. Emilia stopped.

"We should remove the Order altogether. Excommunicate them. Half of their strength marches north. Now is the time to gather our strength, ally with the other Orders, and hang every man who wears the grey," hissed the first voice. "Their every breath insults the Eternal Lord's will and those who fight for Him. Your own ancestor must be roaring his hatred of the Wolves from the Shield Wall in the Sky."

"Fool, boy! You are young, you do not see the precipice the Lands of the Light stand upon. The Wolves are in command. The lord steward is their own. Our king is incapacitated, I am surprised he has not passed yet—"

"The blood of the Eternal Lord flows in his veins, he'll not—"

"Silence!" snarled Trethore. "Do not interrupt your betters. It is foolhardy to imagine the king will live to lead us once more. His body has seen too much agony, his mind has been silent for too long. With no heirs we must assume Thomak will take command of Secunda while this war lasts. After that? Who knows? We cannot affect that outcome. What we can control is the extent to which the Wolves allow themselves to be corrupted, and to corrupt those around them."

There was a silence, then Trethore spoke again.

"Besides, that is moot if we cannot convince the other Orders to side with us. The Wolves are held in high regard after their actions in Gall. The Fifth: by Armenius, they are like the Wolves' private army. Their leaders have aligned themselves to them and Thomak has encouraged it by sending them north."

"But esteemed father, there is an opportunity here surely. We could petition Thomak now, while he has few allies in the grey or of the Fifth around him. Bluff the power and convince him to our cause as a matter of faith. With the last of the Eternal Lord's bloodline failing he'll not refuse us our open investigations—"

"What if he knows?"

"What?"

"What if Thomak knows? What if he is a part of it?"

Emilia held her breath, fearing the rasp of it over her throat or through her lips might give her away.

"What if Thomak *is* the cancer infecting the body of the Wolves, knight by knight, man after man? What then, boy?"

There was a long pause.

"Then we——"

"No. Once more we get ahead of ourselves. Either way we need the rest of the host on our side, or as much as we can gather to our banner anyway, before we strike. We'll not get that without evidence."

The voices lowered further. Emilia leaned in closer.

"The girl?"

"Yes, the girl. I've had little chance to speak with her. It breaks my heart that I must treat her as such, but there is too much a stake. Uthiel knows something, I am sure of it. He or Lord Ryun or the Light Bringer. That is why Thomak has sent them north. Seeing as how we do not have Solanthur's, or either of the Ryun's, wives or lovers with us to give me an insight in to their men, Emilia is our only in. And should the time come, our only leverage."

"Esteemed father, we should put her to the question."

"No. I will speak with her. I will probe her. But I cannot harm her. The Eternal Lord may forgive my many shortcomings, but I am not sure he would forgive that."

"I could do it for you. Blood would not stain your hands."

"No."

"But——"

"I said, no. I'll hear no more on it. I'll not see her harmed. Ever."

Once again there was quiet. Emilia was afraid. Her blood roared with terror. Her heart pounded. Every movement and breath made her feel like she was clashing a spoon and pan together.

"What of the other?"

"By   Armenius,   he's   still   alive?"

"No, we captured another one."

"Did the last one speak to you, boy?"

"He knew nothing. Nobody could have kept their silence through that."

"Remember that information gained through those means is not often true. A man in true agony may say anything to make you stop."

"You don't approve."

"You know I don't."

The next words came out in a sneer that chilled Emilia's very soul.

"You want the Wolves cut out? I promise you, give her to me and I will give you what you need to excise the corruption. She knows. Your prized little Uthiel knows. Scheme and plot and insinuate all you want. They need to scream. They need to burn along with the rest of them. Armenius demands it."

"Get out."

Emilia backed away quickly and then scrambled for the cover of the nearest tent, her hand over her mouth stifling a scream.

CHAPTER TEN

Uthiel ran a hand through his grimy hair, pushing his fingers back around the side of his head to come to rest on the bridge of his nose between his closed eyes. This was the third village in a week where the wind had brought them an expectation. The sickly smell of decay was a foul messenger, a horrid herald, the beginning of the next chapter in the book the Imonetian prince was writing across his stricken countryside in innocent blood. *I thought I'd gotten through to him. Is this my failing?*

The town, from its outskirts, was large and sat upon a large sweeping rise of hard packed earth. There were no walls or fort, just a spread of buildings of various sizes, haphazardly built without much thought to planning. Plumes of black smoke still twisted into the air. Sand stone brick walls, blackened by cleansing fire, sat open-ceilinged, bereft of their coverings as the bodies around them were bereft of life. Roof frames rose blackened like a fired rib cage.

Uthiel spat the taste of bile from his dry lips as he and his men walked past body after body upon the ground. The men of fighting age having left to defend their lands, only the infirm, the old, the women, and the children had remained to face the wrath of Prince Phiti alongside their barbarian captors. To Uthiel, the bodies still wrapped in black chain and leathers were of no consequence to him, but those innocents — *those poor people*. If he should live long enough to survive this war, he would never forget these horrible days.

Captain Darian came to rest beside him as the men of the twenty-second company of the Fifth spread out into the town looking for survivors. Uthiel and Darian stood in silence, watching men duck their heads into doorless homes and more often than not, quickly exit with a hand over their mouths. Some men had taken to wearing scarves and other pieces of cloth stained with flowers or oils wrapped around their faces, anything to lessen the stench of death.

"There will be no survivors," said Darian. "Bastard never leaves survivors. Women, children..."

"Let's not discuss it, captain."

"How many towns have we seen like this? Why can our lord general not stop him? By Armenius, this shall haunt me until He calls me to His side."

"Four towns in a week. Now, captain, talk no more of it. It only serves to anger me," snapped Uthiel.

Uthiel clenched his teeth and tried to find the calm he needed for command. Of late, his calm was becoming harder to achieve.

"Clear the town along with my brothers. Let's move on."

"Captain!"

Both Uthiel and Darian looked up. One of the Fifth stood at a street corner. There was fresh vomit shining wetly down his tabard and splashed upon his boots. As the two captains drew closer, they saw the man's face was pale, drawn and haggard.

Darian put a hand on the man's shoulder. "Soldier, what is it?"

The soldier was sucking in deep breaths, steadying his stomach and nerves.

"My captain. My lord. In there... the women... been up there for months... rotting... something..."

Uthiel was already running past the soldier, Darian in tow some ten feet behind him. His heart hammering in his ears and his mind racing, Uthiel rounded a corner and looked into the town square. None of the Fifth had dared stay there. Rat and vulture droppings littered the hard packed dirt in small mounds.

There were around fifty of them, picked down by vermin and carrion eaters to their very bones and last chunks of rotting sinew and fat. They lay upon trestles seven feet tall, their heads and throats hanging off the end of the wood and stiffly swaying in the wind. Uthiel felt like a ball of lead had sunk into the pit of his stomach. He could feel something against his chest heat up and make his skin tingle, something that swum through his veins and set his blood afire with hate.

The Black Wolves had been here. There were more of them. Uthiel stifled the flashbacks of Gall. Not here. Not now. No, he needed his focus. He needed his anger to smoulder within him, waiting for him to unleash it upon the foe.

"By Armenius, it's like Gall," breathed Darian heavily.

"They lived here, this whole time, with their loved ones rotting in the centre of their town. The barbarians must have chained them and beaten them like slaves."

"And forcefully fathered children upon them."

Uthiel turned to see Tarren striding up to them.

"Again, my captain. That bastard murdered pregnant women, again!" shouted the irascible young knight. "Give me one bout with him. I'll beat him to death with my bare hands!"

"Brother, calm yourself," said Uthiel curtly. "Is the town clear? Can we move on from this horrid place?"

"We should burn it," snarled Tarren. "The whole town. And throw Prince Phiti in to burn with those he failed and then betrayed."

"No better way to announce our presence to the foe," said Darian.

Tarren shot him a look, but Uthiel spoke before the young knight could say anything.

"Captain Darian is right. Though I wish it were as you say, brother, we cannot announce our movements further to the foe."

Tarren didn't speak, just pointed to the smoke columns from the buildings above with a petulant look upon his face.

Uthiel nodded, sticking out his bottom lip. "Fair point also, brother."

He took one last look at the sacrifices. Nobody had come to save these unfortunates from the Black Wolves and their butchery. Nobody had ridden in on a steed with steel bared and fought for them. They had died with their friends and families filling their eyes as the blade rasped through their necks. Uthiel sighed.

"There is nothing we can do. Get the men together on the other side of town. Do a head count, make sure nobody is missing, and lets get our spread right once more before we move on."

Darian and Tarren nodded, the first walking off and calling to his men, the other calling to the Grey Wolf brothers within earshot without bothering to leave Uthiel's side.

Uthiel looked at Tarren and raised an eyebrow.

"Your Shield isn't here to watch you, captain. Can't have you bloody standing here without one," said Tarren gruffly. "Thomak'll have us all hung, drawn and quartered if you get a bloody scratch." Uthiel was a little surprised to see some sincerity in his brother's eyes.

Pavel returned to his side a moment later. "The town is another graveyard, captain."

"I know," responded Uthiel. "We've a few hours to find and make camp, let's get the men moving to scout out suitable ground. When the main force arrives I want combat practice. Tarren?"

Tarren looked to him. "Captain?"

"Get me a training wagon. Blunted blades for us and spears for Captain Darian's men."

Tarren nodded.

"Pavel?"

"Captain."

"You spar with me."

"Happily, captain."

Uthiel tripped, staggered and spun away from the slashing blade, in the fading light, as it roughly hewed its way through the air. Pavel read his move, as he had read all of Uthiel's intentions in their bout, and with quick footwork sidestepped to match Uthiel's spin and hammered his second blade into the captain's pauldron. Uthiel staggered a few steps, caught off balance, but righted himself in time to deflect a follow-up strike.

Pavel stood before him, his face impassive, his exertions well hidden. By comparison Uthiel's chest heaved with the effort of fending off the master swordsman, his own ability well outmatched. Pavel darted in, his movements fluid and sharp like quicksilver. Uthiel parried, averted, dodged, and tried a riposte that was swatted away with little effort and then returned two-fold.

Once more Uthiel staggered, righting himself far more quickly this time, changing tack and calling on his inner reserves of strength as he launched himself forwards, cutting and hacking, deflecting a return blow with his vambrance and almost landing his first strike on his Shield.

"Better, captain," said Pavel, without any hint of arrogance or cruelty.

Uthiel didn't respond, instead launching himself forwards.

"Captain!"

Uthiel pulled up short of Pavel and turned to look who had called for him. Brother Theon stood with Inin and Tarren, watching the display.

"Brother Theon, you interrupt my practice. For what?" said Uthiel.

Theon stood a moment, unresponsive. Uthiel inwardly seethed. He'd had enough of the knight: his demeanour, his arrogance, everything about the knight had frustrated Uthiel since taking command of the man.

Theon's face had reddened slightly in the torchlight.

"He's back. Came in to camp a moment ago."

Uthiel clenched his jaw, feeling the rage build within. He stormed over to the practice equipment wagon and threw his blunted swords in, retrieving his own blades and sheathing them.

"Theon, Pavel, Tarren, Inin. With me. The rest of you, keep practicing. Brother Draven, you command in my absence."

Uthiel marched off in the direction he knew he would find Prince Phiti. His young mind was a tumultuous mix of rage and hurt and duty. His arms ached from his sparring, but fresh life fed into them as he narrowed his eyes upon the tall flag flying from the top of the prince's tent.

"Captain——" started Tarren.

"Shut up."

Uthiel's brothers marched after him as soldiers began to notice them. He saw Darian spy him and wave half-heartedly for a moment before grabbing a sword belt and a few men and running over to fall in to step.

"Captain Caellar, what are you going to do?" asked the old soldier.

Uthiel didn't respond for a moment.

"Captain? My lord?"

"I am going to challenge Prince Phiti to single combat. He must be stopped."

Theon roared his approval, drawing a blade, a vicious excitement coming over his features.

"Damn. I thought as much," said Darian.

"I shall take him, or his champion, for you, my captain," said Pavel dutifully.

"No," responded Uthiel. "I'll not have you fight my battles for me. You may by my Shield by rank, but I've not yet earned the honour in battle or in brotherhood."

Pavel walked beside him briskly for a moment, contemplating his words.

Theon laughed. "You will never earn that from Pavel, he has no soul, no want beyond duty, no love beyond his blade. But damn my tongue to turn black, boy, you're beginning to earn mine."

Phiti's tent came in to view. The men of the prince's bodyguard lazed about, being seen to by the camp followers with string and needle and bandage. There was a hollow look to some of the men's faces. Each had a pallid look of exhaustion mapped across his face, as well as something else. Uthiel knew, this time, that it was shame.

By Armenius, you deserve to feel nothing more.

Phiti's slave bodyguard, Khin, walked out, eating a shrunken apple. The piece of fruit fell to the ground immediately as the man saw the intent in Uthiel's pale blue eyes. A long curved blade rasped out of its sheath and roused the bodyguards around him to immediate action.

Men shouted, apothecaries scattered away from the impending violence, Uthiel drew his blades as Khin strode towards him.

"What is all that noise?" called a voice from inside the tent.

The Imonetian prince walked out from his tent. Immediately Khin tried to usher him back inside to relative safety. The prince's eyes rested on Uthiel.

"Come to challenge me, then?" he asked darkly.

Uthiel nodded, loosening his neck and shoulders.

"No words? No questions of explanation? Just blood, and perhaps death?"

"Certain death, for you," said Uthiel, his voice low and full of malice.

Phiti smiled, his condescension blatant. "A mere captain, thinking he can challenge a prince?"

"A man, standing up for what is right in this blood-soaked world, challenging a foe as evil as the darkness we are all supposed to be fighting."

Phiti chewed a nail for a moment. "I note you have brought few men with you. I could just have my warriors cut you to pieces where you stand. They outnumber you at least two to one, in case you hadn't noticed."

Uthiel smiled, his stare never shifting. "Men of the Fifth, stand to arms, on me!"

Before the prince could speak again the stomping of feet filled the air as almost a hundred soldiers picked up spear or sword and created a circle around the prince and Uthiel's men.

The prince tried to hide his quickly loosening grip on the situation behind a forcedly confident smile, as he held out a hand to grasp a sword and reached for a roundshield with the other. Uthiel ignored the show, turning to his brothers and kneeling before them.

"Should I pass to the Shield Wall in the Sky, Tarren, take my son as your own."

Tarren nodded, reaching down to place a hand upon his pauldron. "Kill this son of a whore, and I won't have to."

"Armenius be with you," intoned Pavel.

Theon looked down upon him. "He's fast, watch yourself. Trust in your armour, it'll take those skinny blades."

Uthiel stood, his eyes narrowing. The prince launched himself at the young knight.

Uthiel didn't even raise his sword, but threw himself forward, leading with his massive pauldron. The prince's blade hammered into his cuirass, but the plate held, and the young knight captain slammed into Phiti's face, smashing his nose and bearing him to the ground. Dropping his swords, Uthiel got to grips with the prince. His left hand held the rim of the prince's breastplate, the right swinging with little back lift to chop a fierce punch into the prince's already blood covered face.

The prince yowled in pain and desperately tried to protect his head. Uthiel slammed one more punch into the man's chin before the prince wrenched his knees up and overbalanced the young knight, sending Uthiel flying into the dirt. Uthiel was up into a fighting stance, fists ready to continue the fight. Khin tossed the prince a curved blade. Phiti grabbed it from the air and spun it around with relish, vengeance coating his face as thickly as his own blood and mucus.

Uthiel didn't hesitate, reaching down and yanking his forearm-length knife from his hip scabbard and moving forward, his vambrances up and ready to deflect the blade of the prince. Once more Phiti leapt at him, the scimitar flashing in dazzling arcs. Uthiel was immediately on the back foot, weaving and dodging, deflecting and blocking, his concentration at its pinnacle as he watched every piece of the prince at once.

The man's footwork and balance was exquisite. The arc and speed of the blade was nothing short of magnificent. The eyes: vicious and menacing and intent on doing him harm.

Sweat dribbled from Uthiel's thickly stubbled chin. In the back of his mind, through his desperate and determined concentration, Uthiel felt a familiar heat: a scorching of his flesh sitting between his collarbones that was more than welcome. Once more, as in the battle of Gall, when he had needed it most, strength and focus leant itself to his mind and limbs.

The prince's movements slowed. Uthiel watched him come forward with the same move he had barely parried a few heartbeats before, but this time he felt as if he had ample time to step in and slam the thick ridge of his vambrance into the prince's forearm, before stabbing forward with the hilt of the knife and cracking the prince's skull with its blunt force.

The prince tumbled to the ground, legs flailing, fear in his eyes. Uthiel followed him down to the dirt, the blade of the knife flicking around and sitting against the prince's throat. Then, there was stillness, only the sound of heavy breathing. The shouting of the men around them was like the far off echo of a thunderstorm.

Uthiel felt something slip from the curve of his gorget. It fell for a moment and then stopped short, the chain around his neck snapping tight as the wolf's head talisman danced up and down for a moment before resolving into a lazy swing. Uthiel could feel the heat radiating from it, the sheer power coursing through his body. It blinked light for a moment, like it had become molten for half a heartbeat and then returned to its solid form.

The young Grey Wolf captain smiled as his eyes burned holes into Phiti's own. There he could see fear, resignation, and an acceptance of death.

"It's done. Finish me. Reduce my line to but one brother," whispered the prince.

Uthiel reached back with the blade, his eyes widening. The prince closed his own. Only when the sound of the blade entering the sheath cut through his acceptance of his defeat did the prince see Uthiel had stood and walked away, back to retrieve his swords. Uthiel spat upon the ground in the prince's direction.

"Stay down a while, with the horses' shit, where you belong," snarled Uthiel. "You may be worthless, but your brother will need your help to rebuild a nation."

"I'll remember this night," promised the prince, familiar venom returning to his voice.

"Best you do, prince. Best you do."

Uthiel turned away once more, his eyes resting on his brothers. Pavel, as usual, was unreadable. Theon nodded his gruff approval. Tarren openly cheered him with most of the youths of his company and the men of the Fifth.

"What is this? Why are you men gathered!?" boomed a voice.

"Damn," muttered Uthiel, his head dropping resignedly.

"Prince Phiti? Look at your face! What happened?"

Uthiel looked from the Lord Ryun over to the prince. *Damn.*

Beside him Pavel dipped his head. Theon and Tarren seemed to move a slight step or two to put at least a little part of themselves between Uthiel and their lord general.

"All is well, lord general," mumbled Phiti, using a water soaked cloth to wipe his flattened nose and bloodied face.

"Another practice duel with our young Captain Caellar, eh?" said the lord general.

The man's face showed how little he thought that fact possible. The prince didn't respond for a while, his eyes resting on Uthiel for a long moment before returning to Lord General Ryun.

"The captain was... helping me resolve an error in my offensive strategy."

Uthiel sniffed loudly, disdainfully, scornfully. The Lord General Ryun turned to him.

"I thought you may like to know, Captain Caellar, that the night scouts report barbarians massing in force to the northeast. Muster your men immediately."

Uthiel smiled, giving the prince one last burning glare.

"Finally," he said, before marching off with his men in tow.

The prince watched the young captain walk away, and then turned and walked back into his tent, not even bothering to look at the lord general again. As quickly as they had appeared, the remaining men of the Fifth disappeared back into the small forest of tents surrounding the Lord General Ryun.

Ryun turned away, a smile on his lips.

CHAPTER ELEVEN

"When did it happen?" demanded the Lord Pomen as he desperately tried to rouse his ailing body to get dressed.

"They say it struck him last night," responded his manservant. "They say his face paled over dinner, then he fainted as he tried to rise from the table. He had to be carried to his bed and there he fell into a slumber from which he has not woken. They say his breathing is rasping, as if the very ghosts of his country tear the wind from his lungs in vengeance for his failure!"

Pomen stopped what he was doing and looked at his manservant. "Calm yourself, Grullen. Stop that foolish talk. Help me get dressed, and let us do away with conjecture and go see for ourselves."

Grullen started and then nodded furiously as he reached for a pair of thick woollen trews and an undershirt. Pomen allowed himself to be dressed, now so used to it that his embarrassment and self-outrage barely even registered anymore as he lifted a thin white leg into the clothes. He took a deep breath to ensure he remained calm, and exploded into a coughing fit.

One foot in the air poised at the top of the trew leg, and the other nowhere near strong enough to hold him, Pomen fell to the ground as Grullen desperately tried to help ease his unstoppable passage downwards. To Pomen, there was nothing outside the world of raw, wet pain as each explosion of air and each rib-crushing clench of his chest and stomach felt like it tore another layer of flesh from within him.

Finally, after what felt like a month of agony had passed in but a long moment, Pomen felt the familiar deadening of his body, the relief of the receding pain, and the chunky wetness upon his lips. Grullen was there, kneeling over him, wiping his face with a cloth in one hand and ladling water into a bowl with another without even watching. For a brief moment Pomen wondered at the skill of the man. *Such dexterity and physical self-awareness. Perhaps the man may have been a knight in another life.*

As Grullen looked away finally to reach for the bowl, Pomen caught sight of the white cloth his manservant had used to wipe his face. There were necrotic black flesh lumps amongst the deep vermillion of his lifeblood and the green and yellow phlegm of one of his many current diseases.

Hah, not yet, my Eternal Lord. Not yet.

Throat still burning, he accepted the water, chilled by the winter.

"You need to take it slow, my lord," said his manservant. "Need to take your time to do things. Your body is failing and if you push yourself, you will speed its demise."

"My apothecarion now, are you Grullen?"

Grullen's face registered a moment of hurt until he saw the smile on Pomen's face, which he reciprocated warmly. The ailing lord was too old to make new enemies now, and with the world going to hell around him it'd be nice to see Grullen amongst whichever brothers still loved him when the Eternal Lord called him to the Shield Wall in the Sky.

It took them some time to get Pomen dressed but eventually the old man and his manservant managed to make it out. As usual it was cold enough to steal the warmth from his bones within a few breaths, but surprisingly, Pomen's four bodyguards were no longer there. Pomen looked around the sides of his tent, but his men were nowhere to be found.

A little angry now, he marched off towards the lord steward's tent with Grullen in tow. His manservant was beside him the entire way, his strong arm there to offer support when Pomen needed it, his voice there to move the throngs of soldiers and camp followers from the mud road.

The density of men thickened as they got towards the centre of the camp. There was a large group of knights thronging the command tent. Some of those knights turned to look at him, odd looks upon their faces. Pomen paid them no more than the shortest heed. His business was within the tent, with the second last king of Imonetia, who lay dying.

He burst through the thick canvas and fur flap to enter Thomak's tent. Immediately the stench of illness hit him like a fist, and a horde of lords and knights turned to face him. Without hesitation, his keen mind noted that only Secundans were within the tent. He dismissed the thought as he breathlessly made his way through the wall of men and to the centre where the king of Imonetia lay upon the lord steward's palette bed. Thomak and the chief surgeon stood over the stricken king.

Thomak locked eyes with Pomen for a moment, took a deep breath and shook his head, a defeated look on his face.

Upon the bed, King Aphiti was a haggard and drawn version of the overweight liege of Imonetia Pomen had seen a day past. Gone was the arrogance, the self-assuredness, and the hardness that made the man a political gladiator. Now there was nothing but a comatose diseased man, thick mucous bubbles upon his upper lip and a labouring chest wheezing breath through cracked and bleeding lips.

Pomen looked to the chief surgeon in disbelief. "How?"

The surgeon looked at him, doing his best to hide his obvious bewilderment.

"I know not, my lord," said the man. "Forty years experience and I've not seen the like."

"Are we at risk, is it the plague?" asked Pomen urgently, suddenly realising the danger to the steward of his nation.

The chief surgeon shook his head. "I and my attendants have been with him since last night when he fell. If the plague could strike down a man of such impeccable breeding so quickly, it should have had some effect on us by now. No, I do not think the affliction of the king to be a contagion."

Pomen clenched his jaw. *But what? What could it be?*

The word crossed his lips before he could stop himself.

"Poison?"

The room went silent and all eyes fell upon him.

The chief surgeon looked to the lord steward. Thomak's stare never broke from Pomen.

"Lord steward? What is going on? Has there been an assassination attempt on the Imonetian king?" asked Pomen.

The lord steward watched him a moment longer before closing his eyes.

"It can only be such. There could be no other explanation. I have neither seen, nor heard of any disease, be it even the dreaded cancer or plague, that could lay a healthy man low so quickly."

The surgeon nodded vehemently. "I can only concur, it must be a poison."

Around them men drew swords. Thomak immediately held up a hand.

"Brothers! Don't be foolish, whoever did this is long gone. Should they try to lay a blow upon me they would be hacked to pieces by you all before their blade was out of the sheath."

There was an uncomfortable silence.

"Though I shall have one of my manservants sample my food and wine, of course," he said with a smile.

Men around him laughed sporadically, most of it forced. That did not please Thomak. The look on his face lasted but a moment as the king's back arched and a fountain of blood sprayed from his wide-open mouth. His bloodshot eyes were equally wide, blind and unseeing as the surgeon and his orderlies tried desperately to get him to lie back down. There were shouts of alarm, and of disgust for those who were close enough to be spattered with crimson. The circle of lords and knights took a few steps back in horrified unison as the king sat up higher and higher from his bed, his breath coming so fast it was almost impossible to tell the gap between them.

Pomen watched the man in abject horror. He could hear the cracking of bones, smell the early onset of rot and the explosive release of the king's bowels as if all the fluids within the man were trying to evacuate through every orifice available. Finally, the king slammed back down into the palette, a final puff of pink mist taking flight from his lips as life left a dead stare aimed blankly at the ceiling above him.

Pomen turned to the lords and knights around him. "All of you, out."

They obeyed him without hesitation, hustling out in an orderly manner, their voices low but urgent as they spoke to one another. Pomen didn't move.

The chief surgeon placed a long and delicate finger on the king's throat.

"He has passed, my lord and lord steward. The king of Imonetia has passed to be judged by his gods."

Pomen ran a hand over his balding scalp. To his shame, his first thought was not of the king, the king's brother, the Imonetian royal family, or anyone who may have been bereaved or hurt by the loss of a family member or friend.

His first thought was of himself as he lifted his hand to stifle a cough.

Armenius, allow me a more pleasant death than that.

He looked over the king's body. It was a horrible sight.

"Chief apothecary, have your orderlies clean and bathe his body. Get some carpenters to build him a regal casket, I'm sure his brother will want him buried in the sand of Imonetia according to the customs of their peoples," ordered Pomen.

The chief apothecary looked to Thomak for permission. Pomen smarted a little.

"Chief apothecary, am I not a lord of the Order of the Grey Wolf?" he snarled, his voice raspy from his earlier coughing attack. "Do as I say!"

The chief apothecary looked back over to him for a heartbeat, his eyebrows raised a little in fear, and then back to Thomak. Thomak nodded and the man set his orderlies to work.

They had been well prepared, expecting the man's death, and water and sponges began their work as soon as the soiled clothes were cut away for burning.

Thomak placed a hand on the man's shoulder, a look of sorrow crossing his features as he watched the king's stilled features for a long moment until an orderly respectfully asked to clean the area. Then he walked around the bed to stand next to Pomen.

"I'll mourn for him. A product of a school of royalty far removed from our own, I'll admit, but the man had an admirable tenacity despite his lack of prowess with blade and shield," said Thomak.

Pomen looked at him, his mind still reeling somewhat from having watched one of two men capable of reuniting Imonetia under the blood of a pure royal pass from this life and into wherever the next was that the Imonetians believed.

"Y-yes," he stammered. "An admirable man. The Lands of the Light will miss his leadership."

Thomak smiled, though Pomen could not tell the sincerity of it. That in itself made him doubt the man. They both stood in somewhat companionable silence for some time, watching the orderlies work.

"May our own king not share the same fate," said Thomak suddenly.

Pomen nodded. "How does he fare?"

Thomak didn't speak for a moment. Pomen could swear there was wetness in the corner of the lord steward's eye.

"He does not improve. He does not fade."

"He is the last of his line. No sired sons, no living siblings with his brother lost at Archenon Creek before the winter. We shall lose our living link to our god, my brother. I never dreamt I should see such horrid times."

Pomen surprised himself with his candour of his fears, and stopped speaking. His eyes on the dead king, he didn't see the look on Thomak's face. A glint sat in his eye, his fierce ambition glowing from his stoic face.

"The king will survive," said Thomak loudly. "He has the blood of a god in him, he will not leave us before he is ready, before we have claimed back Mother Secunda."

Pomen nodded. "I will away, leave the apothecarions to their work."

Thomak didn't respond, so Pomen turned and hobbled off, Grullen rushing to his side to aid him if required. Then he stopped dead, his powerful mind gripping a moment with abject clarity from his rush to the tent.

"Lord Steward Thomak?"

"Lord Pomen."

"Where are King Aphiti's bodyguards?"

Thomak turned and walked over to, and past Pomen, walking to open the tent flap as if he were to leave without having spoken.

"Lord steward?"

"I do not know, lord Pomen, nobody has seen them since last night."

"Could Prince Phiti have..."

"I don't know, my old friend. I don't know."

Lord Pomen watched the man leave, his mind whirling. *The Imonetian royal court is notoriously cutthroat and bloodthirsty, but surely Prince Phiti did not slay his brother!* Re-thinking all the possibilities, all he could keep coming back to was that after weeks of alienation and indignation at the hands of Thomak, the man had once more called him a friend.

He had called him 'friend' with the manner of a wolf on its haunches watching a mortally wounded deer bleed out. Pomen's body may have been failing him, his mind keening for past youth and glory to return, fearing the present and the future, but he was sharp enough to pick up on what had just transpired. *By Armenius, it was you, brother. It was you.*

Hard resolve set within his chest.

I'm not dead yet, you bastard. I'm not dead yet.

Stupid old man.

Thomak smiled as he walked from Pomen's presence. Immediately his Wolves looked to him, his personal guards moving closer. One of the men came to his side, a bull-shouldered veteran of a hundred skirmishes and battles.

"Is it done?" asked Thomak, his voice low enough to be drowned out within a few feet of where he walked.

The man beside him bowed his head. "The six that remained with him came outside when you spoke of plague. We waited till morning, befriended the heathen, and slit their throats. Their bodies are just over there."

Thomak looked over to where the larger mass of his men waited. There was a mound of earth, freshly dug.

"Deep?"

"Enough. We've spread the word they took their own lives when they learnt their master had fallen. Such is the fate of the slave guards of the Imonetian royals when their masters pass," sneered the knight.

Thomak rubbed his jaw.

"Smart, Captain Hogun. And the main host of his guard?"

"We took them to the outskirts of the camp, began skirmish work with them. They took blunted blades. We didn't."

"Losses?"

"Few lads with splits to their faces, a concussion or two and some missing teeth, some dented armour and some tabards that are being washed out as we speak. That's about it," hissed Hogun, with relish.

Thomak smiled. "Captain Hogun, you have pleased me. Organise an additional ale ration for you and your men tonight. You have done well."

Captain Hogun beamed a moment and then dipped his head, his fist coming up to bump against the steel covering his heart.

"Your will is my command, sire," said the man.

Thomak frowned. "Lord steward, captain. Lord steward. You may leave me."

Hogun nodded. "Yes, lord steward."

Thomak's attention was immediately drawn away as the Grey Wolves around him parted to allow Father Trethore through. The man still looked a formidable warrior, tall and broad and proud within his casing of four-century old armour.

Thomak always found himself marvelling at the pieces of polished metal that covered the man. Those pieces of armour had sat upon the shoulders of the standard bearer of their god. The sword at the warrior priest's hip had drawn the blood of Secunda's enemies with their Eternal Lord. Now *that* was something to be in awe of.

Men back then would have appreciated what he was doing. The Eternal Lord would appreciate what he was doing. He would favour Thomak's endeavours: he already had. Thomak walked towards the tent where half of the king's bodyguard stood at attention as they guarded the house of their liege. He stood and watched them a moment, wondering if he should enter.

What would happen if the man woke? Would he approve of Thomak's actions in light of the bigger picture? Would he rise and rage and cast Thomak from the Lands of the Light?

Thomak laughed to himself. *Not likely*. The king was already half in the embrace of Death, his pink and black scorched skin constantly weeping his vital fluids on to his bed. Thomak had not been in to see the man descended from his god in weeks. Why he could not bring himself to do so, he was unsure, though at times his indignation would escalate and he would think of nothing but removing this block to his ascension to the leader of the Lands of the Light.

He sighed, his shoulders sagging a little. There were limits. There must always be, lest he follow the path of men like Kael. Down that path was darkness. Those bloody cobblestones led to servitude to a god more powerful than his own — a god who took direct action to aid those who appeased a being older than the distant mountains, a god whose favour seemed fickle at times when utter strength was needed to win.

"Lord Steward Thomak," came the gruff voice of Trethore. "You seem deep in thought."

Thomak snorted. "That is the lot of my title. I lead the Lands of the Light, father, I lead us to Mother Secunda in our king's stead. There is much to ponder and plan."

Trethore frowned.

"Indeed," was all the old man could manage, a little taken aback by the snarl in the lord steward's tone.

There was an awkward silence.

"I heard of the Imonetian king's demise," ventured Trethore. "A horrid end for a man. A sad day for the Lands of the Light that his family helped to build."

"Yes. Unfortunate." *But necessary.*

"I feel there is more you would wish to say on the matter, lord steward," said Trethore.

"Perhaps, father. Perhaps not, that is between myself, my king, and the Eternal Lord."

"I am His representative on this land, after the king," said Trethore. "To have my ear is to have His. Perhaps I can help you. Perhaps I can provide counsel, assistance, guidance."

Thomak turned on the priest, his face thunderous, his voice hissing. "You think me so inept to lead this crusade that I must rely on a priest to achieve victory? Pah! I don't need either of what you offer. I am of the Thomak house, we were born to lead the likes of you... you *sheep*."

He took a deep breath. It felt so good to let it out, finally. After years of silent manoeuvring and plotting, months of clandestine action, and now murders, it was time. Time to openly declare his intentions. Trethore stood there watching him, his jaw set. Thomak felt the warrior inside rise to the challenge.

"Great plans, far and wide sweeping, are coming to fruition, father. Pieces set in play months, years, ago are now making their move. Secunda will be the kingdom of kingdoms, the jewel of the Lands of the Light, the ruler of all. Should the king awake, he shall awake to a unified land under his rule, delivered by me, his foremost lord."

Trethore continued to stare at him. Thomak could see the man's mind working behind those cold eyes, trying to appreciate the full scope of the things Thomak had set in motion.

The lord steward turned and looked out to the north, a broad smile crossing his face, his back straighter, his shoulders more square and sheer determination and ambition combining to light his eyes afire as he thought, with anticipation, of what would be happening so many leagues away, in the lands of Imonetia.

"Should he not wake, then I shall be the first king of my line, and my sons shall lead a united land with but one ruler."

CHAPTER TWELVE

"Victory, brothers! One step closer to Mother Secunda!"

Uthiel pulled his sword from the skull of the barbarian he'd just brained, and lifted it to the sky. Tinny patters of blood and splattering brain matter against the steel of his helm filled the hot space around his head. His body was still firing on the surge of battle, his breath rasping with the sustained efforts of the shield wall, and his face triumphant.

"Mother Secunda!" he roared to the sky.

"Mother Secunda!" came the cry of his brothers and his company as they echoed his lead.

"Mother Secunda!" came the cry of the men of the Fifth under his command.

Uthiel pulled his helm from his head, shaking out his sweat-soaked hair. His gaze took in the scene around him. He drank it in as he revelled in the glory of battle won.

They had defeated the barbarians. No, they had *crushed* them. The shield wall had been impregnable. Steel and flesh and raw courage backed by years of training and hard-fought selection had held the centre of the Secundan line. The Grey Wolves had been implacable, and the men of Uthiel's company had been at the centre, the Lord General Ryun directly behind them.

The bodies of the foes were littered in an ever thickening mat of the slain leading up to the where the Secundans had received the charge, held it, and then pushed them back. With sword and spear, shield and crossbow they had pushed for all they were worth, and Uthiel had been at the very centre of it, locking shields with Tarren on his right, and Pavel on his left.

He looked to his brothers now. Pavel was cleaning his blade, shield resting against his waist. The sword master had not drawn the blade from behind his shoulder, instead favouring the thicker, double edged sword to stab over his shield whilst in the confides of the shield wall. Uthiel watched him as the tall man cocked his head, looked down and then casually lanced the sword master's blade through the throat of a gutted barbarian who was too stubborn to die.

With a flick of the blade to remove the heavier drops of crimson, Pavel returned to cleaning the shining steel. Uthiel turned and looked for Tarren. As usual the brash young knight had managed to take a wound. One of the brothers was wrapping a piece of cloth around his bloodied elbow where a sword or axe had slipped through between his gousset and vambrance. Tarren looked up, and grimaced as the cloth was pulled tight.

Uthiel nodded to his brother and turned to look at the rest of his company. Most wandered the field in tight groups, checking on friends or seeing to their own wounds. Theon stood stock still about twenty feet away, staring at the ground. Uthiel could see the glint of polished plate in the sun at his feet.

"No," he breathed, the joy of battle receding quickly as he jogged over.

Theon looked up at him. Uthiel was surprised to see a tear on the face of the knight usually so gruff and haughty. The captain looked down at brother Inin. The youth seemed almost peaceful in death. A blade had found its way through his defences and delved deep within his inner thigh, severing something vital within. A pool of blood mixed with the evacuations of his corpse sunk into the sand under him.

Uthiel's emotions raged like a hurricane wind. Sorrow, hurt, memories of losing his father, his best friend, his brothers in Gall, Rouen, Tadel, all the places he had fought in the last year and more, swirled within his chest. They threatened to overcome him. He felt his jaw tremble, and clamped down hard, fighting with all of his spirit not to allow the burning in his throat and eyes well into a single tear.

A massive paw of a hand pressed onto his vambrance. Uthiel looked up.

"He fought well. He fought hard, but Armenius had need of a brother to fill a gap in His shield wall. The Eternal Lord needed young Inin, and our brother heeded the call and even now watches us from above," came the deep, baritone voice of brother Theon.

Uthiel couldn't speak.

"Did you know him well, my captain?" asked the big knight, his free hand resting on the hilt of his black steel sword-breaker.

Uthiel thought a moment.

"No, only as well as you," admitted Uthiel. "Though I had hopes for him. He was a good knight, a reliable fighter, and a man who deserved longer in the plate of our ancestors. He was our brother."

Theon smiled, his bear-like face warming a little. "Captain, I once told you that a Shield is earned."

Uthiel nodded, still looking down at Inin.

Theon knelt before him. "I offer you my shield as your own. My life as your Shield."

Uthiel was more than a little shocked. "Brother…"

Theon stood, thick neck craning back to look Uthiel in the eyes. "It is done. Pavel and I, we may not see eye to eye on… well… anything, but two finer swords you'll never meet and two finer Shields you'll never have watching over your life."

Uthiel's mouth opened and closed a couple of times, looking for the words. There were only two possible.

"I'm honoured."

Before Theon turned and walked away he patted Uthiel on the pauldron once more.

"A great captain earns the respect of his men in battle and in his care for those he commands. A great captain has a heart as well as a strong arm and will. You are young, but you have it in you. Just always remember those who brought you to where you are, those who died so that you may protect our lands and our people. Those men, whoever they might be and whatever you might think your relationship with them was, died not just for their beliefs and their families, captain. They died for you."

Theon nodded to something over Uthiel's shoulder, and then he was gone.

Uthiel turned.

"Truer words I've never heard said, my captain," said Darian as he and ten of his men made their way over to him.

As they walked, a spear flashed up and then hammered down into a body on the ground. There was a sharp gasp of air and another barbarian finally left the battlefield. Uthiel grasped the man's hand in a warrior's handshake.

"Well met, Captain Darian," said Uthiel. "Your men fought well today. Held the line as I asked, never gave an inch. They have done you proud."

Uthiel noticed Darian's men stood a little straighter at the compliment. He smiled a little, having almost forgotten that so many of the Fifth still knew of his legend. He was the hero who slew the warlord in the borderlands of Gall, the Grey Wolf who took on the beast of the barbarians in single combat and emerged bloody and victorious where no hero had managed to be in three major battles. Finally, he was the man whose father had led the Fifth to glory and died defending the king of Secunda in Gall.

For once, the thought of his father wasn't matched with an immediate memory of Tanin's broken body lying beneath the corpses of the barbarians and the Fifth that the charge of the king's guards had strewn across the cobblestones of Gall. Instead it was the warm smiling face of the man who had made him who he was and the man who had been his hero all of his life.

His smile broadened. The soldiers around him mirrored the smile. Once again, the sour thought of casualties brought the mood down. He knew, as captain of a Grey Wolf company and leader of Captain Darian and his hundred soldiers, there always came a time to inspect the butcher's bill.

"How many?" he asked.

Darian's gaze hardened a little. "Fifteen dead, twenty-three wounded badly enough that we'll need to leave them behind if we are to press on. How did your men fare?"

"We lost only one. The shield wall held strong." Uthiel looked to Tarren, needing an opportunity to try to lighten the mood a little as he watched the men with Darian sag at the thought of lost comrades. "Though Tarren somehow managed to get injured again, despite all the armour he has on."

There were a few laughs from the men. Uthiel watched their faces and saw some genuine levity flow over the hurt in their eyes.

"Bloody heard that!" called out Tarren.

Uthiel barked a laugh. The men around him laughed some more. Uthiel noticed Darian nod to him, approval in his eyes.

By Armenius, it is good to lead. Good to be alive under the watchful eyes of my ancestors and brothers from above. This is what I was born for.

"Captain Caellar!" came a loud shout.

Uthiel turned to see Captain Ryun walking towards him.

"The lord general expects your men ready to move within the hour. We will take our wounded and move on to clear the next town and leave them there. The rest of us press on for Imonetia!"

Uthiel nodded. "How did your men fare, brother?"

Captain Ryun ignored him and turned away.

"Arse," said Darian under his breath.

Uthiel shot him a wary look. "He may be an arse, but he is a captain of the Grey Wolves. Keep yourself in check."

Darian nodded. "Fair enough, but watch that one, Captain."

"I'll be wary. Get your men in order. Anyone not assisting the wounded in column behind my company. Expect scout picket duty."

Darian bowed his head. "As you wish it, captain."

Uthiel looked around to his company.

"Wolves, with me!" he called out, and his brothers looked up and moved to him, falling into a semi circle around him.

They settled quickly, as was expected of the knights.

"Brothers, well met," he started.

The semi-circle of men growled their assent.

"A battle hard fought, and a victory won in the crimson of our brother, Inin. May Armenius judge him fit for His Shield Wall in the Sky."

"Armenius be with him," said Theon, the knights around him immediately echoing his sentiment.

Uthiel nodded. "Brothers, we muster once again. There shall be no respite in this march on Imonetia. See to your wounds, your armour, and your blades. Take a moment to commune with the Eternal Lord, you may not have another chance."

His men nodded to him. Theon, Pavel, and Tarren stayed close while the rest of his men cleared the bodies around them and created a small clearing amongst the slaughter. Each man in his own world, they pulled out whetstones to rasp against blades, oil cloths to work on their armour, and bandages and needles to work on their flesh.

Uthiel closed his eyes a moment, allowing his mind to wander amongst the sound of the men who were kin to him through oath and blood and war.

"Armenius' balls," swore Tarren.

Uthiel's eyes snapped open, searched a moment, and then spotted Prince Phiti walking over. The prince's eyes were locked squarely on Uthiel, his diminished bodyguard cadre limping around him. Uthiel's Shields interposed themselves between him and the prince, blades rasping from sheaths.

"No women here for you to murder," snarled Theon.

"Enough, brother," said Uthiel, his voice low.

"Bastard—" started the stocky knight, his shoulders bunching as the prince pushed through the outer ring of lounging knights.

"I said, enough, brother Theon."

The prince stopped before him. His armour was scored and dented, a deep gash cut down his cheek, splitting both his lips before exiting through his chin. The men around him, all five of them, were in a similar state, coated in the blood of their foes as much as their own.

"Where is the rest of your guard, prince?" asked Uthiel.

Phiti looked up, exhaustion written across his face.

"Slain."

Uthiel noted Khin was not amongst those standing before him.

"Khin?"

"Slain also. I shall miss him," said the prince.

"I doubt it. Just enslave another poor bastard to take a blade for you, if there are any of them left after you're done with the people of this land," retorted Uthiel, his voice pure ice.

Phiti looked up at him, his dark eyes flashing. "It is their life's honour—"

"To be forced into a life of butchery and servitude," finished Uthiel.

"You are also a servant, just of a different nation under a different ruler."

"I chose this life. *I chose this life, you bastard!*" snarled Uthiel, doing his best, but failing to keep his cool. "I chose this life because I wanted to protect the lands of my family, my friends, and my god."

"Do you think I had a choice? I was born to this!" snapped the prince.

Uthiel paused a moment. There was a modicum of reason to what the man had said. Uthiel didn't care.

"You had a *choice* when you decided to go rampaging through your homeland and murder all of those innocent women. You had a *choice* when you slew the unborn children within their bellies. Now you have another *choice*. Leave me, or draw your blade so I can give you a cut on your other cheek to match what the barbarians gave you."

Phiti's bodyguards stiffened around him. The prince took a deep, calming breath.

"Captain Caellar, Uthiel, this is not what I came here for."

Uthiel didn't respond as the prince visibly worked his face and mouth around something he was struggling to get out.

"I... I came, in the hope we could speak."

"We are speaking."

"In the hope you would allow me a moment of your time, alone, voluntarily, to treat with me."

Uthiel was about to retort when the prince cut him off and continued.

"I do not expect to heal a friendship. I do not expect to resolve our disagreements. I only hope to help you understand, to see my perspective before you judge me."

"What do you care what a knight captain thinks of you, Prince Phiti? I have no royal blood to match your own station," said Uthiel.

Phiti looked at the ground a moment.

"An Imonetian royal... has no friends, no confidants, no respect to give or receive except through strength and fear. I... respect you, Captain Caellar. I valued your thoughts and our discussions. I know I have lost that, but perhaps..."

The prince's voice trailed off from his uncharacteristically meek form. Uthiel's ire began to wane, but he didn't let it. There was no space within his life for a man who treated the women he was supposed to protect as cattle to be slaughtered at his whim. He thought of Emilia and his own unborn and all of a sudden his rage, pure and burning, flowed back through him.

"I can see your point of view, Prince Phiti," he began.

The prince's eyes flicked up to him. Uthiel was a little surprised to see genuine hope in them.

"You feel these women and their babes represent the raping of your lands and cities by the barbarians. If you expunge them, as is your right to do with those deemed your property, your nation may start afresh. You may start afresh."

"Yes, you see—" started the prince, his face lighting up with hope.

Uthiel cut him off.

"I hate everything that you are."

Phiti's head dropped, his cheeks reddening as his royal mind quickly turned from disappointment and rejection to angry hurt.

"You make me sick to the very fibre of my being. My soul, when it is released from this body, shall carry the stain of what I have witnessed you do with it when I go to be judged by my Eternal Lord," Uthiel spat.

The prince had no retort.

"My lady, with our child in her belly, will only be safe while I dedicate my life to killing those like you. Those whose hearts are black. Those who do not deserve life."

Uthiel turned away, awaiting the tirade of abuse the prince would level at him.

"You are right," came a slight voice. "My heart is black. My soul departed before my body has expelled its last breath."

Uthiel didn't turn, but felt the anguish in the words work away his rage. The self-deprecation was like a greasy balm to his burning anger. Uthiel dropped his head a little as the prince let the words hang, waiting for Uthiel to speak.

"Leave, Prince Phiti. You and I are nothing alike. We have nothing in common. The gulf between us is too blood-soaked."

Uthiel heard a sigh and then the sounds of the prince and his men moving off. He didn't have much time to ponder the discussion as the men of the Secundan host began to move into column formation. The Lord General Ryun approached.

"Captain Caellar," said the lord general. "We move. Three miles north is another town. Your company is the van. Take the town, picket it and turn it into something the wounded can be left and defended at. We'll be a mile behind you."

"As you wish, lord general."

Uthiel turned to his men and called out to them and Captain Darian. Quickly, they moved into their scouting spread, and in the waning sunlight moved off towards Imonetia once more.

First Captain Solanthur Verutus stood amongst his brothers in first company in yet another abandoned small town in the vast desert lands of Imonetia. He watched as the men of the Fifth

157

worked to barricade gaps between houses and dig trenches and ditches into approach roads to turn the town into a fort to house their wounded. Two of his men would be staying behind, their loss of limbs and blood too much for them to carry on. His eyes wandered south, where another of his men smouldered on a pile of Secundan dead.

Brother Theon, his old Shield from before Thomak's removal of the knight to fight in Uthiel's company, walked by and lowered his head in respect. Solanthur returned the man's nod, observing the bear of a man's swagger mixed with his tiredness. Behind him was Captain Caellar.

Solanthur had known the knight for over a year now. The young man was a fierce warrior, his skill far from honed but improving with each conflict. His legend was impressive: the boy who slew the warlord. Solanthur remembered that barbarian warlord, had even clashed blades with him once on the borders of Secunda. He'd been an impressive beast, easily seven foot tall and muscled like a bull, and a fast, brutal, and incredibly efficient killer. One day he'd ask Uthiel how he'd slain such a man. Solanthur chuckled to himself. *One day when I finally accept that it wasn't me to land the strike.*

Solanthur continued to watch the young knight as Uthiel moved in amongst his men, speaking with them, sharing a new camaraderie the first captain had not yet witnessed the youth enjoy. Something had changed in him and the men around him. Battle had beaten him in its forge, fired the steel of his spirit in its great bellows, and he had come out hardened and not brittle. His men saw that. His men respected that. Solanthur smiled and looked away. The boy had the makings of a captain after all.

The staccato sound of beating hooves drew his attention beyond the ramshackle wall being created by the men of the Fifth. Messengers, in the garb of the Grey Wolves, rode hard towards them. He tried to make them out, work out which company they heralded from. Quickly, he saw that the men must be from Gall, from one of the companies still with Thomak at the main front.

The horses drew up at the outer wall, calling out for the lord general to attend them. Lord General Ryun emerged from a small hut, straightening his tabard with one hand while the other rested on his sword. His bodyguards immediately interposed themselves between the man and any potential threat.

The lead rider dismounted gracefully and walked over, pulling out a scroll tube, uncapping it and handing a white piece of parchment to Ryun. The lord general reached out and took the message and unfurled it, taking his time to read it. Solanthur was sure the lord general read it twice, perhaps three times, before speaking to the messenger and sending the man off to water his horses.

Ryun beckoned the first captain over. Solanthur moved quickly and was soon by his commander's side. The lord general spoke to him curtly and then looked over to rest his gaze on the young captain, Uthiel Caellar, and then on to the prince.

Solanthur took a moment to fully understand what was being asked. He looked down at the grey upon his chest as it flapped gently in the cool winter's breeze. His world stopped as he read the orders, his arms dropping by his side.

"What is this?" asked Solanthur. "How could he be so stupid?"

"You're his peer, you're the man he deems a hero," said Ryun. "You make sure it gets done."

Solanthur's mind whirled in the horrid reality of the order, of what he was being asked to do. This went against his code of honour, against every code that he lived his life by.

Then his jaw set. His eyes hardened.

He was Solanthur Verutus, first captain of the Grey Wolves. He was a hero of Secunda and a champion of the Lands of the Light. He was these things because he was a man who did his duty. He was a man who prosecuted the will of his lord general, his king, and his god.

And now he was being asked to be a party to execution.

CHAPTER THIRTEEN

Emilia stood upon the flat stump of a tree that had been long ago carved down for arrow-shaft wood, and stared out in the bleak distance to the north. The light wind kissed her bare neck and her skin goose-pimpled amongst the thick wrappings of her heavy shawl. She shrugged her shoulders up and drew the garment in tighter around her slight shoulders. She wasn't sure what she hoped to see, but looking down and finding her hands encircling the small swell beneath her clothes let her know where her mind strayed.

Uthiel, my love, where are you? Do you stand upon a stump so many leagues north, looking south to the cooler climes and wondering after me? Do you stand, with your eyes closed, thinking of my face? Of my form swelling with your child within your warm embrace upon a bed in a world where there is no war? A world where men do their fighting with blades of words and shields of reason?

Emilia sighed. She knew deep within her soul, as so many millions of soldiers' women had known before her all the way back to the ages when men had fought with crudely shaped stone, that such a world could not exist. Where men lived, there would be greed. Money, glory, power, lust: always greed

160

deceptively turned the acts of the vicious into the lies of honour that men not born to royalty would follow to their deaths.

Her Uthiel was one of those men, following lords and kings who wanted to take land back from those who had taken it from them four centuries ago. Believing that what he did was so righteous was what disappointed her most of all. As always, men only saw one side of a coin. They looked to what served their purpose most of all.

For Uthiel and his kinsmen, it was the loss of their ancestors' home four centuries ago. They cared not whom their ancestors had slaughtered to gain the land in the first place. As she had once told Uthiel, when they had first met, who was to say it was not the Secundans who were in the wrong? Who today saw the Secundans walk into a vast tract of land that no other had set foot upon before and say, *I take this empty land, without the sacking of other civilisations, without murder, without hate, without greed, and I name it 'Secunda'.*

By the absent gods, men were stupid! It was always the men who started these things. Emilia racked her mind for a time, as the sun rose into the sky above the horizon, but could think of no evil queen or conquering woman who had ever been the drive behind such wholesale evil deeds. The queens of the Lands of the Light were reputed as good women. Many were attached to men who did not deserve to have such strength by their side.

They are not evil. They do not bring war. She shrugged to herself. *Their husbands do. Their families do. They are royal, and they are all alike.*

Royalty. She fought the need to spit at the thought. *A sense of divine superiority of character through the simple act of popping out of the right woman, who had either married the right man, or been popped out by the right woman in turn, is a ridiculous idea. A man probably thought of that one.*

What made it worse was when good men, like her Uthiel, put on armour, drew their blades, and marched off to battle, forsaking their families to stand on a stump, on the edge of a camp somewhere near the White Frontier, looking north and wishing she could see him coming home to her. She chuckled to herself. *Stupid girl.*

She'd known what he was when she first approached him. She'd known what sort of man she had lain with when she'd allowed him to spend his seed within her. He had been open of his loyalty and devotion to his god and his Order and the purpose of his lords. In hindsight, she wondered if she'd even listened as she looked into those eyes that resembled ice but were as warm as a fire in a hearth.

Deep in her thoughts, Emilia had not heard the sound of heavy booted footsteps behind her.

"Emilia?" came a voice, soothing, the name well enunciated.

She turned, already knowing who it was.

"Father Trethore, how may I be of service?" she asked, well-practiced in her role now.

He smiled and offered her his hand to help with the short drop from the stump. The offer was unnecessary, but for all the things Trethore falsely portrayed himself as, a gentleman was amongst the foremost qualities. Emilia came lightly to the ground below, her boots crunching into the melting snow.

He stood by her, staring north. She watched him for a short while as his gaze remained unwavering. She knew better than to offer conversation. There was no way to tell what she may accidentally let slip if she freely entered a conversation with the warrior priest, no way to tell what he may glean from the veil of simpleness she did her best to portray to hide the knowledge of a secret so dark her head would most probably be separated from her body and her child die within her falling form before she could finish its utterance in the presence of the old man. *I am so afraid.*

"I have seen you here, Emilia, each day. Sometimes a short time. Sometimes for a while. A great deal of your free time spent simply staring in to the north. You miss him."

Emilia nodded.

"He's a good lad, our Uthiel. He is strong, fast, devout, a great leader and a promising young man. I feel he shall go far."

"Had I gods to pray to, I would wish it so," replied Emilia.

Trethore pondered her comment a moment.

"I've heard of this, the abandoning of your gods by those who remain of your people."

"The gods abandoned *us*, father, not the other way around. True gods would not have left a devout people to suffer in the way we were left to suffer. Our entire nation was put to the sword. Would Armenius allow such a thing to happen?"

Trethore smiled. "Perhaps."

Emilia was a little shocked.

"You forget that we Secundans abandoned our gods a mere four centuries ago, when we were driven from the east, and mighty Armenius took the mantle as our protector and was eventually raised to godhood."

"True, I did forget. Though we did not have such a hero to watch over us when the barbarians came murdering."

Trethore continued. "Who is to say our old gods do not still watch us, while we worship a new deity? Who is to say they are not Armenius, re-forged from our burning anger towards them into something stronger with our Eternal Lord at their fore? The moment we, as simple people, believe we understand the gods as we do our brother, then we are doomed to madness."

"Isn't that your purpose?" asked Emilia, intrigued at the priest's frankness.

"My role is to lead the people of Secunda to Him. To show them what works we have from his mortal life, to teach them of His great plan for our nation, to let them know where their lives of toil and glory lead them. I do not profess to understand the intentions and whims of the Eternal Lord post-ascension."

"You say, 'where their lives lead them to,' you mean the Shield Wall in the Sky?" asked Emilia, thinking back to some of the prayers she had witnessed.

"For warriors, yes, their place after death is by our Eternal Lord's side, beating back the scions of the darkness," responded Trethore. "Theirs is the lot of the watcher and the warrior, ever ready to leap to our spirit's defence from above."

"How can you know it is real, if you know not what happens after death?" countered Emilia.

"Faith," said Trethore simply. "He said it would be so, before His ascension, and therefore it must be. He is our Eternal Lord."

"But what if he was wrong?" she asked, and immediately regretted the question.

"He cannot be wrong."

Emilia's face betrayed her inquisitiveness.

Trethore smiled again. "Many are the writings of our Eternal Lord. Many more are the recordings of his speech by the mortal hands that witnessed his last years. Some pieces are deep and of use, others are of less worth. Some, can never see the light of day."

"Why?"

"A fair question," responded the warrior priest, surprising Emilia once more. "A difficult one to answer, but fortunate that it answers both His role, and mine."

"My Order are the keepers of lore for Secunda. We are the guardians of knowledge, the hard leather sheath over a sharp steel sword — both protector and warrior. Our role in our kingdom is to guide the Secundan people through these times with the recitation of His words as we deem fit."

Emilia frowned. "As you see fit? Why would you withhold the words of your god from your people?"

"Now you come to the crux of my role. While all words from the Eternal Lord speak true, not all words are for the ears of the people. For example, take the recitation of *One Hundred Souls*."

"I do not know it."

"It is a poem saying that one hundred heroes will stand against the great foe when all warriors around them fall."

"I do know it! Uthiel has recited the words."

Trethore smirked. "What you do not know is that those are not the actual words of that poem. Over time, they have changed, morphed, to suit the needs of the people further. As it was written, the poem said that only one man would stand, when all around him fell."

"Why would you do that?" demanded Emilia. "What purpose does changing the words of a god into lies serve?"

Trethore's face darkened. "For the people, Emilia. To bring hope and to steel the hearts of men and women to take up blade and shield and bow when the great enemy marches on us."

"How does lying achieve that?" she asked, her anger growing.

Trethore turned her around to look at the soldiers of the camp. There were thousands of them.

"If you were a fighting woman, standing amongst these men and women on the verge of campaigning into the Black Lands with a finite reserve of courage, skill, and luck, like everyone else, and I told you there was one person in all of Secunda who would stand against the great foe while everyone else died, what chance would you think you had of that hero being you?"

Emilia thought for a moment, trying to picture it and calm herself at the same time. *Be wary.*

"Little."

"Correct. But if I then told you that in this land there are one-hundred souls that could stand against the great foe, what would you think then?"

"Still a small chance. Why not a thousand. Why not ten thousand?"

"Ah! You are a smart one. Why not a hundred thousand?"

Emilia stared back at the warrior priest.

"We can't all be heroes, Emilia. But if something seems achievable, even if at a stretch beyond what you would admit you are capable of, we strive to achieve. And when the men and women of Secunda strive, shoulder to shoulder, they can achieve anything. A small extension of the truth for the greater good.

"One of my, and my ancestors' purposes is to determine where and how to extend a truth to build hope and courage, and where to hide it to save dismay and fear and cowardice."

"Dismay?' ventured Emilia.

Trethore paused before continuing. "There is another piece from the Eternal Lord, one which has not seen the light of day since my ancestor laid hands upon it after the Eternal Lord passed.

"It speaks of a prophecy that is referred to in other texts we have amended. It speaks of a Dark Sun. It warns us of a shining light that turns to evil, a bringer of death for Secunda as a nation, falling from above. It speaks of betrayal, of a god smote from the heavens, of a darkness of spirit to come. It speaks in metaphor and conjecture, and inexact predictions — a text clearly inked during the latter part of Armenius' mortal life when his mind had already partially ascended.

"The light turning to dark could represent the invasion we have staved off. It could represent the smaller one the White Frontier held at bay two centuries ago. Or it could refer to a man, one single man, who may already be dead or yet to be born for a hundred centuries. Perhaps it refers to a group of men, or a group of women?

"It hints at fratricide and of brother turning on brother, though it does not say when, or provide portents of the coming of this time.

"It could also be that the scribe who recorded the verse may have misheard. Perhaps he was tired, or drunk? Perhaps he was already mourning that which Secunda had not yet quite lost.

"In essence, it is a dark fear that may not come true for a thousand years, or may have already come true. It cannot be predicted, we shall not know it is coming nor the scale of that arrival, and therefore it is of no use except to sow fear amongst the people."

"Therefore you have hidden it," said Emilia.

Trethore nodded.

"Why would you tell me?"

Trethore smiled. "None would believe your words. The words of the warrior priests are what the men and women of Secunda believe. Our canon has been established since long before anyone still alive was born."

The silence grew for a short while.

"It must be difficult to speak of betrayal when a nation like Secunda is built upon the brotherhood and blood of its warriors," said Emilia.

"It matters not if the Secundan is a warrior, hunter, cook, servant, wife or whore. Secunda is *family*. You see it in Uthiel and his brothers——"

"Brothers argue. Brothers fight. Brothers betray. We are all human. We wear our fallacies as well as our virtues laid bare under duress. My brothers did all these things, before they were murdered."

"Not those who stand for Secunda."

Emilia didn't respond. *I have ventured too far. I have insulted him.* Trethore continued, his eyes narrowing.

"For the betrayal of your brothers is the greatest crime known to a Secundan. Whether it be abandoning your fellow miners while the struts around you collapse, hiding while a bear attacks your hunting party, leaving your loved one to bear the pain of birth without you there defending her, or out in the field defending her from afar, it is a thought abhorrent to our people."

There was a pregnant pause, a great weight in what Trethore was building up to.

"And there you shall find the warrior priests of Secunda. We are the miners who cut the treachery and cowardice from our people like miners cut steel from the mountains, we seek out the weak of heart like the hunter and strengthen or discard them, we ensure the next generation of Secundans are birthed from the strong and the loyal. We make sure that those who build and defend this nation in His image are His people, and none else's."

Emilia felt a tear build in here eye as her jaw quivered. *He knows. No 'maybe', no nothing, he knows and he is going to kill me.* She clamped her jaw down to stifle a sob and turned away to look out to the north once more, marshalling her courage. *No. He cannot. I have not incriminated myself. I have not betrayed Uthiel. Hold strong.*

Her mind raced through a hundred different interactions with the warrior priest, trying to find anything that may have given her, Uthiel, and the Grey Wolves away. *Nothing.*

She could see Trethore watching her out of the corner of her eye, but refused to make eye contact as she fought legs that demanded she run. The silence grew in both length and awkwardness once more.

"I miss the feeling of gods, father. I miss the safety of their knowledge," she mused, doing her best to portray herself as having passed over his thinly veiled threat. "I miss the safety of knowing the light of good from the darkness of evil through the words of priests."

Trethore watched her carefully before turning away. "The distinction is easy. It shall be made by my word and my blade."

Emilia swallowed hard as the priest walked away. *What can I do?* Tears began to roll down her cheeks as the relief of his departure mixed with the retelling of their conversation that grew ever more dangerous with each reliving. *How do I get my baby out of this alive?* Emilia's face dropped heavily into her hands. *How do I protect Uthiel?* Her shoulders began to shake as sobs that were quickly lost underneath the weight of the sounds of the war camp burst from her quivering lips. *How do I save myself?* The sobs began to flow freely.

She was unsure how long she'd been sitting there, crying into her hands, but eventually the tears just dried up. Her jaw ached from the effort of stifling her own sobs and her eyes were red raw. Looking up and around she took in some long deep breaths to steady herself.

"Sometimes things just seem better after a good cry," said a voice, matronly and strong.

Emilia swivelled around and looked behind her. A stern looking woman in an expensive riding dress and thick winter coat stood tall behind her, staring out past the borders of the camp and into the wild.

Hard eyes eventually looked down at Emilia, and in that stare she could see such strength. Immediately she knew she was before someone above her station in life and dropped to a knee.

"Get up, stupid girl," barked the woman. "Getting your dress wet is a sure way to come down with the chills. A woman with child does not need the added strain."

"How did you know?" asked Emilia.

"You may not be showing yet, but the glow in your skin tells the tale. I have birthed seven of my own, and seen two of those birth me grandchildren. I know the look."

The strange royal stood quiet for a while. Emilia did not know what to say, and sat there feeling a little stupefied. Her more vicious thoughts regarding royalty came to her in that moment. Emilia suppressed a blush of embarrassment.

As she sat, she noticed the armoured men around the woman for the first time. One was a big knight with a well-kept beard. He had a sword and brambles inscribed upon his cuirass. The warrior glowered at her a moment before turning and speaking orders to some other warriors in a hushed tone. Those men marched off. The bearded one returned his glower to her.

The royal's eyes rested on Emilia once more and her feeling of ill-comfort rose hot upon her cheeks.

"I am Valissa," said the royal.

Emilia's eyes widened. "Queen of Lemug?"

Valissa smiled. "Among many things."

Emilia wiped her eyes. "What else would matter against that?"

Valissa looked at Emilia like she was thicker than a tree stump.

"Have I not already said? I am a mother to seven and a grandmother to two. My husband leads a nation at war. My sons are his generals: sons I birthed and fed and raised into fine young men. My daughters are wed to upstanding young nobles. They are fierce young women, sharp and proud with minds like blades given to them by their mother."

Emilia stared back at the woman, trying to hide a feeling of meekness in the face of such fire. Valissa continued, her eyes alight with pride.

"My mother gave me to a king twice my age when I was thirteen."

Emilia shook her head, becoming a little angry once more at the thought of royalty. Her first thought was to speak out, to give voice to her dissonant views on royalty, but she kept her mouth closed. That bearded knight could be asked to cut her throat, and none would be here to save her.

"You must have been so afraid," she managed, lamely.

The queen stared at her for a moment, as if she sensed Emilia was hiding her true thoughts. "I was afraid, but I did my duty and I am now matriarch to the finest family in the realm."

Emilia nodded, averting her eyes.

"Becoming a queen took naught but standing through a ceremony under the sunlight of a glorious day in the morning, watching everyone feast and drink themselves to ridiculous excess in the afternoon, and receiving my husband's seed as the light waned," snapped Valissa. "Motherhood is the true challenge of a woman's spirit. A true challenge to her mettle."

Valissa took a deep breath. "Ah, you must be wondering at the point of my ranting."

Emilia could not bring herself to respond.

"Gods, woman!" said Valissa, her tongue as sharp as any knife. "Have the courage to speak of what you actually think! Do I look like some evil harridan that will have my man behind me walk over and slit your throat?"

Emilia looked from the stormy face of the Lemugian queen, to her bodyguard, and then back. A sly smile broke her lips and she shrugged.

"The worry had crossed my mind, queen."

For a moment, Emilia thought she had trod too far over the boundary. Valissa's face broke into laughter a moment later.

"There you are! There is the woman I saw standing defiant before that belligerent priest! There is some spirit and heart left in the women of Gall after all!"

"You saw that?"

Valissa nodded.

"He is a frightening man," conceded Emilia.

"Who is he to you?" Asked the queen.

"A priest of the Secundans."

"Why should he threaten you?"

"He did not—"

"Do not defend him, girl! I saw with my own eyes. I have been around men of war and butchery my entire life. I have seen every type of man there is to see from the weaselling noble to the mud-covered peasant. He was posturing to frighten you, girl. You know this, be strong enough to admit it. Even if only to yourself."

Emilia looked down. "You are right, he is threatening me. Though his threats are veiled beneath slick words."

Valissa reached out and placed her hand under Emilia's chin.

"Do not be ashamed. Be afraid, if you must. Fear is a good thing. Fear lets you know that you are in danger. But stand tall! Stand and face your fears. Admit they exist, and then face them with all the might you have."

Emilia nodded to herself, feeling her heart lift and her strength resolve itself back into her limbs. She sat up straighter. The queen leaned in. Her eyes narrowed.

"Did he put that child in your belly?"

Emilia rocked back, horrified. "No! He would never!"

Valissa chuckled. "Never say that when it comes to men. They have two minds: one bouncing around inside their heads like a single cow in a large pasture, and one between their legs like a raging bull eyeing the cow from behind the broken pasture fence. When the latter takes control, 'never' is not a term that exists."

Emilia's face darkened. "My child is of Uthiel Caellar, a captain of the Grey Wolves. A hero—"

"A good man?" interrupted Valissa.

Emilia warmed quickly. "The finest."

"What does he look like?"

Emilia smiled, her eyes drifting to the sky over the queen's right shoulder.

"Tall, strong, handsome and blond, unlike his countrymen. Almost clear blue eyes."

"Blond? That is distinctive, amongst his people," declared Valissa with a large smile.

Emilia's gaze came back down to meet the queen's. "You could not miss him. He is all that, but his face is badly scarred from battle. I only saw him twice before he received the wounds. One of the enemy cut him a cross on his face. Here." She traced her fingers in a cross along her nose and cheek and then from her brow to her jaw. "And here."

Valissa smiled. "But yet you love him still."

"Always. There is kindness in his eyes and heart. I don't even see the scars."

"Where is he?"

Emilia looked north. "He marched to Imonetia. I have heard naught since."

"He left you in the care of his priest, did he not?" said Valissa.

Emilia nodded. "Uthiel does not trust the man, but had none other to protect me while he fought."

"If only men cared so much about their families as they did about their fighting, the world would be a safer place."

"Uthiel fights for me. For our unborn," insisted Emilia.

"Yet he leaves you in the clutches of one who threatens you harm?"

Emilia had no response for a while. Valissa's words gave voice to her own thoughts. After a while, Valissa reached out once more, this time putting a hand upon her slight shoulder.

"I speak too harshly at times—"

"No, you speak thoughts I am too afraid to voice."

Valissa was not troubled by the interruption. "It is the same fear the wife, mother and daughter of any man who picks up the blade and marches has had, probably for millennia into history since the dawn of time."

The queen grew serious. "Yet you are with child. Your first?"

Emilia nodded.

"A wonderful moment. It will be painful, but wonderful, to hold your first. I pray your man gets to stand with you when the time comes."

The silence grew once more. Emilia was about to speak when the queen turned to her once more.

"Are you in danger?"

Emilia shrugged. "I do not truly know."

"What does he seek from you?"

"A secret."

"Is that secret worth your child?"

"It is worth the lives of many people, including my husband and my child."

"And yourself."

"I matter not. Without my child I am not alive. Without my Uthiel I do not wish to be alive."

Valissa's face was unreadable, but Emilia swore she could see wetness in the crow-feet in the corners of the queen's eyes. Valissa's bodyguard chose that moment to move forwards and lay a hand lightly on the queen's shoulder to bid her away.

"The life within you is all, girl. Take it from me. All else is worth naught without it. You are bonded. You must do all to protect yourself and it. I cannot help you with whatever dangerous precipice you stand close to. But I shall pray for you. I shall send you my strength, for I like you. You are honest of the face, and love and life beams from you. You remind me of me in my youth."

Emilia smiled.

"I should not like to see that light extinguished."

The queen stood.

"Take care, girl."

Emilia looked up to her. "My name is Emilia. You have given my heart strength. I thank you."

Valissa smiled sadly and then turned away.

Emilia watched the queen leave and then looked down at the hand resting on her stomach.

I shall be strong for you, little one. I shall fight for you. We shall live to see your father. You shall yet draw free air into your little lungs.

We shall yet have life.

Emilia stood, gathering her skirts and moving quickly after the queen. "Queen Valissa!"

The queen stopped and turned. "Yes, child?"

Emilia waited until she up close. "I... there is something..."

"Come girl, take a breath and get it out."

Emilia gathered herself. *I must protect my child and my man. I must do this, no matter what happens to me.*

"There is conflict within the Secundans."

The queen's eyes narrowed. The bearded knight looked around for prying ears. *I am committed now.*

"All is not what is seems between the Wolves and the Priesthood. The priests suspect treachery while the Wolves hide their secret."

Valissa reached out her hand. "What is this secret? What is it that is worth your own life?"

Emilia stopped herself. *Can I break my word to Uthiel for the queen? Can I trust her?*

She stared deep into Valissa's eyes. She could read strength and purpose and pride in that gaze. *Can I trust you?*

Will this gamble cost my child its life before it draws breath?

Valissa blinked, and that broke the spell.

"If you have something to say, Emilia, I would hear it or I must away."

Emilia took a deep breath. "The Wolves."

"A great Order. What of them?"

"They have a treacherous lineage."

"Take care in what you say. They are well respected. Their lord commands the military might of the Lands of the Light. My own king allows his forces to be directed by them."

"I swear it. On the life of my child."

Valissa's piercing stare intensified.

"How can you know?"

"The traitors led the barbarians who destroyed my people. I was captive for months, dragged from my home, beaten and herded like cattle to the gates of Gall and into the horrors within.

"I was trussed up to be sacrificed by men I thought to be barbarians wearing Secundan armour. I watched as these madmen came for me, slicing their way through... my family... my people... in an orgy of vileness. I slew one with mine own hand. I watched my Uthiel kill their leader. I watched his best friend turn and try to kill him. I watched that same man save Uthiel's life a moment later.

"I have seen the great foe in all of their horror. I have seen them in the armour of the Wolves. And I have seen the Secundan blues and tar-black hair sitting on the faces of those I can no longer see as men."

Valissa's mouth had dropped open. "I had heard the Wolves had lost heavily on the Frontier—"

"They lost their honour on the Frontier when Uthiel's older brothers turned on each other. Almost half the Order turned or slain, the black survivors fled in to the Black Lands to scheme and plot this mighty invasion for the last ten years. And Thomak is doing everything to hide it while Trethore is doing everything to find out. When he does, the heart of Secunda will rip itself apart."

Emilia's breath came heavily, such was the effort of getting the weight from her shoulders. Valissa still stared. Her bearded knight's face was pinched as if in pain.

"I can have one of my men take you away."

Emilia closed her eyes. *Yes. Save me. Get me out of here.* "No."

"Emilia. Let me save your child."

"If I leave, Trethore will know beyond doubt that I harbour a secret. He will know it is the Wolves. He will find me and he will break me. Then there will be more war. So much blood has already soaked the Lands of the Light. I cannot be the cause of more."

The queen stepped forwards and grasped her hands, a tear in her eye. "Let me save you. I can protect you."

Emilia took a deep breath. "But then who will protect my Uthiel?"

CHAPTER FOURTEEN

"Halt! Halt the advance!" shouted a voice Uthiel recognised as the first captain's.

He echoed the call to his men as he looked left and right along the line to make sure he was obeyed. His men with crossbows sank to a knee and raised their weapons to watch the ground before them, while swordsmen moved to protect them with their shields. Satisfied, Uthiel turned and looked back, noticing Pavel move to shield his back.

Behind them the whole column had come to a halt. Men stood stock still, blades drawn, shield walls formed, ranks ready to repel any attack that may come. But there was nothing. No screams or clashing of blade and axe head. Uthiel strained to listen.

"What's going on?" whispered Tarren.

Uthiel waved him silent. There was movement, amongst the column where first company stood at the ready. Uthiel heard the hammering of hooves off to the flank. Phiti and his men rode alongside the king's guards, and then broke off to head for Uthiel and his men. Uthiel swore under his breath. He heard both Tarren and Theon loudly unleash choice words.

Phiti pulled up a few lengths short of Uthiel.

"Captain, is there danger?" he asked curtly, his eyes full of fire.

Uthiel looked at him, feeling his ire rise. His first reaction was to snap at him, though he forced himself to hold it in check. They were on the march and this was no time for personal vendettas.

"I did not call the stop. We have seen no danger."

Phiti stood tall in the saddle, his eyes searching out beyond Uthiel's men.

"I see nothing."

"As I said, we have seen no danger, Prince Phiti," snapped Uthiel.

Phiti continued to look out over the land, ignoring Uthiel's terse response. Uthiel shook his head and turned his back on the prince, returning his fraying patience to his men. Pavel stood statue still beside him, but Uthiel could feel the Shield's readiness to draw his blade in defence of his captain.

"I mourn the day I lost your respect, Uthiel," said the prince, all of a sudden.

Uthiel frowned, but did not respond.

"I enjoyed our friendship, short as it was, and—"

"You didn't lose my respect," said Uthiel, his voice almost a whisper. "You murdered it."

The prince did not respond.

"Captain Caellar! Your presence, immediately!"

Uthiel turned and looked back past the prince. The Lord General Ryun stood with his son and the first captain alongside a messenger. The messenger wore the armour and tabard of the Grey Wolves, though Uthiel did not recognise the man. He shouldered past the prince's horse and moved at a run towards the group. Pavel quickly followed.

Uthiel and Pavel made it to the gathered men quickly. Uthiel bowed his head to his brothers in deference to the lord of his Order and the mightiest knight in the Lands of the Light.

"Brother," he acknowledged First Captain Solanthur Verutus, and then turned to Lord General Ryun. "My lord general, how may I serve?"

There was a moment silence, a serious pause by the look on the faces of the men around him. Uthiel could feel the weight of what was about to be said growing like the pressure of a quickly building storm. He looked at the first captain questioningly. The man's face was set deeply with troubling thoughts. Uthiel's feeling of trepidation grew fivefold.

"Brother," began the Lord General Ryun. "The lord steward himself has set us a task that will change the course of history."

Uthiel looked again at Solanthur. The man's face hardened further, his eyes steel as they met Uthiel's unwaveringly.

"We have been set a duty most grave — a duty to excise the disease of treachery from the Lands of the Light. It leadens my heart to demand this of you and your men, but it must be done."

Uthiel frowned, his eyes narrowing.

"But it is an act that will free the lands of the Imonetians from a corrupt leadership caste. It will be a punishment for a treachery most foul in the south, where they have tried to murder our lord steward."

"Murder?" asked Uthiel.

Ryun nodded dismissively.

"How?"

"I know not the details of the attempt," said Ryun, uncertainty underlying his usually powerful voice.

Uthiel read the lie in that moment. Ryun's face betrayed him.

Is this a coup?

"You want us to detain them?" Uthiel questioned.

"They are traitors to the Lands of the Light. I want you to kill them."

Uthiel stood stock still, his eyes never wavering from his lord general's.

"Kill… kill the Imonetian royals… kill Phiti?" he said, his voice unsure.

"And his bodyguards, if you please," said the lord general, quickly showing Uthiel a scroll of paper with the red wax stamp of the lord steward affixed.

Uthiel stared for a moment at the seal. He'd seen it a few times before and recognised it, though the handwriting was too small for him to read from where he stood. Without thinking, he reached his hand out to grab the paper. Lord General Ryun withdrew it, the orders quickly lost within the folds of his tabard with a scowl.

Uthiel looked to Solanthur.

"Go on, brother, do your duty. My men and I will be with you," said the first captain, his voice strained.

Uthiel dropped his gaze in supplication to belay the anger at his action on Ryun's face, and then turned to walk back to his men, his hand falling to his sword hilt. As he turned away, he saw it. It was ever so brief, like the single pound of a heart: no, less, like the blink of an eye: a brief moment of disquiet on the lord general's face. It was a darkness of expression as the shadow of an evil deed passed over a man's soul. Uthiel's stomach jumped up into his throat.

By Armenius! Ryun, what have you done?

Pavel moved in beside him, his unsure stance mirroring his captain's. Uthiel caught the veteran's eye for a moment. For once, for the first time Uthiel could remember since meeting the swordsman, he saw something in his Shield's expression, something that let him know that those quicksilver eyes had seen what he had seen: shame.

"Pavel?"

The tall knight looked down to him, his jaw clenching and unclenching.

"Duty, my captain. Duty before all else," growled Pavel before spitting, as if the words were bitter within his mouth.

There was naught else to say.

Uthiel's young mind reeled. He had seen treachery, bled to fight it, watched his friends fall to darkness with the lure of it, and seen all but one of the rest of them slain by it. He'd spent over a year of his life fighting it for all that he was worth, and now he was being asked to commit it.

He turned and looked back over his shoulder, twisting the tall collar of his pauldron out of the way so he could see Solanthur and the main host following him. The first captain had his head down. Uthiel could read the dogged loyalty in the man. The reluctance to throw away his honour was there for all to see. Uthiel could feel the same in himself.

He turned forwards to his men and thought of what he was about to ask them to do. Could he ask this of them? Could he ask them to participate in an act that may stain their very souls and lessen them in the eyes of the Eternal Lord when it was their time to ascend to the Shield Wall in the Sky?

He'd have to. There was no way he could slay the prince and all five guards single-handed. If he tried, his men would leap to defend him. He shook his head. The result would be the same, though their honour and their souls may evade some of the scorn of Armenius.

I could refuse the order. Challenge the lord general. Stand up for what I believe in. Men would side with me.

It was a beautiful thought and a way to keep his honour. But could he slay a lord general of his holy Order in the place of a man intent on bathing in the blood of the innocent for some insane view of the honour of his people? Could he lead a rebellion? He turned back once more, looking for the lord general. The man was basing this on an order from the highest authority in the land. He was doing his duty.

Solanthur watched him. Would the great first captain side with him? If he made a stand, would the greatest warrior of the Lands of the Light draw blades beside or against him in the schism? Uthiel couldn't tell. Duty versus honour was a question no knight could honestly answer until truly pressed.

Uthiel's eyes flicked to Captain Ryun. There was no question the son would follow the father without hesitation.

A hundred questions and a few stark, bloody possible realities hammered his mind like a hailstorm.

I could convince the lord general. Convince him of...

No. The lord general was the lord steward's man, through and through. Uthiel thought back to the glint in the man's eyes as he handed the order over. *What was happening? Why would we do this? When the largest war of the last four centuries was in full flight, why turn on our allies?*

Like a ray of sickening sunlight, it became clear. Uthiel wanted to throw up and scream in equal measures. He wanted to turn back and draw his blade, take to horse and charge back to Gall to face Thomak.

Bastard! How could you be so short sighted? So bloodthirstily hungry for power?

His fist clenched so hard around the pommel of his sword he heard the leather creak under the strain of his rage.

We could run.

The thought flashed through his mind like a fox through the undergrowth. He could run by himself into a foreign land, discard his armour and lose himself in the dunes and weedy forests of the desert lords.

"Captain?" came Tarren's voice. "A problem, Uthiel?"

Uthiel looked up into his friend's open face, realising he had stopped in his trudge back to his men and the prince. Uthiel looked past the stocky knight and to the prince, who had dismounted with his men and was walking around stretching his back.

"Uthiel, what the bloody hell is wrong with you?" snapped Tarren.

Uthiel blinked and shook his head. "Get me a crossbow. Get the men ready to obey my orders."

Tarren frowned, nodded, and ran off, sensing the urgency in his captain's words.

Uthiel continued to stride towards the prince. He could see the royal looking around at the knights as they readied for battle.

Uthiel heard the stomping of heavy boots behind him as Solanthur and his company caught up to him and spread out beside him, crossbows drawn and bolts locked in.

Prince Phiti finally turned to look at Uthiel and Solanthur as they moved towards him side by side. Tarren made it back to Uthiel quickly and passed him a crossbow. The prince's look turned from questioning, to concern, to outright fear as he saw the intent of action written across Uthiel's face.

"Wolves!" bellowed Uthiel. "Turn and face thy foe!"

Uthiel's crossbow was pointed squarely at the prince's chest plate. At this range, he would be sorely pressed to miss, despite his well-known lack of skill with the weapon. The prince's armour was masterfully made, but a crossbow was designed to be deadly to all but a castle wall at anything less than twenty feet.

His company quickly brought up their arms and fanned sideways to clear themselves of Uthiel's bolt, should it punch straight through the prince. He could see questioning looks on their faces.

"Captain, what is—"

"Traitor!" roared Uthiel: he had nothing else to say. No other lie to give to fuel his hate enough to commit this action.

"I—"

"*Traitor!*"

The bodyguards were shouting, their blades drawn and their roundshields up. One of them ran screaming wildly at Theon. The knight beside the Shield dropped the bodyguard with a single bolt through the belly.

The prince was turning around frantically, trying to find a way out, desperately searching for an ally. Finally, his shoulders sagged, and he turned to face Uthiel. Defeat was written across his face.

"You are the last of your tainted line, Phiti."

A tear welled in the young prince's eye and he fell to his knees.

Uthiel strode three sharp steps forward. Two bodyguards moved to intercept. They died immediately, two and three bolts smashing through their bodies. Uthiel's face never left the prince's. The last two bodyguards dropped immediately after as the Grey Wolves' expert crossbowmen wasted only one bolt each in felling them in a succinct symphony of steel and fire-hardened wood punching mercilessly through flesh and iron.

Phiti's lower lip wobbled and he let out a sob as Uthiel stopped five feet from the prince, his shoulders hunched over the wooden stock of the crossbow as he steadied his aim and his spirit.

"Not... Not like this," blubbered the prince.

Uthiel clenched his jaw. His eyes narrowed, his heart hammered, he wasn't sure he could do this. He begged his soul to dredge up the hatred of the last weeks, to find that red anger at the prince's actions, to gift him purity of purpose and a feeling of righteousness. He prayed for Armenius to bless him, to allow the talisman that sat beneath his gorget to burn against his flesh and lend him strength. *Let me know my action is right!*

Nothing. Nothing but the rushing of blood in his ears and the unnaturally ice cold of the silver talisman between his collar bones. Uthiel felt nothing but emptiness. Phiti's red eyes begged him. His hands clasped before his chest.

"Please. Please. Uthiel, please——"

"I am sorry," he whispered, only the dead bodyguards and the prince witness to his words. "We are slaves to His will."

The crossbow sang.

The bolt punched through the prince's chest and into the sand behind, hammering Phiti on to his back, his knees bent awkwardly beneath him.

Uthiel exhaled the breath he had been holding. He felt something within him take a step over a cliff and into the abyss. In the emptiness he swore he could almost here a primal chuckle. He looked up. Every man was staring at him, a mixture of expressions Uthiel would sooner forget written across their faces.

The prince's hand grasped at a blade instinctively, though his eyes stared blindly into the sky above and his mouth gasped widely to drag air into lungs that were quickly filling with his lifeblood. Uthiel moved forwards, dropping the crossbow to the ground, and stamped a boot on to the prince's wrist to pin it to the ground. The rasp of polished steel against oiled leather heralded the draw of Uthiel's long knife.

He took a knee beside the slowly choking prince and without ceremony slit the last Imonetian royal's throat. He didn't move for some time, nobody did, the wind whispering lightly through them and mixing with the excited or horrified breaths of the knights. Uthiel closed his eyes.

How did I come to this?

The image of his father shaking his head with disappointment fluttered across Uthiel's dark imagination.

Without warning, his vision clouded over red, his mind filled with dark thoughts of horrible – *beautiful* – slaughter. Without thinking, without being able to think, Uthiel lifted his blade to the sky, and with all of his rage drove it through the prince's eye before stalking back to the forefront of the Secundan advance. Pavel moved after him, his face once more nonchalant, though his eyes never dropped to look down at the seven bodies.

Most of Uthiel's company followed him immediately. Theon and Tarren strayed behind a moment. Both knights kneeled down to look at the knife hilt jutting from the prince's face.

Tarren was the first to speak. "By Armenius, what have we done?"

Theon didn't respond for some time.

"I do not know, my brother. But the order could only have come from the lord steward. Something is amiss," said the big Shield as he reached out and yanked the blade from the prince's head.

Theon looked at Tarren, and then back to the advancing lines led by the lord general, and then rested his steely gaze upon Solanthur. The first captain stood unmoving, also staring off into the distance as Uthiel led the way north once more.

"Stick by the captain, Tarren. He needs his company by him. He needs his Shields. Mark my words, brother, he needs his Shields."

<--->

A hundred feet out in front of the column Uthiel stopped, his breath raggedly tearing itself from his chest where his heart thundered sickeningly against his ribs. He closed his eyes, forcing the black thoughts from his mind, forcing his body to slow, to return to normal, desperately trying to reclaim his mind from whatever had driven him to mutilation a moment ago.

He heard it again. The sound was like a whisper of malicious laughter hiding in the background of his consciousness like a stalking hunter. His head immediately began to pound and his teeth clenched at the pain. Uthiel turned quickly, looking for the source. No one stood near him. He was motionless for a long moment, taking in the silence, trying to decide if he should listen for the whisper or to block it out. To search within himself would be to admit... *No*. He stopped himself, his thumb and forefinger already absently toying with the talisman around his neck.

His jaw slowly, painfully, unclenched. Then fear touched him, like an ice-cold blade through his flesh. He had seen such berserk rage before. He had seen it in a man he had loved as a friend from youth, and a brother of another Order, as a young knight. The last time he'd seen that young knight, the man had taken part in the slaughter of the Gallites. Last time, that young man had come very close to killing him.

Armenius save me.

Is this what happened to Nikhael?

CHAPTER FIFTEEN

To my dearest lord general,

I write to you in the most urgent of natures. The King of Imonetia, Aphiti, has fallen to illness. The opportunity for our plans to come to fruition, for the glory of Armenius, has arisen. The time we discussed is now.

End their line. Burn Phiti and his bodyguards' bodies. Send me Phiti's wristbands so that I may know his death has been assured.

Then I expect you to march on Imonetia and take it, in the name of our king. Your son shall remain to govern the lands once owned by the sand lords; I hereby name him lord governor of Imonetia. May his rule be long and his city-state of a new Secunda a glorious image of our own home.

Of note, is that the Lord Pomen is becoming a problem in Gall. His illness continues to see his body fade but his mind will not do the same and he continues to be a nuisance. He will pass soon, however, of that I can assure you.

It would be best if Captain Caellar were to be put into situations less conducive to good health in the hope that he shall also pass — lest he attempt to adopt Pomen's type of approach to our new Order in honour of his fading adopted-

uncle. We can make use of a dead hero's legend far better than a live naysayer's.

Nevertheless, within the month I shall lead the main host forward, beyond the White Frontier, where a Secundan army has not set foot in four centuries. I shall see you at the gates of Mother Secunda, my brother.

There we shall know eternal glory.

My brother, we stand upon the precipice. Secrecy is yet required.

For the glory of Secunda,
In the name of the king,
Lord Steward of Secunda, Gall, and Imonetia,
Under His eyes,

Thomak.

The Lord General Ryun re-read the message. So, finally, the time had arrived. The lord steward had decided to stop manoeuvring, to step from the shadows and announce the intentions of the Grey Wolves to elevate Secunda to the pinnacle of the Lands of the Light. It was time to unify the nations to the west of the White Frontier under the Secundan banner, and to mount the final offensive into the Black Lands.

Ryun crushed the paper in his hand and walked over to where men were hauling kindling and branches to create a bed for the funeral pyre of Prince Phiti and his bodyguards. Blood stained the sand heavily beneath the bodies of the seven Imonetians. Ragged red holes were wide open to the air where the Grey Wolves had pulled their bolts from the flesh of the dead.

Above, vultures had begun their lazy circles, waiting for the post battle meat to be left behind for them.

Not this time, thought Ryun as he watched their broad wings keep their fat bodies and long necks in the air.

"Lord general," came the voice of the first captain.

Ryun looked down to the champion of Secunda. The first captain was a blunt instrument. He was a highly trained, skilled, and motivated killer capable of brilliant tactics at a company level and a ferocious, level-headed combatant when the foe came within reach of his blade. The man was struggling.

"A problem, first captain?" asked Ryun.

"My lord general, I... I..."

"Out with it, first captain. I've not the time to waste on your stammering."

Solanthur's face reddened and hardened.

"My lord general, your orders?"

Ryun grimaced. "It is obvious to me, first captain, that 'your orders' is not what you intended to say when you first approached me."

Solanthur did not respond for a while. Ryun let the moment hang, enjoying the first captain's awkwardness.

"Speak openly, first captain."

"Lord general, I... we..." The man steadied himself. "My lord general, what have we done?"

"Why, first captain, we have freed the Lands of the Light from a traitorous and hapless ruling family. We have done our duty as the lord steward demanded of us. We have made the will of Armenius manifest in steel and in blood and we have taken another step on the road to freeing the land of the cancer that brings it to its knees and prevents us from reaching the doors of our lost home to reclaim what was once ours."

The first captain did not seem convinced. Ryun, his political mind sharper than any tactical or blade skills he still possessed, quickly switched his approach.

"You do not agree with our actions? The man's brother was a traitor to the Lands of the Light. Your lord steward, with the authority of the king, and Armenius himself, decreed it so. Do not all traitors deserve death, First Captain Verutus?"

Solanthur held the lord general's gaze unwaveringly. Ryun changed tact quickly once again, leaning in aggressively, his face darkening. He needed to find a way in to the man.

"Do I need to be convinced of your loyalty?"

"Of course not, lord general."

"Does a lord general often get called to task by his first captain?"

"Lord general, I would not—"

"You are my first captain, Solanthur Verutus. Mine. Behave like it. I do so hate the task of replacing men of your stature."

Ryun watched the muscles on the side of the first captain's jaw work as the man very quickly mulled over the words. The first captain's support was an ongoing and necessary requirement of his leadership. Without the man, taking this army to victory was going to prove just that little bit harder. Despite his words, replacing the greatest hero in the Lands of the Light was not an easy task.

"I apologise, my lord general. The task tested me, but as you can see, my men and I were not found wanting," said Solanthur, gesturing to the bodies upon the ground.

"You may remove yourself from my presence."

The first captain bumped his fist to his heart, then turned and walked away, his expression appropriately contrite.

No, you and your men were not found wanting. Yet.

Ryun's gaze wandered over to his son and the company of knights around him. He felt his heart rise alongside a sudden surge in pride as his only boy looked over to him and waved in welcome. The boy had grown into a worthy captain. He was young, strong and so far his command in battle had been reliable. His father being a lord general had most certainly helped his ascension to his rank, but what sort of a man would he be if he did not help his son? Pushing the boy ever towards the greatness that the name of Ryun deserved to be bathed in, was his job as a father.

Reliable.

At the word his gaze roamed over to the line of men receding into the distance.

Uthiel Caellar. Is the hero reliable?

Ryun rubbed his chin with a gloved hand as he considered the young man. Sure, Thomak had been foolish to elevate the young captain so early on in a career that spanned only a year beyond initiation, but the lad had potential. He was a good knight: he fought well, despite his legend obviously being blown out of proportion by the men around him. He was becoming a good leader, and he had the element of greatness about him. How great he may become would only become clear by how long through this campaign he may live. Ryun took a deep breath and rolled his shoulders.

A moot point. The youth had to find his end out on the battlefield. A dead hero could be worth more than a live one, if the stories of his greatness and the vileness of his death at the hands of the enemy could be played well enough.

Ryun waved his son over. The boy moved well, ever in balance and ever the image of his father at his age with a strong jawline and deep-set blue eyes.

"Father?"

"Captain, before they burn the prince, get me his wrist bands."

Captain Ryun looked at him a little quizzically. "What need have we of gold?"

"None. They are a mark of royalty in Imonetia. They will make a fine present for the lord steward. Bring them to me and see the bodies burned. Not a trace of those men is to be left."

"It shall be done, father."

Ryun smiled as his son left him. Glory for the house of Ryun and the Grey Wolves was but months away. Within days they would march on Imonetia, finally setting eyes upon the yellow stone walls of the sand lords. They would take the city, take the lands, own the people, and then march for Mother Secunda.

They would know glory like none before them.

"Armenius' balls! Uthiel, this talk is madness," hissed Tarren. "Have you taken leave of your senses?"

Uthiel placed a finger over his lips and looked around to see if the irascible knight before him had been heard. The men of his company rested, seemingly casual in their lounging, while they cleaned weapons or repaired damage to plate and flesh.

Uthiel knew better, however. Beneath the veneer of the men relaxing under the shade of a few lank trees, the men of his company, Grey Wolf and soldier of the Fifth alike, were on a knife's edge. Each and every man of them had watched as their captain, the young hero, had walked up to the prince and shot him with a crossbow. Each man had witnessed the end of an alliance that spanned back centuries beyond the sacking of Mother Secunda.

Each of them had witnessed what any man of moral standing would call simply, 'murder.'

"Keep your voice down, brother," said Uthiel.

"Brother?" said Tarren. "Are we still brothers? Do I align myself with a murderer?"

"Murderer?"

"He had no sword drawn, no warning, no nothing. Where was the honour in slaying an ally like that? What will you tell Armenius when you stand before him waiting for permission to join his shield wall?"

"I will tell him that I followed the order of my lord general," hissed Uthiel. "I will tell him that I did not relish the task when I was given it, nor did I enjoy it once done. I will tell him that I expect I shall wear it as a stain upon my honour for the rest of my life, as I wore the stain of the prince's existence while he slaughtered his people, upon my soul."

Uthiel narrowed his eyes. "I will tell him I slew a traitor to the Lands of the Light."

"Traitor? Pah! We were helping the man get his brother's seat of power back! What possible reason would he have to become a traitor? What could he possibly have done?"

"I admit, I know not brother," said Uthiel, pinching the bridge of his nose.

He took a calming breath. Here they came, to the crux and the reason for their discussion. Tarren waited expectantly for him to continue.

"The order came directly from the lord steward."

"Did you see the order?" asked Tarren.

"No. Lord General Ryun relayed the contents on to me. Though I was shown the seal upon the parchment."

Tarren rubbed the stubble upon his chin. Uthiel read mischief in his eyes.

"Brother, I would have your mind spoken openly," said Uthiel in a hushed voice, once again looking up to see if any men had strayed close enough to listen in on their conversation in the waning light.

"I simply question the treachery," said Tarren, his hands creating a triangle beneath his chin. "What was to be gained that was not already being achieved through our marching up here to take back their capital?"

Uthiel clenched his jaw, knowing he had to tread carefully here. He'd known Tarren for a long time. They had fought together, watched their brothers die together, and come out the other side of the meat grinder that was the advance on Gall as one of the few remaining knights of the small regiment of men that had left Secunda's borders under Captain Phyrus. But he did not know if he could trust the man wholly. Not with what he truly wanted to say.

"You question the word and honour of our lord general. Of our lord steward."

Tarren's face darkened. "I... *You* brought this discussion on, captain. Not I. You were... I—"

"I question it also."

The words hung heavily in the air. This was the moment Uthiel had been dreading, the moment when conspiracy began or ended in its infancy. The moment when he and Tarren spoke more, or Tarren drew his blade, as honour would dictate, and brought it crashing down onto Uthiel's unarmoured head.

Uthiel's hard stare flicked between Tarren's eyes. They were cold, they were hard, and they were unreadable. Uthiel could see one of Tarren's hands grasp and then release the leather-wrapped handle of his blade. The tall inner collars of the knight's pauldrons rose as he tensed, and Uthiel prepared to throw himself backwards and away from Tarren's first strike.

It never fell. Tarren's steel covered shoulders relaxed, and his hand cleared itself of his blade. His eyes, however, remained cold and angry.

"Explain yourself, captain."

Uthiel took a deep breath. This was it.

"I hear your concerns on the accusations. I agree. They have nothing to gain. But I would take it further. I would take the theory to the feet of the very man who leads our nation in the king's stead, to the very man who commands the Lands of the Light in the defence of our people. I would place an accusation, one that I cannot prove, at the feet of the Lord Steward Thomak."

Tarren swore under his breath and for the first time looked about to ensure their secrecy.

"Will you hear me out, brother? Or shall you slay me where I sit?" asked Uthiel, knowing full well his life could be ended with a single draw of Tarren's blade. Either an immediate death, or a slow one drawn out by one of the warrior priests, waited on Tarren's decision.

The thought of a warrior priest snapped his focus back on to Emilia. His lady, carrying their child, was in the hands of a man he had once trusted above all else. If Tarren were to turn on him now, then the lives of his family would also be forfeit. And Uthiel had been the one who had put her in harm's way by placing her in Trethore's care.

"I will hear you out, brother, and I will keep your confidence."

Uthiel's attention was wrenched back to Tarren.

"Do not go too far, however, brother," warned Tarren. "I have seen the foul beasts of the barbarians. I have seen the walking dead while I stood alongside you. I have seen the worst the enemy could throw at us. But I know you know of worse that you have not spoken of. Whispers, I have heard, in the darkness of men's dreams as they sleep beside brothers who did not fight within the walls of Gall. The unholy light that drank blood and called for ever more sacrifice. I have heard of the horrors that rose against us in the armour of Secunda. These Black Wolves."

Uthiel clenched his jaw to stay the shock before it reached his face.

Tarren leaned in closer. "I have heard of these horrors, as whispers passed on from one man, to one whore, to another man, and then to another. I have heard the Black Wolves are brothers who have shed their greys. But I did not see them inside of Gall, nor did I hear first hand from a man I trust who was there. You will not tell me, and therefore I will not believe that it exists beyond the frightened fables of camp idle discussion."

Uthiel took an annoyed breath, *You never saw our lord, and yet you believe in him.* Immediately, Uthiel felt like barking out a laugh. That was Emilia talking. Her influence. Even from afar her fair touch still nestled against him.

"Brother, I shall stay within the realms of the known evils. I will not speak of these Black Wolves, as I do not believe they are a party to what I speak of. Yet, you will be shocked at my accusations nonetheless," said Uthiel.

Tarren nodded, his frame still leaning in towards Uthiel.

Uthiel took a deep breath, looked around once more, and plunged into his story.

"I will be blunt, my friend. I believe the Grey Wolves, this very host of men and brothers, to be a party to a treachery most foul. We stand allied to a bid to take over the Lands of the Light through conniving force, a plot to remove the leaders of each of our allied nations and to then claim 'stewardship'. Once this role is claimed over all of the lands, and the nobles of the Grey Wolves placed in governing positions amongst the allied nations, Thomak will rid Secunda of our own wounded leader and name himself emperor of the Lands of the Light and the reclaimed Black Lands. He will rule all from the mountains in the east all the way to the seas in the west, the deserts in the north and the rocky plains of the deep south."

Tarren was dumbstruck for a moment, his mouth working but no words coming out. Uthiel ploughed on ahead.

"Do you not see it, my brother? First, Gall. Imonetia will be next, now that their royals have been executed. Already Thomak rules a quarter of the lands we know to exist."

"What of Lemug and Pandur? Two nations will surely defeat any attempt we could make through force of arms. We have not the men to take them!" countered Tarren.

"They have taken as a bad a mauling as we have, if the stories are true. Think on it. The battle for the White Frontier stands on a knife's edge, all the Lands of the Light relying on the strength of Secunda to hold their lands and then surge forwards in victory. But I ask you this, brother, what if Thomak withheld aid? He could clandestinely help the barbarians while it suits his own purpose. What if he awaited their armies to be dashed upon the fields and then swept down to take up and rebuild what was left?"

Tarren was silent for a while, his face racing and raging from one emotion to the next: confusion, disbelief, denial, anger, and so many more.

"This is madness!" he hissed, spittle flying from his lips. "Utter madness! It could not be possible, there is nobody so insane or bloody stupid to cause a civil war while we are at war with the Black Lands! I knew I should not have stayed to listen. This is fool talk, captain!"

Uthiel reached out and placed a hand upon Tarren's pauldron. "If I am wrong brother, then you have heard a fanciful story that can be forgotten. But think, so many of the facts we do know lead easily to my conclusion. By Armenius, the hand we have played ourselves in those facts cannot be disputed! We slew the Imonetian prince. It was my bolt that sent him screaming to whatever hell is reserved for women slayers and child murderers!"

This time it was Tarren who leaned forward, finger pressed against his lips. By the look on his face, Uthiel could see his brother coming around to his arguments.

"Quiet, brother!" he whispered. "You may have found an ear to listen to you in me but you may find a sword in the others of our company. Men would draw upon you for the words you have spoken. You speak of treason, but the words you speak, in their meaning and where they may take us, are treason themselves!"

Uthiel squinted. Tarren was right. Everything he spoke of, while it made sense to him, may not be accepted by those men around him at all. He could be slain out of hand for what he was saying. But as he watched the hardened young knight across from him, he knew what he was telling the man rang true.

Tarren sucked his teeth, swore under his breath, and then spat upon the ground. "So what now?"

Uthiel leaned in further, his face only a finger's breadth away from Tarren's.

"We need to find out who will support us. Speak to some of the men you know who will side with you or me. Get them on board, then let us work on the others within the company."

Tarren shook his head. "Simple in theory, but I doubt even your two Shields would side with you on this. What you speak of is treason most foul, despite your reasons. You speak of overthrowing the leadership of your brother. You speak of possible fratricide."

Uthiel's head dropped into his hands and stayed there a moment. He rubbed his face and then his eyes before coming up, his mind resolved.

"Do you think I have not considered this, brother?" he said.

"I figured you would have, but thought I would make sure. By not declaring you a heretic outright immediately, I have damned my life to whatever fate you take on as your own," responded Tarren.

"I would never betray you, brother," snapped Uthiel. "Your confidence will never be revealed. If I am discovered before my plan comes to fruition I shall not mention your name or this discussion."

Tarren sneered. "Stupid bastard, do you think I would let you stand alone when blades are drawn?"

Uthiel took a deep breath, some resignation coming out. "No, I imagine you would not."

"I have stood by you through all the great enemy could throw at us for over a year now. I will stand with you, for better or worse, whatever may befall us," finished Tarren, holding out his hand.

Uthiel took it in a warrior's handshake.

"To whatever end we meet brother, I shall value your friendship."

Tarren smiled. "As long as my end is in a beautiful tavern wench with long legs, ample hips, and a bosom I could suffocate in before this all finishes, then I shall value yours also."

Uthiel stifled a laugh.

"If my end is in a dirt ditch, the lime thrown beneath me and the firewood piled above, then I may have a different opinion of this moment."

Uthiel's smile hung for a moment longer and then reset to a more serious visage.

"Speak to our brothers, see who you can gather to our cause," said Uthiel, still holding Tarren's forearm.

Tarren nodded, and then looked away as the sounds of hoof beats thundering off into the distance broke his attention. Uthiel followed his gaze.

The main column was here. Three riders carrying messenger satchels over their grey tabards galloped off towards the south. Uthiel released his brother's arm and rose to walk over to his men. It would be time to move again soon.

CHAPTER SIXTEEN

Thundering footsteps and loud voices broke Lord Pomen's peaceful sleep, bringing him back from the world of his dreams to the burning pain of his reality. Immediately the body spasms and wet coughs began and Grullen burst in from outside with damp cloth in hand. Pomen allowed Grullen to wipe the thick chunks of flesh, blood, bile and mucus from his ratty beard and then accepted some warmed water.

"What is going on?" he managed, his voice dry and raspy, his vision not yet clear enough to make out the details of Grullen's face.

"There has been a battle in the north, lord," said Grullen.

"The result?" demanded Pomen.

"A victory for the Grey Wolves, though not for the Imonetians."

Pomen frowned. "How so?"

"The prince took up position with his men in the front line, next to the shield wall. The barbarians hit with ferocity—"

Pomen waved a hand, disgusted. He knew what had happened. Phiti was gone. The details of the loss were immaterial. The last Imonetian royal had been slain by Ryun and his Grey Wolves. The old lord forced himself up, a scowl upon his face.

"Dress me. I need to get outside immediately."

As usual, it took a while for the Lord Pomen to manage to get dressed and keep down the coughing fits that plagued his every moment. The cold assaulted his lungs as soon as he opened the tent flaps to walk out into the brisk late-morning air.

Winter was slowly but surely yielding to spring and the snows were already beginning to melt after the night's fall. The sun shone above with a little warmth, and Pomen momentarily allowed himself to enjoy the touch of the golden light. A booming voice broke his quiet moment.

"Brothers! Hear me! A great battle has been fought in the north upon the sands of Imonetia!"

A knight with a wobbling second chin sitting atop his gorget stood upon an empty ale barrel as soldiers and knights and camp followers alike began to crowd around. Quickly, the numbers swelled to about a hundred and the knight deemed the audience size worthy of his story.

"Brothers, men of the Seventh, and proud Secundans, I have travelled two weeks without rest to bring the news from the north. Two horses lie lame and dead upon the track behind me, I rode so hard to reach you!"

Someone from the crowd held up a mug of ale. The man grabbed and emptied it in a remarkably quick time to a roaring cheer. Foam flowed down the man's extra chins and onto his sacred armour. Pomen shook his head as the crowd cheered its approval. *Have the men of the Grey Wolves fallen so far?*

The knight held up a hand for silence. Pomen couldn't help but notice the bulge from beneath the man's cuirass, the image reminding him of the top of a muffin being forced from below the holy breastplate.

"A great battle, I say!" the big knight called out, spittle flying. "Secundans and Imonetian royalty stood side by side in the front line against the dark and hated foe. Great heroism from every man in the front line was seen, as ten barbarians fell to every one of ours! Black Lands' blood coated the sands for a thousand yards, spilled by the heroes of our knight orders! Spilled by my brothers in the Grey Wolves!"

Another roaring cheer rent the serenity of the morning.

"Knights such as Solanthur Verutus the Lightbringer, champion of Secunda! Heroes like Uthiel Caellar, slayer of the Black Lands' Beast and legend of Gall! With Lord General Ryun leading the charge there was no foe in this land that could have stood firm in the face of such men. And indeed, those bastards could not stand. They could only die!"

By now almost three or four hundred men and women had surrounded the knight on the ale barrel. They were cheering and roaring themselves hoarse. The plump knight's face grew dark, a well-practiced shadow falling upon it. The crowd noticed it and quickly fell silent.

The knight allowed the silence to linger a while before continuing with a reverent look and a measured breath.

"Battle is both glorious and horrible, in equal measures, my friends and countrymen. Those of us who have stood in the front line, mended the wounded, or burned the dead will know of this."

"Who has fallen?" interrupted a voice.

"Who of our mighty heroes stands with our Eternal Lord in the sky?" called another.

"Fortunate for those of you with loved ones in the north, our casualties were low," continued the fat knight. "However, the royal house of Imonetia was struck a mortal blow. Prince Phiti, the last Imonetian king, though word did not reach him fast enough for him to know it, has fallen. So ends the royal house of Imonetia, the line ended in this war."

"As such," called out another booming voice from the crowd, "Secunda shall take stewardship of the lands of Imonetia until a family of royal or lordly blood can take up the mantle to rule once more."

The crowd parted and the fat knight bowed to a man that Pomen could not see. The reverence on the knight's face could only mean one person, however. Pomen swore to himself.

The Lord Steward Thomak emerged through the parting crowd, his head high and his eyes hard.

"Secunda shall once more play Defender of the Light by taking on the hefty responsibility of nursing a second broken nation back to health before handing it back to its rightful owners."

The crowd cheered as the lord steward replaced the fat knight upon the ale barrel.

"My brothers, my countrymen, it will fall to us as a nation to win this war. Lemug and Pandur fight horrible battles in the south. Their men and women test their immense strength against the immovable force that is the southern barbarian horde. They need our help, as do the Imonetians and the Gallites."

The lord steward steadied his gaze, purposefully staring into many sets of eyes beneath him.

"It comes down to you. Knights, soldiers, tailors, blacksmiths, cooks, apothecaries, hunters, scavengers, butchers, bakers — all of you to win this war!"

There was a roar of approval. Thomak went solemn once more. Pomen could have heard a muffled cough from a quarter mile away. Through the crowd he spied Valissa, mostly hidden by a bearded knight. She was doing her best to mask her horror, but was failing. Pomen caught her eye for a moment, but couldn't hold it as if the weight of shame forced his gaze down to the mud.

"For without us mighty Secundans, this war, and these lands, are lost. Armenius expects each man and woman of you to go above and beyond your duty. He demands your best. Will you give it to him?"

There was one final roar that shook the very ground. Pomen looked around. Almost a thousand men and women stood around the lord steward, a great deal of the remaining companies of the Grey Wolves included. Pomen shook his head sadly and turned away.

He had turned his back on one too many things, and in doing that had become complicit in the beginning of a civil war. He had allowed Thomak too long a line and the man had now gone too far. *How did I let this happen?* He raged at himself. *Stupid old man! You're not worth the grey tabard on your back!*

A tear rolled down his cheek as he walked away from the crowd, back towards his tent. *Years, decades, of honourable service to my nation and our allies, gone. It's all been thrown away. No matter what I do, I shall never be forgotten as one of the lords who was a part of this insanity. I will forever more be one of the men who, when civil war should have been an anathema to our existence, sent our armies to spill the blood of our allies while our greatest threat in four hundred years ravaged the White Frontier.*

I am a part of this. I allowed this to happen. I am forever tainted.

Upon entering his tent, he called to Grullen for a bowl of water. He felt contaminated; he needed to find a way to rinse something away, even if it was just the week's dirt from his face. His servant returned with a bowl of water quickly. Pomen gestured for the man to leave.

He sat for a while, the bowl upon his lap and his mind off wandering, trying to discover the turns upon the trail that led them all to this point. Search as he might, he could not find them all. Some were obvious to him, but many pieces of this puzzle still eluded him. He sighed, where once where his body's strengths had begun to desert him to leave him with just a razor-sharp mind, now his mind had also begun to desert his few remaining strengths. How else could he not have seen this?

His hands reached down, cupping in order to grab some water to wash his face, but they stopped, a finger's breadth away from the cool surface. The water had stilled, and when he pulled his hands away, he saw an ancient man. His hair was falling out, his eyes were sunken and had deep black bags beneath them. Liver spots dotted his thinning and loosening flesh and thick barbs of black hair grew from them.

Pomen sat there and stared into his own eyes for a while. He neither knew nor cared how long he sat there, just watching his face, as if he could catch Time in the act of aging him. He felt something warm and wet gather within the crook of his long nose. It gathered weight for a moment, unnoticed, before spilling over into the bowl.

The fat drop of blood shattered the reflective surface of the bowl. Pomen instinctively wrenched his head back. The blood reversed its course and went back down his throat where the ailing lord spat it out in a bout of coughing that brought him from his seat and onto the ground, curled up into a ball of pain and sorrow.

Upon a long sweeping sand dune, Uthiel Caellar finally looked down at the capital city, Imonetia. It sprawled like a massive sand beast almost as far as the eye could see. Three walls ringed a central keep of unbelievable size. Each wall showed where the city had grown throughout the centuries. Each wall, far more ancient that the other outside it, had only one thing in common: they had all been breached.

There was no smoke of burning buildings or bodies, no siege towers, no long lines of men guarding the walls or patrolling the lands beyond, no charging masses. Uthiel instinctively looked to the sky, watching for the same dark swirling vortex that had caused such havoc above Gall.

The dread touch of Zhar T'Hur was nowhere to be seen. The skies above were mostly clear and blue, a few white whisps of little substance lazily making their way across above. Uthiel returned his gaze to the city as his Shields arrived either side of him with Tarren.

"Glory to the sand lords," mused Tarren.

Theon snorted, though Pavel remained quiet as he looked down at the approach to the outer suburbs of the great city. Uthiel took a quick look around to ensure his men were in position across the scouting line and then checked back on the progress of the main column, his hand raising to shield his eyes from the sun.

The last two weeks had seen the sun rise for longer, and the days progressively get hotter. Gone was the ice chill of the winter, though her cold breath was oft felt throughout the night and in the early morning. A comfortable spring had arrived for the rest of the realm, but in Imonetia Uthiel was already beginning to find an appreciation for the light armour and loose-fitting silks and cloths the prince and his bodyguards had worn.

The column had struggled to forge its way through the loosening sands. Heavy horse, heavy armour, and heavily laden supply wagons made for hard going. It'd taken them almost twice the one week Uthiel remembered his lord estimating to get from the borders to the city.

"Fighting a battle in summer on these dunes must be like holidaying in hell," said Theon.

Uthiel nodded, wiping the back of his hand across his brow. It came away glistening with sweat.

"I was thinking much the same," said Uthiel. "Tarren, Pavel, have the men break along this ridge for water. Find some shade. We'll wait for the main column to catch up. Shouldn't take more than an hour or two. The rest will do us good if we are called upon to enter those outer suburbs."

Tarren and Pavel nodded, heading off to carry out their captain's commands. Uthiel watched as Tarren went to Captain Darian of the Fifth and spoke with him, while Pavel moved among the Grey Wolves. All of the Secundans seemed pleased to be able to sit upon a good vantage point and rest, even if they were unable to relieve themselves of the heavy metal burdens each wore.

Theon looked to Uthiel. "Brother, captain, I have heard whisperings among our brothers. Whisperings of treachery. Some say that you are the source, others say it is Tarren."

Uthiel did not speak, but continued to stare down into Imonetia. He had been looking for safe approaches to the city, and mentally mapping the route through the streets to the wall breaches. His attention was fully on Theon now.

"I would hear it from you, captain," continued Theon, his hand lightly grabbing Uthiel's pauldron. "I would hear it from the lips of the man accused of such words, and not from the mouths of men who heard it from others."

Uthiel weighed his next words carefully. He was not a skilled liar, but his needs required that he become adept, and quickly, lest he be struck down by the bear of a man meant to defend him with his body as if it were an extra shield.

"There is nothing to discuss, brother," was all he could say.

"I believe there is more, captain," pressed Theon. "I believe there is far more to this than I know. We executed the Imonetian royal for treachery, though I know not what kind of treachery the man would have been fool enough to commit given his circumstances."

Theon leaned in close. "I would know what that treachery was, my captain."

Uthiel shook his head. "While I saw the lord steward's seal on the order, I was not permitted to see the writing on the parchment by the lord general. I do not know what act was committed beyond what I was told."

"Which was?"

"An assassination attempt upon the lord steward."

"Then they deserved their fate."

Uthiel raised an eyebrow. "You truly believe that?"

Theon frowned and stared hard at Uthiel. Inwardly, the young captain cursed himself for speaking. *Stupid.*

The silence stretched out.

"I do. There is naught to question. The word came from our lord general."

"Then there is your answer. The lord general's word is sacrosanct. I shall discuss this no further," finished Uthiel.

Theon grunted, standing back. "I still feel that there is more. Whether there is and you are not telling me, I have not decided yet. Just remember what I told you, captain."

Uthiel stiffened as he sensed a threat. "And what was that, brother?"

"I told you to remember the men who followed you in order to elevate you to your position. I told you to remember the men who risk and give their lives so that you may be the great man a captain of the Grey Wolves needs to be. Do you remember that discussion?"

"I remember. What of it?"

"Remember that the men who follow you are the men you are responsible for. All of them: me, Pavel, Tarren, all of your brothers as well as Captain Darian and his men. If you do something that stains your honour, you visit the same upon us."

Uthiel paused. *The Fifth. It's so bloody obvious.*

Theon seemed to get uncomfortable.

"There is talk, captain, after the slaying of the royal. Some are calling it cold-blooded murder. I call it duty, as you have told me. But I hear that others are not so sure. They have not heard your account. They only know you two have drawn each other's blood before and then saw you call out an order and shoot the helpless royal through the chest."

"What would you have me do?" asked Uthiel, distractedly.

"Get back amongst the men. You have been distant of late. They rely on you for cohesion, to unify the company. You are their captain, proven in battle. They are your men, forged in war. Lead them."

Theon stood and patted Uthiel on the pauldron, his heavy touch feeding through the steel plate onto Uthiel's shoulder. As the big man walked away, Uthiel's mind was already working. *The Fifth.*

There were fifty or sixty knights of the Grey Wolf Order in Imonetia, all told. There were *thousands* of the Fifth. He'd been worrying over ways to win his brothers to his cause quietly, without considering the biggest opportunity, or the biggest risk. If the Fifth sided with Ryun, then this was a lost cause from the beginning. If they sided with him, then like as not he would not even need the support of his brothers.

Quickly he weighed up the situation. The Fifth knew him. His father had led them into Gall after their muster and died a hero's death there. He had some personal friends within their ranks, men he had known since before becoming an initiate. The Fifth had been on the field of battle when he'd slain the warlord that brought him his fame. While replacements had been brought in from the thinning population of Secunda, surely there would be men who had actually seen him fight?

On the other hand, he knew very few of the men, against the larger whole of the Fifth army, by name or face. Only one of the men he knew was a captain or of rank. The army captains not seconded to a Grey Wolf captain all reported directly to Ryun. It would be difficult to get enough of the twenty-odd captains across to his cause, but to do it without Ryun finding out would be an almost impossible matter.

Soon enough he could feel the march of the main force coming upon their position, the earth shaking under hoof and boot and wheel. Captain Darian came to stand with him.

"We going in there?" asked the veteran, motioning towards the city.

Uthiel nodded.

The captain turned to walk back to his men.

"Captain Darian," said Uthiel, taking in a deep breath. "I need to speak with you. In private and in confidence."

Darian looked at him, frowning. "Is there a problem, captain?"

"Listen to what I have to say and then you can make that decision for yourself."

CHAPTER SEVENTEEN

Jotel's thick paws ran over the scar on his bare collarbone, tracing the pink flesh back over his shoulder. He stood atop the walls of Imonetia, deep in thought, as his fingers snaked back and forth along the line that marred the pale flesh of his bare torso. His immense pectorals and shoulders rose and fell rhythmically as he otherwise stood statue-still. His baleful gaze, filled with a searing hate and an intense need to do murder, spied the first black silhouettes of the Secundan scouts cross the far off hills and stand to observe the city.

Jotel closed his eyes, his broad jaw clamping and the muscles upon his flat features going taut as he prepared himself for the battle to come. He had faced the foe before, slain their captains and their knights and their soldiers without thought of mercy. He had raped their women in the hundreds, and he had sacrificed them in their tens of thousands. He had worked within the realms of the Black Lands for a decade to bring his god to walk the Lands of the Light in blood-soaked footsteps. And he had failed.

Leather creaked as his anger built and the hand resting upon the pommel of his blade slowly began to constrict with incredible power. His weapon, a piece of steel forged to create fear and rend through the finest armour with ease, was always upon him. His long sword, uncommon to the men of his homeland, who preferred shorter stabbing swords to match their shield walls, was of pristine quality. The steel was as dark as the cloak of Death herself, and the serrated edge as vicious and sharp as the day it was forged by the smithies of Secunda.

He looked down to it and the blade brought him comfort. Yes, he and the Black Wolves he called 'brother' had failed in Gall. *No*, he snarled inwardly, *Kael failed*. But he and some of his brothers were still alive. And while there was still blood in his veins to fight, then there was still a chance to bring Zhar T'Hur to this land so that He could wreak His bloody vengeance upon those who lacked the courage to throw off the shackles of their stagnated civilisations and follow the red path.

As he watched the Secundans slowly begin to file into position, man by man and unit by unit, he felt the lunatic hate begin to take over. He revelled in it, gloried in it, as if their bodies already littered the ground around him. He had not drawn the blood of his erstwhile countrymen for nigh on a year now, not since the assault on the north riverbed of Archenon Creek where he'd led the major assault to break through the White Frontier. Jotel hawked and spat in disgust at the memory of the night Kael had drawn him aside and explained the bigger plan to him.

Kael's planning had been magnificent: a decade spent uniting the thousands of brutal barbarian tribes under the one leader through murder, challenges, blood, mud, conniving, assassination, and misdirection; ten years of sacrifice from the brothers who had cut themselves from the chaff of the Grey Wolves and fled to the wastes beyond the White Frontier.

They had seen so much. Brothers lost to the land, to the blood madness, to the challenges where the barbarian landed a lucky blow or the fur-clad chieftain spied the dagger from the dark before it plunged into his back. They had seen and smelt an ocean that nobody from west of the frontier had set eyes upon for four centuries, and they had slaughtered the expeditionary party from a foreign land that had beached their ships upon the finely grained sands. They had set foot upon the cobblestones of Mother Secunda, read from the scripts stencilled in stone there and seen their own worthiness to take all from this world and place it under their boot heels. They had seen a true god, inside themselves and in each crimson drop that exploded from the bodies of the unworthy as blade pierced flesh.

And on one mighty day they, the Black Wolves, had led hundreds of thousands of barbarians across the White Frontier in a tidal wave of steel and flesh and an excess of slaughter. Here, Kael's tactical magnificence came to the fore, and here the once great Black Wolf out-thought himself and destroyed what should have been.

With their brothers already laying siege to the fortress at Archenon Creek and large elements of their host pushing towards the lands of Gall, Kael had pulled brother Jotel aside.

'Brother' he had said, *'Brother, I have a task to ask of you.'*

Jotel had grunted his assent to continue as a barbarian woman worked a bone needle and thread through his skin to stich up the wound that had broken his collarbone in the previous day's fighting.

'I would not have our great plan rely on only one sacrifice. If we are to fail… Zhar T'Hur would be most unpleased. We must be assured of his arrival.'

Jotel had looked up, incensed by the insinuation that he may fail. Archenon Creek was his front. *His.* He would not fail Kael. He would not fail Zhar T'Hur. When their god looked upon Jotel, the big man would be surrounded by the sacrifice of a hundred thousand Gallite women and Zhar T'Hur would bless him as His champion.

But Kael had continued. Jotel had acceded. And five months later, Jotel had lain siege to Imonetia after leading the northern barbarians to a crushing defeat over the sand lords. A hundred thousand women had bled and coated the ground with innocent viscera. Jotel had stood at the pinnacle of the sacrifice, so blood coated he was almost indistinguishable as a knight, awaiting the light Kael had said would come from the heavens if the sacrifice in Gall failed.

But, nothing. No light. No god. No word from the south. Nothing. A month passed. Two. Then the southern barbarians began to scatter throughout the Imonetian lands. Most were broken remnants of the forces Jotel had left behind over half a year before. They came with stories of the light from above, the dead walking, the Red Father sucking the blood of the slain into the sky in a vortex of hate. They spoke of the signs the Black Wolves had sought for so many years.

They also wailed of defeat. They retold tales of men in steel with grey tabards with fear and reverence. They spoke of the Grey Wolves and they spoke of failure.

Jotel killed most of them with his own blade. The barbarians were a blunt weapon, an immense fighting force of warlike men and hard women who hated each other almost as much as they hated the steel-men. Kael and the Black Wolves had brought them together through manipulation and fear and force. There were so many of them that a few hundred or so more put to the sword mattered not against the possible poisoning of the morale of those camped in Imonetia.

Volatile as they were, they were also a heavily superstitious race and would have taken such tales from the south as signs that the steel-men in grey could defeat the Red Father. Such thought could not be allowed if the Black Wolves were to be victorious. Jotel would not allow it. He would finish what Kael should have. He would bring a god to live amongst them and lead them. He would find another receptacle to the god's liking, if his own body was not suitable. He would see the realm united under one bloody, iron-shod fist.

This was his chance to draw the eye of a god, as old as the mountains and malevolent as the desert sun, upon himself. This was his chance for eternal glory. Kael was no more.

Jotel returned to the present as he felt someone approach him.

"Brother," grunted a deep voice.

A short, powerfully built knight stood beside him, his dull armour glowing deep red in the afternoon sun.

Kael nodded his approval for the man to continue speaking.

"Our brothers are ready. The barbarians have been subdued and they are prepared. Your trap is set."

Jotel nodded once more. "Glory to you, brother. We bring Zhar T'Hur, and all the bloody magnificence that follows will be as a feast to the appetiser we provide this day."

The Black Wolf bowed deeply and backed away a few steps before walking down the battlement stairs towards the city below. Jotel allowed his gaze to follow the man and then wander throughout the city. The streets rotted, a hundred thousand wasted sacrifices almost beyond putrid decomposition atop their seven-foot tall trestles.

No matter, thought Jotel, his gaze returning out towards the gathering Secundan host. *A far more valuable sacrifice awaits you, Zhar T'Hur. With these, the elite of the Lands of the Light, I call you to our lands. I call you to lead us. I call you to bless me with your power as I send soul after soul screaming to you, their lifeblood sucked unto the sky to replenish your body's spirit, which has been starved of wholesale slaughter for many months now.*

Zhar T'Hur, enjoy thy coming feast and set foot upon this realm once more.

CHAPTER EIGHTEEN

"My brothers. Men of the Fifth. To me."

Uthiel's voice was pure strength and dedication. His men responded, as did the men of some of the other companies around them. In a wide semi circle facing the walls of Imonetia, they knelt as one to the young Grey Wolf captain who would be leading the van of the assault. Uthiel closed his eyes and took his time to gather his thoughts.

The first thought to cross his mind was of his child and Emilia, of her warm embrace, and of the child's future. He now knew with almost certainty that he would have no part in that future. He felt that knowledge try to crush him, try to drop him to the ground in wracking sobs and tears, but he would not allow it.

He opened his eyes and exhaled slowly. Hundreds of men looked to him expectantly. They were the tip of the spear being thrown against the stone and wooden walls of the foe. They were the men who would follow him to try to breach the enemy in the most terrible of battles. Many, if not most, of them would be wounded or killed. Uthiel would not allow himself to let these men down.

He was a hero in their eyes. He was a man to embrace Death for. Uthiel could not let them see the shaking in his heart, nor the rage that threatened to stain his soul as he locked eyes for a brief moment with his commander.

Lord General Ryun stared back, his eyes cold and impassive. Those eyes spoke of the knowledge of what Uthiel had been doing. The men surrounding Uthiel gave testament to that knowledge. Every man Uthiel felt he might be able to convince to his cause was in the van. Every man.

His company of Grey Wolves, Captain Darian and his men, and the two companies his father's friends fought with were all there. He wasn't even sure if the men Antony, Argo, and Camen fought with knew what Uthiel had attempted, but they had been sentenced to death by association anyway. Ryun smiled at him and in that smile Uthiel knew defeat. The two hundred and fifty-odd men kneeling before Uthiel were about to pay the price for his attempted coup.

It would die in its infancy, as, most probably, would his child if Emilia were to live long enough to give birth. Uthiel broke gaze with Ryun and looked down to his men. Grizzled, hard faces looked to him, their eyes begging him for inspiration and courage. They all knew what was asked of them. They all knew what was coming.

They had five hundred feet of open ground to cross to reach the weak spot in the wall. Arrows would rain down upon them from above while they charged forward, and then, when they had clambered up the rubble of stone where the barbarians had brought down the wall to take the city, and then piled wood waist-high there to defend it, they would meet the savage axes of the foe. Easily more than half of the faces Uthiel saw before him would be bereft of life within the next two hours: an estimate based upon victory.

"It falls to us, men, to breach these walls," he began. "It falls to us to take back what the barbarians have pillaged from the Lands of the Light. I have no glorious speech for you, no light or uplifting remark, we all know what lies before us: the bloodiest of tasks. We all know the man next to us will likely not see another dusk.

"Yet, we go anyway. We go because we are the knights and soldiers of Secunda. We go because it is right to do so. We go because without men like you and me, willing to lay down our lives, the Black Lands would have wrestled these lands from us centuries ago. Look to the man next to you and remember his face, his name, where he is from. Remember him, so that if you are called to the Shield Wall in the Sky, you have a brother with you who can vouch your bravery to the Eternal Lord.

"I am Uthiel Caellar, my brothers. I am a captain of the Grey Wolves. I ask you to follow me."

Uthiel turned away and rested his eyes upon the thirty-foot wide breach in the immense outer wall of Imonetia. A steep mound of chunky rubble led up to it like a ramp, and carts and various other pieces of wooden rubble had been piled there. A thick line of barbarians manned the defences inside the gap and a host of archers stood upon the walls above to either side.

Behind him Uthiel could hear the men who would join him in the assault stand to order. Without looking, he knew Theon, Pavel, and Tarren would be beside him. His men would form a single long line in the centre of the charge, while the men of the Fifth would pour in behind them.

Pavel spoke. "Brother captain, I still advise you, do not lead from the front. Send some of the Fifth in first to weaken the foe. You are too valuable to the attack to be lost with the first axe-swing."

Uthiel smiled. "I'll not send men where I myself would not go first."

"I would expect no less," said Theon from the other side.

"Neither would I," piped in Tarren. "Uthiel just doesn't seem happy unless he is trying to get me killed."

"Archers to the fore!"

Uthiel winced at the command from the lord general. This was it. He dipped his head and placed his bucket helm over his head. Immediately his view of the world changed to two slim slots and the reverberating sound of his own breathing. He hefted his shield on his left forearm and raised his right hand to the sky.

Dropping his arm forward he called at the top of his voice. "For Mother Secunda! Onward!"

He began at a walk, and felt the ground beneath him tremble a little as his men fell into step beside him. There was no point in running yet, there was no danger this far out of shot. Uthiel didn't even draw his sword. He would need all of his energy should he make it to combat. In that moment, his lips moved silently as he prayed to the spirits of the brothers who had worn his armour before it had been bestowed upon him.

My brothers, shield me from our foes. Allow me to reach combat. Allow me to decide my fate, face to face with the enemy. Do not let the arrow or throwing axe pierce my flesh. Let me lead these men as they deserve to be led, the entire way into the city, or the entire way to the Shield Wall in the Sky.

There was a loud chorus of bowstrings being loosed and he looked up to see the first flock of arrows fly over their heads from the Secundan bowmen behind them. They took a short while to reach the pinnacle of their arc, and to then make their way down. Most of the shafts clattered from the walls or landed short into the dirt. One or two dark shapes upon the wall fell from sight.

Uthiel hefted his shield a little higher as step by step the walls seemed to grow menacingly before him. The first volley of arrows from the barbarians loosed and flew towards the Secundan van. Uthiel watched their arcs as they landed almost fifty feet short of the advancing line. Secundan bows had the longer range against the barbarian short bow, but soon that would not matter.

A second volley of Secundan steel hail flew at the defenders, this time felling a few more as the archers of the Fifth found their range. Uthiel watched the walls intently as he saw the enemy recover and lift their drawn bows to the sky. The barbarians loosed once more.

"Pull in! Shields up! Keep moving forward!" called out Uthiel.

The men around him closed ranks and lifted their shields to the sky, creating a dark shade pierced only by shafts of light.

Uthiel could hear their ragged breathing and their feet pounding upon the ground like their hearts would be hammering inside their chests. They stank of fear: sweat, dried spit, vomit, soiled breaches. There were men praying, men begging to see out the day, men sobbing in abject terror.

Then the first arrow hit like a hammer from above. It was followed a thousandth of an eye-blink later by a few hundred more. The sound was unbelievable, though it lasted but a long moment at best. Steel slammed into wood, plate or chainmail, and for the unfortunate few, flesh. The clatter of shafts glancing away or falling to the ground after hammering down was just as deafening. There were screams. Men fell. Uthiel could hear them like they were shouting in his helmet.

He heard one man call out to his friends not to leave him. It was a squeal of desperation, begging for help.

"Stay tight!" roared Uthiel. "Keep your formation, by Armenius!"

Beside him Theon shouted. "Shields up lads! Only a couple more volleys!"

Uthiel kept pushing his men forward, step by step. They moved in a well-drilled jog, the knights like the steel tip. Uthiel risked a glance above the rim of his shield. The bows upon the walls went up once more.

"Here they come again! Get tight! Brace!"

The arrows slammed down again. Uthiel tripped as an arrow lanced into the dirt before his foot and two more slammed into his right pauldron. The soldier behind him took the following arrow in the gut, the head bursting through the mail and dropping the screaming man to the ground. Uthiel looked back and saw the soldier trying to pull the arrow out as more arrows crashed down. Three more men fell as the break in the shields widened around the sprawling wounded.

Rough hands grabbed Uthiel from either side and pulled him back up. Uthiel glanced up and saw Pavel and Theon protecting him with their own arrow-ridden shields.

"Up my brother, get the men back together. We need to keep going."

"Back together! Shields up!" called Uthiel, all of a sudden out of breath.

He risked one more look. They were only fifty feet from the base of the rubble. There, he knew, it would be time for recklessness. It would be a time for heroism. It was a time for him to lead. Uthiel felt the familiar burning of the talisman against his chest. He felt fresh strength lend itself to his limbs. He welcomed the feeling. Armenius was with him in this bloody endeavour.

Rage began to build as he spotted the stereotypical tall inner collars of a Black Wolf at the centre of the defences in the gap. He clamped his teeth down on a feral growl that threatened to come out before he even realised it was there. He felt his chest burn brighter, his eyes both increasing in clarity and tinging red as if something within fought for supremacy: controlled warfare or a berserk charge.

Uthiel forced his feet to slow as he realised he was beginning to push the front of the men too hard for the men behind to keep up without tripping over the longer stride of the man in front. *Easy. Calm. Eternal Lord, help me. I must be calm to win. I must be cool headed if I am to ever see my child.*

Uthiel drew in a deep, stuttering breath as he felt the men compress behind him. Immediately after another volley crashed down upon them. More men fell, screaming. Uthiel didn't look back this time. At the base of his shield he saw the first chunks of rubble from the wall. He realised he could hear the barbarian war cries. He smiled. His heartbeat quickened and his limbs felt afire with anticipation. It was time.

"Break! Forward for Armenius! Forward for Mother Secunda! Forward to glory!" he screamed at the top of his lungs as he broke rank and powered up onto the debris slope.

An arrow or two flittered past him. Uthiel barely noticed them. He raised his shield and took an arrow flying toward him from above. His legs pumped hard as the men defending the breach before him drew back their tattooed arms to throw axes. Uthiel raised his shield once more, his vision blocked by the wooden backing and leather loops strapped to his forearm.

He saw the sharp edge of the axe burst through the wood of his shield before he felt the bruising impact through his shoulder. Immediately he stumbled off-balance as the additional weight of the axe dragged him down. Without thinking Uthiel threw down his shield and drew a blade with each hand. A few more steps and he launched himself up on to the barricade, parrying the axes of four barbarians and slaying two of them within the blink of an eye.

Blood flashed into the air, along with the screams as the Grey Wolves smashed into the barbarian lines in a cacophony of steel carving meat and crashing into armour. Arrows flashed down, glancing from a knight's armour here, indiscriminately lancing into a barbarian's throat there.

Uthiel ducked an axe and saw Theon crash a blade through the skull of its wielder, then take the haft of another axe on his sword breaker. Uthiel whirled, one blade lancing out to spill the steaming guts of a screaming man, the other angling away the wicked half moon axe of another man while Pavel hammered that same barbarian sprawling into his fellows with his shield.

All around Uthiel was chaos. Men were dying at an unbelievable rate. The wooden wall had only held a moment before collapsing under the weight of armoured men, sending those standing atop it sprawling to the ground to be hacked and stomped to death. Uthiel had lost sight of the Black Wolf almost immediately, but knew he was still out there. He could *feel* the malevolence of the monster.

Uthiel cut and slashed, spinning away from axe blades that searched for weak spots in his armour, carefully watching other blades as they smashed into his plate. Without warning, something slammed him to the ground and his vision went black.

He felt legs kick at him. A body fell on top of him, legs grinding the rubble below weekly and breath wheezing slowly to stillness.

"Captain!" he heard someone yell.

"Get him up!"

"Stand over him damn you!"

"Brothers! To the captain!"

Uthiel rolled away instinctively and felt something smash into the body on top of him. He kicked out and connected with something that reeled away, before reaching up to pull his twisted helm from his head and regain his sight. The Black Wolf was right before him.

Uthiel roared with rage as he saw his men charge in around him, pushing the barbarians and the Black Wolf back with shield and blade. The body atop him was rolled clear by Theon.

"Come, brother captain, we're not finished yet!" he yelled.

Uthiel pushed himself to his feet. An arrow clanged from his pauldron. He looked around, took stock of his position. A shield blocked his view for a moment as Pavel stopped an arrow. He stood atop the wall, in the very centre of the breach. Around his feet, the bodies of the dead and dying were thick.

He watched men scrabble and gouge each others' eyes and try to rip out throats with clawed hands upon the red ground. He saw men try to push their ropy innards back inside the gashes in their bellies, stand around in shock attempting to find severed limbs, place hands over pumping artery fountains as knees buckled.

Uthiel looked back over his shoulder to the plain. The main host was advancing. Uthiel felt his face twist into a wicked grin as his vision once more began to cloud over red, the smell of battle filling his senses. Something pulled at him, coaxed him to action.

Back to the slaughter. It called inside his head. *I want more.*

Uthiel grinned as a group of Darian's men crested the hill alongside him. He revelled in the looks upon their faces as they laid eyes upon his battered plate, blood-sheathed swords and wild face. He grinned, tasting other men's blood on his lips. He could no longer feel the burn of the talisman against his chest.

"Yes," he said to the men in their mail and tabards. "Back to the slaughter."

Turning from the men, Uthiel spied the Black Wolf as the stocky traitor knight slew one of his brothers. The young slain knight fell to the ground, his arms flailing the air above as he reflexively tried to withdraw the blade jutting through his eye slit. The Black Wolf stomped a foot onto the dead knight's helm and wrenched the blade back out, all the while staring down Uthiel from across the field.

Uthiel roared, his voice like thunder, his eyes the very rage of the storm, and threw himself back into the melee. His blades hissed through the air and crunched through flesh and bone. Massive fans of crimson sprouted from his every sword swing. No blow was wasted, not a strike could be parried. He felt more than saw the barbarian getting in behind him and kicked out, sending the man crashing to the ground, knee bent savagely backwards. He turned for but a moment and saw Theon slash the man's throat as he tried to keep step with Uthiel.

Uthiel could see the Black Wolf just five or ten feet away. Three barbarians stood in his way. They died quickly and brutally. The Black Wolf spotted him just as a spear thrust took the traitor full in the chest and sent him reeling backwards through the waiting ranks of barbarians. Uthiel saw the man through the crush of bodies sit up and leap to his feet, a deep dent in his cuirass. Uthiel could feel a powerful rushing through his veins scream for the challenge.

But the Black Wolf would not reciprocate. The man took off his helm, shook out his sweat drenched hair, locked eyes with Uthiel and smiled.

"You!" roared Uthiel, his vision a sea of rage. "You who would shed his grey! Fight me! I'll rip your throat out, bastard traitor!"

In his peripheral vision Uthiel could see the look on both of his Shields' faces. They had heard him, and they had seen the helmetless Black Wolf. Uthiel didn't care, his eyes and thoughts only interested in chasing the traitor as the man turned and backed away through the press of barbarians.

"No!" he screamed as he was showered in the blood of the man he had just decapitated.

Behind him he heard the battle cry of two thousand more voices as the next wave arrived and crested the hill. The fresh men charged down and Uthiel moved to go with them but hands grabbed his pauldrons and held him back. There were too many hands for his powerful body to break free of. He turned, his eyes wild, his swords held in check just barely through sheer force of will.

Concerned and friendly faces looked to him, their mouths moving but no words breaching the rushing in his ears. Slowly his haze of battle-madness seemed to begin to clear, like the first cool autumn breeze breaking through the stifling summer heat.

The first man he recognised was Tarren, then Pavel and Theon. Antony and Argo stood there also. He turned back to try and see the Black Wolf. Camen stood there, his back to the group, ready to defend them. In that moment the men of the second wave poured past them and into the city to fall upon the defenders. The first captain raised his shield in salute to Uthiel as he moved past with his men in tow.

Uthiel could still see the Black Wolf in is mind's eye, could still see that taunting smile. He looked to his friends and brothers once more, their voices beginning to pierce his fog.

"Uthiel, wait! Rest. Your men need rest. We took the breach," said Argo.

"Calm, captain. The job is done."

Uthiel's world came swirling back to him as if a hood had been lifted from his mind. He took a deep breath, turned and sat upon the rubble. He watched the men of the Fifth stream on past him, running down the mound of shattered rock and bodies as they strengthened the line and pushed the barbarians further into the city.

Someone handed him a skin of water. He drank greedily and then passed it on to the man beside him. Uthiel pushed himself to his feet.

"There is no rest until the city is won. Get them men back together. Show me what we have left, then we move into the city," said the young captain, resoluteness covering up the berserk wildness that had ravished his face and mind but a short while ago.

His men nodded to him and moved off, leaving him with only his two Shields and Tarren by his side. Theon moved before him and knelt. Uthiel looked up at the veteran's face.

"My captain. You said something. During the battle. To the barbarian wearing our armour. You accused him of shedding the grey and called him a traitor."

Uthiel's mind whirled as he tried to recall the moment. Then it reeled as he realised what he had done.

He looked up at the faces of his three brothers. The concern was overlaid with something else in their faces now, even Pavel's. He dropped his gaze to the ground. There was nothing else for it. After all this bloodshed, it was time the Grey Wolves knew their own dark secret.

"My brothers. I must tell you something. Something you will struggle to accept. Something that will be hard to hear. Something I must have your utter confidence on until I know what to do."

The three men around him nodded expectantly, each man promising his confidence in his own way.

Uthiel took a deep breath.

"That man is not a barbarian. He once was a brother of ours."

"What?" snapped Theon. "How would you know this and we veterans do not?"

Pavel was calmer. "Has the lord steward been notified?"

Uthiel licked his lips.

"Thomak knows. So does Ryun."

Theon swore long and hard.

CHAPTER NINETEEN

Emilia did her best to hide her fear as she picked up the thick, ornate pauldron and attached it to Trethore's shoulder. She fixed her stare on the leather belt that held the piece to the cuirass and focused on getting the attachment exactly right. Too tight, and the warrior priest would not be able to swing a blade. Too loose, and the gap between cuirass, gorget and pauldron may allow a blade through.

She did her best to steer clear of the warrior-priest's stare, which right now searched her face with a cold and clinical look that chilled her very soul. She turned away and gripped his vambrances and held them out. Her head remained down, pretending to study the intricate etchings of prayer upon the steel.

Trethore's thick forearms pushed into the pieces and, one after the other, cinched the leather straps to hold them secure. Emilia had already turned away to grab his greaves. She knelt down, still feeling those eyes burning into the top of her head, and began to strap them on to his shins. They were beautiful pieces of armour, and were she not so afraid, she may have appreciated the intricate handiwork behind their creation and four centuries of loving maintenance.

"Are you feeling alright?" came Trethore's deep voice.

Emilia held her nerve, stopping herself from visibly twitching in shock at the words.

"You seem nervous today, Emilia," said the priest, his voice like a dagger, offering itself to her to fall upon. "Do you have something weighing down your soul? Something you may wish to speak of?"

Emilia shook her head. Perhaps she had shaken it with too much vigour, but it was all she could do. Her fear had rendered her mouth dry and her tongue useless.

"Look at me, child," said the priest.

This was what Emilia feared above all else. Those eyes, cold hard versions of the stereotypical Secundan blues her Uthiel had, could pierce the very soul. Trethore had been working her down since Uthiel's departure, finding a way into her defences. Within her soul she knew, *she knew*, that Trethore could see that she was hiding something.

Her eyes rose to meet his, slowly making their way over the mail skirt that protected his thighs, the black leather sword belt around his waist, and up the ancient cuirass inscribed with twenty-seven ancestral names strapped to his mighty chest. The gorget around his throat preceded his chin, while his weathered and scarred features followed soon after. His mouth was flat and hard and then finally, she locked gazes with the man she had come to fear most in the world.

All of her courage poured into her face to stop the tears from flowing. Everything she had, anything she had, she used to protect her child and her man. Her face held rigid, her eyebrows raised and her eyes the very image of supplication. Normally this would assuage him. She felt today may be the last day that would happen.

Something had changed in Trethore. Something that told her he would no longer allow her games. Something that told her she was in very great danger. She sat transfixed by Trethore for a while. Even if she had wanted to move, to run, Emilia was not sure that under that gaze she would be able to bring herself to move.

"My lord?" she managed.

Trethore smiled. There was no warmth in the motion.

"Things have come to pass, child. A great shift in the world as we know it," rumbled the warrior priest, his eyes flashing angrily.

"I have not heard——" started Emilia, her voice wavering.

Trethore leant down and placed a finger on her lips to quiet her.

"There is a taint in Secunda. Something that festers from within, threatening to destroy all that four centuries of men and women have fought for."

Emilia could not speak. Her heart raced but somehow, she kept her face from revealing her secret.

"There are men, knights, who know of what is happening."

She wanted to run. Her legs would not respond. Her hand fell to sit on the swell of her belly. She felt trapped, as if he had bound her hands and feet.

Trethore leant in close. "There are knights within the Grey Wolves who know."

Emilia felt a tear escape her eye's grasp. She involuntarily looked past Trethore for Valissa. There was nobody there to pull her from this plight.

"I believe we have found one such man, one insidious beast who holds secrets — secrets that I will find and pull from him. Though we have not been able to break him, yet, I need a task from you. It will be unsavoury. And for that I apologise in advance. But I must ask you anyway."

Emilia almost felt her heart fall from her chest in relief. They couldn't have her Uthiel. Not here. He was many leagues north, fighting in Imonetia. She'd heard the messenger shout of his heroism only a few days before.

Then her mind reeled once more. *What if this man knows of Uthiel? What if he damns the father of her child with his words?*

"What would you have me do?" she asked.

"The man sits in a small holdfast dungeon, only a few miles from here, in the care of the brothers of my Order," said Trethore. "Unfortunately, he is rather sick. I need him well in order to question him properly. I know you worked with the apothecaries, prior to Uthiel asking me to look after you. I would call on what skills you learned now."

"But, I am no healer! I only know how to stitch and bandage. I know nothing of healing the ill."

Trethore tilted his head a little. "There may be some stitching required. I am sure a few herbs and poultices will see him well enough for me to carry out my work."

Emilia was about to object again, to say she was with child and should not be around the ill. Trethore didn't allow it. He leaned in closer, his demeanour increasing in its menace.

"Emilia, I have done Uthiel and you a great service by taking you in to my care. I need this done in secret, away from the eyes of the other men we stand with. If word of this was to spread, we may ignite a civil war. Do you understand the importance of what I ask of you?"

She looked into his eyes, searching for the lie her heart felt was there. All she saw was the coldness of his glare. She could read nothing. For all she knew this was all in her head and she was imagining the danger. For all she knew he was asking her to stand with him so he could lance one of those huge knives the knights carried into her stomach.

She took a deep breath and stood. She really didn't have much of a choice. She had to keep up her charade, lest her body be tossed into the burning pits where she had watched so many post-battle wounded be tossed once their life had fled.

"As you ask, father," she said. "Uthiel and I are forever in your debt. I shall grab some items and meet you there."

Emilia moved to walk past Trethore and leave the tent. Whether or not she would return she had not decided yet. Her instincts screamed at her to flee, while her mind, riddled with fear, told her to obey and wait for the right opportunity. Trethore did not allow her the decision.

"Come, we have the necessary items already at the holdfast."

Emilia nodded to herself and grabbed the priest's white tabard and helped him in to it. Trethore thanked her, and then stared at her belly for a moment. His gaze wandered over her form: not with lust, perhaps regret, she just could not be sure.

It lasted not long before the tall warrior priest whirled away and walked out through the tent flaps into the open.

Emilia followed obediently, walking by his side. Had Trethore been any other old man she felt certain she could have fled him, but she had seen the lean muscle that decorated his frame, she had seen him train with the other knights. She knew that even in full ceremonial plate, he would be able to chase her down. Trethore also had a camp of thousands at his beck and call.

No, she would wait. She would bide her time until they reached the holdfast. Then she could flee, lose herself in the thick forests around Gall where her agility and small stature would help her disappear from Trethore's eyes. She would run to the villages where she had grown up and hide there. She could not wait for her Uthiel to save her. Her life, and that of their child, was in her hands. Nobody else was coming to save her. *It's up to me*.

As the plan formed in her mind she allowed herself the slightest of grins.

"It is a small walk from here," said Trethore. "Back to the east. We shall be safe; the lands have been cleansed of the foe. My Order ensure none travel our roads or hide in our forests."

Emilia forced a smile. "I feel safe with you beside me."

The walk took the better part of the early afternoon. They moved from wide dirt roads, worn by both feet and carriage wheel, to thinner tracks where she was forced to duck under low-hanging branches. Trethore would stand beneath those and brace them for her, his eyes very rarely letting her escape their peripherals.

Emilia took in the details of the forest around her, taking note of possible hiding places and looking for landmarks to try to work out where she was. Twice, her dress caught on brambles, and twice she ripped the fabric free with the help of the warrior-priest. Eventually, they arrived on to an overgrown road which had been disused for many years, by the look of the grass growing thickly upon it.

Quickly after, the holdfast came into view. It was a two-storeyed ramshackle cylindrical stone building. Its crenellated battlement was in severe disrepair, the rotting wood of its frame visible through the holes that fallen stones had revealed. The front door had fallen from its top hinge, and the lower one had rusted and rotted to barely hang on like a partially severed sinew.

A scream rent the air. Emilia instinctively moved closer to Trethore. The warrior-priest put a massive hand on her shoulder to calm her. Two knights in white, two men of Trethore's holy Order, walked out from the door and approached them.

"Brother Trethore," said a vicious looking man, his broad shoulders and lean waist exacerbated by his well-fitted armour.

"Tyran," responded Trethore. "How fares the questioning?"

Tyran's eyes lurked upon Emilia for a moment. Emilia immediately felt sickened by his glare.

"We make progress," said the young warrior priest, bluntly.

"Show me."

Tyran nodded and turned away. Emilia was given a light push forward and followed the youth into the holdfast. Immediately, the stench of the place made her gag and cover her nose. It was the stench of death; the reek of pain and the sheer horror in the air itself was palpable.

It took her eyes the most scant moment to accommodate the dank light from the torches. She froze in fear immediately.

Seven warrior priests stood around the walls. They were of varying ages, heights and sizes, but each had the same terrible look to their faces as they stared at her. Emilia felt stripped bare before their eyes. Stripped bare and incredibly afraid, as if she had just walked willingly into the mountain bear's den.

There were various cruel looking items placed upon or at the base of the circular wall. Racks held gleaming blades, both delicate and brutal. Two braziers were alight. Brands and prods with thick handles sat stuffed in them, shafts reddening. Some buckets sat haphazardly around, some full of water, some full of other, darker liquids with thickening scum-surfaces. An armour stand with gleaming plate upon it stood regal amongst the filth.

In the centre of the room was the cause of the smell. A man, or what remained of him, was strapped to the chair. One of his legs had been removed below the knee. The limb sat upon his naked lap, tied with rope to his chest so that each time the man faded and his head fell forward, his face squashed into the dead open meat of the calf. One of his forearms was just a mess of burnt tissue, while the other had had long strips of skin carved from it to reveal the red musculature beneath.

On his remaining attached leg, three of the toes lay severed upon the floor in puddles of his own excrement and blood, the stumps on his foot cauterised. Chunks of his hair had been wrenched from his bloody scalp and one of his eyes was naught more than a burnt socket. Emilia could see the man's smashed teeth through lips so split they looked more like open flesh than the soft pieces the man was born with. His nose had been crushed against his right cheek, the nostrils so malformed the victim was forced to draw breath through his mouth, over the raw nerve endings revealed in his destroyed teeth.

Emilia screamed and covered her eyes, shying away from the sight and into the arms of Trethore, before she realised what she was doing.

"What did he do?" she sobbed. "What could he have done to deserve this?"

Trethore soothed her, patting her on the back. She pulled back, her eyes red with tears and her lunch trying to force its way back through her lips.

"This man isn't sick, is he?" she asked in a mixture of dumb shock and resigned fear.

Trethore smiled coldly. "No, child. He is not sick."

Another of the warrior-priests grabbed her by the shoulders and turned her to once more face the stricken man.

"But you will need to see this, Emilia. It will be for your own good."

Trethore turned from her, leaving her helpless in the powerful grip of whoever had grabbed her. She tried to close her eyes and look away but the man shook her viciously until she looked again.

Hot breath whispered against her ear. "Don't make me hurt your baby before it is born. It may be a traitor's get, but I would still rather not kill an unborn. It may be held against me in the afterlife."

She stiffened.

"Watch. You shall be fine. I know you have seen worse."

Emilia shook her head, but kept watching.

"I haven't," she whispered.

"What?" the man snarled into her earn, the rough of his stubble brushing her neck.

"I have not seen worse. To watch good men fall so far is worse than I have experienced in my life."

Before she could move she felt the tip of a blade break the skin of her back. She squealed in pain and arched her front away. Trethore turned.

"Tyran!" he hissed. "She is not to be hurt. Put down the blade and just hold her there. Make sure she sees."

Emilia saw and heard the blade clang heavily to the table beside her.

Trethore glowered. "Thank you."

Then he turned his attention to the man strapped to the chair. The man had opened his one remaining eye. Emilia noted, with growing horror, it was blue. Then her eyes rolled down his side to a scar about the size of her palm upon his side. A scar she had seen many times – the wolf's head brand.

The man was a Grey Wolf.

Emilia's heart stopped. They were going to kill this man to get her to incriminate Uthiel. She had to get out. She had to get out now. Her eyes began to dart around frantically.

"When did your Order become traitors?" said Trethore, his voice no different to when he would wish Emilia a good morning each day.

The man shook his head, his mouth too much of a ruin to form coherent words. Trethore shrugged.

"Are your lords traitors? All of them? Or perhaps only a few. Give me a name."

The man made more noises, his head down and shaking from side to side, his one good eye squinting and his body slathered in filthy sweat.

"Not in a speaking mood today, my son?"

The man nodded vigorously, moans and incomprehensible cries coming out with increasing urgency as Trethore walked to one of the racks.

"Pity."

Trethore picked up a slim blade from the rack. The man's cries became more and more fervent.

Trethore knelt before them man.

"Armenius does not look kindly on those who will not help His most holy servants in the most holy of works."

The man was shaking unbelievably now, the chair rocking frantically from side to side as he tried to move himself away. Trethore stood once more, then leant back and kicked the man full in the face, sending him sprawling backwards onto the ground. The unfortunate screamed at the impact. The stump of his severed leg pushed up into his chin. Emilia watched in abject horror as a mix of vomit and blood spewed from his mouth to add to the filth on the ground.

Trethore did not speak further. He grabbed the man's still attached ankle in a vice-like grip and, without preamble, skinned the sole of his foot. Emilia could live a thousand years and never forget the victim's scream. It burned her with its rawness. Trethore grabbed the man by the hair and righted him. As the skinned sole planted in the pool of his own waste on the floor, his screaming renewed in its vigour.

Trethore locked eyes with Emilia. His blade lanced out and the man was silent but for a choking gurgle as his lifeblood spilled from the new mouth across his throat. His actual mouth was wide open, as was his one eye, desperately trying for air that would never come. It didn't take long for his body to stop convulsing. The warrior-priest did not break eye contact the entire time.

"Thus the punishment for treachery," said Trethore fiercely.

"Armenius damn him from our afterlife haven," intoned the other warrior priests.

She could take it no more. Emilia reached out with her hand, quick as lightning, grabbed the earlier discarded knife from the table, and slammed it into the man behind her with all of her force. The blade slipped between his mail skirts and lanced into his inner-thigh.

He screamed and grabbed at the wound. Emilia took her chance and ran. A knight near the doorway ran and dived at her. Emilia leapt high and cleared his searching hands. She burst out through the door, leaving a small chunk of skin from her elbow on the rusted and jagged hinge as she powered past, her feet pounding the earth beneath them with all of her desperate energy.

Shouts followed her, but she dared not look back. Not this time. She spotted a path she had eyed off earlier and pumped her arms hard to lend her more speed towards it. Boots hammered heavily against the ground behind her. She could hear the deep and fast breaths of those giving chase. Those sounds were fading. It lent her heart the optimistic power of possible success in her flight.

She cut away from the path and in to the bush, dodging and weaving through trees and tearing through shrubs. She heard someone swear and crash to the ground far behind her. She was going to make it.

A bush moved unnaturally to her right. An arm snaked out and grabbed her hair. Emilia's feet flew out before her as her head was wrenched backwards. As she slammed into the ground, all of the wind flew from her chest and her consciousness fled from her mind.

Emilia woke a short time later, the sky and canopy moving slowly past her above. Immediately she felt the vicious tugs on her hair and screamed out as some of it tore from her scalp. Her fearful eyes darted around as she felt a stick snag the skin of her thigh and tear it. Her body had been stripped of its dress and was being dragged over the ground.

She looked down at her body, her shaking breasts and swollen stomach, the nakedness of her groin and legs. *Oh no, gods save me, no! Not again!*

She screamed. She screamed for Uthiel, for Tarren, for men who could not save her. Then she screamed for Trethore. Even he would be better than what the barbarians would do to her. She screamed and cried.

Trethore's face came into view beside her. Her eyes went wide with shock.

There was no longer even an attempt to hide his true feelings upon his face. All that remained was pure disgust and absolute hatred.

"Emilia, it is time we dropped all pretences. You are not the innocent woman you proclaim to be. I can no longer be the gentle old man who has protected you. You know something of the Wolves. You know a dark secret that could destroy my people. It is time you and I had a proper talk."

Another face came into view. The man was limping heavily and his face was pale. It was Tyran.

She managed to draw breath, but not to scream, before Tyran snarled his rage and his iron shod forearm slammed into her face and her world went dark.

CHAPTER TWENTY

A Secundan blade sizzled through the air above Uthiel's head. The young Grey Wolf ducked and lanced out with his own sword, scoring a glancing hit against the greave of the Black Wolf. His mind was afire, rage and control each doing their best to claim him in the whirlwind combat.

All around the two combatants was anarchy. Men in their thousands butchered each other without remorse amongst the rotting forest of innocent bodies upon trestles. Smoke rose to the sky along with the cacophony of battle. Imonetia burned once more.

They had fought for three days and three nights, pushing the barbarians further and further into the great city of the sand lords. Street by street, house by house, they had pushed them back, ever under the gaze of whichever rotting eyes the crows had left.

Uthiel parried his foe's blade to a dead stop with one sword and attempted to smash it from the man's grasp with his other. The edge of the Black Wolf's shield interjected itself and Uthiel spun away.

A barbarian reared up to attack Uthiel. Once more one of his Shields saved him. Theon hammered the man to the ground, lancing his blade through a tattooed chest. More of Uthiel's soldiers pushed past him, giving him a moment's respite. Theon nodded to his captain before turning in to the path of an arrow to deflect it from his armour.

Uthiel could see his Shield torn inside. Between his duty as a brother, subordinate, member of the Grey Wolves, and what he believed was right in this world under the sight of Armenius. What Uthiel had told Theon, Tarren and Pavel had shattered their perception of the simplicity of this campaign.

What he had told them would challenge their every ideology and loyalty. He was asking them to take his side and rebel against their commanders. He was asking them to betray the Order's commanders and the lord steward himself, so that they may do what would be deemed right in Armenius' eyes. Uthiel was asking them to dishonour themselves in this life, so that they may go to the next with honour.

It was a hard decision for each man, and one he would have to make for himself. Uthiel had not had enough time to speak fully with the three for the Lord Ryun had stormed up to the breach and barked at Uthiel to get his men moving further into the city. Uthiel could not have been sure, but there was a spark of annoyance in the lord general's tone at seeing him still alive.

The Black Wolf and the battle found him once more and a sword clanged from his pauldron and a shoulder barge sent Uthiel flying to the ground. He parried two thrusts at his head before Pavel slammed his blade into the Black Wolf's back, sending the man rolling away with a deep depression in the back of his cuirass. Pavel looked down to Uthiel for a moment, a pause in his eyes, before looking up and decapitating a charging barbarian.

Uthiel pushed himself to his feet.

Concentrate.

The word came to him as he felt the reinvigorating burning of the talisman between his collarbones. Looking around, he spied the Black Wolf as he felled a spear-wielding man of the Fifth.

Kill him. Offer me his blood. Sacrifice him to me.

A darker voice, ever backgrounded with a malicious chuckle, spoke this time and his eyes began to cloud over red. His heart began to hammer and his feet began to drag him towards his foe. Uthiel stopped and shook his head.

No.

He stopped himself. The haze cleared, the burning on his chest grew stronger as his mind found combat clarity once more. He had only a moment to enjoy the feeling as the Black Wolf charged at him.

Uthiel launched himself at the man and they exchanged blows at a furious rate. Sweat poured down his helmetless face as time and time again he thwarted strikes that would have seen him cleaved and bloodied upon the floor, and then had his own ripostes brought to shuddering halts in return.

Back and forth the two men went, each the equal skill of the other. Both were the product of the same school of combat. Most likely Uthiel had been taught the blade by the men this bastard had once called 'brother'.

Finally Uthiel's blade breached his foe's slowing defences, hammering the helm from the man's head. The Black Wolf tried to turn and duck away in order to tear his helm from his helmet, but Uthiel followed through and stabbed the man through the back of his leg. The Black Wolf cried out and fell to a knee.

Uthiel kicked out and crunched his heavy boot into the man's sword wielding hand, sending the blade cartwheeling to the ground. Before Uthiel could make the kill, three feet of single edged blade lanced through the man's throat. The Black Wolf's helmless head stared up at Uthiel, his eyes wide open in shock.

Pavel stood behind him, his blade arm still outstretched.

"Thank you, brother," said Uthiel.

Pavel nodded, withdrew his sword and turned back to the melee.

The Black Wolf was on his knees, slowly drowning in his own blood. Uthiel cut his head horizontally in half without hesitation. He looked down at the man's sword. It was the standard, straight-edged blade of the rank and file knight. He thought back to something he remembered hearing somewhere. Something about the swords of Secunda slaying her children.

It was standing over his defeated foe that the Lord Ryun found him with what remained of his company.

"Captain Caellar!" roared the lord general. "Is this the second time I must ask you to take your men and pursue the foe? Must I force you to glory?"

Uthiel looked at his lord general. He was tired. Exhausted. His armour was dented and covered in blood. One of his eyes was swollen half shut and he had yet another cut to add to his already impressive collection on his face. The knights with the Lord General Ryun, including his son's own company, were fresh with naught but splashes of red upon their boots. A few companies of the Fifth were also with him. Many looked at the blood soaked visage of Uthiel with more than a little fear and awe.

Uthiel looked at his own knights. He knew of seven he had seen fall. Dead or wounded, he did not know. If more had been slain where he did not see, he was unsure; but only nine stood with him now. Of the three companies of the Fifth who had followed him in to the breach, perhaps a company worth of them, perhaps a little more, stood with him in a ragged group now.

Uthiel spat a fat wad of his own blood from a split lip onto the ground.

"Your men look fresh, why don't you go taste a little of the glory and let me tend to the wounds of mine own."

It was not a question or request. Uthiel was ordering his lord general.

Beside him, Theon gasped. "Brother—"

Ryun exploded. "You would order your masters around as such? You would demand that other sons of Secunda should fall because your cowardice would not see you fight?"

Uthiel shook his head and laughed. It was a dark laugh, with little humour. He looked down at the tattered remains of his grey tabard and the hundreds of scores and dents and rents that lined his own steel skin.

"If my brothers are too afraid to get their hands dirty, perhaps they should give their fresh armour to those who need it most. Then you may sit back and watch those Armenius favours walk back into the fires of battle."

Ryun and the men around him were incredulous. Uthiel heard swords drawn and oaths sworn. He could do naught but smile: his patience was at an end. He heard some of his men move to his side and draw their blades.

Uthiel eyed off the lord general. The man was old, even weak from walking around the battle for three days and three nights. Uthiel knew in his warrior's soul that he could defeat the man. The twenty knights and three hundred men of the Fifth around him would be another matter. Once more he heard the dark chuckle in the back of his mind. Once more he felt his hunger for blood rising. He almost welcomed the feeling this time.

Uthiel took a step forward, flicking his swords through a quick rotation to allow the blood to fan away from them. He felt his senses heighten, even hearing the patter of the blood as it struck the plate of the knights behind him. Allowing one arm to hang lazily behind him he stood side on and brought the other up to point directly at Lord General Ryun.

"I challenge—" Uthiel never got any further.

"Brothers! What is this madness?" roared the voice of the first captain.

Uthiel snapped his head around. Immediately his senses returned, dulled by exhaustion but heightened by a spike of fear. *Is this what I want, deep down in my soul? Did I ache for the bloodletting, for the crimson of my brothers and countrymen?*

He brought his sword down and turned to see Solanthur at the head of his knights and a thousand men of the Fifth. He straightened himself before the man. Solanthur's gaze landed on the thunderous face of the lord general.

"Lord general, the barbarians have fled the city. The king's guards must be quickly pushed onto the plain to chase them down and slay as many as possible. We need fresh men searching the outer suburbs of the city main, down to the rear gate. We need those men, your men, now."

The lord general kept trying to stare down Uthiel. Uthiel huffed, spat at his lord's feet, and turned back to his men.

"Come, brothers, let us anticipate the lord general's orders and move to the rear gate," he said scornfully.

Around him, the nine brothers who could fight stood and began to move with him. The hundred-odd men of the Fifth seemed indecisive. Uthiel turned to them.

"Any of the men of the Fifth who fought with me these last three days has earned the title of 'brother' more so than some of the men wearing holy plate. Let us go."

Those men stood taller for a moment, and then wearily followed him under the baleful glares of Ryun and the knights around him.

Solanthur stood stock still, watching the scene.

"Lord general? I need fresh troops. I need them now. Uthiel and his men have been on the front lines since the start. It would be tactically sound to give them rest and allow fresher troops to take the task of making certain the cleansing is done completely. Give me your son's company. Swap your companies of the Fifth for ones who have seen battle," insisted Solanthur.

The lord general finally gave Solanthur his attention.

"Swap two companies out. My son and his men stay with me. You have command of the king's guards, set them to task as you see fit," he snapped before turning and walking away with his men in tow.

"And what of Uthiel's men?" said Solanthur. "They must be rested."

Ryun turned and stormed back over to Solanthur.

"He stays in the van. At all times. I don't care about the men around him but that little bastard stays in the van until he earns his glory or I watch the flames take his body to be judged as harshly as possible by our Eternal Lord," snarled the lord general with such poison that Solanthur took a step back.

Ryun followed him forward a step.

"We march for Mother Secunda at sunup in two-days' time. Push the men through this afternoon. Cleanse the city as best we can. My son stays to command Imonetia in my stead with his knights and five companies of the Fifth. They shall finish the job our precious Uthiel shall fail to do before we march."

Ryun stormed away. Solanthur swallowed hard. His world of duty and honour was becoming very difficult to uphold. The greatest hero of the land felt true, non-combatable fear for the first time in his life. This was no battle he could control or win. His influence may have little to no effect.

He'd seen the way the men of the Fifth, and indeed some of his own knights, had looked at Uthiel. There was awe and respect in those eyes. Uthiel was a captain to follow to Death's cold embrace. He'd watched the way Theon and Pavel had thrown themselves to the defence of their captain in the battles in the past three days. Their respect was hard to win.

He also saw the way the lord general had been ensuring every bloody task was set upon Uthiel and his men. Darian's company had not been reinforced, nor had the other two who had stormed the breach. Solanthur looked at his own men. Already four reserve companies had been folded into the ten companies that followed him. His men were fresh. Not so Uthiel's ragged band — their blood and loss earning them only disfavour by proxy.

Solanthur shuddered at the thought of the potential schism he may very soon have to pick a side in.

The horse stumbled a moment and Lord Pomen was nearly tossed from his saddle. His manservant reached up and steadied him with strong, sure hands. Pomen smiled his thanks and then erupted into a coughing fit. He could almost feel the thick chunks of his lungs being torn from within through the white pain. He most certainly could taste and feel them as he vomited them onto the ground.

It took some time before he could lift the reins to urge the horse forward once more. The horse, an old mare, supple and obedient and well past her prime, plodded along slowly enough for Grullen to walk beside and support his master. Pomen's eyes, so quickly receding in their clarity during his illness, worked hard and strained to focus on the command tent.

Pomen had a plan.

It would undoubtedly cause the greatest civil war of the age and the deaths of tens of thousands. It mattered not, civil war was already upon the Lands of the Light, there were just factions who did not know it yet. The barbarians had spent their wrath in Gall and north of it and were, or would quickly be, defeated and it was now time for the lands west of the frontier to go to war with each other.

There was nothing Pomen could do about it. His lord steward had set plans in motion that were like the unstoppable slide of a glacier. Imonetia would soon belong to the steward. Pomen feared Thomak would then push forward across all fronts, ensuring the kingdoms of the south did likewise, then he would march south with whatever men he had left and take their capitals while letting the tribes of the Black Lands whither down undersupplied forces.

Within the year Thomak would have Lemug and Pandur in the south, Secunda in the west, Imonetia in the north, Gall in the centre, and Mother Secunda in the east. Thomak would be the first emperor of the realm in five thousand years. If the king awoke from his coma, would the lord steward be willing to hand his empire over to his liege?

Pomen had decided he needed to tell the Lemugians and the Pandurs. Perhaps he could stay their advance. Perhaps they could defend their lands. Perhaps they could prevent tyranny on the grandest of scales. Pomen hoped so.

Though undoubtedly his adopted nephew would have been slain by one of the Ryuns by now, and he had not seen Uthiel's woman in days, Pomen resolved to not leave the world a worse place than he had found it. In his soul he felt Armenius would be proud of him. When he went to be judged by his god, in a few days' or weeks' time, he would not have cowardly inaction staining his honour.

Pomen shook his head.

Daydreaming again. Come on, you old bastard, hold together for just a few more days.

He wiped a hand across his nose as he looked around to get his bearings. There was blood on his sleeve and probably across his face but he cared not for it. He coughed wetly, but for once didn't go into a fit. He was beside the command tent. There were guards all around. Some watched him but most of them dismissed him.

He dismounted with the help of his manservant, the weight of his own body upon his legs almost too much for him to bear. His hip flared with pain as it touched down and he grimaced. Grullen put an arm under his shoulder and helped him stand.

"In there," was all Pomen could manage as he pointed a bony claw at the door of the tent.

Grullen helped him limp to the flap. Two door guards crossed a pair of barb-headed pikes to block his path.

Pomen fixed them with a glare.

"Do your senses leave you? Do you not know who I am?"

One of the guards fixed him with a glare. "You are the Lord Pomen. By order of the lord steward, you may not enter this tent under any circumstance."

Pomen saw the hardness in the glare. There would be no argument to get himself in. He changed tact immediately.

"Brother, you would leave an old lord bereft of his walking cane? Look at me, having to put my weight on my poor manservant."

Pomen allowed his form to sag a little further to exemplify the fact.

"I have ever served the Grey Wolves. Over half a century of battle! Do not leave me the indignity of my last few—"

A few well-timed coughs spat from his mouth, followed by some he had not planned and a long string of red-black drool dripping from his chin.

"—days being unable to walk unaided."

There was a hint of pity in the man's eye. Just a hint. Pomen had him.

"I cannot allow you to pass, venerated lord," said the knight, new respect finding its way into his voice.

Pomen frowned, pretending to be thinking long and hard.

"What of my manservant? I know you would get it for me, brother, but you are at your post on duty. Grullen, here, is sure he knows where it was left and will be in and out in moments."

The guard thought for a while, eyeing off Grullen. Grullen was suitably meek in his appearance.

The guard stood aside. "Be quick."

Grullen ran inside and was back out, walking stick in hand, a short while later. There was a triumphant look upon his face.

"Here it is, my lord. I have it for you."

Pomen smiled and reached out to take the cane, noting the slight bulge under Grullen's shirt. He turned to the guard.

"Thank you, brother. I pray you be at the feast to celebrate my life. You have eased the mind a little for my passing."

The knight smiled genuinely and nodded, but said no more.

Pomen turned and hobbled back to his horse. Grullen helped him climb into the saddle. Together, they walked away in silence until they reached Pomen's tent. As they entered, Pomen struck up an idle conversation.

"The black sable shirt to dine in tonight please, my friend."

"Yes lord, will that be warm enough?"

"Probably not, but I am not long for this world, and I will look my best for the time I have left."

"Will you be wanting matching leggings?" asked Grullen as he tied the tent flap closed.

"I feel all black may be a bit to early, I am not dead yet!" said Pomen, holding out his hand.

"Of course my lord, something more colourful?" responded Grullen as he pulled out the scroll from beneath his shirt and passed it on to Pomen.

Pomen unravelled the scroll, looking around for any shadows against the tent wall before laying his eyes upon its contents. He smiled. It was perfect. Exactly what he needed.

He held proof of Thomak's plan in all of its horrifying detail.

"Yes, my friend, that would be wonderful."

Pomen tightly wrapped the scroll and snuck it into the join where his pauldron overlapped his cuirass on his armour stand.

"That would be wonderful indeed, for I feel tonight may be my last opportunity to dress so."

CHAPTER TWENTY-ONE

Captain Ryun stood atop the west-facing battlements of the keep in the centre of the mighty Imonetian capital city. In the distance he could see the column led by his father trailing off towards the horizon. They marched for the frontier, and, if he was being honest with himself, he was happy to be left behind.

Let men like Uthiel Caellar do the dying for the false glories of the battlefield. In the end it would mean nothing. He would either be bested in combat, or one day be too old to wield a blade with any usefulness. Ryun would relish that day.

From his seat in Imonetia, where he would have many sons and a gorgeous young wife, he would laugh as old cripples like Uthiel came begging to him. He licked his lips and chuckled at the thought. *Where will their past glories be then?*

He looked down from the horizon. Those men were almost a day gone, and he had more pressing matters requiring his attention. He was the lord of an entire land now! *Lord Ryun. Warden of the north.*

Below in the city streets, his brothers supervised the five hundred men of the Fifth he had been left with as they dismantled the horrid sacrifice the barbarians had left. Huge fires roared out of open pits dug into the hard-packed dirt of

Imonetia's streets. Already, in the day since his father had given him lordship of these lands, they had burned thousands, perhaps tens of thousands.

The smell of burnt bone and meat was rank in the air, and Ryun had taken to holding a scented handkerchief to sniff at whenever the desert winds blew the stench his way. It would take many weeks before they could all be burned. He imagined it would take many months before the smell left also.

"My lord," came the voice of one of his knights.

He turned and raised an eyebrow, signalling the man to speak with a quick flick of his hand.

"My lord, we have found something of interest," said the knight. "An aqueduct, running beneath the city. The burning pit diggers dug right in to one. We have a supply of fresh water without having to send men to the river with barrels."

Ryun smiled, this was good news. No more wasted manpower.

"Send a rider out after the last train we sent. Bring them back. Get those men burning bodies. I want this city cleansed before the heat really starts."

The knight nodded and bowed his head. "As you command, my lord."

Ryun turned back to watch his city being rebuilt. Alongside the soldiers clearing bodies and trestles there were camp followers who had also stayed behind to build a new life. Work teams of stonemasons fashioned fresh stone for the gap in the wall the Secundans had attacked through. He could see houses being rebuilt by carpenters and cook fires streaming long skyward trails of smoke as a small group of women started a cookhouse.

He watched a scantily clad woman, some five or six streets away, lead a man into a small house. Ryun chuckled. *The oldest services are often the ones first to rear their heads.*

At last he'd had enough of the smell and withdrew within the keep of his newly acquisitioned palace. Inside, four of his men awaited him. They were the men he had designated his personal bodyguards. They were his best, veterans tested in battle for many years.

Two stood at the doors of his bedchambers.

"Has she arrived?" asked Ryun, licking his lips greedily.

One of the men at his door simply nodded and turned, his arm reaching out to open the door.

Ryun walked in. She stood there before him. A see-through shift clung to her figure from her shoulders to her ankles. The young new lord found arousal quickly. She was young, pretty, and had a look about her that said she would please him immensely.

"Your name?"

She made to reply, but Lord Ryun lifted his hand.

"It matters not."

He watched her for a moment, admired her form, her beauty, enjoyed the way her cheeks flushed as he let the silence grow ever longer and just stared.

"Your dress."

She slipped her thumbs under the shoulder straps and slipped them off. The material floated down and pooled around her feet. Long legs daintily stepped from the light cloth, towards his bed. The bed was covered in gaudy Imonetian silks. *I shall have to change those.*

"On the bed."

The girl took a few steps backwards and lay back. Ryun unbuckled his pants and pulled his shirt awkwardly over his head.

"Hands and knees, turn away from me."

She obeyed while he placed a knee on to the sheets. *Soft. Silky. Marvellous. I shall be keeping these sheets. Perhaps a little tailoring to my taste is all that is required.*

He smiled as he reached out a hand to touch her.

"I'm going to enjoy you."

Captain Ryun awoke while the torches burned low upon his walls. By his side the girl lay curled up, facing away from him, beneath the covers. He pulled down the covers a little and could see the bruises his attentions had left across her flesh. She breathed evenly, fast asleep.

Ryun stood and reached under the bed to grab the chamber pot. He walked out on to the bedroom balcony and leant against the battlement as he relieved himself. He breathed a long sigh of release. On the horizon the sun was making itself known, providing a golden-orange line between the night sky and the shadowed lands.

My first night as a lord. Not a bad one. He shook himself dry, wincing a little at his tenderness. *Not a bad night at all.*

He was about to turn back when he noticed movement. About six blocks away a man and a woman were dragging something out of a small house. Ryun could only just make them out in the distance. The darkness hid them well but some of the corpse fires still raged into the night and the flickering flames lent enough light for him to see.

He shrugged his shoulders. *Probably just another body for the fire pits.*

Thinking no more of it, he turned and walked back in to the bedroom. The girl had rolled and pulled the sheet down in her sleep. Ryun felt himself harden once more. The door burst open. One of his guards ran in to the room. The girl sat upright, eyes wide with confusion and fear.

"My lord!" exclaimed the knight.

"What is it?" snapped Ryun.

"Seventeen night patrolmen have not checked in to exchange with the dawn shift. I fear we are not alone in this city."

"Barbarians?"

"Unlikely, lord. More likely Imonetians come out from hiding in the desert to try and reclaim their city."

"Insolent bastards!" yelled Ryun, his face reddening with anger. "Armour and all the men you can rouse. Immediately! I'll show these bastards what it means to mess with a lord of Secunda!"

He heard a noise behind him. The girl was getting dressed.

"No! You stay here. I'm going to need something to cheer me up after I've finished with this."

Ryun held out his arms as one of his manservants ran in and began to help him into his armour. Outside, he could hear his men shouting and gathering soldiers to the palace keep. *Ungrateful bastards! I'll show them! I am the lord of Imonetia by rights and I will get the respect of these people if I have to hang, draw, and quarter it out of every one of them!*

It was not long until it was done. Before he left the room he looked back at his whore.

"Whatever you are normally paid by the men per week, double it and lie with no other. You are mine."

He didn't bother to wait for her reaction, but turned to his waiting bodyguards and followed them out of the palace and in to the keep where around forty men had assembled before a red faced brother Grey Wolf. The air was rank with fear.

"Where are the rest of my men?" stormed Ryun.

The knight looked at him. His face said it all. It was disbelief. Complete and utter disbelief.

"Gone. No trace."

Ryun stared at him until the knight looked away.

"That is ridiculous," said the lord. "These men will be enough to get started. Let us move out in to the city and find the rest."

One of his bodyguards reached out and placed a hand on his pauldron.

"My lord, we need to get you back inside. You need to be safe. Let the men conduct the search."

Ryun battered the hand away. "No! I will not hide in fear! This is my city! Mine!"

He marched into the loose group of soldiers and began to push through them on his way to the gate. The men let him go. Nobody followed him. Even his bodyguards lagged behind. He walked up the to gatehouse of the keep and kicked the counterweight lever. The iron shod door shot up.

He stood at the dark opening to the city.

"See? No ghosts. No ghouls. No Imonetians, and no bastard barbarians. Now grow a spine and help men find the other men!"

Ryun's voice was by now a heady mixture of hysteria, fear, and indignant anger. His bodyguards followed him first, and then the rest began to trickle after him. Ryun smiled and walked out of the keep walls that enclosed the palace.

He marched his men aimlessly through the streets while the sun began to make its way up. He'd call out snap commands and his men would obey, kicking down the doors to houses and storming through them. At first he sent in ten man groups, but as he gained confidence, Ryun split them in to smaller and smaller groups to search more and more houses.

He marched through his city, pointing left, pointing right, and barking out more orders as the sun reached its pinnacle above. He felt every inch the lord. He had made it through Grey Wolf initiation. He had become a captain under his father's eye. He was now a lord and commander of a city and its surrounding lands. There were women begging for his attentions back in his bed chambers. *By Armenius, this is what I was born for!*

"Lord!" one of his bodyguards yelled at him.

Ryun stopped. Evidently the man had been shouting at him for some time. He looked around, blinking a few times to clear his thoughts. Two bodyguards. Twelve soldiers. He didn't recognise the buildings. Where was he?

"Where are they?"

The bodyguard looked at him blankly. "Never returned, lord."

"Why did you not go in after them?"

"You did not wait for them, lord. I could not stop you."

"You would blame me?" Ryun drew his sword.

The bodyguard took a step back. A scream rent the air. The men of the Fifth looked to each other, their feet already shuffling away.

Ryun pointed his blade at them. "Don't you—"

It was too late. The men fled in to the city. Ryun was left standing with his two bodyguards. There was a clash of steel a couple of streets over. He heard screams. Ryun kept turning in circles, backing away in random directions. His bodyguards tried desperately to keep track of, and close to, him while watching the shadows at the same time.

All of a sudden, without warning, one of them was gone in a clattering of armour and feet. Only a few drops of blood remained on the ground to show he was ever there. His second bodyguard chased a few steps around a corner. Nothing.

Ryun began to weep. The bodyguard walked over to him, sword up, eyes both fearful and wary. Ryun turned from him as the guard passed the open door of a building.

As he looked away he heard the unmistakeable sound of steel shearing through steel. He turned.

His last guard stood transfixed, four feet of serrated dark-steel sword protruding from the centre of his chest. Blood bubbled from the man's mouth as his life slipped away. Behind the bodyguard, from the shadows, an immense figure in a horrible parody of Secundan armour walked out. The beast was head and shoulders above the guard, filling the doorway completely. The sword lowered and the body was kicked from the sword.

Ryun fell to his knees and pissed himself, the last vestiges of his courage evacuating with the contents of his bladder.

The monster took two steps towards him. That immense serrated sword, dark as coal and dripping with Secundan blood, swept up towards the sky, as if the man was pointing at the sun above.

The beast spoke, his voice reverberating like a collapsing mountain within Ryun's chest.

"For you, Zhar T'Hur. The blood of a weakling empire for you, my Red Father!"

The sword swept down.

Serrated Secundan steel met Jotel's long tongue and cut a little way in. Not enough to split the muscle, but enough to draw blood. Fresh crimson mixed with the clotting viscera of the young knight upon the black steel. He withdrew his tongue and swallowed, revelling in the power that came with the metallic taste. He enjoyed the mixing of his own life with that of his fallen foe as a gift to Zhar T'Hur.

He could feel the touch of the god upon his shoulders. Kael had failed, drawing the Red Father's eye away from Imonetia for a plot that eventuated nothing. Now Jotel was one of three remaining Black Wolves. He was one of three men with the ability to bring their god, a god of blood and slaughter, to walk these lands. He was one of three men capable enough to lead the thousands of barbarians he had ordered hidden in the sewers and aqueducts beneath the city in the trap he had set for the Secundans.

They would never see this coming.

Jotel would swarm over their camp from behind, striking at night when they were off guard, hammering home his advantage until he could pile the bodies of his erstwhile brothers and their soldiers in a mountain a hundred high to honour the Red Father. From there, upon that pinnacle of his proven martial might, he would call for Zhar T'Hur's favour.

No. He would *demand* it.

His god could not refuse him this time. This time he would not be able to look away. Jotel had found the champion of the light. He had seen him, from the very balcony from which he had seen the coward lying slain at his feet come from this morning. He had watched the knight take the breach in the wall. He had watched the man butcher and kill with unbelievable speed and skill, his pair of swords carving their way into Jotel's memory.

Three days later, as he had committed the last of his more expendable barbarian forces and wished a loyal brother a good death, he had seen the same man stand up to a lord general of his old, weak Order. He respected the man and his fortitude and his skill and savagery in combat. Were the situation any different, he would try to turn him away from the Lands of the Light.

But this man was to be his ultimate sacrifice, his final offering in blood and martial prowess. He would lead his forces in pursuit of the Secundans and he would crush them. In the midst of this battle he would find this champion of the light and he would challenge him atop the bodies of fallen, worthless barbarians and his own countrymen. He knew Armenius would favour this man. Zhar T'Hur would favour Jotel and together they would crush the light from these lands.

He had been marked by the shamans, cut his own flesh, and ripped the life from countless men and women to slake His thirst. He salivated at the possibilities of what was to come.

"Brothers!" he shouted.

Immediately the last two Black Wolves walked towards him.

"Rouse the horde. We move at dusk."

His brothers nodded to him and turned away. They shouted to the buildings around them. Barbarians began to appear. First came the thousand that had partaken in the slaughter of the lord and his men, then, more began to climb from beneath the city. They were Jotel's last elites, the last and best of the savages he had brought across the frontier with him in to Imonetia. They were covered in filth, soaked in water, and they were hungry for war.

Each man carried his own provisions: a sack of water and a separate sack of dried and plundered food tied to their belts. There would be no slow moving train. Each man carried enough for two, maybe three days. That was all the time that Jotel would need them for.

Jotel and his brothers marched down the main street to the eastern gate, the horde growing larger and larger by the moment behind them. He knew he would have almost seven thousand axe-wielding men at his back by the time they marched. Seven thousand would be enough. He'd counted the Secundans at more than half of that, but not at two-thirds. He had almost a two to one advantage, plus the element of surprise.

It would be more than enough to wipe out the Secundans. More than enough to create an immense altar of slaughter he could climb up. More than enough to welcome his god into his body and become the greatest and most terrible champion these lands had ever seen.

Klyra watched them go from the safety of the balcony door. In their thousands they had spewed from beneath the city, adding the stench of their unclean bodies to the reek of burning and still-decaying corpses.

Her body ached from the young Lord Ryun's rough rutting. Her pale skin would be bruised for many days before it cleared once more. She thanked Armenius that none of the barbarians had found her. She'd heard some of the stories to come out of Gall. Heard them from people she knew that knew survivors of the sacrifice there. She'd seen the rotting corpses outside.

That would not happen to her. Klyra walked out on to the balcony and watched the horde from afar. She was too far away and too deep in evening shadow to be seen now.

Looking down she saw her would-be employer. His body had been carved into seven different pieces. He lay in a small pile of chunks that held up one of his severed arms, bent fingers pointing to the sky.

She had become accustomed to such things. She'd seen the corpse pits after battles. She'd stitched gashes and bandaged amputations. She'd earned her keep a thousand times and more in both the apothecary tents and on her back allowing men in their hundreds to enjoy her.

She looked around at the city for a moment. Many would have been cowed. She did not feel so. There wasn't a person nearby who could hurt her. She owned a city by the right of being the only person alive in it. There would be months, maybe years of food stored in the granaries. She smiled sadly at her haven.

The realm of Imonetia was dead, and Klyra would be the last beat of its heart.

CHAPTER TWENTY-TWO

A hot, sandblasting wind had ripped down from the north since early morning, scoring bare flesh and parching mouths. Uthiel trudged forwards through the storm, a scarf wrapped around his face and his recovered shield strapped over his back. He looked side to side and could see most of his men, as well as most of Darian's and the other two brutalised companies that had now fallen under his command.

He stopped and waved the men to trudge further on, and took a moment to pull down his scarf and take a sip from his water. He stared malevolently back in the direction where the sand storm blotted out the following column.

That his position was perilous was beyond obvious. He had a little over a hundred men who would stand by him in the coming schism. A hundred of his men could do little versus the thousands still at the beck and call of the corrupt lord general. He swore out loud. That same lord general was doing a very good job of keeping him away from the rest of the column, away from speaking with the men who may have come over to his cause.

Ryun had cunning. There was no doubt to it. The man knew how to run an army where dissent was manifesting.

Another battle or two, without having his men reinforced, and Uthiel would fall. Of this he had no doubt. He would simply run out of men to hold the line and he would be overwhelmed.

He knew how Ryun would play it once he fell. Uthiel would be the glorious fallen hero. Ryun could not discredit him, could not call him traitor or coward. Too many had seen his heroism and combat prowess for such a lie to stick. But if he fell, Uthiel's legend would do his dead husk no more good while it would benefit Ryun in pulling this fracturing army back together.

Uthiel smiled. Were he not the focus of Ryun's rage, he imagined he could quite admire the lord general's acumen. He spat as he began to make the outline of the approaching column out, and his anger railed at its chains. He could see a man atop a tall stallion surrounded by knights.

Ryun.

A time was coming. Not today, though perhaps tomorrow or the day after. But a time was coming when Uthiel would have to challenge the lord general, when brother would draw upon brother. Crossbows would be levelled and a single volley would rip through either side before — *fratricide*.

There was no other word for it. Uthiel had witnessed it. He'd committed it. He was no stranger to the slaying of his oath brothers. But now it was the end of the road. Few men in holy plate would walk from this fight. Uthiel just needed to pick his time and place.

If he could not win the Fifth, then he needed to remove them from the equation before they could intervene. He needed a lighting coup. The blood of Ryun and whoever locked shield beside the lord general would need to be slain upon the ground before any of the Fifth had a chance to intervene.

Uthiel took a deep breath and turned away.

Patience.

Challenge him now!

Uthiel shook his head. The two different voices were becoming more insistent.

As he resumed walking, quickly catching up to his men, he allowed his mind to wander. He thought of Armenius and wondered how many times in history two men with opposing goals had thought themselves the benefactor of the same god's favour?

Perhaps I am wrong? Perhaps I am the one with treachery staining my soul.

Uthiel looked up to see if he could see the sky through the swirling sands. Thick tinges of blue cut through the dark gold drifts. He smiled.

Do I have your favour, my Eternal Lord?

Only a chuckle answered him within his head as he felt a small ache begin under his eyes. The headaches had been growing worse. Whenever he thought of his Eternal Lord they would come, like the aftermath of a fist fight. They would grow worse, and then they would disappear. Often he would feel the warmth of the talisman against his chest as the pain receded. It would comfort him, but his mind ached and his soul felt weary.

Uthiel rolled his shoulders and massaged his eyes, enjoying the pressure of his hands upon them.

Am I in the right?

The young captain nodded to himself, thinking of what his father would have said. He knew, though he had never asked the man the question.

Secunda was here to protect the Lands of the Light, assist and defend her allies, as her allies had defended her people four centuries ago.

She was not birthed by a god to become a tyrant.

To the allies of Secunda,

You are in the gravest of danger.

The Lord Steward Thomak moves to rule the Lands of Light and Dark. He moves to unify the realm under his own hand. He moves to deceive and take that which belongs to you and a hundred generations of your forefathers by force of arms while you march away from your homes to his plans to conquer the Black Lands.

I beg you, heed my words. Thomak has planned the downfall of Lemug and Pandur. Gall and Imonetia already kneel at his feet. He owns them in all but appropriate title. His 'stewardship' is a horrid lie —a lie our lands shall wake up from only when he slays our dying king and assumes the mantle of emperor.

Do not allow your men to move from your lands. Barricade your roads and defend your cities. I say this without false pride: do not engage the Orders in open field battle. The shield walls will crush you. Stay in your cities.

While it hurts me to reveal this to you, Secunda is at the extent of its manpower and supplies. There are few more men to be drawn from the mines and fields and towns. The granaries will begin to run dry within the year. Thomak will not be able to maintain sieges, and hold on to his lands won during this campaign at the same time. His plan relies on you obeying him and marching forth.

Time, years, a decade perhaps at most, will replenish his granaries. Two decades will replenish his manpower with three to five generations of fresh young men yearning for the glory of their fathers.

Then he will be at your door once more. Whether terms shall assuage him, or you shall find yourself bending the knee to avoid the scale of bloodshed he would bring to your lands, or you find a way to defend yourselves from the forces of the three major kingdoms and whatever support he draws from the Black Lands, is up to you.

By that time I shall no longer be able to help you. As you read this, it is doubtful that I still draw breath.

May Armenius be with you.

And may He forgive me this transgression against my people,

Lord Hubritan Illiar Pomen,
Grey Wolf to my death.

Pomen finished the letter and dropped the quill as if his bony hands could not bring themselves to touch it once more. He sat back and read over the parchment. His scrawl was not the easiest to read, but it was legible. He looked up to Grullen. His man nodded.

Pomen folded the letter.

"My friend, the wax, if you please."

His manservant tilted a stick of grey-dyed sealing wax into the flame of a small candle. Fat molten blobs fell upon the letter and began to dry. Pomen grabbed an iron seal and pressed into the wax. Without warning he coughed. He tried to cover his mouth but he was too late. Small red, black, and dark yellow specks flew onto the white parchment.

Pomen swore and raised his hand to scrunch up the paper. Grullen reached out and held his hand back.

"It shall add to the urgency of the message, my lord."

Pomen stared at it for a while.

Then he nodded.

"True."

He turned and looked up to Grullen.

"My friend I am not long for this world—"

"A sad piece of knowledge for all of us, I assure you," came a cruel voice.

Thomak walked in through the tent flap. A Grey Wolf entered either side of him to create a menacing trio. The lord general sneered at them openly. Pomen started coughing again.

"Silence!" yelled Thomak. "I tire of you and your illness!"

Grullen moved to help Pomen, leaning down and shifting the letter to place some water upon the table before his master. Thomak gave one of his knights a look. The burly Grey Wolf stepped forward, grabbed Grullen by the shirt and dragged him out of the tent.

Grullen cried out and looked to his lord. Pomen just shook his head as the manservant disappeared.

Thomak leered. Pomen took a deep breath as the lord steward reached down and grabbed his letter from the desk. Thomak ripped off the seal and opened the letter and began to read its contents.

"Lord Pomen, I had thought you better than this. I had thought you a loyal Secundan. This is no way to end your career. Though this will be the way you end your life. As —"

The lord steward stopped. He dropped the letter on the ground and stepped upon it, twisting his boot to grind it into the hard ground and smudge the ink. Pomen strained to look at it but his eyes would not focus as age and a hammering heart took their toll.

Thomak's eyes narrowed. No words were spoken but Pomen knew his life was now measured in hours. The lord steward had played his hand and lost somehow, else Pomen would have been dragged out to be hung, drawn, and quartered by now. Thomak growled and stormed out. But the man would be back.

Pomen bent down and picked up the ruined parchment from the dirt floor.

To the lords of the Grey Wolves and any family I may have,

This is my last testament and will. I have some coin collected from a lifetime of service, as well as some arms and armour I have commissioned. These I bequeath to my adopted nephew, Uthiel Caellar, should he survive to claim it.

Should he pass—

Pomen chuckled. *Grullen.*

The lord steward had no evidence to damn Pomen in the eyes of the lords of the other Orders. He'd nothing substantial to show them at all. Grullen's quick hands and mind had seen to that. Thomak could make an initiate, or perhaps a rank and file brother disappear, but not the Lord Pomen. Pomen knew that, for once, his age had saved him. Too many people knew of him for him to simply disappear.

One of two things would now happen before Pomen had a chance to see anyone who may support him, face to face.

Thomak would fabricate evidence against him. His seal was not hard to replicate. His scrawl was similar to so many men who had been taught by the same teachers. He would be dragged out in front of a baying crowd. He would be executed.

Or, a strong set of hands would find their way to him while he did search out help on foot. His bodyguard had been withdrawn. Grullen was not a warrior. Undoubtedly they would both be found dead somewhere in the camp, perhaps having drowned in the river, or been kicked to death by a horse. There would be an inquest. Thomak would have his men putting on a right old show as they rampaged around trying to find pretend murderers. Some poor bastard might even hang for it.

Either way, Pomen would be dead, his message undelivered. There was only one hope left to him. It galled him to ask this of Grullen, but this was bigger than both of their lives.

"Grullen!" he called.

The manservant entered the tent. He had a black eye, a split lip, and a broken nose.

"Grullen, my friend. I have something to ask you."

Grullen looked afraid, yet resilient.

"I have the most grievous task to ask of you."

"Anything, my master," said the servant, his voice wavering.

Pomen raised a hand. "No my friend. Hear me out. It is a choice; I can only but ask you to do this. I am a lord only in name now. I have hours to live at best. I cannot force you to do as I ask."

He thought for a moment, closing his eyes.

"Grullen, you have been beyond loyal. You have saved my life just now. I can only repay this debt in one way."

Grullen frowned, a little confusion playing across his features.

"Grullen Baferian, I free you of your duties."

Grullen stood stock still, his jaw working but struggling to make sound.

"My lord—"

"No longer. You are a free man. And as a free man I must ask something of you. You may refuse, if you please."

Grullen made to speak. Pomen silenced him with a hand.

"Hear me out, before you decide. If you take the gold and silver in my personal belongings box — it's in a small pouch — say your goodbyes, and walk from this camp, I shall see you and welcome your with warm friendship when you join me in the afterlife. Most probably, you will not join me for many years."

Grullen's eyes turned to look at Pomen's small oak box where all of his small valuables and trophies were kept. They swept back to Pomen.

"What would you ask of me, my lo... My friend?" asked the man.

Pomen sighed.

"You have seen the letter I just wrote. It must make it to the hands of the Lemugian or Pandur ambassadors. They must be convinced to flight. They must be convinced to flee and fortify their lands. If not, Thomak will win. The Lands of the Light shall fade into history."

"There will be risks," said Grullen thoughtfully.

"Risks you know full well, and I do not deny. You must weigh them up for yourself. I'll not tell you what to do.

"On the one hand you have probably twenty gold pieces and perhaps forty silver and a few bronze there with my best wishes. You could run a farm, sire sons, or find a ship somewhere and flee this realm to start a new life. You could live for twenty years with sound investments when commerce begins once again.

"All you would need to do is turn around, walk out, sneak past the perimeter guards, and flee for all you are worth. I do not imagine they will know you have fled for a few hours. If you flee back to Secunda, you could lose yourself in the great city until the war is over."

Grullen nodded, still thoughtfully watching Pomen as his mind worked.

"On the other hand, I offer you a chance to do what I believe is right, and I think you believe it also. Though to do this, you will most probably end up in a ditch or hang next to me."

Grullen sat upon Pomen's bed.

There was a long pause. The manservant looked about to say something, and then stopped himself, more than once. Pomen just sat there and awaited Grullen's decision with patience. Finally, Grullen nodded to himself, his decision made.

Then he stood and walked over to the oak case, opened it, and removed the leather sack of gold.

Pomen looked at the ground. "Ah, I truly spoke myself out of that one."

Grullen smiled and delved into his shirt, pulling out the letter.

"My lord. My friend. It has been my honour to serve you these years. Truly it has. I shall carry the letter for you. I am a servant and know how to move about this camp in the shadows and away from eyes. I shall survive, though I shall not return. I shall flee, as you have suggested, and I shall live."

Pomen smiled, a tear working its way down his cheek.

"I thank you, my friend."

Grullen beamed. "I have had crueller masters before you. You have always treated me well. Seen me fed and warmly clothed. Treated me with as much dignity as any manservant I know. I shall not forget it. I shall tell my sons and daughters of you as they grow. I shall tell them of the greatest lord to walk these lands since Armenius. I shall tell them of the man who saved the Lands of the Light from a tyrant."

Pomen forced himself to his feet and offered Grullen his hand.

The man gripped it with a smile. Without further word he turned, grabbed one of Pomen's dark cloth cloaks, and moved out into the waning light.

"Can the old bastard just die?"

Thomak walked into his empty command tent and kicked over a small sweets table, sending it cartwheeling. Small plates and piles of food flew to the floor. His heavy tread destroyed the slight wooden table upon the floor with a few vicious stomps. His eyes looked up hungrily for something else to destroy. Then they calmed coolly.

I am not some hot-headed youth. No, I am the lord steward, the most powerful man in the Lands of the Light. A calm mind will see me through.

"Hogun!" he barked out.

A Grey Wolf entered the tent.

"My lord steward."

"The Lord Pomen. I am done with him. I'm through with playing games to catch him at the treachery I know he commits. I have not the time to waste on evidencing his downfall. See him dead and gone. I want none to know of his disappearance. I shall deal with that at a later time."

"As you wish it, my lord steward."

The knight turned to walk out.

"And Hogun?"

"Yes, lord steward?"

"I'll have your oath of secrecy in this matter. Now, if you please."

"You have it, lord steward."

"Good. Make sure nobody sees you. His manservant would not be missed either."

Hogun nodded, turned and left.

Thomak smiled. To openly move against his old friend felt good. Finally, he was able to act like the conqueror he was. Finally, he could conquer in the open. He had the Secundan armies under his control. Even if the knight Orders did not side with him, he would still win by weight of numbers. Even if a third of the armies did not side with him, he would still win. The lands of the light would be his.

He stopped a moment. It was a real possibility that some of the armies would side with the Orders they had fought beside. Losing those men would see his forces drained for the marches on Mother Secunda, Pandur, and Lemug. This would not do.

"Aestepos!" he yelled.

An elderly manservant entered.

"Yes, lord steward?"

"I need you to scribe. Now. Bring many pieces of parchment."

The elderly man bent his head and nodded, quickly shuffling from the tent.

Aestepos was back quickly, his back and head hunched over a hand-held slate with parchment and angled quill-dip ready. Thomak thought about his words, thought about the weight and grandiosity he should put into his letters. He was, after all, demanding that probably innocent men hang for treason. He was demanding that officers kill their commanders,

commanders kill their heroes, and men in chainmail slay those in plate on the chance the victims would not side with him.

Thomak took a deep breath. Here was the opportunity to decide if his plans for the conquering of the realm lasted a few years or a few decades. If he did this right...

He needed a starting point, something to get the words flowing. A message to one of the loyal commanders who would have no issue completing his orders would start him off well. Thomak cleared his throat.

"To my beloved friend and loyal brother, Lord Ryun,

"It is time to sever the lives of those who may rise against us from within the ranks of our brotherhood.

"Put Uthiel Caellar to death immediately.

"The men of the Fifth, or our Order, cannot be allowed to rally behind him. Any brothers or company commanders you feel are partial to him are to be put to death also. If their men are of the same mind in your opinion, they die alongside those they foolishly follow.

"This is to be done immediately, upon receipt of this order."

Thomak nodded to himself. *That was easy.*

With an anticipatory smile Thomak launched himself into the remainder of his missives. Between two and three went out to all of the major forces under his command. It would not be long before those orders, with his seal upon them, would be galloping away to the distance.

Some orders would be carried out within the next few days. Some would not reach their intended recipients for almost a month.

Thomak took most of the afternoon to complete his work. By the end of it he could see Aestepos visibly sagging. Whether the old man's weariness came from continued effort, or the burden of writing the death warrants, Thomak did not know. He wasn't sure he particularly cared.

With a wave of his hand he dismissed the manservant. Aestepos left the parchment piled neatly upon the main command table, and left without a word. There was but one thing left to do. *One last roadblock to my empire.*

He huffed, *my empire*. It was not so long ago he'd dreamed of handing this thing he was creating to his king. *No, not anymore.*

The Faramon line was at an end. The king would not heal, yet he would not die. He would never again be fit to rule Secunda, let alone an entire realm made up of four more conquered nations and the tens of thousands of tribes that roamed the Black Lands. Thomak's mind became resolute. It was time to make sure the king did not wake up. It was time to claim all he had striven to earn.

It was time to become an emperor.

CHAPTER TWENTY-THREE

"How many do you think?" asked Uthiel.

"Must be close to fifty thousand down there," said Theon.

Uthiel nodded, satisfied with the answer. The battlefield was thickly littered with skeletal remains, all but picked clean by scavenger birds and rats. Rotting, sun-bleached banners fluttered atop spears. Rusted steel had begun to decompose into the darkening sand. Only the scraps of leather armour of the barbarians could pick them out from the steel-band armoured fallen Imonetians.

"Even from here, all these months later, the bodies tell us of what the Imonetians did wrong," came the deep voice of the first captain.

Uthiel looked back to the veteran.

"How so, first captain?"

"See where the ridges of bodies are on the field. There is where the heaviest fighting occurred. Look."

Solanthur pointed his arm and ran his finger past a few mounds of corpses being slowly lost to the sands for Uthiel to see.

"The first impact was there, just to the right of the centre of the field. The killing must have fearsome. The Imonetians held there a while, their hardiest and most stalwart troops to the fore."

Uthiel tried to picture the battle. He tried to imagine fighting in the middle of the line without the discipline and strength of the shield wall and his brothers around him.

"That, however, is not what lost them the battle," continued Solanthur. "Look, see the small ridge to the left, then the long carpet of bodies, and then the larger hill back behind where the centre was holding?"

Uthiel once again followed his arm.

"They lost the left flank and the barbarians rolled them back into their own forces," said Uthiel. "There, with nowhere for the units to manoeuvre, the battle was lost. With nowhere to run, the loss became a slaughter."

"The Imonetian commander made one of two mistakes," said Solanthur. "Either he put weak troops on the left flank, or he greatly underestimated the strength of those troops that attacked him there."

"I'd expect nothing more from such inbred scum," growled Theon.

Solanthur ignored Uthiel's Shield.

"My concern is only for the latter of the two possibilities."

Uthiel suddenly understood what Solanthur was getting at, horrid memories of the sheer power of the undead beast Carn had become ripping through his calm. He shot a look at Solanthur. He could see the same trepidation in those eyes.

"If the foe have managed to rouse more of the fallen, then we are in dire trouble. Especially if they have them in the numbers necessary to turn the tide of a major battle in such a manner."

"Why?" said Theon. "If they have these beasts once more we shall face them in the shield wall. They shall charge our fortress of steel and courage and they shall fall."

"Yes, brother Theon, a sound theory. That would be to suggest that the enemy defeated the Imonetians here, then charged forward to the capital, leaving behind their most fearsome troops to guard a frontier they probably cared naught about. I'm sure even the most useless general would have seen the logic behind that."

Theon glowered a little, realising he was being made fun of.

"No, my brothers, those monsters would have taken part in the sacking of Imonetia."

"So where were they when we took back the capital?" asked Uthiel.

Uthiel blinked as he heard it again. A chuckle in the back of his mind that made his head began to pound again.

"That, my brothers, is what I would fear most."

Uthiel looked back over his shoulder. Rank upon rank of the Fifth stood stalwart and at the ready, their eyes casting over the battlefield. The Lord General Ryun stood in conversation with a few of the captains, every now and then stopping to point at routes through or around the battlefield.

Sitting low between two immense sand dunes the two-mile front was just a morning's march short of the Imonetian White Frontier fortress. Sand consistently shifted across the ground this far out into the desert and the heat was beginning to creep up in intensity as the days between the capital and the frontier slid by.

"Just what in Armenius' name were they doing fighting a battle here?" snapped Uthiel, his eyes narrowing.

Solanthur frowned, a little taken aback by Uthiel's tone.

"They waited for their strength to grow for too long before marching. Had they left the day before they may have made the fortress before it was overrun and held there," said the first captain.

"That's what happens when men are born into positions of leadership, instead of earning them," Uthiel retorted.

Solanthur's eyes narrowed, but Uthiel walked away before he could respond. Theon gave the first captain a weary look before marching off in Uthiel's wake. Uthiel took deep breaths, attempting to stem the growing tide of bloodlust and rage, desperately trying to get the image of him stomping on the first captain's chest and yanking his sword from flesh out of his mind.

"My captain!" came the voice of Theon. "Uthiel, what is the matter with you?"

"With me?" roared Uthiel, spinning around on the spot to face his Shield, bits of saliva flying.

Theon stopped, shocked by the outburst. Uthiel took a calming breath and held up a hand, focussing on the burning of the talisman against his chest, allowing it to soothe him.

"I am sorry, my brother. I truly do not know. Forgive me."

Theon watched him for a moment.

"Uthiel, something has not been right with you of late. You've been distracted ever since you slew the prince. Something happens behind your face that you do your best to hide. The men who know you best see this. I see this, as does Tarren and the first captain."

Chuckle. *They see it. They see nothing. They know not who you will become when you embrace me.*

Uthiel shook his head. Theon was staring at him.

"Even now! Even now you are so put off by something you will not even listen to me."

"No, brother, no. I am fine. Find me—"

Uthiel stopped as a figure upon one of the almighty dunes caught his attention. It stumbled and fell, righted itself, then stumbled once more. It was a man in armour. Uthiel looked to Theon.

"With me, brother."

Both men hefted their shields and ran for the dunes. It took them some time to arrive at the base of the sand mountains, and then even longer to ascend, their heavy tread sinking deep into the sand.

The figure above them fell, one last time. Chests heaving and faces soaked in sweat, Uthiel and Theon arrived at the stricken man. He was a Grey Wolf. Uthiel knelt by him and pulled out his water skin, dabbing some across the unconscious man's lips with his thumb.

"Do you recognise him?" asked Uthiel, looking up to Theon.

The big man shook his head. The knight was young, perhaps a summer older than Uthiel at most. He was of average

271

build and had a face ravaged by thirst. The knight's eyelids snapped open and for a moment the man struggled meekly.

"You are with your brothers, my friend. Be calm. Drink. Rest," soothed Uthiel.

The man shook his head. "No, my brother. I must not. I need to deliver a message to the lord general immediately."

Theon leant down. "Let me bear your burden for the rest of the journey."

"It is for the eyes of the Lord General Ryun himself, my brothers. You must help me the rest of the way."

The knight tried to get up, his face straining with effort. Without warning, his body went slack and he fell back to the ground. Uthiel leaned down, his ear next to the man's mouth.

"He breathes, still. He needs water," he said distractedly, his attention drawn to the leather satchel the knight had been lying upon.

Theon knelt down beside Uthiel and began to dab more water onto the knight's lips. Uthiel reached out and opened the leather satchel, retrieving a folded piece of parchment from with the lord steward's wax seal upon it. As he laid eyes upon the seal his head began to pound. He could feel the talisman's cleansing burn once more, as if something within fought for supremacy over him. It was a feeling he was struggling to become accustomed to of late.

"Brother," came the warning voice of Theon.

The big Shield was looking at Uthiel's hands. The young captain had broken the wax seal without even realising what he was doing.

"That missive is not for your eyes, my captain," said Theon.

Uthiel's body immediately wound up, ready to do violence. He felt its need as his own desire, the message in his hand forgotten, his gaze reddening. Once more he could hear that infernal chuckle, ever taunting him, ever enraging him further — ever telling him blood would slake his thirst.

"You would stop me?" snarled Uthiel. "You would stop me though you know its contents may help our cause?"

"Our cause?" questioned Theon.

"Yes, my Shield. Our cause. To depose the lord general."

Theon stared at him, hard. Uthiel fought within, desperately trying to calm himself in order to speak reason.

"You assume too much through my silence, captain. I am not sure I can do what you ask of me."

Uthiel shook his head. "You still doubt me, brother?"

Theon returned his stare. "What you spoke of... It goes against all I have lived, all I have fought and killed and bled for. You speak of a world where my brothers and I become the evil the Black Lands once was. You speak of Black Wolves as men who wore the grey."

Uthiel gathered himself, marshalling his scattered thoughts. He would not get another chance with Theon.

"I speak of many things, my brother. I speak of one chance right now, however. One chance to recognise the danger of what our great nation may become. One chance to prevent war from tearing the realm apart."

"It already tears this realm apart, brother," interrupted Theon.

"I agree. Though imagine what will happen when the lord steward turns on Lemug and Pandur, slays our king, and claims the world for his own."

"He would not turn on such allies, nor spill the blood of the ancestor of the Eternal Lord. I have met the man, fought beside him. I can see this. He is honour personified, glory emboldened. He is all it is to be a knight," insisted Theon.

"That is an illusion," snapped Uthiel. "The man is a political animal. He has given away those virtues that once made him a great knight. He has naught but determination for victory—"

"A virtue in itself."

"Not when that victory is the betrayal of our allies and domination of the people we were meant to protect."

Theon sat upon the sand, the man beside him forgotten. Uthiel took to the sand beside him, taking the time to tip a quick splash of water onto the unconscious knight's lips. Before them, the Fifth had begun to march across the battlefield in scattered companies.

Theon sighed. "Open it."

Uthiel looked across at Theon.

"The seal is broken, he shall know we opened it whether you read it or not now."

Uthiel didn't wait for the big man to change his mind and pulled out the letter, reading it aloud.

My oldest friend and brother,
Put Uthiel Caellar to death immediately.
The men of the Fifth or our order cannot be allowed to rally behind him. Any brothers or company commanders you feel are partial to him, are to be put to death also. If their men are of the same mind, in your opinion, they die alongside those they foolishly follow.
This is to be done immediately, upon receipt of this order.

For the glory of Secunda,
Lord Steward of Secunda, Gall, and Imonetia,
Under His eyes,

Thomak.

Uthiel looked at Theon. He could see the big man's mind working feverishly to grasp their weight of the missive Uthiel had just read out to him — a missive that most probably spoke of his death alongside Uthiel's. Dark blue eyes looked up to the young captain. Uthiel could read the confusion, the anger and the hurt in them.

"We need to make our move. Right here. Right now," said Uthiel.

Theon nodded dumbly.

Uthiel reached over and grabbed his Shield by the gorget roughly.

"Theon! This is when I need you most. This is when Secunda needs us most. Armenius is relying on us to keep this stain from our history's honour. Our forefathers are watching us in this moment, waiting to see what we shall do."

Theon still stared off into space.

"Are you going to just sit there and let this happen?" snarled Uthiel.

Theon's face came around quickly, hard and resolute.

"No."

"Then we need to find a way to defeat Ryun."

"We are but nine brothers and a hundred-odd men of the Fifth. What hope do we have against all that?"

Theon pointed down to the hundred-strong companies of the Fifth that were making their way across the field below them. Uthiel took a deep breath.

"We must strike the head from the dragon and hope the body falls behind it."

"Kill Ryun?"

"I can think of no other option. Were it not for the pure chance of finding this messenger, both you and I would not have seen this sun's setting. While he lives he commands the Fifth. Should he fall, command would pass to Solanthur."

Theon assented. "The first captain may not see this your way. He is a man who stringently sides with duty over all else."

"Without Ryun, he has no duty to stand against us. He may be swayed."

"Perhaps. I do not think it likely."

Uthiel shrugged. "What else would you have me do? Strangle this brother who lies by our side, bury him, and pretend the message never arrived while Ryun ensures we lead every attack until the last of us falls? No, I cannot. I have a duty to the men who fight for me and are consigned to death beside me."

Theon looked at the unconscious messenger beside him.

"Stay with him. I shall confront Ryun," said Uthiel, standing and dusting some of the sand from his cloth pants.

Theon stood also, his stare boring into Uthiel, fresh anger written across his face.

"I am your Shield."

Uthiel shook his head. "Not in this. You need to decide what is right for you. Fight by me, against me, or stay upon this dune. I must away, to do what I see as right, lest I be judged poorly when I reach the Shield Wall in the Sky."

"What of the others? What of the men you are so willing to assume will fight by you?"

"They are with me."

Theon looked surprised. "Truly?"

"Tarren tells me you are the last of the men to withhold a decision on where your loyalty rests. Either you are with me, or you are with Ryun."

"We shall die in this schism."

"It is most likely," conceded Uthiel.

Theon huffed and stood to walk down the hill.

"You are with me then," asked Uthiel.

"I am your Shield. You cannot discard me whenever you feel like it you bloody young upstart," snarled Theon.

Uthiel smiled. "Then I have a task for you."

Uthiel reached his men quickly, having told an apothecary where to find the unconscious messenger on his way past. His men, eight brother knights and just over one hundred men of the Fifth, picked their way through the deluge of bones, rotting cloth and rusted steel. Darian, Tarren, and Pavel made it to him first.

Uthiel looked to them, and then down at the parchment in his hand. All read his gaze and its meaning.

"It is time, then?" said Captain Darian.

Uthiel nodded.

The captain of the Fifth sighed. "I cannot believe it has come to this."

"Bloody hell," swore Tarren.

More of his men gathered around him.

"My brothers," he began. "A great treachery has stained the honour of our nation and all the men and women who came before us. The time has come, when brother shall slay brother in order to wipe the stain clean. The blood of the sons of Secunda shall spill on to the sands, spilt by the swords She has released to us from Her bosom."

The men around him looked grim. They were tired, exhausted, many beyond his company did not know what he spoke of. He could see it in their eyes. Each man courted Death by standing beside him. From the back he saw a few break off and walk away, if not through knowledge, then by instinct. He did not blame them.

Looking through the midday heat haze he spied the lord general. He stood with Solanthur's company, gesturing and speaking to runners from the companies of the Fifth that moved across the battlefield. There was not a company within three hundred feet of the lord general, and only one within a thousand. The king's guards were nowhere to be seen.

Uthiel felt the wind pick up, the sand beginning to rustle audibly as it shifted and whorled. Visibility began to shorten. Uthiel heard a whisper on the breeze.

Now.

He smiled.

"On me, my brothers. Armenius is with us."

The men moved to stand by him. Uthiel dipped his head a moment. This was it. His head began to pound. A low growl fell from his lips. The red rage began to creep upon him once more. He suppressed it viciously within. He would need all of his control to win. If the first captain stood against him it would stand to him to fell the greatest hero of the Lands of the Light.

He donned his helm and hefted his shield. Tarren and brother Ralan took up position either side of him. He could not see Pavel but took some comfort as he began to march into the growing maelstrom around him and he heard the steps of men form up beside and behind. They were men of the same mind, and his brothers, whether they wore the grey or not.

Uthiel felt the weight of the wind grow heavier, and looked skyward as a dark shadow fell across him. Clouds stormed their way across the sky, centring in above him as they began to shift into an inverted whirlpool. He felt the malevolence of a god bring his horrible bearing upon the killing field they stood upon.

Uthiel looked at Axom. The knight had fought beside Solanthur in Gall and had seen the similar presence of Zhar T'Hur above the city. Ralan nodded to him. Uthiel licked his lips, feeling some trepidation and fear overcome his zealousness. He saw a few men hesitate in their steps as the air grew heavy with malice and foul whisperings lent their weight to the winds.

"Hold strong, my brothers!" he roared. "We do the work of Armenius!"

A few men stood straighter at that. A few did not.

Up ahead they had almost lost sight of Ryun, though Uthiel knew he could not be more than fifty or sixty paces away. He waved his men in, shoulder to shoulder, the howling of the wind rising to a fever pitch.

Then there was stillness, like the eye of a hurricane. All around them a wall of shrieking sand screamed and above clouds as black as a starless night roiled. And in the centre stood Ryun, a tall knight by his side, Solanthur and his company behind him, and two companies of the Fifth either side.

Uthiel paused in his advance as the captains of the two companies of the Fifth shouted and the soldiers lowered their spears at Uthiel. The Lord General Ryun looked up from his conversation with the tall knight and smiled.

Uthiel was outnumbered two to one. Ryun's companies were not the veterans that Uthiel had by his side, but it would not matter. They would be hard pressed to win. The sound of twenty shields clashing together create the centre of the line around Solanthur was like a death-chime amplified a hundred fold.

The tall knight beside Ryun turned, cold, dark eyes, so much like Nikhael's, looked at Uthiel impassively. Pavel.

"You bastard piece of shit!" roared Tarren. "You swore an oath!"

Pavel cocked his head a little. "I do my duty. As always, though it does me no pleasure to do so."

"I'll gut you before I fall!" yelled Tarren, taking a step forward.

Uthiel reached out and grabbed the man's pauldron. "Hold brother. Not yet."

Pavel smiled. It was sickeningly smug. "I shall take pleasure in one thing, my little brother: teaching you one last lesson in swordplay."

Tarren took a step back and moved himself into the shield wall his brothers had formed around Uthiel.

"Come and test me."

There was silence as none moved. Uthiel did not have long. Their best chance of surviving was to defend, but he had to make the enemy come at them. If two companies had already arrived to fight against him, then more could already be on the way and further delay would only lengthen his odds.

"Are you one of them?" he yelled at Ryun.

Ryun did not respond for a while. Uthiel called out to him again.

"I do not waste words on dead men!" yelled the lord general.

"Are you a Black Wolf?"

The lord general hesitated. Many men turned to face Uthiel from across the field.

"Did you shed your grey tabard and slay your brothers a decade ago? Did you stand beside Kael in mutiny and return to us as an agent of darkness? Have you waited for this opportunity to slay more?"

Ryun looked around himself. Men were eyeing him warily now. Uthiel smiled to see questions start flying around the opposing ranks.

"Have you told them? Have you told them that the men who led this incursion that has cost us all so dearly were once Grey Wolves? Have you told the men of the Fifth, who lost sons and brothers and fathers at Archenon Creek, that the Black Wolves were once your brothers?"

Uthiel could see his words were having an effect.

"You would know of betrayal!" responded the lord general. "You commit it with each breath!"

Uthiel pushed harder, shouting over the lord general. "You have fooled our brothers and countrymen far too long! When I discovered it, you tried to have me and my men killed. Pushing us to ever greater bloodshed at the forefront of the army with no reinforcements! Did you pray for my death? Pray for the deaths of the men around me?"

The fighting men around Ryun were shifting. Uthiel could see it. Ryun would not wait any longer, he could not draw this out for fear of losing the morale and perhaps the loyalty of his men. They had all seen Uthiel's men pushed harder and harder with no respite and no reinforcement. Uthiel was swaying them because what he was saying was, at least in part, true. Ryun was looking around, sensing what Uthiel was seeing.

"Forward at the march!" Ryun screamed, his voice cracking with effort as he shoved the man beside him forward.

There was hesitation as some advanced, but others did not immediately, before running forward to fall in to step. Uthiel smiled. He'd manoeuvred the lord general just where he wanted him. His heart beat rhythmically and slowly, his excitement held in check. He could feel the burn of the talisman against his skin, sweetly searing the flesh.

"Armenius is with us!" he yelled as he steadied his stance, shield locked to the fore.

He drew a blade as the enemy line advanced to within a spear-throw's distance.

"Is he really a Black Wolf?" whispered Tarren beside him.

Uthiel shook his head. "More's the shame, my brother. We shall be slaying our brothers this day."

Ryun locked eyes with Uthiel from behind the lines of the Grey Wolves' shield wall.

"Kill them all!"

CHAPTER TWENTY-FOUR

Uthiel instinctively ducked as a crossbow bolt clanged from the rim of shield, jarring his arm with its brutal power. He could see his brothers across the break in the lines from him. Solanthur marshalled them with skill, looking left and right to make sure his line impacted at the same time. For a moment, Uthiel swore he could see the first captain's hard stare lock on his own. There was sadness in that gaze.

Uthiel allowed none of the same emotion to settle within his own visage behind the steel face of his helm. If he was going to kill the greatest warrior in the land he would need nothing but his most ferocious cunning.

Around him men were calling to each other. They yelled to and at men beside, behind, and in front of them. There was no rage, no all-encompassing or cold hate that they fought the barbarians with. There was only a great sense of tragedy as the men who Armenius had chosen to defend Secunda marched towards fratricide, one half-step at a time.

"Crossbows!" called out Uthiel.

Only two of his men carried the weapons. They were raised over the line of the shields and loosed their bolts together. Both slammed into raised shields only ten feet away.

One of the knights in the front line of Ryun's force screamed and dropped to a knee, the bolt piercing through the shield and the bearer's forearm. The knight quickly disappeared behind the advancing line as the man behind him took up his place.

"Spears!"

Either side of Uthiel, one hundred spears were levelled at the approaching line. Uthiel raised his blade and laid the flat of it atop his shield. His men mirrored him. A moment later, so did Solanthur's. It was fearsome to see the steel wall from the wrong side.

Uthiel looked at Solanthur.

"Brother! You can stop this!"

Solanthur's helm did not move.

"We need not all die!" shouted Uthiel. "We can take this army and march back south to our own brothers and our own people."

"Forward brothers! Slay the traitors! Kill those who would stain the honour of Armenius and the Grey Wolves!" shouted Ryun, his voice booming above the sounds of marching feet.

Four feet.

"Solanthur!" shouted Uthiel desperately, drawing back his blade to strike.

Uthiel and Solanthur, captains of the Grey Wolves, lauded heroes of Secunda, struck each other at the same time. Uthiel's blade slammed into the tall inner collar of Solanthur's pauldron while the first captain's glanced from Uthiel's helm. Then, crushing impact: shield pushed upon shield in the centre, spears stabbed in to chainmail either side.

The horrid music of battle filled Uthiel's ears as he pushed with all his might to hold his spot in the line beside his brothers. He could see Tarren beside him as he stood tall and stabbed over his shield with his sword. Uthiel ducked a moment as Solanthur's blade tried to find his helm and three spears responded from the line of soldiers behind him, forcing the first captain to duck.

In his peripheral vision, Uthiel watched Tarren's blade slide into the eye slit of the knight opposite them. There was an intense scream as Tarren's steel plunged deeper.

A sword hammered into Tarren's vambrance and creased the steel. Tarren cried out and pulled his blade back, lucky the cramped conditions of the battle had robbed the strike of real power. The knight he had just slain remained standing upright, blood pumping down over his gorget and his head sagging as the press of bodies held him up.

It was a mad crush, the worst of battles, fought upon one of the most blood-drenched battlefields of the frontier. Uthiel stabbed and stabbed, his eye-slits in line with the top of his shield, his feet desperately trying to keep him upright and his shield strong. Legs kicked out to try to trip him while swords and spears tried to find a way through his armour. Screams filled the air all around them and clashing steel kept rhythm to the symphony of death, which he stood at the epicentre of.

Uthiel could see nothing beyond the few men beside and in front of him. His shouts of encouragement were lost in the cacophony of violence. His world shrank to the brutal struggle before him. The crush of the lines was immense; it would have to break soon.

And in that moment, it did.

Without warning one of Uthiel's brothers, two men down the line, fell, blood pumping from where a blade had slipped between his helm and gorget. The knight beside him turned as a foe kicked into his shield and three blades carved into the weak spots in his armour, pitching him to the ground. The line held a moment, a fraction of a heartbeat as the men of Darian's company tried to surge forth to plug the gap, and then it collapsed.

Solanthur's men forced their way into the hole, hacking and slashing as Uthiel's left flank quickly turned into a series of melees as the line broke down and men died screaming. Uthiel knew he was done as he and Tarren were pushed back, the weight of numbers of the foe finally winning over their dogged defiance. He felt the men of Darian's company desperately trying to halt the reversal, but they were too few and they were spread too thin.

"They are behind us!" yelled a voice.

Uthiel ignored it as Solanthur opened up enough space around them and slammed his blade into the younger captain's hastily raised shield.

Uthiel stumbled backwards, cannoning into the man behind him and sending the poor soldier careening to the ground. Uthiel rolled in time to avoid Solanthur's blade, though the soldier Uthiel had knocked over was not so swift and the knight beside Solanthur stabbed his Secundan steel through the man's neck.

Argo, wrapped in the colours of the Fifth, leapt forwards and thrust at Solanthur with his spear. The first captain took the spear point on the shield and cut the haft in half with his blade, his boot slamming in to the old soldier's knee and felling him with a scream of pain. Tarren rushed in, having slain a second of his brothers from the Grey Wolves' first company, and he and Solanthur traded three blows before the young knight fell back with a grunt, blood streaming from the hip when his chain had been parted below the cuirass.

Uthiel had retained his feet and drawn his second blade, the red once more seeping over his vision, his hatred burning as strongly as the talisman against his chest. There was a roaring in his ears. His heart hammered painfully and wonderfully and he began to laugh within the confides of his helm, blood seeping from his nose.

He spied Solanthur as the first captain carved his sword into the throat of one of Darian's men and then smashed another to the ground with his shield. Through the blood thundering around his head Uthiel heard a roar, a cry of hundreds of voices, and then a clash of steel amidst screams of fear and pain.

He did not have time to look for the source, instead leaping to hammer his shoulder into Solanthur's shield. He whirled, Ghurkar's blade carving through the back of a knight's knee and following through to block the downward stroke of Solanthur's blade. His second blade hammered into Solanthur's helm. Solanthur staggered back, trying to right himself. Uthiel spotted a soldier closing on Tarren with intent, and without hesitation, wrenched his own helm from his head and hurled it at the man with a cry.

The helm took the soldier on the side of his head. The man did not have time to live out his surprise as Tarren turned at the noise and lashed out. The soldier fell, desperately trying to stem the flow of crimson from his jugular. Uthiel did not see it, having already turned back to leap across two bodies, and a wounded soldier grasping at his lower jaw that had been cloven in half, to once again clash swords with the first captain.

As the men around them butchered each other, Uthiel and Solanthur cut and stabbed, parried and dodged with unbelievable speed. Neither could land a blow as their feet twisted and transferred weight, ever dodging the fallen of this battle, and the last, with preternatural speed. To those unnoticed men around them, it was like watching two gods of the blade do mighty battle.

Uthiel spun away from another onslaught of blows. Solanthur used his shield much like Uthiel used his second sword, with brutal efficiency and unequivocal grace and balance. The young captain took a moment to get his breath. His eyes, burning like cauldrons of ice fire sat within them, never leaving the first captain as the man slowly advanced upon him.

It was only then, through the building haze of rage, that he noticed the stinging pain and the warm trickle that ran down the side of his face. He cocked his head as a little found its way into his mouth. He looked down. Upon the ground between he and the first captain was a tuft of dirty blonde hair matted with blood. Attached to the hair was a half-palm sized chunk of his scalp. Pain seared upon his head as he realised the wound.

He felt heat burn upon his chest, firing his limbs and clearing his mind for a moment. That clarity brought the full horror of the field around him. Men screamed as soldiers and knights they had fought beside for a year drove blades into their flesh with grim faces. The wounded were mercilessly put down. The living hesitated as friends ran at them. Blood fanned out in all directions as the lines between friend and foe blurred

285

and mixed as soul after soul was torn from mortal flesh to fly to be judged by a god no doubt watching in dismay.

The burning upon his chest grew more intense, searing his skin. Uthiel grimaced as he smelt his own flesh blister. Uthiel's world stopped a moment, slowing as if all around him waded through water. He had felt this before, when Armenius had blessed him in Gall and against Kael, but this time it was different.

Come to me. You are mine. A dark voice chuckled, echoing like an insidious soul in the darkest recesses of his mind. It hid behind his own battle-sharpened thoughts, tantalising the darker nature that every man of the blade held in check. Uthiel felt his control beginning to slip.

He felt a torrent of hate building within, a rage so unchecked that even the iron chains made of his training and indoctrination would not be able to hold it back. His mind swam in a fathomless ocean of searing anger.

He saw Solanthur stop a moment in his advance, something in his eyes looking akin to fear, and then the red and blackness tunnelled his vision. Before he could control his actions, Uthiel had darted forward, his swords snaking out like lighting and striking like mountains collapsing, sending chunks of Solanthur's shield flying into the air.

The burn of the talisman was but a far off, distant memory as he heard himself scream in rage and pleasure as the narcotic of heedless battle assaulted his senses. Solanthur was on the back foot, desperately defending himself as Uthiel hammered him time and time again.

Finally, his blade found a way through. The power of the stroke found a way past Solanthur's defences and also through his cuirass, a fan of crimson spraying out. The first captain fell and Uthiel leapt upon him, his blade driving almost to the crosspiece into the sand where Solanthur's head had been a moment ago.

A knight threw himself to the first captain's defence. Uthiel ducked under a blow and slammed his blade up and under the man's mail skirt, skewering him through the groin and deep into the belly. The knight let out a strangled cry and crumpled to the ground, dragging Uthiel's blade from his grasp.

There was a loud cheer. Uthiel looked up to see Tarren's face. The knight Uthiel had known since being a novice was lending his voice to the roar of victory, pumping his fist in the air. All around them soldiers of Darian's company were lifting their spears to the sky while the men who had supported Ryun fell to their knees.

In his berserk state, Uthiel could not grasp the moment, his head down and his teeth clenched around the taste of blood in his own mouth, his eyes screwed shut. A huge paw of a hand grabbed his pauldron. It took all of what was left of his self-control to stop himself from killing Theon.

"My captain, we are here," said the big knight solemnly. "The day is—"

The big knight stopped as he saw Uthiel's face contorted with rage and disappointment at the ending of the bloodshed.

"My captain?"

Uthiel looked up in time to see a long blade stab through Theon's throat. The steel was single edged and etched with words of Armenius worship. As Theon fell, his massive hands grasping his throat, Pavel stood over him, blade still in hand and a smile upon his face.

He never saw Uthiel coming. Despite the weight of his armour, Uthiel's knees hammered into Pavel's chest as he leapt and bore the sword master to the ground. His forearm-length knife flashed out and before the tall knight could react, had been driven up to the hilt in to Pavel's eye socket.

Uthiel grunted with the effort as he tore the blade out and slammed it home again and again. He didn't know when he had released the blade, but until his fists were hammering against the bowl-like remains of Pavel's skull he was unable to stop himself. The desire to slake his thirst for slaughter fought to take him over like two thousand pounds of raging bull. Images of mass-murder rifled through his mind and with each one came a rising bloodlust and an almost unstoppable urge. His breathing became more ragged as something dark tainted his mind with each passing moment.

He felt the presence of more heartbeats, more lives begging for him to stop them. He fought for all he was worth to hold onto a sense of self through the red haze. Someone was speaking to him.

"Uthiel, what is wrong with you?"

"Come back to us brother, the day is won. Ryun has fallen, we have him captive."

"My friend, breathe! Calm!"

The voices faded into a swirling morass of sound he could make no sense of.

You are mine. Take their lives. Give them all to me.

Uthiel screamed, his mind shredding under the sheer power of the voice of a god.

Give them to Zhar T'Hur. Become mine and you shall know glory and pleasure like never before. Become my champion and rule the world by my side.

Through the fog of pain and rage, Uthiel could feel his eyes and ears and mouth beginning to bleed.

His mouth opened wide into a scream as his back arched painfully to push his face to the swirling darkness above.

"No!" he screamed, over and over, his voice breaking as his own men stepped back from him in horror.

Above, the clouds turned darker and fat chunks of dark ice began to fall with the shrill buffeting winds. They began to slowly swirl lower towards the earth as sickening red lightning lit the epicentre like the blood-slicked eye of pure evil.

Whispers, like a million enraged souls craving the lives of the living, began to lick the ears of all who lived with barbed tongues. Men who had, but a moment ago, felt themselves victorious looked to the sky and shook with fear at what they saw above.

Theon's corpse twitched as the first pieces of ice struck steel.

Pomen sat upon the bed in his tent. He was the most alone he had ever felt. There were no brothers nearby to watch over him, he had yet to hear of the Lemugians leaving or to receive word from Grullen. Blood tricked from his mouth, his chest was searing with white agony, and mucus bubbled from his nose.

His body felt on the verge of collapse, it was all he could do to remain sitting upright. Outside, he could hear the hammering of cold rain against the canvas tent. He wore only his grey tabard, that loyal cloth that had sat upon his armour in so many battles, some leggings, boots and his thick fur coat. Even with just these items he was genuinely wondering if he would be able to stand.

His cataract-covered gaze rested upon his armour. It sat gleaming in the darkness, resplendent with its last coat of polish that Grullen had applied only days before. He tried to stand, but his legs failed, pain roaring through his ankles, knees and hips. As he slumped back on to the bed, his lower back flared and he cried out weakly.

"No."

His weak voice trembled with the word.

"No!"

His declaration grew with defiance as his eyes narrowed, still locked on the armour before him, trying to draw strength from the holy plate that had been a second skin for so many decades.

I will not go quietly to His side. I shall have one last moment of glory. One last—

Pomen doubled over in pain as he exploded into a coughing fit. It lasted for what seemed an age, leaving him curled up in the foetal position upon the dirt ground, hands like claws over his face. When the fit finished, he lay upon the ground for some time, his face covered, sobs bursting from between the fingers as his breath wheezed like wind across sand coated rotting flesh.

Tears streamed down his face to mix with the snot and blood and rot that stained his palms. It was only in this moment, when he looked at what sat in his hands in the dim candlelight, that he saw the tips of his fingers had begun to go purple and black.

He'd seen this before, in his father when he had been but a boy. The old man had lain there, suffering an affliction much the same as Pomen suffered now. His father had remained unmoving, bereft of the ability to speak, his eyes almost closed but their blue still moving between the family members around him.

Pomen, only seven summers old at the time, had been holding his father's hand. He'd felt the hand clench his own, and had looked down in surprise. A moment later, he yanked away in revulsion as he spied the darkening fingertips.

In the last few breaths before his father died, Pomen remembered seeing intense hurt in the man's eyes. That look would haunt him for many years. What would haunt him more was that now Pomen would die without the only family he had known since being an initiate.

He took a deep, shuddering breath, the last of his sobs breaking through his bone-dry lips. Dead weary arms pushed beneath him, trying to lever his body up. It took almost all of what he had left to push himself back into his original seating position. Time was of the essence, now.

He reached out a liver spotted hand, the flesh so thin he looked ghoulish, and grasped the supporting pole of his tent. Gritting his teeth, the Lord Pomen pulled himself to his feet. His head swam with nausea and his body shook with effort. His lungs fought to make him splutter and explode into another coughing fit.

Pomen would not allow it.

If this is my last night, it shall be doing what I have always done.

Pomen took a shaky step towards the tent flap, his hand still holding the supporting pole.

I shall defend Secunda and the Lands of the Light.

The dying lord released the pole and stumbled a moment before righting himself desperately. His hand reached out and opened the canvas flap, the wind and rain rushing in.

I shall go to the Shield Wall in the Sky with my honour intact and my conscience clear.

He stopped as he heard footsteps.

"—Pomen. Where—"

"—Close by."

He heard his name, picked out over the sound of the hammering rain. They sounded only a few tents away.

Pulling his hood over his head, Pomen moved out into the driving downpour, his feet urgently trying to hold him upright and stop him from slipping or becoming bogged in the quagmire.

Looking behind him, as he staggered in the direction of the Lemugian tents, Pomen caught the glint of cold steel in the dark.

CHAPTER TWENTY-FIVE

The chanting had run non-stop for the better part of the morning and had gone well beyond driving Jotel to the point of madness. The voices of the hundred barbarian shamans swept around him as if they had physical weight. His could almost see shadows that swirled around him, punching through his body, reducing in size upon their exit.

Were it not for the power building behind his eyes as Zhar T'Hur turned a small portion of his attention to a chosen warrior, Jotel would have taken his serrated blade and slain them all. He could feel the Red Father's attention. Aeons old, the lightest touch of his essence was almost enough to make the Black Wolf scream with equal measures of rage, agony and ecstasy.

Upon his knees, he looked up to the swirling clouds above and smiled as red lightning lanced down and vaporised four of the shamans, tendrils of barbed power licking Jotel's armour, leaving vicious runes imbued in the steel. Power resonated within him, power like nothing else he could have experienced in a thousand lives. He would dominate this battle in the name of the Red Father. He would bring Zhar T'Hur to the earth so he could rule at His side.

Reaching his hand up to the sky he roared, the sound of his voice lost in a rolling clap of thunder that reverberated with the thumping heart within his chest. His hand clawed and shook with strength. Jotel's eyes were wide as he looked down to the woman he had pinned with his free hand. Her eyes were wide with fear and her naked body kicked and writhed in desperation.

Lightning lit the sky a sickening red and purple once more as ice began to fall in thick, bruising chunks upon her pale flesh. Jotel smiled. It was time.

"For you Zhar T'Hur!" he thundered.

Lightning surged down from the sky, covering Jotel in unholy fire.

The woman in his grasp screamed in terror and torment as her skin bubbled and burnt under the fire. Jotel stood, dragging her up while his flesh lit, but did not burn. His hand clamped around her throat, holding her aloft before him like she weighed nothing more than a scroll of parchment.

In that moment, as he locked eyes with the terrified woman, his world became becalmed. This was it.

Give her to me.

With relish, Jotel swung his arm down in a broad and theatrical arc, slamming it into the woman's stomach. His clawed fist punched through the flesh and drove up into the rib-cage, ripping and rupturing organs as it sought its prize. The woman gasped in agony, her mouth wide open but soundless, tiny hands grasping Jotel's wrist feebly.

With a crunch of bone and a sound of ripping flesh Jotel ripped his cocked arm and hand backwards, separating the rib cage and creating an exit wound from belly to throat. The heart in his hand pumped once more before going still.

The woman's face fell slack and her head lolled, her eyes clouding over in death. Jotel roared to the skies, demanding the favour of his god.

It was granted.

It smashed him to the ground like he was nothing. His body burned and he screamed in agony, his hands tore at his face and his muscles wracked with involuntary spasms. The chorus of chanting around him swelled with power at every moment.

Then the screams began. Wails of terror and rage and fear pealed off into the night. Jotel heard none of it. Shamans turned and tried to run, their mouths beyond their control cracking open and snapping jawbones loose as unholy words spewed from lengthening tongues. Eyes misted grey, then white, and knees cracked backwards while hands desperately tried to tear out their own throats.

Then, in a moment, it was over. Every shaman detonated, showering the air in viscera before it was swept up and into the sky above, leaving only bloodless meat-chunks peppering the ground.

Quiet. Nothing moved.

A Black Wolf, the last of Jotel's brothers, emerged from hiding with twenty barbarians in tow. The knight could not disguise the horror in his eyes as he walked through the deluge. The sand was stained pink and red. The woman's body lay twitching before the hunched form of their leader.

He stepped warily forwards, reaching out to touch Jotel.

"My brother—"

A hand snapped out and grabbed his cuirass, bending the steel in its grasp. With a flick, he was thrown twenty feet through the air as Jotel rose. The flying Black Wolf's spine snapped as he slammed into a stone wall. The barbarians before Jotel cowered in abject terror, mewling and crying out in fear in their guttural language, like sheep trapped before the alpha wolf.

Jotel's face was drawn back over his sharp and pronounced bones, his flesh white and taut, his eyes black with tears of pitch rolling down his cheeks. Teeth, now sharp as a wolf's, gnashed behind drawn-back white lips, and a stabbing tongue flickered between them.

He felt the air around him heavy with power and drew from it, willing his strength into the brother he had just slain. The corpse shivered a moment and then rose as if a great hand had picked it up by the head. It turned, grey eyes regarding its master, black fluid dribbling from blue tinging lips, legs pushing it forward. Still warm hands drew a blade. Jotel watched the creature with relish, instinctively knowing it would obey his whim with the power of three men.

With a flick of his head he motioned the beast forward, into the group of barbarians. The barbarians realised his intent all too late as the Black Wolf tore in to them with blade and hand, his jaw cracking open beyond man's capability and releasing a mind-rending howl.

It was over quickly. Few had managed to lay axe head upon the monster Jotel had once called brother. Jotel again poured a thimble-full of his malice into the fresh corpses and they rose, twenty undead beasts with grey eyes, gaping wounds still dripping lifeblood. In unison their mouths cracked and snapped open, blackening tongues whipping out, and roared in feral rage.

With a sharp-toothed grin of anticipation, Jotel turned and pointed west, where the Secundans were less than a few miles distant and his own host was but a mere three-hundred feet away. His minions obeyed immediately and turned to hunt down the sacrifice.

Lord Pomen tripped and fell to the ground with a groan of pain as one of his ribs cracked. He was soaked through, his body shivering uncontrollably, mud covering him from head to toe. He could hear them, behind him, splashing through the mud and calling his name.

He could not get up. His strength was spent. He was about to die before finishing his mission. He sighed, his face dropping to the ground and sinking into the slush. His nose and mouth filled with the taste and scent of foetid soaked earth and his lungs began to scream for air.

Take me. Just take me, he willed the Eternal Lord. *I am done. I can fight no more.*

He felt his body relax and his lungs wrenched a mouthful of liquid into themselves. Searing pain drove down his throat and his right arm as his mind dulled.

There was naught else I could have done. I have failed my people and all they stand for.

Pomen felt himself begin to float as the pain receded into warm nothingness.

Forgive me for what I could not do.

Hands roughly grabbed his shoulders and wrenched him from the slurry he was drowning in. Agony flared all over his body as a fist slammed into his breastbone, cracking it audibly. His mouth, filled with black water, opened wide as his vision opened blurry before him and shadowed smudges of figures leant over him.

"Come on. Breathe!" snarled a voice as a fist hammered into his breastbone once more.

"Breathe!"

Pomen coughed, mud spitting from his mouth, and then vomited violently. He heaved in a deep breath and then vomited again, red and yellow mixing with the deluge of water his body repulsed from itself.

Knights in dark steel, their armour so alike his own, leaned over him. They reached down and dragged him to his feet. He could see a lady, water streaming over a thick black coat she wore and plastering her light hair to her face, looking over the shoulders of her men.

"Lord Pomen, what has happened to you?"

Pomen could not speak. He blacked out, his vision lolling to the ground.

There was darkness: an eternity and a moment in blackness.

"Lord Pomen."

"Lord, wake up."

Pomen opened his eyes. No longer did the cold rain hammer down around him. No longer were the figures around him shadows. The steel of the Lemugians loomed over him and the wet material of a tent ceiling flapped above them. A damp cloth was wiping his cheek and working the gritty sludge from the corners of his eyes. His head was tilted up and a bowl of water put to his lips. He managed only two sips, before coughing up more dirt.

The dying lord's lips worked soundlessly for a while, his mind thinking of only one thing.

"Gr...Grullen?"

Queen Valissa moved into sight between the hard faced warriors.

"My Lord Pomen, we must speak. Do not leave us yet," her voice soothed him.

Pomen noted the tension in her face, the worry creasing her handsome features.

He repeated himself, "Grullen?"

Valissa hesitated a moment.

"Where... Where is he?"

"I am sorry. He is gone."

"How?"

"He is nailed to a tree fifty feet from the lord steward's tent. He has been hung and drawn."

Pomen's face crumpled and a sob bit out.

"I am sorry, lord. He must have been a fine servant."

"He was... my friend."

The queen's lips drew tight, and her eyes glimmered with wetness for a moment. She reached up and rubbed them with a thumb and forefinger.

"I am sorry."

Pomen could not respond. Memories of the man who had served him to the end flashed through his mind's eye, clamping his chest and constricting his throat as tears began to stream down the side of his face.

"We need him to speak, my queen. We need him to speak, now," came a harsh voice.

Pomen opened his eyes. A man with a thick, but well kept, beard stared down at him.

"Lord Pomen, what is going on? Just what in the name Nemamian's balls and the Twelve Chasms of Hellfire is happening?"

Pomen looked at him, confusion muddling his mind.

The bearded knight swore and looked back at his queen.

"He is too far gone. And far past is the time for us to leave. You are in danger. On my life, you are in grave danger."

The queen looked at Pomen for a while longer, and then to the knight.

"No, we cannot."

The bearded knight made to respond. The queen raised her hand.

"Without an aid caravan our front will eventually crumble. We may march out during the winter, our strength falling on the disparate tribes scratching out a living in the snow, but summer will come once again. The tribes will return. Without food and steel and more men, we will fail.

"We have this one chance to rid the realm of the barbarian race. One chance. I will not stake it all on your gut, or what I perceive. I shall go and speak to the lord steward. I shall confront him and I shall wrest the truth from him. He cannot have victory without the south. He will not betray us lightly."

The bearded man grimaced with frustration, but acceded.

"What of what the girl said? Civil war is coming. Secunda will tear itself apart."

"It may be so. Even so, the potential for reward outweighs the risk." The queen was quiet a moment. "Have you seen her again? Emilia?"

The bearded knight shook his head. "What does it matter? She is a low-born girl in a realm drowning in blood. She matters not. "

"You are a harsh man. Every life is worth something to someone."

"Your life is all that matters to me, my queen. We must away and we must do it *now*."

The queen sighed. "Blue eyes, blond hair, tall, strong, worthy of the heart of a pure and innocent young girl that reminds me of my youthful self."

"What? My queen——" The bearded knight was incredulous and growing more desperate.

"We can only hope she makes it back to her knight," snapped Valissa.

There was an awkward silence.

"What of him?"

The queen looked to Lord Pomen.

"Bring him with us. It hurts me to do so, but the man is in disfavour, his guards nowhere to be found and his manservant publicly executed. I shall hand him over to the lord steward. Perhaps buy a little favour to speed our exit with a supply train."

"No—" sputtered Pomen.

"I am sorry."

"Listen—"

The queen turned away. The bearded knight reached down and hauled him painfully to his feet. His broken rib and ruined body screamed in pain while his mind reeled with vertigo.

"Queen... please. Hear me."

The queen stopped, and then turned.

She sighed. "What?"

"You are in grave danger."

The bearded knight grabbed him harder and pulled out a knife, resting it against the sagging skin of his throat. Pomen winced as the blade drew blood.

"Speak."

"The lord steward has plans for the south."

"He has promised—"

"Plans that do not involve you or your bloodline ruling the people."

Pomen felt the blade press deeper into his skin. He did not allow himself to cry out. If he could just speak his piece then this knight could end his agony.

The queen's face was unreadable.

"Thomak will wait for you to push on beyond the White Frontier. You will spend your strength there. He will take your lands from behind you then. If he cannot, he will consolidate for a year, maybe two, maybe ten, maybe twenty. Then he will march down and take your lands by force and not subterfuge."

The bearded knight looked back to his queen.

"Either way, with the combined weight of the lands of the light and dark behind him, he will conquer the south eventually."

None spoke. Outside, the rain had stopped hammering against the canvas tent. Men could be heard walking around, swearing about the swamp the camp had become.

"Why should she believe you?" Pomen took the words of the bearded knight as if he had been physically struck.

"What?"

"I said, why should we believe you, Lord Pomen?"

Pomen could not think fast enough to respond. He'd not considered his warning would be ignored.

"You are in disfavour, an outlaw or traitor by the looks of it. You may be sowing dissent amongst the lands of the Light."

"Why?" asked Pomen, trying to convince the queen and the knight of his innocence with his face. "Why should I lie?"

Valissa looked to her knight, wiping her wet hair across her forehead. "I know not. I wish it was as simple as believing you but your knight Orders are a different breed to our own men of steel. Each faction is a law unto themselves. Each is a political powerhouse of elite warriors with the best arms and armour available. You have fortresses that you own and answer only to each other and a lord steward you are now trying to convince me is going to betray my husband?"

Pomen shook his head, desperation in his eyes.

Valissa looked away. "Take him to my quarters. I want to know more."

"My queen, what of the supplies?"

Valissa grimaced. "I need to know more. He won't be missed for a day. If he knows more, then I need to know more." She looked back down to Pomen. "You're going to come with us. You have more to tell, I can see it in your eyes. If civil war is brewing, and you have information that can save my people, then I need to know."

Pomen reached up. "I—"

In that moment something flashed through the canvas. Pain exploded through the hanging flesh of his arm and a knight grunted, falling to the ground. Pomen looked down at his arm. Blood flowed freely where something had punched clean through his bicep. One of the Queen's guards lay on the ground, feebly trying to wrench a crossbow bolt from his gut.

Outside there was an uproar.

"Stop shooting!"

"The Queen of Lemug resides within! Hold fire and stand away!"

Pomen heard the unmistakable twang of more bolts being unleashed. There were cries and screams of pain as heavy, armour-clad bodies fell to the ground. A battle cry erupted and steel clashed.

There were more screams.

"No," snarled the queen. "No! Treacherous bastards!"

The bearded knight dropped Pomen to the ground and slashed his blade through the tent from the opposite direction of the sounds of battle. Another knight stormed out first and then the bearded warrior shoved the queen out unceremoniously.

The last Pomen saw of her, queen Valissa looked back at him. She seemed sorrowful. She mouthed something to him as the bearded knight grabbed her roughly and dragged her away. *Thank you.*

Pomen was sure she mouthed the words '*thank you*'.

He hauled himself up against the support pole of the tent, his hands weakly grabbing at his wound as he bled out onto the floor. Before him a figure in armour stepped through the tent flap. The sounds of battle outside had faded. The guards the queen had left outside had died to cover her escape.

"She'll not get past the camp perimeter," came a familiar voice, a voice Pomen had once enjoyed hearing.

Thomak squatted down before him, sword lying across his mail-covered thighs.

"Our brothers chase her as we speak."

Pomen smiled as he heard more shouts and then the thundering of hooves.

Thomak pulled his sword back and placed it against Pomen's breast.

Pomen laughed painfully. "You are undone, old friend. They have the fastest horses in the land."

Thomak's eyes widened in anger and his jaw clenched hard, the muscles on the side of his face bulging. There were more shouts and then a second group of pounding hooves, much larger than the first, set off and receded into the distance.

"Know this, traitor," snarled Thomak. "My men shall hunt her down to the ends of the realm. They shall not fail, they shall not falter. They shall have her slain."

Pomen coughed, and smiled again. There was no longer any pain in him. Darkness played on the edge of his sight.

"They... won't... catch her."

Thomak's face darkened with anger. Then it eased, sadness drooping the lord steward's shoulders.

"We were brothers once," he whispered.

Pomen opened his mouth to respond.

Thomak never gave him the chance. Using both hands he drove the sword into, and through Lord Pomen. The old man's body offered little resistance as he watched the blade driven through up to the crosspiece.

A speckle of blood coughed from Pomen's lips, but the old man was already gone before his head sagged forward.

The Lord Steward Thomak stood, pulling his blade from Pomen's chest. Walking through the hole cut in the side of the tent he moved out into the night once more. A body of one of the Lemugian queen's guards lay before him, a bolt jutting from his back. Thomak kicked the corpse without much enthusiasm.

Rain began to patter down upon his armour and head. He looked to the sky.

Armenius, let me catch her. Let me deliver you this realm.

There was silence in response. He took in a deep breath, allowing the rain falling upon his face to cool his temper enough for him to think.

If his men did not chase down the queen, his plans would be foiled. This war would drag out for a decade.

For a moment he thought of committing more men to the chase.

It was pointless.

The Lemugian cavalry was legendary for its speed and tenacity. Their horses were unequalled in strength and stamina, their riders' horsemanship even better.

Deep down, within a mind that had marshalled half the known realm's men to war and had orchestrated one of the mightiest campaigns in recognized history, Thomak knew his men would not catch the queen. He looked at the corpse once more, doing his best to stay calm to think the problem through. His brilliant mind, that had not yet failed him, quailed for a moment, fear threatening to take over reason and logic.

A knight came running over to him, out of breath. Thomak barely looked up at the man, his thoughts a whirlwind of changing logistics, timeframes, supply needs, troop strengths and dispositions. Imaginary maps flowed over his mind and already broad campaign details were beginning to flow into place.

"Lord steward?"

Thomak looked up, his face resolute.

"The queen, a bearded knight, and two handlers escaped. I have sent scouts and hunters with our brothers to chase them down."

Thomak did not show his disappointment.

"Brother-Captain Hogun, it matters not."

"We shall catch them," said the knight, defiantly.

Thomak shook his head and blew out his cheeks, running his hand over his stubble. "No, we will not."

"But, lord steward—"

Thomak rounded on the man.

"No longer."

"Lord?"

"Gather the Order."

Thomak's gaze moved in the direction of the king's tent. His eyes narrowed. It was time for his final move.

"I am lord steward no longer."

Hogun grinned and dipped his head, darkness blanketing his face. Thomak frowned, it was like looking at a completely different man. He thought for a moment. He'd known Hogun for two decades. The man had been in his company while he had been a captain, had fought in three major battles with him, had been at Archenon Creek when the Black Wolves had risen, and had been by his side all this long incursion.

As he stared at Hogun, things began to come a little clearer. Whatever dark deed he'd needed done, Hogun had been there. *Aphiti's bodyguards, for starters. Pomen's manservant as well.* So many more little items he'd thought nothing of that had helped him get to this point. Hogun stood tall once more, his eyes red-rimmed with deep crows-feet folding in the corners. The knight's eye twitched and Thomak could almost swear he could hear teeth grinding.

Thomak straightened his back and assumed his most regal face.

"I am Emperor Thomak, the first of my line, ruler of the Lands of the Light."

Hogun leered. "As you wish, my emperor."

CHAPTER TWENTY-SIX

Uthiel looked down at the fallen bodies of his two Shields. Their corpses were quickly being lost to piling chunks of ice. He wanted to feel sadness as the wind whipped Theon's hair from his eyes. Try as he might he could feel naught but bloodlust. His heart still hammered and he struggled to focus on what those still living around him were trying to say. A hand reached out and grabbed him roughly.

Uthiel looked up, his face murderous. A captain of the Fifth he had yet to meet glared at him. The man's mouth moved but Uthiel heard nothing. A man he once knew, *Tarren*, interjected himself between the two and shoved the captain away. Uthiel watched with greedy anticipation as his brother hefted his sword to threaten the man.

The captain who had grappled with him earlier managed to push past Tarren. Uthiel didn't even recognise what he had done until he saw his forearm length blade in his hand and the man lying on the ground, a bubbling hole in his chest. Tarren looked at him in shock. The sounds of the world around him began to coalesce once more.

"What have you done!" said one muted voice.

"In the name of Armenius, what is going on?"

305

"You killed them! You killed them all!"

"Untie me!"

This last voice caught Uthiel's attention. It stuck out, sparking his mind to rage as easily as fire caught to tinder. His head turned and he shouldered through the mass around him until he found the Lord General Ryun.

The man looked vicious, even as a prisoner. Uthiel grabbed his hair and chopped a punch into his face. Teeth and blood exploded from the man's mouth. All eyes were on Uthiel, but he did not notice them. To him, there was only Ryun's pulsing neck, stretched backwards and waiting to shower him in glory, and the forearm length blade in his other hand.

Ryun choked out a scream of terror. Uthiel's senses, heightened beyond a mortal man's, could smell his fear over the stench of releasing bowels. In that moment, that one magnificent moment, he truly felt the power that was on offer. He truly understood and accepted why Nikhael had turned to darkness.

And in that moment, he finally knew it was a power born of the darkest evil. A small part of him shoved back within the dark recesses of his mind by months of slow shadowy infusion, screamed with effort as it shone bright gold. The talisman burned brighter and brighter, scorching his flesh and lighting the sickening, rage-fuelled features of his face from below as two gods fought over one champion, like a pair of tectonic plates vying for supremacy.

"Uthiel. Uthiel, my brother."

A hand pushed lightly against Uthiel's knife-wielding arm. Uthiel's head snapped around, his eyes only just barely his own, his body shaking with restraining effort.

Tarren knelt before him, his face fearful, his temperament submissive and non-confrontational.

"My brother, what has become of you?"

The question echoed around within. Uthiel's hand clenched harder as he fought within himself, ripping a scream out of Ryun as some of his scalp tore up.

What has become of me?

He looked to Tarren, his mind struggling to find words.

"To... me?"

Tarren nodded earnestly. "Where does my brother fly? And who battles to reap a bloody tally with his body?"

"I... I am not... myself..." admitted Uthiel. "Something is wrong... Since the prince."

Tarren's concerned look deepened.

"Like Nikhael," said Uthiel, saliva dribbling from his lips and veins sticking out on his forehead as he warred the darkness within.

Tarren froze.

Another knight appeared over his shoulder. Solanthur.

Uthiel shuddered.

"Lead us... home," he growled through clenched teeth.

Solanthur frowned.

"Brother, I cannot hold for much longer... Take these men, and get us home."

Solanthur nodded. A knight handed him a sword.

"Barbarians!"

Uthiel's world broke into chaos once more as screams and clashing steel mixed with thousands of thudding feet.

Solanthur looked to him once more and then turned away, barking out orders. Uthiel could not yet see the battle, but the men who had circled and watched him had all turned away and were forming up quickly into companies and battle lines, their feet crunching through the piled, red-stained ice.

Uthiel stood and drew his blades, his teeth clenched so hard his jaw cracked. He looked above, to see that the clouds had drawn lower and shapes flitted amongst the banks while red lightning lanced out and turned chunks of sand to black glass and chunks of men to red ruin. A sound like thunder, but shaped like a voice, rumbled from the epicentre above.

The men around him and Tarren were being pushed hard. Uthiel stood tall and tried to see over their heads by standing on a corpse. Barbarians: paling flesh rent by blade and claw, greyed eyes and lolling black tongues dripping viscous blackness. They came in their thousands. An animal growl flowered from Uthiel's lips as the addiction of battle began to take over once more. His blades were light in his hands as they begged him to take lives.

The undead crashed into the Secundans again and again like the mighty breakers of the ocean slamming into granite cliffs. Men died at a prolific rate, and soulless undead were hacked to pieces in their hundreds.

A roar split the air and Uthiel watched as three soldiers flew from the front line and slammed into the ranks behind them, trailing blood and intestines. The sound of steel destroying steel clanged out sharply above the sound of battle and a Grey Wolf slammed backwards through the lines of soldiers, his body cleft almost in two as it flew through the darkness.

Then Uthiel saw him.

Seven feet tall, wearing the armour of the Grey Wolves and wielding a massive two-handed sword with a serrated edge, the Black Wolf was a thrilling sight. The undead beasts around him tore into the ranks of the Fifth with unequalled fury. The Secundans died in their droves as they pulled back into a defensive circle where Uthiel and Tarren stood.

Uthiel felt the talisman burn through his haze. He launched himself forward into the gap the massive Black Wolf was forming, but it was too late. The monster crashed through the lines and came at Uthiel. The speed and power of the beast was horrific. Uthiel nearly died seven times within the first two heartbeats of the fight. Three men around him unfortunate enough to catch the backswing or follow through of the evil blade fell screaming.

Tarren threw himself at the Black Wolf. The monster slapped the stocky knight away as if he were no more than a child. Uthiel leapt into the attack with a cry, using his fury to cut and thrust beyond his own capability. He wove under a wild slash, spied an opening, and lunged forward.

Like being struck by a giant forge hammer, Uthiel was slammed from his feet. His cuirass crumpled and crushed into his chest, his strength flowing out with his blood through the immense gash in his plate. He hadn't even seen the blow. It had been too fast.

His vision blacked out a moment and then came to, his hand scrabbling amongst the bodies around him to find his blade, his chest screaming agony. He tried to breathe and blacked out once more. He awoke for another moment. It was long enough to see the immense beast before him pick up Tarren by the throat and launch him into a crowd of the Fifth forming up.

Uthiel's vision went black once more. A voice spoke with him, a voice of duty, of reason, of loyalty. That voice warred within Uthiel against raw hateful emotion that promised the strength for victory. *Succumb and you shall be victorious.* Blackness tried to swallow the light within the young captain. *You are mine.*

He wrenched his eyes open.

"No!" he screamed.

"You shall not have me! I defy you, Zhar T'Hur!"

Blood flew from his mouth at the mention of the name.

His lifted his head up. Bodies were piled up and around him. Three lay atop him and he struggled to push them off. The Black Wolf stood atop the pile, only twenty feet to his right, mercilessly annihilating all who came within his grasp. Uthiel felt his heart near wrench from his chest as he saw Argo's face carved from the rest of his head by the serrated sword.

Fury tried to bubble forth once more but he held it in check. With all of his might and the help of Armenius, he held the wrath of a dark god in check. Up above the clouds thundered ever harder, continuously rolling waves of ear-shattering sound upon the combatants, licking out more frequently with red lightning to destroy friend and foe as Zhar T'Hur unleashed his fury.

Uthiel gathered his swords, his feet quickly becoming accustomed to the hill of bodies and frost he stood upon. Some men grasped at him, moaning for help, while others reached out to drag him down to where they wrestled with clawed hands and biting teeth, but he ignored them as he tried to focus his ravaged mind away from the nightmare of this existence. Reaching within his gorget, he pulled the wolf head talisman over his head and wrapped it around the handle of Ghurkar's sword.

Light, golden and pure, struck out from the silver of the talisman. Uthiel raised his hand, bathing the bodies, the thickly falling hail, and the screaming warriors in light.

Soldiers drove up the mound of bodies to stab at the Black Wolf with spear and sword. Their bodies were quickly and brutally added to the hill of the dead and dying by the champion of slaughter standing at the summit. Others ran, terror mashing their features before they were cut down. Down below, some six feet to the ground, Uthiel could see Solanthur desperately battling with the scant few Secundans who would stand with him. They were dying by the second.

Solanthur looked up to see the light. Uthiel raised his blade.

"For Secunda!" roared Solanthur, launching himself forward.

"Armenius is with us! Fight for him!" the soldiers and few knights around the first captain defended with increased gritty vigour.

Uthiel looked out beyond those men. There were still thousands of barbarians out there. He could barely see some more pockets of Secundan resistance through the tearing rain. Even as he watched, another was overrun.

A screaming barbarian ran at Uthiel. He decapitated the man with barely a conscious thought. Another came at him. He died also, clawed hands trying to scoop his guts up while a soldier without legs reached out to tear the pink innards further out with frost-blue hands. Two undead beasts ran at him. Uthiel rolled forward, the remains of his tabard torn off by searching claws, and clove his blades through the backs of their heads.

All the while the Black Wolf slew more and more, like a whirlwind of destruction. The monster was indiscriminate in his killing. Barbarians. Soldiers. Knights. Undead. He slew them all mercilessly. Uthiel took one, then two unsteady steps up the hill. A hand grasped his calf. His sword snaked out to cut it from its limb. A man screamed in agony, one voice of pain amongst thousands.

Uthiel pushed himself further and further up the incline of bodies, his legs surging with more strength each step. The Black Wolf sighted him and launched his massive frame down toward Uthiel. Their blades met with an ear-splitting clash of steel.

The hands of wounded and dying men grasped at them from below as they pushed with all their might at each other; a champion of the light against a champion of the dark in the most fearsome of struggles. Uthiel's talisman burned brighter. The Black Wolf's darkness deepened as lightning struck and detonated bodies all around them.

The Black Wolf hammered Uthiel with a punch. The Grey Wolf rolled with the blow and then deflected the serrated blade with his vambrance. The blow jarred the blade from his grasp with its power, but it gave him an opening. Ghurkar's sword snaked out and bit deep into the Black Wolf's side, piercing the dark steel cuirass.

The monster roared in rage and pain, his free hand whipping down and grabbing Uthiel's wrist with bone-grating strength. Uthiel cried out in pain and then was cut short at the Black Wolf dropped his sword and clamped his free hand around the young knight's throat and lifted him from his feet to the sky.

Uthiel kicked and punched as his lungs screamed for air. Sharp-edged hail beat against his face and cut his flesh as darkness began to creep in from his peripheral vision. He beat his free hand against the arm that held him. It was to no avail, the beast was too strong.

He saw the monster's black orbs, and tried to punch harder.

The Black Wolf ignored him, raising him higher as if his weight was nothing.

"Zhar T'Hur!" thundered the Black Wolf. "Red Father! My sacrifice to you!"

Uthiel could no longer hold his arms up to strike at the Black Wolf.

"Take me! I am yours! Walk this earth once more and let the soil run red under your victories!"

Uthiel blacked out, his last vision being the endless darkness above as a god looked down, through the eye of a hurricane of death, upon his champion.

CHAPTER TWENTY-SEVEN

Uthiel opened his eyes. Immediately he squinted as black sludge splashed against his blood-covered cheeks. The first thing he heard was the tinniness of the rain hammering against his pauldrons. The next, a roar of battle the like unheard on the planes of man in all of history. He reached for his throat and found nothing. The Black Wolf was gone.

Before him, lines of men in steel plate or chain marched towards darkness in their hundreds of thousands. Their tread shook the black sludge covered ground as they moved in tremendous regiments into the maelstrom of destruction. Uthiel stood and watched in wonder as line after line and column after column of stalwart men with black hair and blue eyes, mostly hidden beneath helms, followed glorious champions, captains and generals onward to battle.

His gaze followed them as they strode in to reinforce the line almost a mile distant just over the crest of a hill, and it was then that he felt the first life blink in to nothingness. It was followed immediately by another, then a hundred more, in less time than it took him to blink. He could feel them dying, souls sent screaming to some sort of eternal darkness.

Uthiel tried to focus on the distant hill crest, but the falling black rain made a shadow of anything that far off. He began to walk toward it, as if his spirit was being inevitably drawn to the conflict that raged there between the steel-shod bodies of men and whatever horrors hid in the darkness beyond.

"Secundan!" roared a voice.

Uthiel turned, his hand rising to shield his eyes.

A formation of men some three or four thousand strong were marching by him, eyes towards the line and spears held high. A soldier had broken off and was walking toward him. The man looked familiar, though Uthiel could not place him.

"Where are your brothers?" asked the man, reaching up to remove his helm.

"I... I know not. Where have you come from? Where are the sands of Imonetia?" said Uthiel, noticing for the first time that the land he stood upon was not that of the Sand Lords.

The soldier looked at him a while, and then frowned. With a cry of anguish the man leapt forward and tried to hug him. Uthiel swung away and avoided the man's grasp, drawing one of his blades. The man held up a hand.

"Why are you here? What has happened?" asked the man.

Uthiel's frustration began to grow. "What? I am in Imonetia! I fight the foe! How do *you* come to be here? Where were you while we were dying taking back the city? Where was this army when we marched on the horrors of Gall?"

The man took a deep breath, lifting his shirt to try and wipe some of the black rain from his face. A mile distant, there was a great cry and a thunderous clap of power and the earth trembled.

Uthiel took a step towards the man. "Tell me! Where am I? What is happening?"

The man reached up and placed a hand lightly on his pauldron.

"My son, do you not recognise me?"

Uthiel stopped, his face and body frozen in shock.

"Who?"

If his heart could beat in this place, it would have cramped with grief. Uthiel's head dropped.

"Then I have fallen. I have been slain in Imonetia. I have failed my god as his champion and have been brought to the Shield Wall in the Sky to face his wrath."

Tanin reached forwards and hugged his son.

"You have fallen to a place where once again, Secunda is on the brink of destruction."

Uthiel looked up.

"How?"

"He   found   us."

"But this is the Shield Wall in the Sky. This is where we protect the souls of our people for eternity. Where are its green pastures and sweeping hills? Where are the clear skies and the polished armour of my brothers? Where is the shining golden light of our Eternal Lord?"

Tanin looked to the distant line of battle. A pale nimbus of light could be seen at the centre.

"The Eternal Lord is at the forefront of the battle, as He has always been. Your brothers stand by his side. That is where my men and I go."

Uthiel stared at the far-off maelstrom.

"Your men?" he said, turning back to his father.

"Four thousand, three-hundred and twenty-two men, every life lost under my command while I lived."

Uthiel watched as the column of soldiers continued to march by.

"So many. Such fear in their eyes. Yet they march still."

Tanin nodded. "They do. They may no longer be living, breathing men, but they are the spirits of men and carry all of the fears, hopes, dreams, cruelties, and courage of the men they once were. They know what they march to. And yet they go anyway."

"But they are of the spirit," said Uthiel, confused. "What can harm them now?"

Tanin clenched his jaw.

"The foe is the purest evil, older than the mountains. He shall outlive the sun. His malevolence outstrips all the horrors men and women could heap upon ourselves in a million years of life and more. A hundred fold more. A thousand fold. Such is his evil that those spirits slain by his minions fall forever, lost to the darkness.

"My men are afraid, because their very souls are on the line."

Uthiel felt fear and a swelling of pride rise within his breast at the same time.

He paused a moment, memories of his life coming to the fore.

"Have you been watching me, father?"

Tanin waited a moment, weighing his words. "I have, son."

"I have done and seen many things, not all of them good."

"I know. I have watched you."

"By being able to walk these fields have I been judged worthy?"

Tanin's face swung to look at the battle, his eyes focussing on the dim light of the Eternal Lord.

"I know not. His attention is occupied at present. But I am proud to call you my son, for what that is worth."

Uthiel smiled with genuine warmth, reaching out and placing a hand on his father's mail-armoured shoulder.

"Then I shall march with you, father."

Tanin smiled. " I'd like nothing more."

They began to walk side by side, the sound of raging warfare on an unprecedented scale matched only by a constant staccato rhythm of rain slamming into their armour and boots marching side by side towards war, filling their senses.

Uthiel turned and studied his father's face as they walked. He could see fear in the man's features.

"How does the battle fare?" he asked.

His father did not answer for a while.

"Father?"

"Not well, my son. The Eternal Lord calls ever more souls to the front lines. We cannot last much longer. Our reinforcements are finite, the great foe's are not."

"How can that be, father?"

Trethore swore under his breath. "Our god is a young one, and our people have been coming here for sanctuary for a mere four centuries. Their god is old, and men and women have been dying for him since time immemorial."

Uthiel shook his head as he tried to take it all in.

"You're saying that we may lose the Shield Wall in the Sky? We may lose the final refuge of our people?"

Tanin stopped and turned to his son.

"I'm saying that every Secundan soul since the founding of our people may blink into the everdeath within the next few hours, and that those who die on the white frontier will fly screaming through the void while Zhar T'Hur's minions hunt them down one by one and shred them to pieces slowly over time everlasting.

"We fight to defend the souls of our nation before they even pass from mortal flesh."

Uthiel's first thought was of his son. His face trembled and tears began to roll down his face.

His father moved to hug him. "Be brave my son. The fight is not over yet."

Uthiel pushed him away. "No, da. I have a child. *Had* a child. An unborn child. I shall never see him into the world."

Tanin's face scrunched up in anguish.

Uthiel moved in and wrapped his arms around his father. A few of the marching men looked over to them. Uthiel recognised Argo. The soldier broke rank and walked over.

"General! We near the lines!"

Uthiel turned to look at the battle line ahead. The sounds of men fighting and the hammering pull of their everdeaths were almost overwhelming. Uthiel drew his blades.

Tanin put a hand on his wrist.

"Not yet, my son. You won't need those yet. Come on, one last hill and we shall see the foe and our Eternal Lord as he stands against it."

Uthiel nodded and sheathed his swords. He fell into step beside his father as they topped a rise to finally lay eyes on the great battle. It took Uthiel's breath away with its enormity and savagery. Truly, it was the war to dwarf all wars. And he could see his brothers and countrymen losing.

Regiments of men marched forth while others drew back, severely mauled, to regroup or be reinforced. Men like his father stood upon rotting tree stumps and empty carts and ordered men in to battle, relaying orders from the Eternal Lord and making intricate changes to troop and reinforcement displacements by the minute. Immense cavalry wings drew up, the hair of their mounts dripping with tar and their flanks heaving in fear.

Blocks of soldiers moved into the line below, joining the butchery of the final frontier, where light met dark in the world that existed beyond that of men. He could see the beacon light of the Eternal Lord at the centre of the line, now, thousands of knights, unmistakeable to his eye even from this distance, around him. To the flanks and to the rear, huge numbers of soldiers in their chainmail fought and died and waited to fight and die. A piece of the line would break, and a fresh regiment, directed there but a moment before, would charge in to straighten the line once more.

It was here, that Uthiel finally laid eyes upon the great foe. They were an ocean of black, pulsing and pushing at the line. He could just make out unarmoured limbs and heads amongst the slashing dark blades and axes. So many did the great foe have that he did not bother to armour his worshippers with anything more than one item to kill a foe with.

Uthiel's eyes swept out over the sea of darkness behind. He could see no end to them. Even where the falling tar rain completely stifled his view the foe were still crammed in, shoulder to shoulder, chest to back, salivating to get at the Secundan shield wall. Uthiel knew true despair then.

His father had not noticed him stop for a few steps. He turned.

"Uthiel?"

Uthiel felt as if in a daze. "We cannot win."

Find me at the front, my champion.

Uthiel looked to his father. "Did you——?"

Tanin smiled sadly. "He speaks with you?"

"I believe so."

"Then the Eternal Lord has called you to the fore, my son. This makes me proud. If the everdeath should come for me today, know that I shall die smiling that you were at His side. You were the light of my life, and now my afterlife, my son. Never forget that."

Uthiel embraced his father once more.

"I shall see you after, father. I shall not let us fall."

"Farewell, my son."

He turned to leave, and then stopped, returning his gaze to his father for a moment.

"Have you seen Branor? Does he fight with this army?"

Tanin shook his head. "Branor's presence is not known to me in this realm. I have seen Carn. I was saddened. He seemed a good man."

"But not Bran?"

"Sorry, son. Perhaps he still lives."

Uthiel sighed. "He could not."

With a half-hearted wave, Uthiel broke away in to a jog, moving in and around companies at a steady pace. With every step towards the maelstrom of battle ahead, he could feel the presence of the great enemy grow within his mind. He could feel the horror of the souls sent to the everdeath, feel the screams as they were lost to the spirit world the Eternal Lord had built.

As he neared the front, the regiments waiting to move into the line grew denser and he had to start pushing his way through the spirits of his countrymen. He passed a block of dark-haired women clad in stiff leathers wielding longbows. The front rank would raise and shoot, turn sideways and take a step back. At the same time the back row would pluck an arrow from a quiver or from the mud, turn sideways as they notched, and then move to the fore. A constant rain of arrows flowed off into the darkness. Uthiel could only imagine the death tally they had caused.

He recognised a face there for a moment. She was young, beautiful, but could not be. *Is that——? No!*

"Emilia!" he screamed.

319

Her face disappeared as the ranks of archers shifted and changed their angle of fire to a further flank.

"Emilia!"

To me, my champion.

Tears streaked down Uthiel's face as his legs began pushing him towards his god once more. *It can't be. It can't be. It's not her. She can't be here, she doesn't believe. She isn't dead. Trethore would watch over her. Would protect her. Would protect my child.*

He felt warmth within his chest as a god spoke to him once more. *Uthiel, my champion, I need you at the front. Emilia is fine, your child's heart still beats. You can see them again. But I need you now. If we are to win this battle and save our people, I need you at the front now, with me.*

Uthiel tore himself from staring at the archers as they sent flight after flight of arrows into the maelstrom. Finally, he reached the press of men awaiting combat. He watched them shift and hustle, their steps short as they tried to keep a constant weight on the man in front. Every now and then the line would bulge outwards and the rear men would lean into those forward of them and push the line straight. Here, the physical screams of the dead mixed with the psychic. Uthiel felt his blood fire at the sounds of battle, though his mind did not beg to unhinge itself from honour and duty as it had during life.

He reached into his gorget for his talisman. It was not there. Grimacing, he began to move into the push, calling out to his brothers to be let through.

At first men resisted him, and then they tried to push him through and past them while not taking the pressure off of the man in front of them. His movement forward was slow but soon he found himself a mere twenty ranks back from the shield wall. It was there he found his brother knights.

He could just see over their heads to the front. Blades flashed in their thousands, shields rose and fell to take the brunt of axes, crossbows were held up over heads and released. Men fell, and the press of the foe pushed them back step by bitterly lost step. The rain from above slammed down as if Zhar

T'Hur was using it as one more weapon in his arsenal against the Secundans.

And then there, at the epicentre of the battle, was Armenius. His armour shone bright gold, brilliant pauldrons untouched by the dark rain. His sword and power were unheard of, each swipe carving five and ten bodies to pieces as he darted out from the shield wall time and time again. Uthiel's heart lifted like never before, glory shining in his eyes.

"Our father calls me to his side!" he yelled, his voice disappearing into the roar of battle.

He grabbed the pauldron of a knight in front of him and yelled again, bringing his face close to the man's head. The bucket helm of the knight turned. The eye slits regarded him a moment and then his arm snaked out and pulled Uthiel into the line. Row by row, Uthiel made his way to the front line. Finally he was but five rows back from this fighting and could go no further, so great was the pressure.

Uthiel leaned his weight into his shoulder, his shield lying somewhere behind him. For a moment he railed at his own stupidity, he would be a weak point in the line. Even Armenius was bearing a shield. A hand grasped him from behind. He turned and a shield was thrust to him.

Uthiel looked up to see a grim face watching him, a face he had not seen for many months.

"By Armenius little brother! Did I not teach you anything?" roared Ghurkar Storm, forcing a shield to him through the press.

Uthiel smiled as he slipped his forearm into the shield straps, his legs braced and his back pushing hard into the man behind him.

"You need a shield, my friend!" yelled Uthiel.

Ghurkar grinned and squatted down, driving his hand into the calf deep slurry of mud and tar below. The knight roared with effort as he yanked up a shield from below and pulled in on to his arm. With a nod Uthiel turned and put his weight back into the line. Up ahead, the brother standing next to the Eternal Lord fell, dragged down by a screaming berserker and his body hacked and trampled to death.

Uthiel felt the line give a little before the three men in front of him leapt forwards to plug the gap. Uthiel looked out beyond the front line to the untold masses that waited out in the darkness. Up close, he could see that under the tar they were of all shapes and sizes, skin colours, nationality stereotyped features, and of both sexes.

There were men, women, and children. Some were broad and muscled, others old and infirm, barely able to wield their blades. All had the same expression on their faces: undiluted hate. Uthiel could understand it no other way. Eyes of all colours that faced him were lit with such fires of hate that it brought horror to his heart. Of all the things he had seen and done in his life, all the people he had killed and seen killed, this moment showed him how it could all be possible.

In the eyes of those who worshipped Zhar T'Hur, Uthiel saw the hate that was a part of every person who had ever lived and ever would live. He saw what became of people when all other pieces of their personality were stripped away and the bare, raw, consuming rage was left to stand alone. He saw the true horror of the darkness that Secunda and the Lands of the Light fought against.

To the left of Armenius, another knight fell. A humongous berserker stormed into the gap, his immense form rippling with bulky muscle and his thick arms wielding a double-handed sword. Two more knights were cleaved into the everdeath as more men and women stormed into the gap, leaping upon shields and trying to drag them down. The man in front of Uthiel was one of those men, falling face down and struggling to rise. Uthiel deflected two blades from the man, but was shoulder-charged as another sword stove in the knight's head. Uthiel gathered himself and charged forwards into the gap with Ghurkar Storm at his heels.

A form leapt at him, breasts wobbling as she tried to bring a cleaver down on to Uthiel's head. Uthiel took the blade on the shield and then kicked out, sending the slight woman flying, screaming, backward. Taking another blade on the shield Uthiel lunged and drove his sword into a man's belly, ripping sideways to release the innards to the ground.

322

Uthiel could see the Eternal Lord battling with immense fury, his war cry reverberating in the chests of the men around him, his blade like lightning. Uthiel led a wedge of knights as they tried to close the gap and re-form the line. As he marched on, his shield locked and his shoulders hunched, he stabbed out again and again, slaying and slaying.

"Forward!" he roared as he drove the tip of his sword into a youth's face. "Forward to the Eternal Lord!"

The knights beside him let out one sharp cry, the line of steel they presented taking a high tally on the naked forms running at them. Fingers wrapped over the top of Uthiel's shield, trying to pry it down. Uthiel lowered his stance instinctively, using his knee to stop the shield pivoting around his forearm, his bicep screaming and tearing with effort. Ghurkar lashed out and the fingers separated from their hands, releasing the pressure.

Uthiel chanced a look down and amongst the bodies spied that of a young girl not ten summers old. His fury rose, cold and controlled. Armenius battled a mere few feet before him, desperately trying to keep his battle line intact. Uthiel called to his brothers for more effort, and they gave it to him, one blood-soaked and bulldoggish half step at a time.

With a roar of victory, Uthiel and his men closed the gap in the wall. Uthiel stood shoulder to shoulder with his god, their shields locked and his soul basking in the radiant glory of Armenius. His spirit afire with cleansing light, he killed and he killed, reaching up to pull out his second blade from over his shoulder when his first was lost to his grip, lodged in a man's ribs.

Armenius turned his gaze towards him. Approval was replaced with confusion a moment later.

"My Champion? Why are you here?"

Uthiel frowned. "You called me here, my Eternal Lord."

"I did not, for you have not fal—"

Uthiel did not hear the rest of the sentence as far out in the ocean of black souls something began to bear down on them, throwing bodies flying into the air as it smashed its way toward the Secundan line. Like some sort of subterranean beast it burrowed through its own forces with no thought for them. Uthiel could feel the malice building in his body.

Beside him, Armenius called to the spirits of his countrymen.

"This is it, my brothers and sisters! Hold for Secunda! Hold for each other! The souls of your sons and daughters and all of your lines need you now! Hold with me!"

Uthiel felt the great ripple of fear flow through the men around him. And then a voice slammed him to the ground. Gripping his head in agony, he didn't see the knight behind him leap his form to take his place, nor feel Armenius try to reach for him. His eyes squeezed shut, the world around him ceased to exist.

You are mine.

You can only win through me, in this world, or the lands of the living.

Your people are mine.

Your father is mine.

Despair, for your child is mine.

I am Zhar T'Hur, and you shall be my champion, or I shall tear the soul from this world in a rain of blood.

Uthiel screamed wordlessly.

You still live, Uthiel Caellar. In the lands of hearts beating you are on the cusp of death. You will die there. The men who trusted you will die next to you. I shall tear their minds from their bodies and feast upon their spirits.

Uthiel screamed.

A sinister voice chuckled within his mind, each octave tearing into his sanity.

Become mine. Become my champion and you shall live. You shall have power beyond compare. Armies in the millions shall stand at your beck and call. You shall be the champion of this realm and shall lead my forces until your have conquered a world in my name. Drench the world in blood and I shall give your men their lives to war by your side.

Uthiel's mind raced through the roaring ocean of pain, ducking away from the faces of the men he had fought with and led in his short life. Branor. Argo. Antony. Carn. Eliem and

Umbar. The faces raced by. Some of them begged him for life. Others screamed at him.

"I'm sorry. I'm sorry my brothers," sobbed Uthiel. "I cannot. All you have died for will be for naught."

A fresh wave of pain exploded within his mind.

You would have glory beyond compare.

A picture was pushed into his mind. He felt it as though it was a violation of his physical body. A mound of bodies, a Black Wolf at his feet, hundreds of the Fifth standing around the battlefield cheering him on, the strength of an immortal fling through his body; power like no man had wielded before.

For a fleeting moment, he imagined this world and wondered at turning the power back on Zhar T'Hur. He could embrace it for but a moment, long enough to win, and then he would renounce it, throw the dark god from his mind.

Yes. You could. It would be your only chance. A mortal cannot win. A mortal cannot defeat a god. Take my power. Turn it against me.

Let the blood flow.

"My brother!"

A voice broke through the darkness of his mind. Uthiel opened his eyes. He could taste the copper of his own blood upon his tongue. A golden figure stood over him.

"Resist him. Resist him for all you are worth. Stand with your countrymen. Do not let him take you," cried Armenius, his hand gripping Uthiel's gorget and pulling him up face to face.

Uthiel felt the blood bubble over his lips. "He shall not... have me."

Armenius smiled. "You are my champion, *mine*. You are a champion of the light and Secunda, a man who shall lead our people back to the light. Secunda needs you. Your daughter needs you."

Uthiel groaned as he thought of the child he would never see into life.

"My daughter..."

"She is not lost to you yet."

Armenius hesitated a moment, doubt clouding his open features. His face hardened, his light diminishing a little.

"You shall find her, I swear it."

Uthiel frowned, and then blacked out again.

A vision flickered before his unconscious gaze.

Torches guttered. Dull light swam over armour, white tabards, flesh and stone. Blue eyes watched. Blood dripped to the ground, splashing in a steady rhythm that echoed in the hushed silence. A slender hand hung limply, two fingers severed, covered in crimson flowing down from above.

A man stood hunched, withdrawing a corkscrew from the dead flesh of a woman's thigh. Seventeen inch-long nails came out next. The man shook these out, flinging the blood from them to the ground. He turned away, his white tabard was red from below his pectorals to where it ended just above the knee.

An old, wizened face looked at Uthiel. *Through me, like I'm nothing but invisible spirit.* Uthiel could see coldness in those eyes, a line crossed in the name of duty. There was a hardness of spirit there, required for what the man had just done.

Trethore spoke to a man who stood behind Uthiel.

"It is done. She will speak no more."

Trethore dropped his gaze and took a deep breath before walking away, showing Uthiel what remained of the unfortunate behind him.

Uthiel screamed. He screamed and screamed.

Emilia.

A rough hand shook him, and golden light once again filled his vision. Uthiel's mouth was wide, his voice crying out to the limit, his throat dry and raw.

"It is a vision!" yelled Armenius. "It is the great enemy turning you against me!"

Uthiel reached out and grabbed his god with his left hand. He saw the lie in his god's face, watched as Armenius' aura dimmed for the briefest of moments.

"You lie!" he roared, his voice hate filled.

His forearm length blade lashed out and scored Armenius' cheek. His god reeled away.

Something immense impacted the front line, sending knights flying into the sky and barrelling toward him.

A lamprey mouth exploded from the rank in front and opened wide, the darkness inside ready to engulf him.

Armenius' form changed with a clap of thunder and a spear of light, brighter than the sun, lanced into the forest of teeth before Uthiel.

Something stabbed Uthiel in the side, white pain carving through his body.

He looked down and saw blood, but no blade.

Uthiel's world exploded into blinding light.

He was ripped from the Shield Wall in the Sky and cast from the world of the spirit.

His eyes opened in the world of the living and looked straight into the red orbs of Jotel.

CHAPTER TWENTY-EIGHT

Eyelids snapped open before Jotel, revealing orbs darker than the night. He met the pitch-black eyes of the Grey Wolf he held in his grasp with surprise. He reached down, his hands cutting themselves on the razor edge of the sword that had pierced his back straight through, and lodged in the side of the young knight before him. He wavered a moment, blood bubbling over his lips, the metallic tang filling his mouth and nostrils. He looked to the sky.

"Zhar T'Hur... give me strength..."

His arm began to weaken, the weight of the champion of the Lands of the Light he was strangling the life out of growing by the moment. A sick smile spread across the face before him, red and black drool lolling from the man's split lips. Two scars that formed a great cross on one side of the man's face moved through hues of sickening red to blue to purple before his very eyes. His hand, and then his arm, and then his shoulder began to shake as he resisted the weight on his arm fruitlessly.

The knight before him reached up with a hand and grasped Jotel's thick wrist with unbelievable power. That red-toothed grin getting wider, Jotel screamed as he felt the bones of his forearm begin to groan under the crush of the knight's grip. He looked to the skies, the red haze receding and fear beginning to work its way in to him for the first time in over a decade.

"No!" he roared to the skies through clenched teeth.

"No!" he spat down his outstretched arm at the knight before him.

"Zhar T'Hur!" he screamed. "Empower me! I am your champion! You are my god!"

Using his weight as a counterpoint, the champion of the Lands of the Light drove his palm up into the Jotel's elbow. The joint snapped upward. Jotel screamed in pain, dropping the knight to the ground, his mind a roiling sea of overwhelming confusion and fear, all of a sudden bereft of its rage-fuelled assuredness and sense of bloody purpose. Jotel wailed, his voice almost not his own, as he fell to his knees, eyes locked on his reversed elbow joint. White pain lanced through him. He looked up at the champion of the light. The man stood above him, eyes black as pitch, his forearm length blade in his cocked-back hand, blond hair swirling madly in the tempest, a wordless snarl upon his lips.

Golden light burned from beneath the knight's gorget, reddening pale skin like flame and casting a nightmare shadow up the knight's face. With every moment, Jotel's horror grew. It was not the knowledge of his impending death. It was not the blue-eyed monster before him. It was not the blade rushing down to his forehead. It was not the clarity of his sight and all that he had done and witnessed done in the last decade.

In that moment, right before the tip of the blade drove into his brain and sent him screaming from this life, Jotel knew horror like he'd never before known in all his years.

Jotel realised that he had been replaced.

Zhar T'Hur had a new champion, and for all his dedication and effort, his blood would be nothing amongst the rest of the crimson that flowed into the sky to feed Zhar T'Hur, the Red Father.

<--->

Uthiel looked up from the body of Jotel, the handle and crosspiece of his blade jutting from the beast's forehead.

Solanthur sat on a dead man's chest before him, trying to pull his sword from Jotel's back. Solanthur held out a hand, waving Uthiel forwards for help. Uthiel's unhinged mind saw nothing but Trethore.

"My brother, my sword. Help me."

Uthiel tried once to wrench the blade from Jotel's skull. It came out on the second attempt, trailing pulped brain matter. His lip rose in a snarl as his body curled like a spring.

"Brother?" said Solanthur.

The first captain saw Uthiel's black eyes a moment too late.

"Brother... your eyes—"

"Bastard! You killed her!"

Uthiel roared and leapt forward. Solanthur's vambrance came up and blocked the blade, his shock almost costing him his life.

They wrestled, the knife only an inch from Solanthur's head, Uthiel's strength growing by the second as his rage turned into a berserk fury. His fist pummelled Solanthur's defences mercilessly, breaking bone and denting armour where it struck. His knees smashed into Solanthur's legs and teeth gnashed before the first captain's face.

Finally a vicious punch took the light from Solanthur's eyes. A second broke his cheekbone and a third crushed his jaw. Teeth flew from the first captain's mouth and were driven through his lip as Uthiel's fist rose and lanced down again and again, destroying the first captain's face.

Something impacted Uthiel. He rolled with it and threw the man off him. Looking down he grabbed a sword, a face no longer his own grinning to see the serrated edge of Jotel's broadsword.

Darian stood before him.

"Uthiel! What have you done?"

Uthiel couldn't find words. He couldn't form them in thought or with his mouth. A demon's rage engulfed him. His only communication was death. He leapt.

Darian was a good soldier, experienced and ever battle ready. He had fought in many skirmishes and met the foe sword to axe more times than he could remember. The young Grey Wolf before him had been a friend as well as a commander and a pupil. The man had been like a member of his family.

Uthiel cut him in half.

The serrated blade entered through the top of his head and exited through his crotch. His own blade clanged uselessly from Uthiel's pauldron.

In an explosion of blood the two halves of Captain Darian fell onto the mountain of limbs and corpses to become just another lifeless husk of flesh.

Uthiel roared to the skies, crimson cascading from his armour. *Yes, my champion! Give them all to me! Every one!* The dark voice inside his head was no longer a clandestine whisper or hidden chuckle, it roared through his body with the power of the sun.

Emilia's scream echoed through his mind like a mail-shod punch to every major organ he had. Uthiel buckled and screamed in agony and rage. Then he stopped, and stood.

Uthiel's slack-jawed, red-toothed grin slid over his features.

"For you, Zhar T'Hur. The blood of those that betrayed me for you, my Red Father!"

An undead beast leapt at him, jaw distended, claws reaching for him. Uthiel slew him without thought. He spun, his pauldron smashing a blade in half, and his hand entering a soldier's chest through the chainmail to claim his heart. Another soldier and a barbarian were next, the serrated blade cleaving them both in two as they grappled with each other desperately.

More and more of the dead beasts ran at him, charging up the growing hill of the slain. Uthiel slew them, joy upon his face as he revelled in the slaughter. Soldiers ran to him, thinking to stand beside him. They ran to a man they thought was a Secundan hero.

Uthiel killed them indiscriminately.

Above the slaughter the maelstrom of the dark hurricane whirled ever harder, winds screaming with the pleasure of

Armenius' champion turned and the baptism of darkness in blood and martial fury.

Inside the eye of the storm, directly above Uthiel, light began to slice down the insides of the ravenous cloud tunnel. A cry of anguish so loud it silenced the clapping rolls of thunder followed a spear of light as it carved through the eye of Zhar T'Hur above. The clouds of the eye began to constrict, rushing inward like a body curling around a belly wound.

Uthiel stood oblivious below, his blade slaying with impunity all who approached him, his eyes becoming darker and darker until they sucked what little light there was in to them. His laughter echoed over the killing field below where a great tide of barbarian undead stood waiting their chance to climb the mountain of bodies and give themselves to Zhar T'Hur's champion. Uthiel moved with inhuman speed, revelling in the bloody offering his new god put before him. Bloodshed through combat, his greatest desire and unsated addiction, grew at an exponential rate alongside a burning need for revenge quickly being lost in a mind drowning in death. Then, he was bathed in golden light.

Uthiel looked up at the last moment, right before the spear of light lanced into him. He saw a face. *Armenius.* His rage spiked at a split-second memory of a lie: a betrayal. His sword struck upwards. Even his reflexes were far too slow.

Armenius struck him from above, his own spiritual essence slamming into Uthiel and seeking out the darkness. Zhar T'Hur's presence in the young knight was obliterated in a heartbeat, overpowered as a god of the light suffered the everdeath for a chance to cleanse the realm of dark taint.

Above, the clouds snapped back and forth spasmodically as the great enemy was struck a blow like no other it had suffered it its time. A colossal explosion of golden light tore out from the kneeling form of Uthiel, bright like the death of a star, its heat felt only by those whose souls were not tied to a body of flesh and bone.

Uthiel knelt, silhouetted at the heart of the light. His mind was empty as Armenius' death echoed over the battlefield in an ever-expanding halo of light a hundred miles tall, the god's wrath tearing the un-life from those Jotel had brought with him. Bodies already bereft of life-force collapsed to the ground to add yet more to the feast Death had enjoyed this day.

Above, the clouds retreated into the sky with shocking speed. Across the lands for thousands of leagues, both light and dark, shamans looked up to the sky. They were allowed one moment of horror before their souls were ripped screaming from their bodies as Zhar T'Hur fled the realm in agony, reaching out with a thousand taloned hands to pull the balms of powerful souls to his wounds.

CHAPTER TWENTY-NINE

Trethore walked from the holdfast, rolling his aching shoulders and stretching his back. He looked to the sky for a moment and frowned. A cloud front above shone with light for a moment with a flash of brilliance coming from the north. It was there for a heartbeat before it died.

He placed a hand on his chest, feeling a sudden emptiness there, though what was missing he could not guess. Moving his head from side to side he let the muscles there loosen and stretch.

His heart stopped a moment.

What if the Eternal Lord has judged me wrong?

What if, even now, after all I've done for Secunda, my soul is damned forever?

Is this emptiness what it feels like to be spurned by the one you loved and worship above all?

Trethore shook his head. He had done the right thing. He had found the cancer at the heart of the Grey Wolves.

The emptiness within me must be something else, perhaps some weak remorse for a traitor? The thought of Uthiel made his eyes grow ever colder.

Trethore looked down at his hand. It was red.

Reaching down, he pulled his blood-soaked tabard from his body.

No, it is the child. I was forced to take its life along with the mother's.

Stretching his back once more, Trethore looked back through the door to the holdfast. He could still see her.

She had lasted many days. She had held out where many men would have succumbed. In the end the unborn child had been his way in. She had spoken then. Oh yes, she had spoken of all.

Uthiel.

The Black Wolves.

Her discussion with Queen Valissa.

Trethore's eyes gazed over the ruin of her body. He watched the blood drip from where he had cut trenches in her flesh and shown Emilia her own ribs. He had cut pieces off her and cauterised the stumps with heated iron from the braziers. He had cut out her eyes. Removed her nose.

It had been a mercy when he had driven a knife into her belly.

Yes, he said to himself, *it had been a mercy.*

A warrior priest walked up to him.

"What now?"

Trethore's eyes narrowed as he looked in the direction of the host camped at Gall.

"Now, brother Tyran, we cut the cancer of the Grey Wolves from the body of our beloved Secunda before this land tears itself to shreds."

EPILOGUE

Solanthur woke, pain wracking his body, his face feeling like a bull had stomped on it. One eye was blind and his lips were raw. He opened his mouth and groaned as the hole where his teeth had punched through his flesh opened afresh. He reached up and felt his face.

He cried out as his fingers felt the broken and shattered bones. Something hard had stuck out through the skin and hairs of his eyebrow. The sound of a scream of anguish grabbed his attention. The sound was primal and rose above the groans and cries of the agonisingly wounded.

He lifted his head. Vertigo slammed in to him and he rolled on to his side as vomit dribbled from his mouth, the acid from his stomach burning his open wounds and gums where teeth once sat. There was another roar from nearby.

His vision began to swim slowly in to view as his one good eye sought the sound of the cries. Solanthur wrestled himself up onto his elbow, unconsciousness doing its best to lull him into its embrace once more. He lay amongst a pile of bodies and injured. To his left they receded down, like the side of a hill, and to his right it rose a few feet to a summit. Arms waved for help, legs kicked out in suffering and panic, heads swivelled and wide eyes searched for help. Hundreds of bodies must have lent their volume to the pile's size. Perhaps thousands.

He spied a face he recognised, arms desperately trying to pull off a badly misshapen cuirass. Maybe Tarren, or one of the other men from Uthiel's—*Armenius save me. Uthiel, what did you do?*

Solanthur levered himself up a little further. At first, he didn't see the knight amongst the deluge. But then the man raised his head to the heavens and screamed, the veins in his neck standing further and further out.

Eyes, stained grey but still almost translucent blue, came down and looked at him. There was pain in those eyes, fathomless depths of agony lying upon the spirit.

Solanthur's heart began to race. He looked around, growing dizzier by the moment. His hand reached out and grabbed a blade. In that moment his elbow gave out and his head crashed into the steel plate of a dead knight under him.

The first captain's head rolled to the side. A soundlessly screaming face met him, jaw distended beyond what a man's jaw should have been capable of. He turned away in disgust.

Uthiel Caellar knelt before him, his foot upon the flat of the blade Solanthur held.

His face was pure torment. Tears rolled down his face.

"My brother, they killed her. My Emilia and my child, they killed her."

Solanthur's disgust grew as images of the punches raining down upon his face and the reddening eyes behind them came back to him.

He spat. The blood and tooth mix that came out didn't make it on to his target, spilling down his cheek instead.

"You... are not... my brother," he mumbled, the pain excruciating.

Uthiel didn't seem to hear him.

"They killed her. Trethore, the priests, they tortured her to find out the secrets of the Grey Wolves. The secrets Thomak bade me keep in the dark. They murdered my child within her."

Solanthur coughed, crying out in agony.

"Traitor. You... betrayed us."

Uthiel's eyes hardened.

"Armenius is gone."

It was as if Uthiel had stomped on Solanthur's face. In his unconsciousness he had felt something scream across the void of his mind. Then there had been emptiness, like something was missing from his chest.

Uthiel pulled something out from within his blood and gore coated armour. It was small and upon a silver chain. It shone dully. If steel could die, Solanthur was looking at a small corpse the shape of a wolf's head.

Uthiel smiled.

"He's gone. Sacrificed himself to defeat the blackness. We are alone in this world once more."

"What have you done?"

Uthiel's jaw clenched.

"I have been betrayed by my people. By those I loved and trusted. I have done nothing to stain my honour, though I shall have vengeance for what has been done unto those I love."

Solanthur coughed a laugh. "You... slew your brothers."

"I saw what they did to her."

"How? She is in Gall!"

Uthiel snorted, but did not respond. He squatted quietly, breathing evenly, staring out at the destruction around them.

Solanthur spoke once more. "Ven... vengeance? Upon who? No one... left."

Uthiel looked south.

"There are some brothers and fathers who require my blade."

"Secunda... we need those men. Without them... we could... fall."

Uthiel looked back to Solanthur.

"The problems of the people of Secunda are no longer my own."

The first captain grimaced and spat again.

"You are a traitor... to your people. Your father would be disappointed."

Uthiel didn't respond, his gaze far off, his thumb absent-mindedly testing the edge of a long sword with a serrated edge.

Solanthur closed his eyes. "Get it over with. Kill me."

Uthiel looked down at him and shook his head.

"I think not, first captain. I am not a cold-blooded murderer."

"Damn you, traitorous bastard! You *are* a murderer, look around you!" snarled Solanthur, his pain fading in the face of his anger. "My god is dead. My army is dead. This land is dead. Yours is the fault. The blood of our brothers and the soldiers who followed us here is on your hands! Kill me! End this nightmare!"

The knight before him stood, his gaze swinging towards the white frontier and then back down.

"No. I shall leave you to decide your own fate."

"I shall survive this. I shall hunt you down. I shall kill you, for you are Secunda's Dark Son," swore Solanthur.

Uthiel smiled mirthlessly.

"Not before I bring down those who betrayed me."

ABOUT THE AUTHOR

Thank you for reading Swords of Secunda, my second novel. I hope you enjoyed the reading this treacherous, blood-soaked ride as much as I enjoyed writing it.

I'm a pretty average guy from Sydney, Australia, with an obsessive (and probably compulsive) approach to all things reading and writing.

I grew up reading Gemmell, Tolkein, Abnett, McNeill, Abercrombie, and so many more. History, fantasy, sci-fi, thriller, horror, anything I could get my hands on, I read – and in turn was influenced by.

Come find me on my website, Twitter, or Facebook. I look forwards to getting to know you a bit better on this crazy ride towards becoming a full time author.

- Adrian Collins
www.adriancollins.com.au
https://twitter.com/ACollinsAuthor
https://www.facebook.com/AdrianCollins.Author?ref=hl